RANDOM
HOUSE

LARGE
PRINT

THE GIRL
WITH THE
LOUDING VOICE

THE GIRL
WITH THE
LOUDING VOICE

• A Novel •

ABI DARÉ

RANDOM HOUSE
LARGE PRINT

Copyright © 2020 by Abi Daré

Published in the United States of America by Random House Large Print in association with Dutton, an imprint of Penguin Random House LLC.

Cover design by Christopher Lin • Cover illustration by Vikki Chiu Cover lettering by Jason Booher

The Library of Congress has established a Cataloging-in-Publication record for this title.

ISBN: 978-0-593-33986-2

www.penguinrandomhouse.com/large-print-format-books

FIRST LARGE PRINT EDITION

Printed in the United States of America

10 9 8 7 6 5 4 3 2

This Large Print edition published in accord with the standards of the N.A.V.H.

To my mother, Professor Teju Somorin,
not just because you are smart and beautiful
and became the first female professor of
taxation in Nigeria in 2019,
but also because you made me see the
importance of education and sacrificed
so much for me to get the best of it.

THE GIRL
WITH THE
LOUDING VOICE

Nigeria is a country located in West Africa. With a population of just under 180 million people, it is the seventh most populous country in the world, which means that one in seven Africans is a Nigerian. As the sixth largest crude oil exporter in the world, and with a GDP of $568.5 billion, Nigeria is the richest country in Africa. Sadly, over 100 million Nigerians live in poverty, surviving on less than $1 a day.

**—The Book of Nigerian Facts:
From Past to Present,** 5th edition, 2014

CHAPTER 1

This morning, Papa call me inside the parlor.

He was sitting inside the sofa with no cushion and looking me. Papa have this way of looking me one kind. As if he wants to be flogging me for no reason, as if I am carrying shit inside my cheeks and when I open mouth to talk, the whole place be smelling of it.

"Sah?" I say, kneeling down and putting my hand in my back. "You call me?"

"Come close," Papa say.

I know he want to tell me something bad. I can see it inside his eyes; his eyesballs have the dull of a brown stone that been sitting inside hot sun for too long. He have the same eyes when he was telling me, three years ago, that I must stop my educations. That time, I was the most old of all in my class and

all the childrens was always calling me "Aunty." I
tell you true, the day I stop school and the day my
mama was dead is the worst day of my life.

When Papa ask me to move closer, I am not answering him because our parlor is the small of a
Mazda car. Did he want me to move closer and be
kneeling inside his mouth? So, I kneel in the same
place and wait for him to be talking his mind.

Papa make a noise with his throat and lean on
the wood back of the sofa with no cushion. The
cushion have spoil because our last born, Kayus,
he have done too many piss inside it. Since the boy
was a baby, he been pissing as if it is a curse. The
piss mess the cushion, so Mama make Kayus to be
sleeping on it for pillow.

We have a tee-vee in our parlor; it didn't work.
Born-boy, our first born, he find the tee-vee inside
dustbin two years back when he was working a job
as dustbin collector officer in the next village. We
are only putting it there for fashion. It is looking
good, sitting like a handsome prince inside our
parlor, in the corner beside the front door. We are
even putting small flower vase on top it; be like a
crown on the prince head. When we have a visitor,
Papa will be doing as if it is working and be saying,
"Adunni, come and put evening news for Mr. Bada
to watch." And me, I will be responding, "Papa,
the remote-controlling is missing." Then Papa will
shake his head and say to Mr. Bada, "Those useless childrens, they have lost the remote-controlling

again. Come, let us sit outside, drink, and forget the sorrows of our country, Nigeria."

Mr. Bada must be a big fool if he didn't know that it is a lie.

We have one standing fan too, two of the fan blade is missing so it is always blowing air, which is making the whole parlor too hot. Papa like to be sitting in front of the fan in the evening, crossing his feets at his ankles and drinking from the bottle that have become his wife since Mama have dead.

"Adunni, your mama have dead," Papa say after a moment. I can smell the drink on his body as he is talking. Even when Papa didn't drink, his skin and sweat still smell.

"Yes, Papa. I know," I say. Why is he telling me something I have already know? Something that have cause a hole inside my heart and fill it with block of pain that I am dragging with me to everywhere? How can I ever be forgetting how my mama was coughing blood, red and thick with spit bubbles, inside my hand every day for three months? When I am closing my eyes to sleep at night, I still see the blood, sometimes I taste the salt of it.

"I know, Papa," I say again. "Have another something bad happen?"

Papa sigh. "They have told us to be going."

"To be going to where?" Sometimes I have worry for Papa. Since Mama have dead, he keep saying things that didn't make sense, and sometimes he talk to hisself, cry to hisself too when he think no-body is hearing.

"You want me to fetch water for your morning baff?" I ask. "There is morning food too, fresh bread with sweet groundnut."

"Community rent is thirty thousan' naira," Papa say. "If we cannot pay the moneys, we must find another place to live." Thirty thousand naira is very plenty moneys. I know Papa cannot find that moneys even if he is searching the whole of the Nigeria because even my school fees moneys of seven thousand, Papa didn't have. It was Mama who was paying for school fees and rent moneys and feeding money and everything money before she was dead.

"Where we will find that kind money?" I ask.

"Morufu," Papa say. "You know him? He come here yesterday. To see me."

"Morufu the taxi driver?" Morufu is a old man taxi driver in our village with the face of a he-goat. Apart from his two wifes, Morufu is having four childrens that didn't go to school. They just be running around the village stream in their dirty pant, pulling sugar cartons with string, playing **suwe** and clapping their hand until the skin about to peel off. Why was Morufu visiting our house? What was he finding?

"Yes," Papa say with a tight smile. "He is a good man, that Morufu. He surprise me yesterday when he say he will pay community rent for us. All the thirty thousan'."

"That is good?" I ask the question because it didn't make sense. Because I know that no man will be paying for another somebody's rent unless he is wanting something. Why will Morufu pay our community rent? What was he wanting? Or is he owing Papa moneys from before in the past? I look my papa, my eyes filling with hope that it is not the thing I am thinking. "Papa?"

"Yes." Papa wait, swallow spit, and wipe his front head sweat. "The rent moneys is . . . is among your **owo-ori**."

"My **owo-ori**? You mean my bride-price?" My heart is starting to break because I am only four-teen years going fifteen and I am not marrying any foolish stupid old man because I am wanting to go back to school and learn teacher work and become a adult woman and have moneys to be driving car and living in fine house with cushion sofa and be helping my papa and my two brothers. I don't want to marry any mens or any boys or any another per-son forever, so I ask Papa again, talking real slow so he will be catching every word I am saying and not mistaking me in his answer: "Papa, is this bride-price for me or for another person?"

And my papa, he nod his head slowly slow, not minding the tears standing in my eyes or the opening wide of my mouth, as he is saying: "The bride-price is for you, Adunni. You will be marrying Morufu next week."

CHAPTER 2

When the sun climb down from the sky and hide hisself deep in the crack of the night, I sit up on my raffia mat, kick Kayus leg away from my feets, and rest my back on the wall of our room.

My head been stoning my mind with many questions since this morning, questions that are not having answers. What is it meaning, to be the wife of a man with two wifes and four childrens? What is making Morufu to want another wife on top the already two? And Papa, why is he wanting to sell me to a old man with no any thinking of how I am feeling? Why didn't he keep the promise he make to Mama before she dead?

I rub my chest, where the too many questions is causing a sore, climb to my feets with a sigh, and walk to the window. Outside, the moon is red, hanging too low the sky, be as if God pluck out his angry eye and throw it inside our compound.

There are fireflies in the air this night, their body is flashing a light of many colors: green and blue and yellow, every one of them dancing and blinking in the dark. Long ago, Mama tell me that fireflies are always bringing good messages to peoples at night. "A firefly is the eyesballs of a angel," she say. "See that one there, the one perching on the leaf of that tree, Adunni. That one be bringing a message of moneys for us." I didn't sure what message that firefly was wanting to bring that long time ago, but I know it didn't bring no money.

When Mama was dead, a light off itself inside of me. I keep myself in that dark for many months until one day Kayus find me in the room where I was sorrowing and weeping, and with his eyes round, full of fear, he beg me to stop my crying because my crying is causing him a heart pain.

That day, I pick up my sorrow and lock it in my heart so that I can be strong and care for Kayus and Papa. But sometimes, like today, the sorrow climb out of my heart and stick his tongue in my face.

When I close my eyes on some days, I see my mama as a rose flower: a yellow and red and purple rose with shining leafs. And if I sniff a deep sniff, I can catch her smell too. That sweet smell of a rose-bush sitting around a mint tree, of the coconut soap in her hair just after a washing at Agan waterfalls.

My mama was having long hair which she will

plait with black threads and roll around her head like a thick rope, looking like two or three small tires around her head. Sometimes she will remove the threads, let the hair climb down to her back so that I can brush it with her wooden brush. Sometimes, she will take the brush from my hand, make me to sit on a bench in the outside by the well, and twist up my own hair with so much coconut oil that I go about the whole village smelling like a frying food.

She didn't old, my mama, only forty-something years of age before she die, and every day I feel a paining in my spirit for her quiet laugh and voice, for the soft of her arms, for her eyes that say more things than her mouth ever speak.

She didn't sick for too long, thank God. Just six and half months of coughing and coughing until the cough eat up her whole flesh and make her shoulders be like the handle of our parlor door.

Before that devil sickness, Mama was always keeping busy. Always doing the-this and the-that for the everybody in the village. She will fry one hundred puff-puffs every day to sell in Ikati market, sometimes picking fifty of it, the best of the gold-brown ones from the hot oil, and tell me to take it to Iya, one old woman living in Agan village.

I didn't too sure of how Iya and Mama are knowing each other, or what is her real name because "Iya" is a Yoruba word for old woman. All I know is my mama was always sending me to give food to Iya and all the older womens who are sick in the village around Ikati: hot amala and okra soup with crayfish or beans and **dodo,** the plantain soft, oily.

One time, I bring puff-puff to Iya, after Mama was too sick to travel far, and when I reach home that night and ask Mama why she keep sending food to peoples when she is feeling too sick to travel far, Mama say, "Adunni, you must do good for other peoples, even if you are not well, even if the whole world around you is not well."

It was Mama who show me how to pray to God, to put thread in my hair, to wash my cloth with no soap, and to change my under-cloth when my monthly visitor was first coming.

My throat tight itself as I hear her voice in my head now, the faint and weak of it, as she was begging Papa to don't give me to any man for marriage if she die of this sickness. I hear Papa's voice too, shaking with fear but fighting to be strong as he was answering her: "Stop this nonsense dying talk. Nobody is dying anything. Adunni will not marry any man, you hear me? She will go to school and do what you want, I swear to you! Just do quick and better yourself!"

But Mama didn't do quick and better herself. She was dead two days after Papa make that promise, and now I am marrying a old man because Papa is forgetting all the things he make promise to Mama. I am marrying Morufu because Papa is needing moneys for food and community rent and nonsense.

I taste the salt of my tears at the memorying of it all, and when I go back to my mat and close my eyes, I see Mama as a rose flower. But this rose is no more having yellow and red and purple colors with shining leafs. This flower be the brown of a wet leaf that suffer a stamping from the dirty feets of a man that forget the promise he make to his dead wife.

CHAPTER 3

I didn't able to sleep all night with all the sorrowing and memorying.

At first cock crow, I don't climb to my feets to begin my everyday sweeping or washing cloth or grinding beans for Papa's morning food. I lie there on the mat and keep my eyes close and listen to all the noise around me. I listen to the crying of a cock in the afar, a deep mourning cry; to the blackbirds in our mango tree singing their happy, every-morning song. I listen as far away, somebody, a farmer maybe, is hitting a ax at the buttocks of a tree; hitting, hitting, hitting. I listen as brooms are making a swish on the floor in one compound, as one mama in another compound is calling her childrens to wake up and go baff, to use the water in the clay pot and not the one in the iron bucket.

The sounds are the same every morning, but today, every sound is a blow to the heart, a wicked reminding that my wedding is drawing close.

I sit up. Kayus is still sleeping on his mat. His eyes are close but he look like he is having two minds about waking up. He been doing this shaking of his eyeslids in a struggle since the day we bury Mama, throwing his head left and right and shaking his eyeslids. I move near to him, press my palm on his eyeslids, and sing a soft song in his ear until he keep hisself still.

Kayus is only eleven years of age. He use to bad behaving many times, but he has my heart. It is me Kayus come to and cry when the boys in the village square was laughing him and calling him cat-fighter because Kayus, he was all the time sick as a child, so Papa take him to one place and they use razor blade to slash on his cheeks three times this way and that, a mark to chase away the spirit of sickness. When you are seeing Kayus, it is as if he was in a fight with a big cat, and the cat use his nails to scratch Kayus on his cheeks.

It is me that was teaching Kayus all the schoolwork I know, the Plus and Minus and Science and, most of all, the English, because Papa is not having school fees moneys for even Kayus too. It was me that tell him his futures is bright if only he can push hisself to learn.

Who will be caring of Kayus when I marry Morufu? Born-boy?

I sigh, look my older brother, Born-boy, as he is sleeping on the bed, a vexing look on his face. His real name is Alao, but nobody is ever calling him that. Born-boy is the first born, so Papa say it is respecting for him to be sleeping on the only one bed in the room three of us are sharing. I don't mind it. The bed have a thin mattress foam on top it, full of holes that bedbugs are using as kitchen and toilet. Sometimes, that mattress be smelling like the armpit of the bricklayers at the market square, and when they are raising their hand up to greet you, the smell can kill you dead.

How can Born-boy be caring for Kayus? He don't know how to cook or clean or do any work except of his mechanic work. He don't like to laugh or smile too, and at nineteen and half years of age, he look just like a boxer, both his hands and legs be like the branch of a thick tree. He sometimes is working all night at Kassim Motors, and when he come home too late in the night, he just throw hisself inside the bed and sleep. He is snoring now, tired, every of his breath is a shot of hot wind in my face.

I keep my eye on Born-boy a moment, watching the lifting up and down of his chest in a beat with no song, before I turn to Kayus and give him two soft slaps on his shoulder. "Kayus. Wake up."

Kayus pinch open one eye first, before the second one. He do this all the time when he want to wake up: open one eye first, then the second one a moment after, as if he is fearing that if he open the two eyes at the same time, he will suffer a problem.

"Adunni, you sleep well?" he ask.

"I sleep well," I lie. "And you?"

"Not well," he say, sitting up beside me on the mat. "Born-boy say you are marrying Morufu next week. Was he joking me?"

I take his hand, cold and small in my own. "No joke," I say. "Next week."

Kayus nod his head up and down, pull his lips with his teeths and bite on it. He don't say one word after that. He just bite his lips and grip my hand tight and squeeze.

"Will you ever be coming back after the marriage?" he ask. "To be teaching me? And cooking my palm oil rice for me?"

I shrug my shoulder. "Palm oil rice is not hard to cook. You just wash the rice in water three times and keep it in a bowl to be soaking. Then you take a fresh pepper and—" I stop talking because the tears is filling my mouth and cutting my words and making me to cry. "I don't want to marry Morufu," I say. "Please beg Papa for me."

"Don't cry," Kayus say. "If you cry, then I will cry too."

Me and Kayus, we hold each our hands tight and cry with no noise.

"Run, Adunni," Kayus say, wiping his tears, his eyes wide and full of a fearing hope. "Run far and hide yourself."

"No," I say, shaking my head. "What if the village chief is catching me as I am running? Are you forgetting Asabi?"

Asabi is one girl in Ikati that didn't want to marry a old man because she was having real love with Tafa, one boy that was working in the same Kassim Motors with Born-boy. The day after her wedding, Asabi was running away with Tafa but they didn't able to run far. They catch Asabi in front of the border and beat her sore. And Tafa? They hang the poor boy like a fowl in the village square and throw his body to Ikati forest. The village chief say Tafa was stealing another man's wife. That he must die because in Ikati, all thiefs must suffer and die. The village chief say they must lock Asabi in a room for one hundred and three days until she is learning to sit in her husband's house and not running away.

But Asabi didn't learn anything. After the one hundred and three days of locking inside a room, Asabi say she is no more coming outside. So she stay in that room till this day, looking the walls, plucking hair from her head and eating it, pinching her eyeslashes and hiding it inside her brassiere, talking to herself and the spirit of Tafa.

"Maybe you can be coming to play with me in Morufu's house," I say. "I can be seeing you in the stream too, even at the market, anywhere."

"You think?" Kayus ask. "What if Morufu is not letting me to come and play with you?"

Before I can think to answer, Born-boy turn

hisself in his sleep, wide his two legs apart, and push out a loud mess that fill the air with the odor of a dead rat.

Kayus sniff a laugh and cup his hand on his nose. "Maybe marrying Morufu is better than staying in this house with Born-boy and his smelling mess."

I squeeze his hand and drag a smile to my lips.

I wait till Kayus is sleeping again before I leave the room.

I find Papa in the outside, sitting on the kitchen bench near the well. The morning is beginning to light up now, and the sun is just waking up from sleep; be like half a orange circle peeping from behind a dark cloth in the sky. Papa is not having any shirt on, just his trousers and no shoes on his feets. He is eating a short stick in the corner of his mouth, his black radio in one hand, and with the other hand, he is banging a stone on his radio to wake it up. He do this every morning to wake the radio up since before Kayus was born, and so I low myself to the sand and keep my hand in my back and wait for the radio to wake up.

Papa bang the stone on the side of the radio three times—**ko, ko, ko**—and the radio make a cracking noise. A moment pass, and a man's voice in the radio say, "**Gooood** morning! This is OGFM 89.9. The station for the nation!"

Papa spit his stick to the sand beside me and look me like he want to slap my head for bending low in his front. "Adunni, I am wanting to hear six o'clock morning news. What is it?"

"Good morning, Papa," I say. "There is no beans in the house. Can I go and borrow from Enitan's mama?"

I have beans swelling inside a tin of water in the kitchen, but I am needing to talk to somebody about this whole wedding coming because Enitan and me, we been best of friends since we been able to read ABC and count 1-2-3. Her mama is also having a small farm, and many times, she like to give us beans, yam, and **egusi,** and she will tell us to pay for it whenever we are having moneys for it.

Papa shock me when he laugh and say, "Wait."

He set the radio on the bench ever so gentle, but the radio make a cracking noise two times, and then it just die dead like that. Give up spirit. No more OGFM 89.9 voice. No more station for the nation. Papa look the radio a moment, the silent black box of it, then he hiss, slap the radio from the bench, and smash it to the ground.

"Papa!" I say, putting my two hands on my head. "Why you spoil your radio, Papa? Why?" The tee-vee didn't ever work, and now, all that is remaining of the radio is a broken plastic with yellow, red, and brown wires peeping out of it.

Papa hiss again, shift his left buttock up, and dip his hand in his back trouser pocket. He bring out two fifty-naira notes of moneys and give me. I wide my eyes, look the money, dirty and soft and stinking of **siga.** Where is Papa finding moneys to give me? From Morufu? My heart is twisting as I fold the naira inside the edge of my wrapper.

I don't say, **Thank you, sah.**

"Adunni, hear me well," Papa say. "You must pay for the beans with that money. Then you tell Enitan's mama that after your wedding, me your papa"— he slap his chest as if he want to kill hisself— "will pay for all she been ever give us. I will pay it all everything. Even if it is costing thousan' of naira, I will pay it all. Every naira. You tell her that, you hear me?"

"Yes, sah."

He look the scatter of his radio on the floor and bend his mouth in a stiff smile. "Then I will buy a new radio. A correct one. Maybe even a new tee-vee. A cushion sofa. A new— Adunni?" He slide his eye to me, strong his face. "What are you looking at? Off you go! Quick!"

I don't say one word as I leave his front.

The path to Enitan's house is a thin line of cold, wet sand behind the river, with a bush as tall as myself on the left and right side of it. The air on this side of the village is ever cold, even with the sun shining bright in the sky. I am singing as I am walking, keeping my head and voice down because behind the bush, childrens from the village are laughing as they are washing and splashing theirselfs in the river. I don't want nobody to call my name, to ask me about any foolish planning for any nonsense wedding, so I quick my feets, cut to my right at the end of the path, where the ground is dry again, and where Enitan's compound is.

Enitan's house is not like our own. Her mama's farm is doing well, and so last year or so, they begins to cover the red mud of their house with cement and begins to fix it so now they have a sofa with cushion and a bed with a good mattress and a standing fan that don't make a loud noise when it is turning. Their tee-vee is working correct too. Sometimes, it even catch the Abroad movies.

I find Enitan at the back of her house, pulling a bucket out of the well with a strong rope. I wait till she set it down before I call her name.

"Ah! Look who is in my house this early morning!" she say, putting her hand up in the air like a salute. "Adunni, the new wife!"

When she make to bow her head, I slap her right up, right in the middle of her head. "Stop this!" I say. "I am not a wife. Not yet."

"But you will soon become a wife," she say, twisting her wrapper out from her chest to wipe her forehead with the edge of it. "I was greeting you, special one. You can like to be angry sometimes, Adunni. What is worrying you this morning?"

"Where is your mama?" I ask. If her mama is in the house, then I cannot be talking to Enitan about the wedding because her mama is worst of all for not understanding why I am not wanting to marry Morufu. One time she hear me talking my fears of marrying any man with Enitan, she pull my ears and tell me to eat my words of fear and be thanking God that I am having a man to care for me.

"In the farm," Enitan say. "Ah, I think I know why you are sad. Follow me. I have some beans in the—"

"I am not looking for food," I say.

"Then what is all this worrying face for?"

I put my head down. "I been thinking about . . . begging my papa to don't let me marry Morufu." I am speaking so quiet, I am nearly not hearing myself. "Can you follow me to beg him? If you follow me, maybe he will change his heart about this whole thing."

"Beg your papa?" I can hear something strong in her voice, something confuse, angry too. "Why? Because your life is changing for better?"

I dig my toesnails into the sand, feel a sharp stone pinch my toe. Why is nobody understanding why I am not wanting to marry? When I was still inside school and was the old of all in my class, Jimoh, one foolish boy in the class, was always laughing me. One day as I was walking to sit on my table, Jimoh say, "Aunty Adunni, why are you still in primary school when all your mates are in secondary school?" I know Jimoh was wanting me to cry and be feeling bad because I didn't able to start my schooling on time like the other childrens, but I look the devil-child inside his eyes and he look me back. I look his upside-down triangle-shape head, and he look me back. Then I sticked out my tongue and pull my two ears and say, "Why are you not inside bicycle shop when your head is like bicycle seat?" The class, that day, it was shaking with all the laughters from the childrens, and I was feeling very clever with myself until Teacher slap her ruler on the table three times and say: "Quiet!"

In the years I was in school, I was always having a answer for the peoples laughing me. I always fight for myself, always keeping my head up because I know I am in school to be learning. Learning is not having age. Anybody can learn, and so I keep to my learning, keep getting good marks in my work, and it was when I was getting more better in my Plus, Minus, and English that Papa say I must stop because he didn't have money for school fees. Since then, I keep trying to not forget my educations. I even been teaching the small boys and girls in the village ABC and 1-2-3 on market days. I am not collecting plenty money for the teaching, but sometimes, the mamas of the childrens will give me twenty naira, or a bag of corn or a bowl of rice or some tin sardines.

Anything they give me, I collect it, because I like to teach those childrens. I like the way their eyes be always so bright, their voices so sharp, when I say, "**A** is for what?" and they say, "**A** is for apple, **AH-AH-APPLE,**" even though nobody is ever seeing any apple with our two naked eyes except of inside the tee-vee.

"Who will be teaching the small childrens in the village on the market days?"

"The childrens have their own mama and papa." Enitan cross her hand in front of her chest, roll her eyes around. "And when you born your own childrens, then you can be teaching them!"

I bite my lips to lock the tears inside my eyes. Marriage is a good thing in our village. Many girls are wanting to marry, to be wife of somebody, or of anybody; but not me, not Adunni. I been cracking my mind since Papa tell me of this marriage, thinking that maybe there is a better options than to be a wife of old man, but my head, it have refuse to cooperating with ideas. I was even thinking to run away, to go far, but where will I go that my papa will not be finding me? How can I go and leave my brothers and my village just like that? And now, even Enitan is not understanding how I am feeling.

I raise my head, look her face. She herself was wanting to marry since she was thirteen years, but I think because her top lip is folding and bending to the left from a accident when she was small, nobody is talking marriage to her papa. Enitan don't care about schooling or learning book. She is just happy to be plaiting hair, and now she is thinking to start a makeupping business as she is waiting for when a husband will find her come.

"You cannot come and beg my papa for me?" I say.

"Beg him for what?" Enitan hiss a loud hiss and shake her head. "Adunni, you know how this is a good thing for your family. Think of how you been suffering since your mama . . ." She sigh. "I know it is not what you want. I know you like school, but think it well, Adunni. Think of how your family will be better because of it. Even if I beg your papa, you know that he will not answer me. I swear, if I can find a man like Morufu to marry me, I will be too happy!" She cover her mouth with one hand, laugh a shy laugh. "This is how I will dance on my own wedding." She pinch her cloth by her knees and hold it up, begin to pick her feets, putting one in front of the other, left, right, right, left in a song only she can hear. "You like it?"

I think of Papa smashing his radio this morning, of how he is planning to buy new things with Morufu's moneys.

"You like it?" Enitan ask again.

"You are dancing as if you have a sickness in your two legs," I say to Enitan with a laugh that feel too heavy, too full for my mouth.

She drop her cloth, press a finger to her jaw, and look the sky. "What can I say to make this Adunni happy now, eh? What can I—Ah! I know what will make you happy." She pick my hand and begin to drag me to the front of her house. "Come and see all the fine, fine makeups I am planning to use for your wedding. Do you know there is a color green eyespencils? Green! Come let me show you. When you see it all, you will be so happy! Then, after that, we can go to the river and—"

"Not today," I say, collecting my hand and turning away to hide my tears. "I have too much work. All the . . . the wedding preparations."

"I hear you," she say. "Maybe I should come to your house in the afternoon for the makeups testing?"

I shake my head, begin to walk away.

"Wait! Adunni," she shout. "What color of lipsticks should I bring? The red of a new wife or the pink of a young—"

Bring a black one, I say to myself as I turn a corner. **The black of a mourner!**

CHAPTER 4

Two years before my mama was dead, one car drive inside our compound and bring itself to a stop in front of our mango tree.

I was sitting under the tree, washing my papa's singlet, and when the car stop, I stop my washing, shake the soap from my hand, and keep looking the car. Is a rich man own, this car, black and shining with big tires and front light like the eyes of a sleeping fish. The car door open, and one man climb out, bringing along the smell of air-con and **siga** and perfumes. He tall like anything I ever see, with skin the brown of roasted groundnut, and his fine face and long jaw make me think of a handsome horse. He was wearing costly trouser cloth of green lace, with a green cap on his slim head.

"Good morning, I am looking for Idowu," he say, talking fast, fast, voice smooth. "Is she around?"

Idowu is the name of my mother. She didn't ever use to have visitor, except of the five womens from the Church Community of Praying Wife every third Sunday in the month.

I roof my eyes from the morning sun. "Good morning, sah," I say. "You are who?"

"Is she around?" he ask again. "My name is Ade."

"She have go out," I say. "You want to sit-down wait?"

"I am sorry, I can't," he say. "I only came to Ikati village to visit my grandmother's burial site. She, uh, passed away while I was abroad. I thought to say hello to your mother on my way back to the airport. I fly back tonight."

"Fly? Like **aeloplane**? To the Abroad?" I have been hearing of this the Abroad, of the Am-rica and the London. I am even seeing it inside the tee-vee, the womens and mens with their yellow skin and pencil nose and hair like rope, but I have never see anybody from there before with my two naked eyes. I been hearing them in the radio sometimes too, talking fast, fast, speaking English as if they are using it as special power for confusing everybody.

I look this tall, fine man, at his skin, which is the brown of roasted groundnut, and his short black hair like foam sponge. He is not resembling the peoples in the Abroad tee-vee. "Where are you from?" I ask him.

"The UK," he say, smiling soft, showing white teeths in straight line. "London."

"Then why you don't look yellow like them?" I ask.

He strong his face, then laugh ha-ha. "You must be Idowu's daughter," he say. "What is your name?"

"Adunni is the name, sah."

"You are just as pretty as she was at your age."

"Thank you, sah," I say. "My mama have travel far to greet Iya, her old friend that is living in the next village. Till tomorrow before she is coming back. I can keep your message."

"Now that's a shame," he say. "Can you tell her Ade came back to look for her? Tell her that I didn't forget her."

After he climb inside his car and was going, I keep thinking, who is this man, and how he knows my mama? When Mama return and I tell her Mr. Ade from the Abroad of the UK come and see her, she shock. "Mr. Ade?" she keep asking as if she deaf. "Mr. Ade?"

Then she was starting to cry soft because she didn't want Papa to hear. It take me another three weeks to be asking her why she shock and cry. She tell me that Mr. Ade is from a rich family. That many years back, he was living in Lagos, but he come to Ikati to be staying with his grandmother for holiday season. One day, Mama was selling puff-puff and Mr. Ade buy some. Then he just fall inside love with her. Big fall. She say he is her first man-friend, the only man she ever love. The two both of them was suppose to have marry theirself. But my mama didn't go to school, so Mr. Ade family say no marriage. When Mr. Ade say he will kill hisself if he didn't marry Mama, his family lock him inside **aeloplane** and send him to the Abroad. After Mama cry and cry, her family force her to marry Papa, a man she didn't ever love.

And now, my own Papa is wanting to do the same to me.

That day, Mama say, "Adunni, because I didn't go to school, I didn't marry my love. I was wanting to go outside this village, to count plenty moneys, to be reading many books, but all of that didn't possible." Then she hold my hand. "Adunni, God knows I will use my last sweat to be sending you to school because I am wanting you to have chance at life. I am wanting you to speak good English, because in Nigeria, everybody is understanding English and the more better your speaking English, the more better for you to be getting good job."

She cough a little, shift herself on the floor mat, keep talking. "In this village, if you go to school, no one will be forcing you to marry any man. But if you didn't go to school, they will marry you to any man once you are reaching fifteen years old. Your schooling is your voice, child. It will be speaking for you even if you didn't open your mouth to talk. It will be speaking till the day God is calling you come."

That day, I tell myself that even if I am not getting anything in this life, I will go to school. I will finish my primary and secondary and university schooling and become teacher because I don't just want to be having any kind voice . . .

I want a louding voice.

✂

"Papa?"

He is sitting in the sofa, keeping his eyes on the tee-vee, looking the gray glass face of it as if it will magic and on itself so that he can be watching the elections news.

"Papa?" I move to his front. It is nighttime now and the parlor is having dim light from the candle sitting on the floor, the white of the stick is melting itself and making a mess beside the sofa leg.

"It is me, Adunni," I say.

"My eye is not blind," he say, speaking Yoruba. "If the food is ready, put it inside plate and bring it come."

"I am needing to talk to you, sah." I low down and hold his two legs. My mind is shocking at how his leg keep thinning more and more since Mama have dead. Feel as if I am grabbing only cloth of his trouser leg.

"Please, Papa."

Papa is one hard man, always stronging his face and fighting the whole everybody in the house, and this is why I was wanting Enitan to follow me come beg him. When my papa is in the house, everybody must be doing as a dead person. No talking. No laughing. No moving. Even when Mama was not dead, Papa was always shouting her. Long times ago, he beat her. Only one time. He give her one slap, swelling her cheek. He say it is because she talk him back when he was shouting her. That womens are not suppose to talk when mens are talking. He didn't beat her again after that, but they didn't too happy together.

He look me down now, his forehead shining with sweat. "What?"

"I don't want to marry Morufu," I say. "Who will be taking care of yourself? Kayus and Born-boy are boys. They cannot be cooking. They cannot be washing cloth and sweeping the compound."

"Tomorrow, Morufu will bring four he-goats to this compound." Papa hold up four thin fingers and start to speak English: "One, two, ti-ree, four," he say as spit fly from his mouth and land on my up lip. "He is bringing fowl too. Agric fowl, very costly. Bag of rice, two of it. And money. I didn't tell you that one. Five thousan' naira, Adunni. Five thousan'. I have a fine girl-child at home. At your age, you are not suppose to be in the house. You are suppose to have born at least one or two childrens by this time."

"If I marry Morufu, that means you are throwing

all my futures inside the dustbin. I have a good brain, Papa. You know it, Teacher know it. If I can be finding a way to go to school, I can be helping you when I get a good job. I am not minding to go back to school and be old of all in the class, I know I can learn things quick. Soon, I finish all my educations, become teacher, and then I will collect monthly salary-moneys to build you a house, buy you a fine car, a black Benz."

Papa sniff, wipe his nose. "There is no moneys for food, talk less of thirty thousan' for community rent. What will becoming teacher do for you? Nothing. Only stubborn head it will give you. And sharp mouth, because the one you are having is not enough, eh? You want to be like Tola?"

Tola is Mr. Bada child. She is twenty-five years and look like a agama lizard with long hair. Mr. Bada send her to school in Idanra town and she is now working inside bank there and is having motorcar and money, but she didn't find husband. They say she is looking everywhere for husband but nobody is marrying her, maybe because she is looking like a agama lizard with long hair or maybe because she is having money like a man.

"She is having plenty money," I say. "Caring for Mr. Bada."

"With no husband?" Papa shake his head, slap his hand two times. "God forbid. My sons will care for me. Born-boy is learning mechanic work at

Kassim Motors. Very soon, Kayus will follow him. What will I do with you? Nothing. Fourteen years going fifteen is a very good age to marry."

Papa sniff again, scratch his throat. "Just yesterday, Morufu tell me that if you manage and give him a boy as first born, he will give me ten thousan' naira."

A load roll on top my chest, join the other load that was there since Mama have dead.

"But you make a promise to Mama," I say. "And now you are forgetting the promise."

"Adunni," Papa say, shaking his head. "We cannot be eating promise as food. Promise is not paying our rent. Morufu is a good man. This is a good thing. A happy thing."

I keep begging Papa, keep holding his leg and wetting his feets with my tears, but my papa is not hearing me. He keep shaking his head and saying, "This is a good thing, a happy thing. Idowu will be happy. Everybody will be happy."

When Morufu come the next morning, and Papa call me to come and be thanking him for the fowl and he-goats, I am not giving them answer. I tell Kayus to tell Papa that my monthly visitor have come. That I am sick with pains in the stomach. I lie on my mat and use my mama's wrapper to cover my head as I am hearing Papa and Morufu in the parlor, snapping open the cover of schnapps gin bottle and cracking groundnut.

I am hearing them as Morufu is laughing loud laugh, talking in Yoruba about elections coming next year, about Boko Haram stealing plenty girls from inside a school just last month, about his taxi business.

I lie there like that, wetting my mama's wrapper with tears, until the night is falling, and until the sky is turning to the black of a wet soil.

CHAPTER 5

M e and Enitan are in the backyard of our house behind the kitchen.

She is doing the makeups testing for the wedding tomorrow, slapping white powder on my cheeks and pressing black eyespencil deep inside my eyesballs.

Our kitchen is not like the ones I use to see inside tee-vee with cooking gas or anything electrics. Our own is just a space with three log of firewood under a iron pot and one white plastic bowl which we are using for kitchen sink. There is one short wood bench, the one I am sitting on top of now, a very handsome bench that Kendo, our village carpenter, builded for me with the wood from the mango tree in our compound.

"Adunni, now you look like a real **olori**," Enitan

say to me now as she press the pencil inside my head as if she want to wound me. "The wife of the king!"

I can hear laughing inside her voice, the joy of a friend that must be so prouding that she is doing wedding makeups. She push up my chin and press the pencil into the middle of my forehead, like those Indian people we see on the tee-vee in the village town center. Then, she draw the pencil on my eyesbrows, left and right, and paint my lips with red lipstick.

"Adunni," Enitan say, "I count one . . . two . . . and three, quick! Open your eyes!"

I blink my eye, open it. At first I am not seeing the looking-glass Enitan is holding to her chest because of the tears inside my eyes.

"Look," Enitan say. "It is fine?"

I touch my face here and there, say "Ah, ah," as if I am very happy with how she make up my face. But the black inside my eyes is looking as if somebody elbow me on the eye.

"Why are you looking sad?" Enitan ask. "You are still feeling sad to marry Morufu?"

I try to give her a answer, but I think I will just cry and cry and not talk anything sense and mess up all the makeups she is putting on my face.

"Morufu is a rich man," Enitan say with a sigh, as if she is just tired of me and all my troubles. "He will be taking care of you and your family. What more are you finding in this life when you have a good husband?"

"You know he have two wifes," I manage to say. "And four childrens."

"And so? Look you," Enitan say with laugh. "You are having luck to be marrying! Be thanking God for this good thing and stop all this nonsense crying."

"Morufu will not help me to finish school," I say, my heart swelling so full up, it push the tears down my face. "Hisself didn't go to school. And if I am not going to school, then how will I be finding a job and having money?" How will I have a louding voice?

"You can worry, eh," Enitan say. "School is not having any meaning in this village. We are not in Lagos. Forget about schooling this and that, marry Morufu and born fine, fine boys for him.

"Morufu's house is not far. I will be coming to play with you and go to the river with you when I am less busy from my makeupping work." She bring out wooden comb from the pocket of her yellow-of-sun dress and start to be combing my hair. "I want to weave it in **shuku** style," she say. "Then I put red beads here, here, and here." She touch my head in the middle of my head, near my left ear, and behind my right ear.

"You want it like that?" she ask.

"Do it anyhow you want," I say, not caring.

"Adunni, the new wife of Ikati," Enitan say, making her voice sound like a singing song. "Give me one big smile." She dip her finger into the side of my stomach and twist it until a smile is crawling to my down-face, until I cough a laugh that pinch my chest.

Afar off in our compound, beside the mango tree, Born-boy is putting a iron bucket into the well with a long, thick rope. The well, it was belonging to my grandfather-father. He builded it with mud and steel and sweat, and my mama, when she was not dead, she was telling me story of how my grandfather-father kill hisself inside the well. He just fall inside one day as he was fetching water. For three days, nobody knows where he was. Everybody was finding him, looking inside the forest, the farm, the village square, even the community mortuary, until the well was starting to give foul odor of rotten egg and somebody mess. The day they find my grandfather-father's body, it have swell up as if his leg, nose, stomach, teeths, and buttocks is all pregnants at the same time. The whole village, they mourn him, wailing cry and beating their chest for three days. As I am watching Born-boy now, small part of me is wishing he will fall inside the well so that the wedding will cancel. But that is bad way of thinking of my brother, so I change my mind.

Born-boy draw the water and set the bucket down and wipe sweat from his eyesbrow as Papa is pushing his bicycle with one hand and holding a green rag in his second hand. He is even wearing his best trouser cloth, the blue ankara with drawings of small red boats on it, looking as if he is going to visit a king. Born-boy lie flat on the ground, forehead touching the sand to greet Papa, before he collect the rag from Papa and is starting to shine the bicycle. Enitan put the comb inside my hair, cut the portions, and start to comb it fast and hard.

"Ye," I say, feeling the pinching from my hair to inside of my brain. "Slow your hand, **jo**."

"Sorry," Enitan say as she press my head down and begin to plait the hair. After the first line, I up my head. Born-boy have finish shining the bicycle. Papa spit on the floor, rub the spit inside the sand with his feets, before he jump on his bicycle and ride out of the compound.

When Enitan finish the makeups and hair and I wash off the nonsense on my face, I stay in the same place outside the kitchen, sitting on the same bench, tearing green leafs off a stick of corns, plucking the seeds into a bucket.

I been like this since middle of afternoon, and the moon is now so high up in the sky, the night hot and stiff. My back feel like a shell of egg about to crack and my fingers are corn yellow and sore and I want to stop the plucking, but the plucking is keeping my mind from running up and down, from thinking too much.

When the bucket is nearly half full, I shift it to one side, stand to my feets, and stretch myself until my back make a click, and then I pour a bowl of cold water into the bucket before I cover it with a cloth.

Tomorrow morning, Aunty Sisi, who is always cooking for peoples in our village, will come to our house. She will mix the soaking corn with sweet potato and sugar and ginger and grind it all together to make a **kunu** drink for the wedding.

I kick off the rest ten sticks of corn to one side, not minding that the floor is full of red sand. If she wants more corn tomorrow, then she can peel it herself. Not me. My fingers feel too sore, and my body is crawling with the white, thin hairs of the corn, feel like little snakes climbing up and down my whole body.

I find Papa in the parlor, snoring, his cap perching on his nose. Three cartons of small stout, gifts for the wedding, are sitting by his feets. One of the cartons is missing a bottle, and I see it rolling on the floor beside a stick of a burning candle, dark and empty. I wait a moment, thinking to talk to Papa one more time, to try and maybe make him think sense before tomorrow, but I think of the corn soaking outside, of the big yams inside the kitchen, the bag of rice and red peppers, of the two agric fowl and four he-goats in the back of the house.

I think of Aunty Sisi, of Enitan and of all the other peoples who will be coming here early tomorrow, wearing costly dress and shoe and bag because of me. I look the stout bottle by Papa's feets and sigh, low myself to the floor by the parlor door, and blow out a breeze on the candle to kill the fire.

I leave Papa by hisself in the dark, and when I reach my room, I off all my dress, shake it for the rest of the corn hairs, and keep it to dry on the window.

I tie a wrapper around my chest and lie down on the mat near Kayus. I try to put my head down on the mat to sleep, but my whole head be breathing by hisself, feel as if Enitan pump hot air inside my head when she was plaiting it to cause a wicked pounding. I sit with my back to the wall and listen to the wind hissing soft outside. Sometimes, I want to be just like Kayus, to have no fear of marrying a man, to not have any worry in this life. All Kayus ever worry about is what food to eat and where he can kick his football. He don't ever worry about no marriage or bride-price money. He don't even worry about schooling because I been the one teaching him school since all this time.

Enitan say that Morufu have a house. A real working car. Plenty food to eat, moneys to be giving Papa and Kayus and even Born-boy. Money for Kayus is a good thing. I can try, like Enitan say, to be happy.

I stretch my lips, force it to smile. But my chest feel full of birds flapping their wings inside of it. The birds are pounding their feets and pecking their beak and I want to cry so loud and beg the birds to stop making my heart to jump. I want to shout at the night and tell it never to become a tomorrow, but Kayus is sleeping like a baby, and I don't want to wake him, so I take the edge of cloth, make it like a ball, and bite on it hard and taste the corn from this afternoon and the salt of my tears.

When my spirit cannot cry any more tears, I spit the cloth from my mouth, sniff up my nose. Tomorrow will come. Nothing I can do about that. I lie down and close my eyes. Open it again. Close it. Open it. There is a sound beside me, a shaking. Kayus?

I sit up, touch him soft, say, "Kayus, everything all right?"

But my baby brother, he just slap off my hand as if I pinch him with two hot fingers. He pick his-self up from his mat, kick off his slippers from the floor, and run outside in the dark before I can think to ask him what is chasing him.

So I sit there and listen: to the sound of his feet as it is kicking the door outside of our room.

Kick. Kick. Kick.

I listen to his voice, the sad and angry of it, as he is screaming my name over and over again. And I listen to Papa, who is shouting a curse from his sleep and telling Kayus to pick one: keep shut his noise-making mouth or come to the parlor to collect a nice, hot flogging. So I drag myself from my mat and find Kayus in the outside, sitting on the floor with his back to our bedroom wall. He is rubbing his left feet with his hands, rubbing and crying and crying and rubbing.

I low myself to him, pluck his hand from his feet and hold it tight. Then I pull him close, and together, we stay like that, saying nothing, until he fall into a deep sleep with his head on my shoulders.

CHAPTER 6

My wedding be like a movie inside the tee-vee. My eyes was watching myself as I was kneeling down in front of my father, as he was saying a prayer to be following me to my husband house, as my mouth was opening, my lips parting, my voice saying "Amen" to the prayers even though my mind was not understanding what is happening to me.

I was looking everything from under the white lace cloth covering my face: the womens and mens standing in our compound under the mango tree, all of them wearing the same style of blue cloth with no shoe; the old man drummer holding a talking-drum under his armpit, pulling the rope on the side of the drum and banging a stick on the face of it, **gon! gon! gon!;** my friends Enitan and Ruka, laughing, dancing, singing. I was looking all the food: the palm oil rice and fish and yam and **dodo;** Coca-Cola and **kunu** and **zobo** drink for the womens, palm wine and schnapps gin and stout and strong **ogogoro** for the mens; bowls of choco-sweets for the small childrens.

My eyes was watching myself as Morufu was putting his finger inside a small clay pot of honey and lifting up the cloth to press the honey-finger on my forehead three times, saying, "Your life will be sweet like this honey from today."

I keep looking, even when Morufu lie down and press his head to the floor in front of Papa seven times and Papa collect my hand, cold and dead, and put it inside Morufu's own and say, "This is your wife now, from today till forever, she is your own. Do her anyhow you want. Use her till she is useless! May she never sleep in her father house again!" and everybody was laughing and saying, **"Congra-lations!** Amen! **Congra-lations!"**

My eyes was just watching myself, watching as the picture of schooling that I put on top a table in my heart was falling to the floor and scattering into small, small pieces.

As Morufu is driving his taxi-motor away from our compound, he is putting his hand outside the window and shouting, "Thank you-o! Thank you-o!" to the peoples lining the road to the left and right of us, waving us bye-bye and wishing us good home.

I am sitting beside him in the car, my head down to my chin, my eyes on the henna Enitan drawed on my hand this morning and thinking how it is resembling what my mind is feeling: plenty twisting and turning of a thin black road so that it is looking beautiful from the afar, but when you look it well, then you are seeing all the confusions.

"You feeling fine?" Morufu ask when there are no more peoples on the side of the road, when it is just trees and bushes on our left and right side; when, outside, the world is turning, and darkness is now where the sun use to be, and the sky is just a big blue cloth with plenty shine-shine holes inside it. A breeze is blowing my face, and another bride, a happy bride, will be full of smiles now, looking the stars and thinking how she is having lucky to be marrying. But me, I am keeping my head down, trying to be locking the tears behind my eyeslids so it will stay inside my eyes and not come out. I don't want to cry in front of this man. I never, never want to show him any feeling of me.

"You are not answering me?" Morufu say, cutting the road to the left, and soon we are nearing the areas that is close to the village border. "Come on! Look me!"

I push up my head.

"Good, very good," he say. "Because you are now a married woman. My wife. The other two wifes in the house, what is their name again? Yes, Labake and Khadija, they will be jealousing you. Khadija is having small sense, but Labake, she will want to make you to be sad. You will not allow her, you hear? If Labake do you anyhow, talk you one kind, call me and I will flog her very well."

My head is not understanding why he wants to flog his wifes. Will he flog me when I do bad?

"Yes, sah," I say. The stupid tears is not behaving hisself. It is running down my cheeks.

"Eh. Am I hearing your tears?" He remove the wedding **fila** from his head and throw it to the back seat.

"You are sad?" he ask and I nod my head yes, because I am praying it will make him pity me and he will slow down on one side of the road and tell me sorry, it is a big mistake and he is not wanting to wife me again, but he sniff his nose and say, "You better wipe that tears and begin to laugh. You know how much it is costing me to marry you today? You better open your teeth for me now and start to be laughing. Come on! Why are you looking at me? Did I kill your father? Are you deaf in the ear? I say OPEN!"

I open my teeths, feel as if I tear my face.

"Very good," he say. "Be laughing. Be happy. A new wife is always happy."

We are driving like two mad peoples, me showing my teeths, and him talking to hisself about how he was paying thousands and thousands of naira for bride-price until we pass the junction beside Ikati bakery, and the smell of rising bread is filling my nose and making me to think of Mama. We pass the village mosque, where there are peoples coming out from the iron gate of the mosque: mens wearing white **jalabiya,** holding prayer beads and plastic kettles, and womens covering their heads with hijab, all of them walking as if something is chasing them.

After nearly twenty minutes of driving from our house, Morufu cut a turn by Ikati canteen, drive enter inside a compound that is big like one half a football field, a cement house in the middle of it. The house is dark, no light in the four windows. There is no door in front, just a short wooden gate. In front of it, a curtain is flapping in the stiff evening wind. Morufu bring his car to a stop near a guava tree with branch that look like a man's hand, the leafs on it spreading out over the compound like too many fingers on the hand. I see there is another car in the compound, green, a blue nylon bag instead of glass in one of windows in the back.

"This is my house. For twenty years, I build it myself," Morufu say. He point to the other green car. "That is my other taxi-car," he say. "How many people are having two cars in this village?" He jam his shoulder to the car door, push it open. "Come down and wait for me there," he say. "Let me collect your load from the boot."

I climb down from the car, kick one or two

rotting guava on the floor from my path. My ears pick a noise from the house, the sound of a door opening and closing itself. A woman, thick in flesh and round at the hip, as if she hide a paw-paw inside of her hips under the black **iro** she is tying around her waist, bring herself come out from the house. Her face is white, be like she mash up white chalk and use it as a powder. In her hand is a candle sitting on a plate, and under the dancing candle flames, she be looking like a ghost with hairnet.

She carry the plate of candle like a offering to one god, walking slow, her feets sounding as if she is marching on eggs-shells until she stop in my front.

"Husband snatcher, welcome-o," she say to the candle, breeze from her mouth making the fire to sleep. "When I finish with you in this house, you will curse the day your mother born you. **Ashewo.**"

"Labake!" Morufu shout from behind the car, "You have started your trouble again? You are calling my new wife **ashewo**? A prostitute? I think you want to die this night. Adunni, don't mind her-o. She is having mental problem. Her head is not correct. Don't mind her!"

The woman, Labake, she hiss, drawing it, so that it is doing echo around the whole compound, before she turn around and walk away, her buttocks rolling.

Me, I am just standing there, feeling a cold climbing up to my head, until Morufu come to my side.

He drop my box on the floor, spit beside my feets, and wipe his mouth with the back of his hand.

"That is Labake, the first wife," he say. "Don't mind her at all, at all. All her talk is empty. Now, follow me inside, come and meet Khadija, the second wife."

CHAPTER 7

I count six peoples in the parlor.

There is a sofa resting by the wall, a wood table in the middle of it with a empty cup sitting on top. The tee-vee in the corner beside the sofa is holding a kerosene lantern which is spitting dark orange light inside the parlor.

I throw my eyes around the womens first. There is Labake, the one with white face, standing near the tee-vee, slapping her stomach as if there is evil inside of it. Beside her, another girl. She look like half a adult, and is wearing long robe, a green-black color in the light of the lantern. I look her from the low-cut hair on her head to the swollen of her stomach. As if she is thinking I will use my eyes to be plucking her baby out from her stomach, she turn it from me and face the wall.

I look the childrens sitting on the floor, all four girls. They are blinking eyes at me as if I am tee-vee movie with too much flashing light. The most young of them look like she is one and a half years of age. All the girls are not wearing correct cloth. Only pant. Even the one with kola-nut-size breast is not wearing brassiere. I use to see that one at the stream, wearing just pant, dragging water inside clay pot. Me and her have play **ten-ten** before, long times ago.

Just then, her name enter my brain: Kike. She is fourteen. Same age of me. When she give me look as if she is shock of seeing me, I hook my eyes on the lantern on the tee-vee, on the flame of fire dancing inside the glass bowl.

"That is Khadija," Morufu say, pointing to the tiny one with pregnant. "She look small, but she is still your second senior wife. Kneel down and greet her."

As I kneel to greet Khadija, Morufu chase away the childrens. "Inside, all of you, inside," he say, kicking their legs. "Up, up on your feets. Kike, Alafia, up, up. You have seen new wife enough! Inside to your mat. No noise today. No fighting if you don't want to see my red eyes!"

The girls tumble on top each other, scatter away from the parlor.

"Labake, Khadija, sit down." Morufu say. "Sit down, let me talk to all of you."

Labake throw herself inside the sofa, fold her

hand on top her chest. "We know what you want to say, so talk quick," she say.

Khadija is not moving from where she is standing.

Morufu yawn and low hisself inside the sofa beside Labake. Under the lantern light, his skin is the rough of sandpaper and slack with aging old, the teeths in his mouth brown and bending left. I manage to count all five of it before he snap his mouth close. He must be around my papa age, maybe fifty-five, sixty years, but he look like Papa's father.

"Adunni, this is your new house," Morufu say. "And in this house, I am having rule. There is respect of me. I am the king in this house. Nobody must talk back to me. Not you, not the childrens, not anybody. When I am speaking, you keep your mouth quiet. Adunni, that means you don't ask question in my front, you hear me?"

"Why?" I ask. "Where should I be asking you question? In your back?"

Khadija make a noise in the corner. As if she is fighting to hold a laugh.

"Adunni, you think I am making joke here? I hope your mouth will not put you in trouble," Morufu say. He is smiling, but his smile is giving me warning. "You cannot be talking anyhow to your husband," he say.

"I have special cane for flogging bad mouth. I don't want to use that cane for you, you hear? Now what am I saying? This is your new house. I swear,

I have gray hair before I marry my first wife. Why? Because I was busy making plenty money and learning my taxi business. First, I marry Labake, but she was not having any child. It is after we have sacrificed two goats for the gods of Ikati river that Labake was able to born one child, a girl." He say this as if it is bitter something to remember, as if girls-childrens are a curse, a bad gift from the gods.

"Kike is her name. My first born. She is your age, Adunni. Since then, we have done many more sacrifice, but I think the gods of the water vexed for Labake. No another baby. I marry the second wife, Khadija. Big mistake! Big mess! Why? Because Khadija is having three girls: Alafia, Kofo, and I forget the name of the last born now. No boy. Adunni, your eyes are not blind, you can see very well that Khadija is carrying a new baby. I have warned her that if it is not a boy-child inside that stomach, her family will not collect food from me again. I swear I will kick her back to her hungry father's house. Not so?"

"God is not wicked," Khadija say to the wall. "This is a boy-child."

"I want two boys," he say. "If I have my boys, I will send them to school. They will become English-speaking taxi driver and make plenty money. Girls are only good for marriage, cooking food, and bedroom work. I have already find Kike a husband. I will use her bride-price to repair my car window, maybe buy more chickens for my farm, because I use too much plenty money to marry my sweet Adunni.

"But I don't mind spending for my Adunni. I don't mind at all! Now, you three wifes, all of you hear me well. I don't want you to fight. Labake, mind yourself. You are always finding trouble. If you don't give me peace, I will chase you out from my compound. I am getting old, I want peace. Let me see. How will three of you be sleeping with me?"

Morufu scratch his gray beard, pull out a hair, put it inside his mouth, and eat it. "Yes. We will do it like this. Adunni will sleep in my room for three nights in the week, Sunday, Monday, Tuesday. Labake for two nights, Wednesday and Thursday. You with the stomach, one night, Friday. Me, I will keep the last night to myself, to gather energy. Adunni is a new wife with young blood. She must born a boy-child for me. Not so, Adunni?" He laugh, but no one is joining him in the laughters.

Is he meaning to say we be sleeping on the same bed like a lovers? Is he wanting to see my naked? To do me the nonsense and rubbish things that adult people use to do? I shiver, put my hand around my-self. Nobody ever see my naked. Nobody except of my mama. Even when I am baffing in Ikati stream, I am using the water as a cover-cloth, wrapping my whole body inside it. I don't want Morufu with his rag face to be touching me. I don't want a husband. I only want my mama. Why death collect her from me so quick? My eyes pinch with tears, but I bite my lip till I break the skin of it.

Morufu push hisself to his feets and remove the **agbada** he was wearing for the wedding. He is not a fat person, but he have a round stomach. It look hard too, like coconut. Maybe there is a disease inside it. I forget the name of it, but Teacher say, in class of Science, that this sickness is causing stomach to be hard when you are not pregnants and when you are not eating a balancing diets. I think Morufu is having this sickness.

"Khadija will show you the kitchen and baffroom and everywhere in the house. Nothing to be afraid of, you hear me?" he say. "Let me go and prepare myself for you. You have any question?"

I want to be asking if he can release me go back to my papa. I want to tell him to don't touch me this night, or ever, ever. But I am shaking my head, shivering, shivering. The cold is colding me, even though Labake's head is shining with sweat, and Khadija is using her hand to be fanning herself.

"No question, sah," I say. "Thank you, sah."

When Morufu leave us be, Labake stand up, tight her cloth around her waist, as if she is making preparations for a fight. "You and my Kike are of same age," she say, eyes blinking fast. "Your dead mother and me, we are age-mates. God forbid for me to share my husband with my own child. God forbid that I am waiting for you to finish with my husband before I can enter his room. Ah, you will suffer in this house. Ask Khadija, she will tell you that I am a wicked woman. That my madness is not having cure."

She click her finger in my face, and push my chest so that I am falling inside the sofa. "I will suffer you till you run back to your father's house."

I shock so much, I start crying.

"Don't cry," Khadija say when it is just me and her in the parlor. She peel herself from the wall and come and sit down beside me. "Labake is just talking. She have a big mouth, but she will not do anything. No woman is happy to share her husband. Don't mind Labake, you hear? Stop crying." She put a hand on my shoulder, her touch soft. She is speaking better English than me even, and I think she go to school before they force-marry her for Morufu.

"Is not so bad," she say. "Here, there is food to eat and water to drink. I am thankful for it, for the food."

I look her face. Her eyes is far inside her head, as if she malnourish, and when she smile, her cheeks is swallowing her eyes so that it is almost disappearing. But I see a kind spirit in the deep of her eyes.

"I am just wanting my mama," I say, talking whisper. "I didn't want to marry Morufu. My papa say I must marry him because he pay our community rent."

"Your own is even good. Me, my father give me to Morufu because of bag of rice," she say.

"After sickness have cut my father's leg. You know **diabetis** sickness?"

I shake my head no.

"Sickness of sugar," she say. "The **diabetis** bite his leg bad, and the doctor, they cut my father's leg just here—" She put her hand on her knee and make a slice around it, as if she is cutting yam. "The hospital money is too much, and he cannot work again, so we are suffering to eat. At first, Morufu was helping us, but he soon get tired and he say he must marry me or no food. He buy my family five **derica** of rice, and my father bundle me into Morufu car and wave me bye-bye. We didn't even do any wedding party like you." She force a laugh, dry. "I was in school before that time, learning well. I have been here for five years now. Now he is saying he will not give my family food until I give him a boy-child. I am just tired of everything. I know this one is a boy-child so I can rest."

"How old are you?" I ask, looking her as she rest her back and put her hand on top the swell of her stomach.

"I am twenty years," she say. "I marry him when I was fifteen years, and I have three children for him, three girls that he didn't want because they are girls. Is not a easy thing, to be wife of Morufu. If you want peace in this house, Adunni, don't let our husband be angry. His anger is a evil spirit. Not good."

I am not liking it, the way she is saying "our husband," as if it is title, as if she is saying "Our King."

"Cheer yourself," she say. "Smile a smile, be
happy. Now, follow me, let me show you everywhere in the house, because our husband is waiting
for you. Tonight, you will become a true woman,
and if God smiles on you, in nine months' time,
you will born a boy."

She push herself up and rub her back. Then she
hold out her hand. "I think rain is coming. Can you
hear it? Follow me, let me show you our kitchen."

The sky clap a thunder, and it feel as if it strike
me, right inside of my heart. I collect Khadija hand
as if I am collecting sorrows, then I am following her.

CHAPTER 8

The rain is coming down with anger, be like the roof of the kitchen is a drum, and the rain is drumsticks in God's hand. Khadija is standing under the roof shade of the kitchen, pointing to the here and the there.

"That is the kerosene stove," she say, pointing at the iron stove in the left corner of the kitchen, her voice loud because of roaring rain noises. "For cooking food," she say, as if anybody will use kerosene stove to cook a motorcar. "There is two of the stove. One for me and one for Labake. You can be sharing my own stove if you want."

"Thank you," I say as I wrap my hand around my body and look around all the kitchen areas. There is the remainder of fish stew in a bowl on the floor, the bone of fish looking like a thin white comb inside of it. There is one small wooden chair beside the bowl, and on the floor, a raffia sponge with a cube of black soap melting inside it. The kitchen is not having a door, just a space and two wooden pillars holding the roof.

Afar off, I see a door. One half of it is having paint, the other is just showing wood, as if somebody was painting it and he change his mind and leave it. Or maybe the paint is finish. The smell of old piss is rising over the rainwater smell and hitting my nose.

"Baffroom?" I ask.

"Yes," she say. "You see the well at the front of the house? You fetch water there, cut from the kitchen here to go to toilet there. Everybody is using baffroom anyhow they are wanting it. Just use it as you want." She say this as if it is wonderful thing, to be using baffroom as we want.

"But I must tell you that our husband must be first," she say. "Very early in the morning, once the mosque call for prayer, or when the cock crow, around five in the morning. After that, anybody can use it. Our husband must do everything first. If he has not eaten food, nobody can be eating. He is king in this house." She smile stiff, keeping her eyes on me and holding it strong. No blink. I wait for her to say something more, but she clap her hands, say, "That is okay for one night. Let us go back inside now. This rain is much."

By the time we walk in the compound under the

rain and go back inside the house, my cloth is wet of rainwater, my **iro** heavy.

"Let me take you to our husband's room," Khadija say. We walk along the corridor, my shadow dancing behind Khadija as she is walking and swinging the lantern; pointing Labake's room to the left, her own room to the right, and the room for all the childrens near her own.

"Don't ever enter Labake's room," she say, talking whisper. "One time, Alafia, my daughter, she go to her room to give her food. That witch, Labake, she beat my Alafia till the girl was almost bleeding. If you like yourself, don't go near her room."

We reach the end of the corridor and stop in front of one door. There is a curtain over the door, smelling as if it need a strong washing with soap and water. Behind the door, I am hearing low whistling, a sneeze, something ruffle like paper.

"This is our husband's room," Khadija say. "You will sleep here for three days. After that, me and you will share my room. Is okay?"

"I am afraid," I say, talking whisper. My heart is inside my stomach, and I feel like I want to vomit it out. "Please stay with me."

She laugh, and in the dark of that corridor, I am not even seeing her eyes again. Only a flashing of her teeths. "This is your first time of sleeping with men?"

"I never see any man naked," I say. "I am afraid."

"It is good honor," she say. "To keep yourself for

your husband. When you go inside there, and he is ready for you, close your eyes because that thing will pain you, but when it is paining you, you must think of something you like. What do you like?"

"Mama," I say as tears is filling my eyes and climbing down my cheeks. "I just want my mama."

She touch my shoulder, knock on the door two times, and drag herself away.

"Come inside, come inside." Morufu is standing in my front, holding the door open.

Behind him, I see two lanterns sitting on a newspaper on the floor beside one kerosene stove. There is a mattress on the floor, the box of my clothes resting on the gray wall.

"Why are you just standing there, looking?" There is a carpet of hairs on his chest, thick and curling and gray. He step to one side, and I carry my leg, one after other, and enter the room, my nose twisting to sneeze at the smell of old **siga** smoke. Even with the two lanterns giving light, the room is like a burial coffin. As if it is going to close itself around me and squeeze all my life away. My breathings is rushing out fast, my heart running and turning, running and turning.

"Join me on the bed," he say as he climb the mattress, tilting it with his body, the spring inside creaking. He lie down, rub his stomach, belch out the smell of gin.

"Why didn't you dance today in your father's parlor?" he ask, put his two hand behind his head and give me smile. "Sit down, sit down. Are you not too happy to be marrying me? I am not a wicked man, you know."

"I am feeling cold," I say as I sit on the mattress. There is no bedsheet on top it, no wrapper to cover the foam where the mattress is tearing or having hole. My eyes catch a dark plastic bottle on the floor. It contain cuttings of a tree bark and green leafs inside dirty water. I try to read the words on the bottle, slowly, picking each word one by one: **Fire-Cracker Bitters. Wake Up Sleeping Manhood.**

What is it meaning to have a sleeping manhood? And is Morufu drinking it because of me? Why?

Fear lock me inside of itself. "My body is paining me," I say. "I was inside rain with Khadija. It is making me cold. Please let us sleep now. Today I am feeling sick."

"I just finish drinking Fire-Cracker." He laugh, shift for me on the mattress. "You know how petrol is for car? That is how Fire-Cracker is for a man's body. It is making my whole body to stand. You want to drink small Fire-Cracker? It will chase away all the cold. Lie down, rest your back."

I shake my head no.

"Come on, lie down for me," he say, patting the

bed two times. The mattress cough out dust, give that foul odor of a cloth that didn't finish drying before folding and keeping inside wardrobe. When I am not giving him a answer, he call my name, voice sharp.

"I am coming, sah," I say. Vomit is climbing up my throat again as I lie down beside him. He shift close, put a hand on my stomach. I stiff.

"Relax yourself," he say. "Relax."

He put a hand on my breast, pinch and squeeze it hard through my **buba.** Then his breathing is louding, running fast, as he move his hand up and down my body as if he is trying to find something that is missing. When he pull off his trouser, I start to be crying, calling for Mama. He climb on top of me, shift my legs apart as if it vex him.

A spit of light enter the room, a quick flashing from the window that fill the room with a strange blue-white glow. Is it Mama? Sending her light to suck up all the dark inside of Morufu?

Mama, help me.

I try to hold the light with my eyes, to keep it with me, but it is too quick, half of a blink and nothing.

The pain is suddenly, it snatch my thinking, my breathing, and send me out from my body to the ceiling. I stay up there, watching myself as I am biting my bottom lip, scratching his back, fighting him with every of my strong. But it is useless, my power is not having power because Morufu is be-having as if a devil is inside of him. The more I am fighting, the more he is pressing hisself inside me, pouring hot heat inside my under until he make a loud grunting noise and collapse hisself on top me. Then he roll off to one side, breathing fast.

"You are now complete woman," he say after small moment. "Tomorrow, we this do again. We keep doing it until you are falling pregnant and you born a boy." He climb down from the mattress, wear his trouser, and leave me and my burning under alone in the room.

I lie there with my tears running down the side of my face and into my ears as I am looking up the ceiling, looking the bulb with no light in the center of it.

CHAPTER 9

The early-morning air feel like a rope around my body.

It is a too-tight, too-thick rope that been twisting around me all night, squeezing my head down to my both legs, making it hard to walk, to breathe, to think. I am wanting to just tear my whole body and throw it away as I am dragging myself from Morufu's room.

My under is on fire, feeling as if I sit on top a burning coal for many hours. I cannot remember many of what happen to me last night, my head is full of a dark cloth, blocking every of the evil Morufu was doing, until this morning when he say, "Adunni, go and bring me my morning food."

Afar off, in front of the kitchen, one cock is scratching the floor with his nails, scattering the red earth, his neck brown with dirty feathers. When it see me coming, he stop his scratching and greet me with a loud **coo-koo-roo-koo.**

Two of Khadija's childrens, their name have escape from my brain now, they run outside from the kitchen area, iron bucket dancing in their hands. It make me think of a time when I use to run to Ikati stream in the morning, laughing as I am going to fetch water for Papa, of a time when my mama was not dead.

I wipe the tears running down my face as I reach the kitchen. Khadija is sitting on a wooden stool in front of the stove. The pot on the stove is boiling something that is making the cover clap.

"Adunni." Khadija raise her head, wave a fly away from her face. "Good morning."

"Your husband say I should bring morning food," I say, searching for something to keep my eyes on, until I see the yam peels on the floor, the knife with wooden handle near the stove. The knife make me wonder evil a moment. Make me think, if I take that knife and keep inside my dress, then when Morufu want to rough me this night, I just bring it out and slice off his man-areas. "You are cooking something?" I take my eyes from the knife, hook it on her face. "Yam?"

"Yes, fresh yam. Did you sleep well?" She tilt her head, look me up and down, as if she is finding what I have push down inside of me. "You have pain anywhere? You bleed blood?"

Shame make itself a hand, squeeze my throat tight. "I bleed small blood," I say. "In my under."

"I know how it feels," she say, voice kind. "**Ibukun** powder is good for pain. When our husband leave for his work, I can boil hot water, press the part for you, and rub you some palm oil. The pain will go." She look behind her shoulder, as if checking sure that nobody is coming. "He drink that Fire-Cracker?"

I nod my head yes.

She wave off another fly, shake her head. "First time he used it for me, I died five times and wake up again. He needs it to give him power for the bed-work. You will eat yam and onion?"

"I want to wash my whole body," I say. My body is smelling of a foul odor, the **siga** smell of Morufu, and my mouth is bitter, as if the bitter seed inside of me have full up and is now pouring into my mouth.

"Go," she say, pointing to the baffroom behind her head. "The children have put a bucket there with water for me. Use it. They will fetch another one for me."

The baffroom is a room of square shape, with walls that have green carpet grass climbing down it. There is a iron bucket full with water on the floor, the smell of piss strong in the air.

I touch the water, draw my hand back with a shout. Is ice-cold, shock my skin. My whole body is shaking as I peel off my wedding cloth and hang it on the door. Dipping my hand inside the water and pouring it on myself, I begin, slowly, to wash the smell of **siga** and Fire-Cracker away from my body.

When I finish washing myself, I lie naked on the cold, wet floor of the baffroom. I am afraid that if I come out, the morning and afternoon will pass too quick, and soon it will be nighttime, time for Morufu to fill me with his bitter fire. So I lie there and curl myself up like a worm and keep my eyes tight shut.

Don't cry, Adunni, I warn myself, **don't you never, ever cry for any nonsense foolish old man like Morufu.**

CHAPTER 10

Since I been in this house nearly four weeks, my eyes have see things I can never wish for the worst of my enemy.

There is a devil inside Morufu, a madness that come out when he drink that devil Fire-Cracker, or when one of the childrens is causing him to be angry.

I have see him remove belt from his trouser and flog Kike and her sisters until their skin is bursting, until Labake and Khadija are begging him to not kill their childrens. There is a small devil inside Labake too, a devil that is only coming out when I walk in her front. Just two days back, early morning, after cock crow, I was baffing, taking time because it is the only time I am by myself, the only time I can be thinking sense, when Labake bang on the door and tell me come out because she want to baff quick before she is going to market. When I tell her that I am nearly finishing, that she should wait, she hiss a angry hiss, jam the door open, and drag me with my naked self outside in the open.

Then she begin to pick sand from the floor and paint my body with it. I never feel shame like that. Khadija's childrens gather around us and was laughing as Labake was using sand to scrub my body and curse me. I am giving her respect, so I didn't fight back. When she finish beating me, she turn to the two of Khadija childrens and slap the laughters from their mouth.

Khadija say I should bite Labake next time she try that kind of a thing. That respect is not answer to Labake's madness. She say that before her stomach was swelling with this baby, that she and Labake will fight and fight until one of them is bleeding blood. She say next time, I must keep a bowl of red, hot pepper beside me in the baffroom so that when Labake come and find my trouble, I can pour the pepper in her face and bite her breast.

Khadija make me feel a pinch of comfort in Morufu's house. She keep to caring for me in between caring for her three childrens and the one swelling in her stomach. "Adunni, you must eat this yam," she will say, giving me the bowl of yam and fish soup with a smile. "Eat it and be thanking God that we are having food to eat." Or, "Adunni, come, let me put oil on your hair. You want me to wash it for you?"

And I will say, "No, no, thank you, Khadija, I wash it myself." Or, "How is that thing now with Morufu? Is it still paining?" And I will say no, it is no more paining me in my body, but in my heart and spirit and mind, the pain is never going away.

Me and Khadija are sharing bedroom now, except of when Morufu call for me. It make things easy, sharing room with Khadija. When sad feelings are catching me in the night, Khadija will rub my back, her hand going around and around, as she is telling me to be strong, to be fighting to keep my mind. Sometimes, when her baby is kicking too hard on her stomach, I press my mouth to her hard stomach and sing a song to the baby inside until she and her baby will fall inside a deep sleep, and Khadija say that when she born the baby, I must keep singing to him too, because the baby is already knowing my voice.

Just yesternight, she was comforting me with her words. "When you begin to born your children, you will not be too sad again," she say. "When I first marry Morufu, I didn't want to born children. I was too afraid of having a baby so quick, afraid of falling sick from the load of it. So I take something, a medicine, to stop the pregnant from coming. But after two months, I say to myself, 'Khadija, if you don't born a baby, Morufu will send you back to your father's house.' So I stop the medicine and soon I born my first girl, Alafia. When I hold her in my hands for the first time, my heart was full of so much love. Now, my children make me laugh when I am not even thinking to laugh. Children are joy, Adunni. Real joy."

But I don't want to born anything now. How will a girl like me born childrens? Why will I fill up the world with sad childrens that are not having a chance to go to school? Why make the world to be one big, sad, silent place because all the childrens are not having a voice?

All night, my mind was busy thinking, thinking on the medicine Khadija was taking, on if I can stop my own pregnant from coming.

This morning I find Khadija in the kitchen, where she is sitting on a bench by the stove and plucking **ewedu** leafs into a bowl by her feets.

"Adunni," she say, "good morning. You feeling good today? No more crying for your mama?"

"I been thinking of what you say last night," I say, my eyes on my feets, on my toesnails, which look like they need a clipping. "About childrens."

"Ah," Khadija say.

I peep behind me to check it sure that no one is coming, then I tell her. "I am having a real fear to born childrens," I say, my words climbing each other, rushing fast. "I was thinking of what you say . . . about medicine for not wanting baby. I am just . . . not wanting to born a baby now. What can I do?"

Khadija stop her hand on the plucking of the leafs and nod her head.

"Adunni, you know that our husband is wanting two boys? One from me and one from you. You know this?"

"I know," I say. "I just want to wait." I am hoping that maybe if the pregnant is not coming ever and ever, maybe Morufu will send me go back to my papa. But I don't say this to Khadija.

"You are fearing?" she ask after a long moment, pity in her voice.

"Very," I say. "My stomach cannot be swelling every year because I am looking for boys to give Morufu. The only thing I want to be swelling is my head and my mind with books and educations." I bite my lips. "I am not strong like you, Khadija. I cannot be borning a baby at this my age."

"You are strong, Adunni," she say, her voice low. "A fighter. We are the same, only you don't know it. You want to fight with your educations—good for you, if you can do it in this our village. Me, I am fighting with what I have inside of me, with my stomach for getting pregnants. With it, I can fight to stay here so that my childrens will keep a roof on their head, and my mama and papa will keep having bread to eat and soup to drink."

I stand there, looking her, at the small hill of leafs in the bowl which is rising with each falling leaf from Khadija's hand, at her fingers which are dark green and wet from the pinching and twisting of the leafs from the branch.

"Do you know how to count the days for your

monthly visitor?" she ask. "You know when it is starting every month?"

"Yes," I say. "Why?"

"There is something you can take. A mixing of strong leafs."

"It will help me?" I ask, my heart lifting with hope. "It will stop the pregnant?"

"I am not making you any promise, Adunni, but I will see if I can find the leafs for it in Ikati farm. You will add it to ten paw-paw seeds and mix it with gingerroot and dry pepper. Put it all in a dark bottle and soak it in rainwater for three days. You must drink it five days before and five days after your monthly visitor and every time you and Morufu are doing the thing."

She lift up her head and thin her eyes at me. "Morufu must not know you are drinking medicine. You understand me, Adunni?"

My heart is melting as I look the round of her face, the kind spirit in her eyes. "Thank you, Khadija," I say, bending to pick up one branch. "Can I pluck this one for you?"

"Adunni," she say, taking the branch from my hand with care and setting it down on the floor. "Your mind is so full of worry, it is pouring all over your face. Forget about housework for today. Pull that bench, sit here with me, and let us talk."

CHAPTER 11

With Khadija, the days in this house are short and sometimes sweet.

We talk together, laugh together, and with her stomach swelling so big and making her sometimes sick, I am helping to do her washing, cooking, everything. I am helping with her small childrens too, baffing for Alafia and her sisters, and feeding them food and washing their hair and dirty cloths. They are good childrens, Khadija's childrens, ever happy and laughing and looking for Labake's trouble.

Me and Morufu, we don't talk much. He is always so busy with his farming and taxi-driving work from early morning till night. Sometimes, he will call me to his room, make me to stand in his front with my hand in my back, and ask me question as if he a doctor. He will ask me if I am having pregnants yet or if my monthly visitor have come because he want me to quick and carry pregnants and born a boy, but most times, he just want to rough me and eat food. I keep to drinking the drink Khadija make for me, from a dark bottle full of bitter leafs and ginger.

When it is my turn with Morufu, I will take a quick cap of it, go to his room, and watch him swallow his own Fire-Cracker, before I am making myself a dead body so that he can rough me. I am hoping that maybe after six months or something like that, he will see that no pregnant is ever coming, and he can send me go back to my papa. Maybe.

Labake is still fighting me. She will stamp her feets and curse if I am too long in washing the plates in the kitchen, or if I am too quick to sweep the compound, or too slow in grinding beans. She is always looking for my trouble, that Labake, always finding a way to fight me.

But today is the second Tuesday in the month.

The day for market womens and Ikati farmers meeting, which means the two both of Labake and Morufu are not in the house. Because of it, I am feeling one kind of a free I didn't feel in a long time, and as I am cleaning the parlor this early morning, I feel a pulling in my heart to sing. To just be happy. To not think of sorrow or worry things. So I start singing a song I just make up in my head:

Hello, fine girl!
If you want to become a big, big lawyer
You must go to plenty, plenty school
If you want to wear a high, high shoe
And walk, ko-ka-ko
You must go to plenty, plenty school

I take the thick newspaper that been sitting under the lantern on top the tee-vee, fold it this way and that until it look kind of like the paper lawyer-wig I sometimes see inside the tee-vee. I put it on top my head, hold it down with one hand. Then I stand on the tip of my toes as if I am wearing a too-high shoes on my feets. I begin to walk on my toes up and down the parlor, singing:

Walk, ko-ka-ko
In your high, high shoe!

As I say "ko-ka-ko," I stop my walking a moment to twist my buttocks left and right to the beat, then I keep walking on my toes, swinging one hand up and down, the other pressing the newspaper to my head so it don't fall off.

My voice is happy and clear like a early-morning bird, and I don't even see Khadija peeping her head into the parlor, looking me with the newspaper on my head, laughing silent.

"Adunni!" she say.

I shock, stop singing, then give her a big smile when I see that she didn't angry.

"Sorry," I say, "I was just—"

"Did you finish your morning work?" she ask.

"I finish it all," I say as I remove the newspaper from my head, fold it, and keep it back on the tee-vee. "I make up a song about a girl wanting to become a lawyer. You want me to sing it for you? **Hello, fine girl**—"

She wave her hand to stop my singing and rub her stomach. "No, not now. I am still feeling a little sick. Maybe at nighttime."

"Okay," I say. "Did you see the okra I cook for you this morning?"

"I will drink some now," she say. "Thank you."

I look around the parlor, then nod my head yes. "All of this place is very clean. Now, let me go and start washing—"

"No," Khadija say. "Leave the cloth in the back-yard, I will wash it for you when I am better. The rains of last week must have swell up the river. Can you go and bring water from Ikati river for me? My clay pot is beside the well. Use it."

"You want me to go to Ikati river?" I press a hand to my chest, blink. "Me?"

Morufu don't ever allow me to go anywhere far like the river. He say that new wifes is didn't suppose to be going up and down everywhere until after one year, after I have born a baby boy for him.

Khadija nod her head yes, then smile soft. "Adunni, I know your friends be always playing in the river around this time. The house is free of Labake and Morufu. It been too long since you seen them all. So go quick. Come back before afternoon."

"Oh, Khadija," I say, jumping up and down and clapping my hand. "Thank you, thank you, thank you!"

I don't think I ever run so fast since the day my mama born me.

I skip on my feets, jumping the rocks on the floor, not stopping to greet some of the womens carrying firewood on their head as I pass them on the way, or the childrens selling morning bread in a tray on their head. I keep my eyes to my front, holding Khadija's clay pot in one hand, my wrapper tight in the other hand until I am near. Afar off, near the fence of banana leafs by the edge of the river, I see Ruka and Enitan.

There are five or six boys in the other far end of the river, playing a boxing match and shouting and laughing, but I keep my eye on Enitan, who is drawing a square in the wet sand with a stick. Her bucket is on the ground beside her, and Ruka is perching her buttocks on the back of her feets, watching what Enitan is drawing.

I stand there a moment, feeling my heart swell as

I am thinking back to the time when I didn't have a husband, when I was free to be playing like this.

Enitan is now drawing another square. I know she will draw about six or seven squares in the sand for a game we are calling **suwe,** which is my best-of-all game. I will throw a stone inside one of the square, then be jumping on every square with only one leg, trying to not fall until I pick the stone, while Enitan and Ruka will be clapping and singing **"Suwe! Suwe! Suwe!"** from outside the box. But all of that was all before in the past.

I set down Khadija's clay pot, shout, "Enitan! Ruka!"

Ruka turn her head to where I am standing, wide her eyes, and smile a big smile. "Look! Adunni!"

Me and Enitan and Ruka, we run to embrace ourselfs and begin to laugh and talk all at once.

"Our wife," Enitan say, pulling my hand to sit down on a rock by the river edge. Ruka sit on the other side of me so that I am in the middle of the two both of them. I feel as if my heart will just burst from the smile on their face, the bouncing happy in their eyes.

"How is life as a wife?" Enitan ask, eyes shining as if a bulb light is inside her head. "Tell us everything, tell us everything!"

"Look your cheeks!" Ruka say, pinching my left cheeks. "Adunni, you been eating too much bread and milk. You are living well!"

"There is plenty to eat there," I say.

"And how is your senior wifes?" Enitan ask. "Morufu? How is he doing to you?"

"Wait, let me ask her one too!" Ruka say. "Tell us, Adunni, did you do that thing with your husband?" She wink her eye like something gum her eyeslids together. "Did it pain you or was it sweet?"

"Are you cooking every day?" Enitan ask.

"Tell us about that thing!" Ruka say. "I want to hear it!"

"Too many questions," I say, laughing at Ruka, who is still winking. "The first wife, Labake, she is just a very wicked somebody. She always be painting her face with white powder like a ghost. She keep fighting everybody too."

"Kike's mama?" Enitan say, pulling her wrapper to cover her knees as a quick cold breeze blow us. "I know that woman. She is always doing like something is worrying her. What of the second wife? What is her name?"

"Khadija." I touch my chest, look my friends left to right. "She is just like us. Only six years more old, but she have three childrens and a new one on the way. She is so kind. She cook for me, teach me plenty things. I sing for her too, at night. She likes to hear my singing. She be just like another mama to me."

My eyes pinch with tears as I am thinking of it. Khadija be like another mama to me. A mama! I been praying long for God to bring back my mama, even though I know she don't ever be coming back, but for the first time since then, I think that maybe Khadija be the answer to my prayer.

"See!" Enitan is saying, clapping. "It is not so bad to be a wife!"

"No," I say, talking slow, "it is not so bad, but only because of Khadija. About that thing you ask of me—" I turn to Ruka with a twist in my stomach. Maybe if I tell them how it is, they will not be hurrying so much to marry. "It is too much pain, make it hard to walk sometimes. I even bleed blood after, and many times, it make me feel so sick. Don't rush and marry, I tell you!"

But Ruka, the foolish girl, she laugh a shy laugh and push my knees to one side. "Lie! Lie!"

I am wanting to ask her why she think I am lying, but Enitan point to the back of us, shout, "Look who is coming from the boys' side of the river! Kayus!"

I jump to my feets and look. True, true, my Kayus is coming, running fast, shouting my name. It is the first time I am seeing Kayus since I marry Morufu two months back, and I pick myself and begin to run to him, leaving Enitan and Ruka. We meet just before he reach the girls' side, and he pick me up, turn me around and around in the air until the sky become ground. He so strong sometimes, Kayus!

"I was hearing the girls shouting your name from afar," he say as he set me down. "And I say to myself, 'No, it is not my Adunni,' but when I look well, I see it is you!"

I steady myself on my feets, then cup his face in my two hands. "My Kayus!"

"I didn't talk to Papa since you marry that goat Morufu," he say, fighting to remove his head from my hands, but I hold it tight because I want to soak up his whole face with my eyes: his long, thick eye-slashes, the thinning marks on his cheeks, his two front teeths that have a chipping on the edge of it from when he smash his mouth in a fall.

"When I start working at Kassim Motors," he say, voice hard, "I swear, I will make plenty money and come and collect you from that Morufu. I will pay back all his foolish bride-price and we will build our own house and live there forever, just me and you!"

I pull him close and press his head to my chest, my heart.

"I know you will," I say. "But till then, I will manage myself. Things is not so bad at Morufu. Come and sit with me, let me tell you everything about it."

Around midday, I leave the river, say my bye-bye to Kayus and Enitan and Ruka, and begin my trek-king back home.

The sun is a shining hot plate in the sky, rest-ing itself among balls of white cotton wool. I carry Khadija's pot of fresh water on my head, my heart skipping in a dance at the sound of Kayus's laughters still in my ears.

As I am nearing the house, my heart stop the skipping and begin to feel as if I put rocks inside, heavy rocks that press me down on my feets and slow my walking. I feeling to just run back to Kayus, to take him to our house and cook palm oil rice for him and sing him to sleep at night, but I know that Papa will give me a beating for it, so I turn to the path behind the house and keep walking to Morufu's house.

A throwing-stone away from the house, the bush make a crunching noise so sudden, I stop my walking. "Who is there?" I say, thinking to put the clay pot down and peep. "Who?"

Labake climb out from the bush, a brown cloth tight around her chest, eyes wide with something crazy. In her hand is a thin, long stick, the one with short wooden nails on it, same one she like to keep at the back of the kitchen for scaring away Khadija's childrens when Khadija is not in the house.

"Good afternoon, ma," I say, trying to not show my fear at the stick in her hand. "What are you doing in the bush?"

"Waiting for you," she say in Yoruba. "I want to catch you by yourself so that Khadija cannot save you. Now, tell me. Why is the kerosene in my stove low?"

I think of the okra soup I cook for Khadija early this morning. She been drinking a bowl of okra every morning since two weeks now, say it help to wake up baby when it is stiff in her stomach. I cook it with Khadija's stove, the green stove beside the washing bowl.

"I don't know why your kerosene is low," I say.

"Did you cook?" she ask. "In the kitchen?"

"For Khadija," I say.

"Which stove did you use?"

"Khadija's stove."

Did I mistake and use Labake's stove? I check my mind, search it everywhere before I shake my head no. There are two of the same kind of green stoves in the kitchen, one beside the washing bowl and the other one behind the bench, and every evening, after cooking, Labake will take her stove to her room. No, I shake my head again, I didn't use Labake's stove because it was not even inside the kitchen this morning.

"Please move from my way," I say. "I want to take this water to—"

"My stove is the one beside the washing bowl," she say, moving more close, eyes thinning with anger. "The green one. I didn't take it to my room last night. Khadija's stove is not working, but I think her pregnant stomach is worrying her brain, so she didn't remember telling you that Morufu take it for fixing. Now, I ask you again, did you use my stove?"

"Your stove is the which one?" I ask, my heart beginning to jump, my hands sore from gripping the clay pot too tight.

She put a hand on my chest and push me. Just a small push, but the water in the pot sway this way and that, drops of it pouring on my face, inside my cloth, the cold of it shocking my chest.

"You are still asking me which one?" She crack the air with the stick, and I feel a slicing on my skin from the sound.

I lick my lips, take two steps back, the pot of water on my head like a pot of fire and stones and troubles.

"I think maybe—" I start, wanting to beg her to don't be angry, to don't flog me, when I hear the voice of Kike, Labake's daughter, from behind us: "Mama!"

Kike come running up the path, breathing fast. Me and her don't talk much since I marry her father. She keep to herself in the house, and me, I don't even look her face. She is tying a cloth around her chest and holding a wooden spoon with white dough on the tip of it. Be like she was turning **fufu** in a pot and just leave it to come running to us. What is she finding here? Is she coming to join her mama in beating me?

"Mama," Kike say, dipping her knees into the sand to greet Labake. "It was me, Mama. It was me that use your stove to, to boil garden-eggs this morning. Not Adunni."

"Kike, it was you?" Labake say, looking her daughter down and eyeing her as if she is not believing her. "Are you sure?"

"I swear, Mama, it was me."

Labake hiss, pushing my chest again. This time, the pot of water jump out from my hand, smash to the floor, and scatter to pieces.

I keep my eyes on the pieces of Khadija pot, watching the sand turn to a deep, dark red as Labake is walking away; her feets sending dust up in the air, her voice loud, full of cursing for me and Khadija.

When it is just me and Kike by ourselfs, I turn to her, where she is still kneeling on the floor, still holding the wooden stick in her hand, looking like she herself is not understanding what she is doing here.

"You lie for me," I say, my heart swelling with a mixing of thank you and a sad surprise. "Why?"

But Kike is not giving me any answer, she just shrug her shoulders, and, picking herself up, she shake the sand from her knees and run off fast, calling for her mama, begging her to wait for her.

I watch the dust settle back to the ground a moment, thinking maybe Kike will come back, before I sit on the floor, spread my wrapper between my two knees, and begin to use my hands to pack Khadija's broken pot and all my happy feelings from seeing Kayus today into my wrapper.

I don't know how long I stay there, sweeping everything into the wrapper: the wet sand, the pieces of a bone that a dog eat and spit out a long time ago, a tin of milk that been crushed under a car tires, weeds from around the bush. I keep packing things, keep putting them into my wrapper, not minding the stinking smell from it all or my dirty hands.

When I cannot pack any more, I try to stand to my feets, but I cannot. Something be pressing me down, and I didn't too sure if it is all the rubbish inside my wrapper, or the sorrow swelling heavy in my heart, so I stay there like that, sitting on the floor, until someone say my name in a whisper.

"I been waiting for you to come home." It is Khadija, her voice soft, concern. "Look how dirty you are."

"It was Labake," I say, pushing myself to my feets, as everything inside my wrapper tumble to the floor like a rain of rubbish. "Labake push me and now your pot is smash up and I was picking it for you, picking everything and thinking of how to fix it, to fix everything that be all mess up since my mama was dead, but it is too hard. Everything is too hard."

"Oh, Adunni," Khadija say as she press a warm hand to my cheeks and wipe the tears I didn't know was there.

"Come with me, child," she say. "You need a hot baff, a bowl of sweet yam, and a deep, deep sleep."

She take me by my hand and drag me and my heavy heart back to Morufu's house.

CHAPTER 12

Since last week, my heart been feeling one kind of soft for Kike, and when we see, we sometimes greet each other with our eyes, but this morning, she find me where I am sitting on the floor and grinding pepper in front of the kitchen.

She stand in my front, hand on her hip, and tilt her neck. "Adunni," she say, "good morning."

"G'morning," I say as I pick the grinding stone and pour water on it to wash away the dirty, before I begin to roll it on the ball of peppers that is sitting on another wide gray stone in between my legs.

"Thank you for . . . for that day in the bush," I say, keeping my eyes on the grinding stone. "I been wanting to say thank you, but your mama, she keep watching me, watching to see if I will talk to you."

"She is in the market now," Kike say. "Till sunset before she is coming back."

"Why you tell a lie for me that day?" I ask.

"Because of . . . nothing," she say.

I look up, roof my eyes from the sun. "I didn't want to marry your father," I say. "You know it."

She bend herself, sit on the stone beside me. "I know it. I know you want to go to school. You have a good brain, Adunni. Good for learning school. Everybody in the village is saying so."

"Then why is your mama fighting me?"

"My papa did a bad thing when he marry Khadija and you because of no boy-childrens. She is using that pain to fight the two of you. You . . . you are my age, it make it all very hard for her."

"I hear you," I say.

"My father find me a husband," she say. "He been looking since I was ten years. He tell me yesterday that he collect my bride-price. Tomorrow, I go to my husband's house."

"Who the man?" I pick up another pepper, tear it into two, put it on the grinding slate, and begin to roll the other stone on it. "You meet him before?"

Kike shake her head. "His name is Baba Ogun. He is selling medicine for sick peoples in his village. He have one wife before. She die six months back of coughing blood. He is finding another one, a young girl like me to make him feel like a young man. We are not doing real wedding because he have a dead wife before, but my papa and mama will take me there soon."

Kike is not vexing; it seem as if she didn't mind it to be second wife of a old man with a dead first wife.

"You happy to marry this man?" I ask as I spoon up the pepper, check it. The white seeds among the pepper is like sand in my hand, so I pour it back on the stone, keep grinding.

"It make my papa happy." She shrug her shoulder. "My mama want me to learn tailor work. But Papa say he didn't have money to send me for training. He will use my bride-price to fix up the other taxi-car." She lean back, watching as my hand is rolling the stone over the peppers, front and back, front and back.

She sigh. "I wish I am a man."

I stop my hand. "Why you wish that?"

"Because think it, Adunni," she say. "All the mens in our village, they are allowing them learn school and work, but us the girls, they are marrying us from fourteen years of age. I know I can be a good tailor. I can draw fine, fine style." She take a finger, draw something in the sand. When I tilt my head and look, I see a long dress, fishtail shape, sleeves like two ringing bells.

"That is a very good style," I say.

"Every day, when I come back from market with my mama"—she wipe the style, and press her finger into the sand, draw another—"I draw a dress of many styles. When I close my eyes"—she press her eyeslids close—"I can see all the womens in the village wearing my style."

She open her eyes, give me a sad smile. "I wish I am a man, but I am not, so I do the next thing I can do. I marry a man."

I think on what she say a moment, the sense of her words.

"I am praying to God that my husband is kind so that he will send me to learn tailor," she say. "And you, Adunni. What you want to become in life?"

"Teacher," I say. I been wanting to be teacher since I was two years of age. Even before my mama was dead, I was always teaching the trees and leafs in our compound when Mama is frying her puff-puff for selling. I will slap my stick on the root of the mango tree and say to it: "You, Mango, what is one plus one?" Then I will answer the answer myself: "One plus one is equals to two, Teacher Adunni!"

I smile at the memory of it. "I want to keep teaching the childrens in the village," I say to Kike. "To give them better life. But now that I marry your father, all of that is didn't possible."

She shake her head. "Close your eyes and be doing the teacher in your mind," she say. "Do it, close your eyes. Think it with your mind."

At first I am only seeing the dark cloth, but as I shift the cloth and I look deep, deep inside of me, I bring myself out and put myself inside the classroom, then I am holding chalk and writing on the blackboard. Behind me, the childrens are wearing white and red uniforms, sitting on the bench and hearing me as I am teaching them all the things that Teacher was teaching me before I was leaving school.

I feel a rush of something free in that moment. Is so strong that I open my eyes quick. A laugh jump out of my mouth, shock me.

Kike give me another smile. "See? I tell you, Adunni, even if you marry my father and you think all your hope is finish, your mind is not finishing. Inside of your mind, you can be the teacher you want." She stand to her feets. "You like to be reading books, so feed your mind with reading of any book you find, maybe in the dustbins of Idanra town or some cheap ones in the market. One day, maybe you become that teacher, maybe not. Tomorrow I go to meet my new husband's family, but inside of my mind, I am Kike the tailor. Wish me well."

When she leave me be, I close my eyes a moment, trying to become teacher in my mind, but the dark cloth is everywhere in my head, and the pepper in my hands is pinching my skin.

CHAPTER 13

Yesternight, Khadija ask me to follow her to midwife.

Her pregnants is nearing eight months. Since last week, she be walking as if there are two tires between her legs. She also keep moaning when she is in the kitchen, keeping her voice down, thinking nobody hear it. But I hear it, and when I ask if all is okay with her baby, she say yes. But yesternight, as she climb the mat and fold herself near me and I start to sing for the baby, she shake her head, say, "Stop, Adunni. No singing for today, please." When I ask her why, because she didn't ever, ever ask me to stop singing before, she say, "I am afraid, Adunni. I am afraid that maybe this baby is coming too early."

"Why?" I ask when she talk about baby coming down. "Is something not correct with baby?"

"Yes," she say.

"You think it or you know it?" I ask.

She sort of frown, big her eyes. "I know it. This is my number four pregnant, Adunni. I know when a baby wants to come out and when it want to stay up. This one wants to come out. It need another four or five weeks before it is a strong baby to come out. Not now. I must see midwife tomorrow morning. This baby is a boy-baby. It cannot die."

"How you know it is a boy?" I ask. "Someone look inside your stomach, check it sure?"

"I know it," she say. "When Morufu say he will not give my family food if this is not a boy-child, I do something to make it sure." She low her head, like she is sad somehow. "What I do is a shame, but I didn't have choice. I cannot born another girl-child, Adunni. You know it. What will my papa and mama eat if I born a girl-child? This one is a boy. It cannot die. Follow me tomorrow morning. First light."

I didn't sleep well after that. I keep thinking, what she do to make sure her baby is a boy? I keep my eyes open, thinking far deep inside the night, sometimes checking Khadija, checking her stomach, because I am fearing what if the baby just climb out and die? If I call Morufu, Labake will beat me stupid because tonight is her night to sleep with Morufu.

But thank God, the baby manage and keep his-self till this morning.

"Where is the midwife's house?" I ask her after my morning baff. "Will you tell your husband that I am following you to midwife?" I am talking whisper to her, even though we are in her room, far from Morufu and Labake. I been his wife nearly three months now, but I cannot be bringing myself to call Morufu "our husband." Is just something my mouth cannot never talk. When I try it last time, my tongue hook itself, so I keep it to calling him "your husband" when I am talking to Khadija. She understand it, I understand it.

She shake her head. "I tell him I am going to visit my mother," she say. "That you are following me to help me carry my bag."

"Why didn't you tell him we are going to midwife?" I ask, confuse. "Anything bad in that?"

"You cannot understand," she say as she rub her stomach and twist her face as if it is still paining her. "Are you ready for us to be going?"

I wear my black sandal-shoe, tight my dress-belt behind my back, and follow Khadija.

Morufu and Labake are inside the compound, standing in front of the taxi-car. Today is Kike's wedding, so I know they are making preparations to carry her to her husband's house.

Morufu is wearing the same **agbada** he was wearing for our wedding, and Labake is wearing something like a brown sack. She hiss, turn her back on me. I hiss too, loud for only my ears to hear.

"Where are you going this early morning?" Morufu ask, hooking his **agbada** sleeve on his shoulder. "You are not following us to Kike's wedding."

"God forbid," Labake say. "They cannot follow us. Today is my day to shine. No witch can spoil it for me."

"We are not following you," Khadija say. She look as if her spirit is climbing out from her body as she wipe her front head, which is full of sweat. "I am going to my mother's house. She so sick. I must take Adunni with me. My bag is heavy to carry."

Why is Morufu blinding to what Khadija is feeling?

I bend my knee, greet him. "Good morning, sah."

"Adunni, my young wife," he say. "Do you want to follow Khadija to go and greet her mother?"

I look Khadija, she sway a little on her feets, nod her head. I nod my own too. "Yes, sah."

"You must come back this night," he say. "Because, tonight, I want to spend one special time with my Adunni."

"By God's grace," Khadija say, "we will come back before sunset."

"Till then," Morufu say. He enter the car, on the engine.

We watch as Kike come out from the house. She is wearing a new **iro** and **buba,** there is a flower on the neck area of the **buba.** It is nice-looking, maybe she style it herself? There is a lace cloth on her head, on her **gele,** and it hang over her face, a curtain. She peep from under the cloth, her eyes filling with hope under the black **khajal** around the eyeslids.

"Go well," I say to her when she reach my front. "Go well, my tailor."

Me and Khadija get to walking the two miles to the bus garage.

The bus garage is not a far distant, but Khadija be walking ever so slow, moaning and groaning, rubbing her tummy as if she about to born that baby right there on the road to the garage.

She keep saying she want to shit, she want to piss, she want to sleep.

I am very fearing for her, but I hide my fear and tell her to keep walking, to don't stop, to don't piss or shit. The bus is not full, just market womens holding basket of bread, orange, beans, making preparations for selling morning food. We sit in the front seat, me near the driver that is smelling of early-morning spit, and Khadija near the door. I hold her bag in my laps, keep my eyes on her, as if my eyes will hold the baby inside her stomach. When the driver is starting the bus and is leaving the garage, I ask Khadija how she feel now. "Baby staying up?"

"Still coming down," she say as she rest her head

on my shoulder, squeeze my hand. "My eyes are closing. We are going to Kere village. Wake me when we reach."

Before I can say don't sleep, she close her eyes, and is starting to snore.

CHAPTER 14

We cut through the forest road, the bus driving between the tall mango trees with thick branches and leafs to the left and right of it.

The branches are leaning close, covering the road like a umbrella, light from the sun entering through a crack in the umbrella. We pass farmers riding their bicycle to the farm, the bells on it ringing to chase away peoples, chickens, and dogs from their road. We pass the womens with trays of firewood, bread, and green plantains on their head, their childrens sleeping in the wrappers around their back. They are just coming from the farm, taking the firewood and food to the house for cooking. I think about this, why the mens in the village are not letting many of the girls go to school, but they are not minding when the womens are bringing firewood and going to market and cooking for them?

We pass Ikati border, and soon a line of red hills be surrounding us like a embrace. Some of the hills is having mud houses perching on the edge of it, looking as if it will fall off the hill and just kill all the peoples inside any moment now.

Black goats, about fifty of them, are climbing up one of the rocks. There is a man at the bottom of it, holding a long stick, flogging the goats up, up. To the left of me is another hill that look like it is crying real tears; and a line of clear water, the blue of the sky, is running down the face of it, the top of the hill egg-shape and smooth like a man's head.

One hour or so after the hills, we reach Kere garage, and Khadija, who been sleeping all the way, snoring deep too, is talking nonsense inside her sleep.

The driver bring the bus to a stop near a cocoa tree. The air have a smell of roasting nuts, and when I look around, I see a man turning walnuts in a wheelbarrow sitting on top a firewood flame. There are one or two peoples in his front, waiting to buy the walnut. It is a small village, this Kere place, half of Ikati, it seems, with one or two round houses that they builded with red sand here and there and the rest houses are nearly falling off the hills.

Across the garage, there is one shop selling choco-sweet, **siga,** newspapers, and bread. A woman is sweeping the front of the shop, the broom doing swish, swish as she is going front and back on the floor and singing, her voice climbing across the road to come and meet us:

In the mornin'
I will rise and praise the Lor'

"This is reach Kere village," the driver say with a shout. "We stay here for ten minutes, then we move!"

My stomach is starting to tight itself as I elbow Khadija. "Open your eyes," I say, but she just drop her neck to one side. Why she sleeping so much? I lick my lips, feel as if I lick a fire, and elbow her again. "Khadija?"

Why, why, why did I follow her to this place? What was I thinking in my brain? What if she keep sleeping on and on, forever and forever?

"Khadija, wake up!" I shout and the bus driver look me. "She didn't wake up!" I say to the driver, and the sound of my tears in my voice shock me.

"Adunni?" Khadija open her eyes slow, look around the place, and wipe spit from her mouth. "I am waking up. This is the place. Let us come down."

"You doing fine?" I ask. The twisting in my stomach stop a moment as I wipe her face with my hand. "I was fearing you were sleeping too deep. You feeling well?"

"Very well," she say, collecting my hand. "Follow me."

Together, we climb out from the bus and walk, her stopping and moaning, me telling her to try keep going, until we cut across the bus garage, pass the singing woman in front of her shop, and find ourselfs on one road. There is a guava tree on the side of the road, and one brown goat with red thread on his neck is eating the grass around the root of the tree. The goat look up, see us as we are coming, tear a grass, and run away. Khadija stop, rest herself on the guava tree, the fruit on top of the tree dropping low to near her head, looking yellow, ripe for plucking.

"You want to sit down?" I ask, putting her bag on the floor. "Rest yourself."

Khadija bend herself until she is sitting on the tree root. "I will wait here for you." She point a shaking finger the round house in the afar. "Cross this road and go to that house with red door. Knock it three times. If a woman open it, tell her you are selling leafs, then turn back and come here. But if is a man that open it, tell him you ask for Bamidele. Tell him Khadija send you. Bring him come to me."

I strong my face, confuse. "Where is the mid-wife's house?" I ask. Bamidele is the name of a man. I never see a man-midwife in my life. "Khadija?"

There is new sweat on her forehead now, beads of water spotting her up lip.

"Please don't ask too much questions now," she say. "If you want my baby to not die, please go and ask for Bamidele. Tell him . . . Ah, my back, Adunni. My back is paining me."

I give her a long look, wonder again why I follow her come. Why didn't I stay in Ikati and mind my own matter? But Khadija help me with the drink for not having pregnant, she keep my mind free of worry in Morufu's house, she fight Labake for me. And if she die here, everybody will say I kill my senior wife. They will say jealousy make me carry her to Kere village and kill her dead and leave her by a guava tree. They will kill me too, with no question, because in Ikati, they kill anybody that kill or anybody that steal.

I remember when one farmer, Lamidi, he kill his friend because of farmland fight, and the village chief tell his servants to be flogging Lamidi seventy lashes with palm frond in the village square every day until he have die dead. They burn his body after he finish dying. No burial. They just throw his black body inside the forest, a burning offering to the gods of the forest.

I carry my legs and cross the road quick, hurrying my feets until I reach the front of the clay house.

When I look back, Khadija raise her hand and wave me bye-bye.

The door is the red of blood, angry-looking. I fold my fingers and knock it one time. No answer. I can hear something inside, somebody is hearing radio, the morning news in Yoruba.

I knock again.

The door open slow. I find myself looking a man. He is tall, young, fine-looking. He is wearing a trouser cloth, no shirt on top. No shoes on his feets too. Radio inside his hand.

"I am looking for Bamidele," I say. "Is it you?"

He off the radio with one button on the side of it. "Yes, I am Bamidele. How can I help?"

I keep my voice low. "Khadija. You know her?"

His face shift, and he look back inside his house as if checking sure nobody is coming. "What happen to her?" he ask.

"She say I should call you come," I say. "She is sitting afar off. Not well."

"Not well?" He strong his face. "Wait."

He close the door.

I stand there, shifting on my feets, feeling much confuse. Who is this Bamidele man? What he and Khadija have with theirselfs? And why she tell me she is going to see midwife, and she tell Morufu she is going to see her mother? The door open again, cut my thinking. The man is wearing a shirt now, matching material with his trouser. "Take me to her."

We walk small, run small, until we reach Khadija. There is much sweat on her face now, and she is turning her head this way and that. I stand to one corner, and the man, this Bamidele, he kneel down, take Khadija's hand.

"Khadija," he say. "It is me. What happen?"

Khadija open her eyes, a struggle. She tilt her lip,

as if she want to smile. "Bamidele," she say, talking whisper so low, I am bending my head to hear what she is saying.

"The baby is giving me trouble," she say. "I am afraid I will die."

Bamidele wipe her face with his hand and I shock. Look around the areas. Who see us? There is nobody on the streets, only that goat is in the afar, bending its two back legs, doing hard shit; small black balls falling like bullets of rain from his buttocks.

What is this man thinking he is doing, touching Khadija's face like that? Didn't he know Khadija is another man's wife?

"**Aya mi,**" he say. "You won't die."

He mad? Why is he calling her **"aya mi,"** "my wife"?

"Khadija," I say, "what is this man talking all this nonsense for?"

Khadija don't give me answers. Is as if she is not even hearing me. So I stand there, looking like a big fool, waiting for the thing I am finding to find me.

"The baby is pressing to come out," she say to the man. "I am afraid that if I born it, it will die. Remember the curse you tell me about? The ritual me and you must do before the baby is reaching nine months?"

What curse? Which ritual? I stamp my feets, feeling more and more confuse, angry. Why are they talking like this? Making no sense?

Bamidele nod his head yes. "We can go today," he say. "Together. Me and this girl will carry you."

He throw me one look, and I step back. Which girl is he talking? Not me. I am not following anybody to go and do anything stupid ritual.

"I am going back to Ikati," I say.

"Please," Khadija say. "Help me. My strength is finishing now, I cannot even stand. You and Bamidele must carry me to go and do this thing."

"Tell me what happen first." I eye the man up and down as if he is smelling of a spoiling something. "Who is this man to you?"

The man push hisself to his feets. "You are who to her?" he ask.

"She is my **iya ile**," I say. "I marry Morufu after her."

"Ah," he say. "Adunni."

How he knows my name?

"Khadija tell me about you," he say, giving a sad smile. "She say you are a good person. Good girl. She say you—"

"Talk sense please," I say. I don't have time to be hearing about my good self when Khadija is looking as if she is inside a bus of death.

"Khadija is my first love," Bamidele say. "She didn't tell you?"

"No," I say. How will she tell me? Is this Bamidele having foam in his head instead of a brain?

"Five years back, me and Khadija was doing love. Real love. We suppose to marry ourselfs," he say, "but her father fall sick, so he sell Khadija to Morufu to help them. Me, I didn't have money that time. It pained me that they carry my love and give her to old Morufu, but I take it like a man. I leave Ikati, come and settle here in Kere to do my welder work. After four years of marrying Morufu, Khadija come and find me. She say she love me. Me and her, we begin our love again."

He drop his head, look her as she is twisting with pain on the floor. When he look me back, tears is shining in his eyes. "That baby in her stomach is for me. It is a boy inside. I know it."

"Help me," Khadija say, talking so weak now.

"Which ritual are you saying she must do?" I ask. "In which place?"

"In my family, we have a curse," Bamidele say. "We must wash every pregnant woman inside the river seven times before the baby is reaching nine months. If the woman didn't do this, she will die with her baby as she is borning it.

"In my family, we don't born many girls. All our womens always born boys. As I am like this, I have six brothers. I know that she is carrying my baby inside her stomach, that it is a boy-child, my son."

He sigh a sad sigh. "Kere river is not far from here. She can use that one. I have one special black soap she will use. I have it in the house. But let us take her first. Help me."

I look Khadija. "Is it true what this man is saying? The baby is not for Morufu?"

"It is true," she say. "This baby is for Bamidele. Morufu is a foolish, wicked man. He wants boy-children, but he cannot give me pregnant for boys. So I come to Bamidele, and he help me with a boy. But because of this curse, I cannot born the baby until I baff . . . but now the baby is wanting to come out, so I must be quick to . . . Carry me up, please."

I keep my feets to the ground. "Khadija, why will you give another man's baby to Morufu?"

Khadija throw her head left and right, twisting her face.

Bamidele look me, worry in his eyes. "We must go quick," he say. "Take her hand there and let me take it here. When I count one, two, three, we lift her up."

"I am not doing ritual," I say, folding my hand on top my chest, feel it beating fast. "Let us just carry her to the midwife. The midwife will help her. The midwife will—"

"She will die!" Bamidele shout so sudden, the goat in the afar stop his shit, take off, and run.

"Please," he say, voice down. "This thing is in our family for many years. I know people who die because they didn't do this baff. Even my mother, when she was pregnant of me and my six brothers, she do the baff. We must be quick."

I don't like this ideas at all. I don't like that Khadija bring me come here and put me inside this nonsense mess with her. But she look as if she about to die, and if it will save her, then I must be helping her. I must. I think back to when I first come to Morufu's house, how Khadija will wipe my crying tears every night and give me pepper soup to drink. How, even when she was feeling sick, she make a hot water for me to baff that day after Labake was breaking her clay pot.

It was Khadija that make living with Morufu not so bad. Because Khadija was there, I been able to smile and laugh on many days. Now I must help her smile and laugh and see her baby boy too.

I must.

My heart is sounding **boom** in my ears as I bend down and pick Khadija's hand. It feel like a ice block as I hook it around my neck. "Where is this river?"

"Not far," Bamidele say. "One mile walking."

"Why don't we just take taxi or motorcycle?"

He look around, shake his head. "I have a new wife," he say. "What will people say if they see me with another pregnant woman inside a taxi or motorcycle?"

I swallow the curse in my mouth. So the foolish man have a wife, and he also give Khadija pregnants? What was Khadija even thinking when she was doing all this? And how is she even sure she is carrying a boy-baby when the midwifes or the doctors have not check it?

In Idanra town, which is not far from Ikati, there is one doctor there, he will come once in the month to help pregnant womens. I hear he have a magic eye-glass and tee-vee for checking if a baby is a boy or girl. I must ask Morufu to carry Khadija to the doctor.

"We must go now," Bamidele say. "We can take the back route over there."

He bend down on the other side of Khadija, pick up her hand. "One, two, three . . . carry her!"

Together, we drag Khadija to where Bamidele say the river is.

CHAPTER 15

Khadija is warring with God for her soul. Me and Bamidele, we are holding her, begging her to be talking. To not be sleeping. I get to talking too, I talk to her about Mama, about Kayus and Born-boy, about Papa. I tell her more things that I want her to know, and things I am not wanting her to know. When I ask her, "You are still here? Khadija? You are still here?" she will make a moan, and I will get to talking again, saying anything that is entering my mind.

I think of Death, how it come and take my mama and kill her dead.

Death, he tall like a iroko tree, with no body, no flesh, no eyes, only mouth and teeths. Plenty teeths, the thin of pencil and the sharp of blade for biting and killing. Death is not having legs. But it have two wings of nails and arrows. Death can fly and kill the bird in the air dead, strike them from the sky and fall them to ground, scatter their brain. It can be swimming too, swallow the fishes inside the river.

When it is wanting to kill a person, it will fly, keeping hisself over their head, sailing like a boat on top the water of the soul, waiting for when it will just snatch the person from the earth.

Death can take form of anything. It clever like that. Today, it can take form of a car, cause a accident; tomorrow it can shape hisself as a gun, a bullet, a knife, a coughing-blood sickness. It can take form of a dry palm frond and flog a person until the person is dying. Like Lamidi the farmer. Or as a rope to squeeze all the life from a person, like Tafa, Asabi's lover.

Is Death following Khadija now? And if Khadija die, will it begin to be following me too?

We take the path that Bamidele is showing us, the floor is so full of mud, it is sucking our feets inside it and we are fighting to pull it back out, making the walking even more hard for us, until I see the edge of water. I never feel so much hope in my life.

"Khadija," I say. "You do well, we have nearly reach."

She groan, a weak sound.

"This is Kere river," Bamidele say as we cut out from the path and find ourselfs in front of the river.

The water is spreading out like a big field of glass, the top of it shining under the early-morning sun.

There are two girls drawing water with their clay pot from the edge. One of them look up and see us, nod her head and continue to draw the water. One fisherman is paddling his canoe in the river, throwing the fishing net, spreading it like a peacock wing over the water.

In my hand, Khadija slack herself. I slip on my feets, catch myself before me and her will be landing on the floor. Me and Bamidele, we make her to lie down. I make her bag a pillow and put her head on top it. I kneel down in her front, take the edge of my cloth, wipe her face.

"Let us do the baff," I say to Bamidele.

Bamidele, he is sweating now too. He swing his head around the river, turn his face to me. "I will go and bring the special soap."

I look Khadija. Her eyes are closing.

I pinch her, she open the eyes, close them back.

"How long?" I ask him. I don't want him to leave me and Khadija here, in front of a river, inside a strange village. "When you will come back?"

"Soon," Bamidele say, wiping his hand on the side of his trouser. "Five minutes."

"Too long," I say. "Two minutes. Run quick and come back."

"I take a shortcut," he say. "Off her cloth for me before I come."

"I am not offing her cloth," I say. "How will I

naked a pregnant woman by myself?" Part of me want to head-butt this Bamidele in the nose for talking like a fool. "I am not doing anything for her until you are coming back. You hear me?"

"I am coming," he say. He bend his head, say something to Khadija's ear. She nod her head, be like ten minutes before her head move.

Bamidele stand to his feets. "I am going now," he say, and before I can talk anything, he turn around and start running back to the path we just come from.

Just then, a thunder scatter boom from the sky.

It is Death, making a announcement, giving us big, big warning.

Many minutes pass, and Bamidele have not come back.

I hold Khadija's hand, counting the seconds, the minutes, and watching the river. The two girls by the water are helping each other, putting their clay pot on top each of their head. When they reach my front, they stop. They look like twins childrens. Their face is the same round of tomato, the same hole in their left cheek when they smile, but one of them is having skin the color of cocoa powder, and the other, her skin is the yellow-brown of fresh bread.

"Is all okay?" the dark one ask, talking the way

Kere people speak, clicking her tongue with every word she speak, making it a bit hard for me to be understanding.

"What happen to her?" she ask. "You need help?"

"She is sick," I say. "I am waiting for"—I think a moment—"for the **Babalawo.** He will give her cure when he reach here. Thank you."

"May the gods be with her," they say together as they walk pass my front.

The sky have eat up the morning sun. Everywhere is gray, dark. The breeze is whistling, the air cold. I shiver, grind my teeths together. The fisherman have take his canoe and go far, far inside the river. Who will I call to help me?

I wipe Khadija's face again, her cool head. "How is the pain?" I ask. Fear have become a wall around my heart, it is wanting to squeeze my breath out, but because of Khadija, I am climbing the wall of fear and making myself strong. "You feel better?" I ask.

"Yes," she say, move her lip, as if she is thinking to smile. "The pain is going."

"Good," I say. "Remember that lawyer song I been wanting to sing for you but didn't able to because me and you been so busy with housework?"

She don't answer, but I keep talking. "I want to sing it for you now. I think you will like the song. Is a very sweet song, Khadija. You will hear it? **Hello, fine girl . . .**" My voice break a little, but I strong myself, keep singing:

If you want to become a big, big lawyer
You must go to plenty, plenty school
If you want to wear a high, high shoe,
And walk, ko-ka-ko

My voice is shaking, fulling with tears, but I keep trying, keep pushing myself to sing: **"Ko-ka—"**

"Adunni," Khadija say.

"Yes, Khadija," I say, "I am here. Singing. Singing for you and for Baby. Are you liking the song? Is Baby liking the song?"

"Where is Bamidele?"

"He have not come back," I say.

"When will he come back?" Khadija ask. "It been too long now. Where is he?"

"He is—" I stop my talking. What if Bamidele have run away, and he is not never coming back and he is leaving Khadija here to die?

Khadija drag her breath. "Will Bamidele cheat me?" she ask. "Will he leave me here like this?"

Before I can check my head for a correct answer, a deep cry come out from her, the howl of a dog in trapping. I look up, look Death sailing up there, and I tell it to be finding somebody else. I tell it to go and form a car and kill that shitting goat. But when I look Khadija, I know she is welcoming Death with her eyes. She and Death are becoming one, husband and wife.

"Adunni, take care of my children," she say, her voice so small, so weak.

"No," I say, and gripping her cold hand, "Khadija, not me. You. You take care of your childrens. You take care of my childrens too. Me and you, we stay together, we fight Labake together. We laugh Morufu together. Me and you. Not so, Khadija, not so? Okay, wait, wait a moment, let me sing another song. A song about—" I shake her shoulders.

Her body is moving, shaking, but her eyeballs, wide-open, be looking the gray of the sky, seeing only what the spirit can see. I put my face on top her breast, which is swelling with new milk for her dead baby, as I am starting to cry more hard and shake her shoulder.

Wake up, Khadija, I beg her with all of my soul. **Wake up. Wake up. Wake up.**

But it is of no use.

Khadija is dead.

And Bamidele have **not** come back.

CHAPTER 16

I push myself up and look around me.

The fisherman is starting to come back. I am wanting to wait for him to come, to ask him to help me so we can carry Khadija and take her to Morufu, but my head is sounding a warning. If I wait for him, he will think it is me that kill Khadija. He didn't see when Bamidele follow me come here. He will carry me to the village chief of Ikati. I think of Lamidi the farmer. Of how they flog him for seven days. I will find Bamidele. Must. I will find him first, then me and Bamidele, we will come back here, and we will carry Khadija go home for burial. He will tell the village chief, Morufu, and Khadija childrens what happen. He will tell them he give her pregnants. That his family have a curse. That there is a soap to baff the curse away, but he didn't come back to give Khadija the soap.

I wipe my face and make the decisions.

Bamidele will suffer for Khadija.

Not me. **Not me.**

I walk many miles, passing many paths, finding myself in front of another house, a lean tree with no leafs, a wild bush with red cherry fruits, beautiful for looking but poison for eating, but I am not finding Bamidele's. Where is it? I walk fast, the pictures of Khadija's body fueling my mind. It is lying inside that sand, by the river edge. The thunder is booming again in the sky and I know the rains are gathering to begin falling.

If the rains wash away Khadija's body into the river, then she will lost forever. What will I say to Bamidele? Or to anybody? How will I tell them that Khadija is dead if I don't have the dead body?

I beg the sky to hold hisself, to not rain, to give me more time to find the house. When I see that goat, the one with the red thread, sitting under the shade of the guava tree, I know I am nearing Bamidele's house. I thank the goat, and keep looking until I find the place, the red door.

I pick a stone from the floor, knock it on the door. There is no answer from inside. I knock it again. Then I am starting to shout, "Bamidele, come out! Bamidele!"

The door open, slow.

The pregnants stomach show hisself first, before the woman's face. Fair skin, face like a hungry dolly baby. Her hair is full of twists, all pointing up to the sky, be like thorns on a crown of flesh. Her round stomach, about the same size of Khadija's own, seem to change itself in my eyes; it become a folding fist and blow my chest. This is why Bamidele is not coming back. Because he have a pregnant wife.

"I am looking for Bamidele," I shout, breathing fast, trying to not cry. "Tell him to come out. Tell him Khadija is dead."

"Bamidele?" She blank her face. "In which house?"

"This house," I say as I look around, see the goat. It raise his head, look me, and I know the goat know it too. This is Bamidele's house. "I come here this morning. He open this door, this red door. You are his wife?"

She thin her eyes, as if she is checking me well, before she nod her head yes.

"But Bamidele have travel," she say. "He travel since three weeks now for . . . to his mother's village. What do you want? Who is Khadija?"

"No," I say. "Bamidele didn't travel. He is here. He open this door for me just this morning."

I jump forward, trying to push the door, but she come out of the house, close the door behind her, gripping the door handles.

"Bamidele is not here," she say. "Go your way."

"But he allow Khadija die!" I am wailing now, stamping my feets. "Her body is in front of Kere river, dead. Very dead. We must go and bring her come! Bamidele, come out! You kill a woman! Come out!"

The next house door open, one man peep out, look us.

"Are you having hearing problem?" the woman ask, her voice low. "Bamidele is not in this house. Please go before I call you **ole.**"

Ole. Thief.

That word is a commanding inside the ears of people. They hear it, they begin to run around, looking for the **ole.** If she call me that, nobody will ask any question. The whole village will come out and be chasing me. They will throw old tire on my head and put fire inside. They will burn me.

I look up, see Death. He is sailing on top my head, shining his teeths, flapping his wings, having two minds about which form to take me: as a cane or as a fire.

But I think of Khadija. I think of her childrens, Alafia and the other ones. Her sick father.

I fuel up my voice, shout again. "Bamidele, come out! Bamidele, you kill a woman! Come out!"

"Ole! Ole! Ole!" the woman is starting to shout now, her voice covering my own.

The man in the second house is looking a village fighter with his big, big hands and wide, strong chest.

"**Ole?**" he ask, but he is not waiting for answers as he is coming out from his house. My face is a stranger here. He know it is me. He too is starting to shout. "**Ole! Ole!** Everybody come out! There is a thief in our area!"

The man and the woman, they join their voice, slam my own down.

In no time, the whole place will be full of peoples.

I look my left, my right. There is a path to my right, leading to the bus garage.

I look the woman's face, and she look mine. She slow her voice a moment, giving me a chance to run, to go and never come back.

But Khadija. Oh, Khadija.

"Bamidele!" I shout again. "I know you are inside that house. God will judge you! You kill a woman! Come out!"

"**Ole! Ole!**" the woman is starting to shout again. The man is nearly reaching my side. He is holding something rough and thick and brown, a branch of a tree?

I turn, see another two peoples coming out of their house.

Four peoples. One thief: me.

I close my mouth; begin to run.

CHAPTER 17

I climb the motorcycle at the bus garage and beg the driver to be driving me to my house.

I cannot be going back to Morufu's house because what will I tell him when he ask me where is Khadija? What will I tell her childrens?

So I tell the driver to be driving me to my papa's house. I don't even know when we reach my house because my mind is not thinking correct. It been nearly three months since I leave this place as wife of Morufu. And now I am coming back as a what?

Papa is sitting in the sofa when I enter. He is sleeping dccp, putting his head back on the sofa wood, his cap on his nose. His snoring is loud, it shake the whole parlor. He jump awake when I enter, open his eyes wide as if he have see a evil spirit.

"Adunni?" He wipe his eye, shake his head. "It is you?"

"Sah." I am shaking too much, it is hard to be kneeling down. "It is me, sah. Good afternoon, Papa."

Outside, the driver press the horn of his motorcycle, **peen.**

"The driver want to collect his money, sah," I say, and before Papa can answer, I run to the room I was sharing with Kayus and Born-boy and take the money I was hiding inside my mat since long time ago, run outside, and pay the driver twenty naira.

"What did you find come?" Papa ask when I am back inside the parlor. He is standing on his feets now, hands on his waist. "You run from your husband's house?"

"No, sah. I didn't run from my husband's house." I bring myself to the floor, kneel down, and hold his leg. "Papa, help me."

"What happen?" Papa ask when I begin to cry. "Why are you crying?"

As I am talking, I feel his leg slack, feel as he remove hisself from my hand and fall hisself inside the sofa. "Khadija is dead?" he ask, talking whisper. "Your senior wife is dead?"

"It is Bamidele," I say. "She have a man-friend, a lover. Bamidele is his name. He is a welder from Kere village. He give her pregnants and now he is leaving her to die because he didn't come back with soap to baff away evil curse." Even as I am talking,

I know it is sounding as if I am telling lies. "I am talking true, Papa. God is seeing my heart! God knows it is true! Bamidele have a soap and he didn't come back and Khadija is dead because of him. It is true, Papa!"

Papa put his head inside his hands, he didn't talk for a long, long time. When he up his head, his eyes are red, watery, look as if hisself about to cry too. "Who see you when it happen?"

I shake my head. "See me? Nobody. Bamidele's wife say he is traveling. She will not talk true." I remember the twins that was fetching water. But I don't even know their name, or if they see me and Bamidele with Khadija. They see **me,** that I know. Everybody see me. Everybody will say it is me that kill Khadija.

"I am talking true. I swear it," I say.

"Ah," Papa say, touch his chest three times. "Ah. Adunni, you have kill me, finish."

"I swear I didn't do anything, Papa!" I am crying too much and coughing out my words. "Help me, Papa, help me!"

Papa remove my hand from his knees, sigh a sad sigh. "Adunni, I must go to the village chief. We must tell them what happen."

"No, Papa, no!" I pull his trouser cloth. "You know what will happen. They will not give me a chance to talk myself, they will just kill me. They will not hear what I am saying about Bamidele."

"We cannot leave Khadija by herself," Papa say.

"Somebody must go and bring her body come. I cannot do it, because they will say I kill her. So, let me go now to the village chief and tell him what happen."

"If they ask you to bring me come, what will you tell them?"

Papa give me one look, and I never see him look so sad, so confuse.

"Then I bring you come," he say, voice so soft, so breaking. "Khadija have her peoples, they must know that she is dead. The village chief must know that Khadija is dead. Morufu must know. Let me go and find all these peoples. The village chief will not kill you when I, your Papa, is alive. I swear it that nothing bad will happen to you. But first, stop your tears. Go inside your room and wait for me."

Papa look left and look right, tap the side of his trouser, as if he is finding something but didn't know what it is, then he put his feets inside his slippers and leave me kneeling by myself in the parlor.

My heart is still turning around inside my chest as I am standing in the room I was sharing with Kayus and Born-boy. I go to the window, pull Mama's wrapper that we use for curtains to one side, to check it sure that nobody is coming. Outside, the sun is starting to climb down from the sky, the color is changing to the red of Papa's eyes when he is drinking too much. The compound is empty, quiet too, only the leafs from the mango tree are dancing in the evening breeze and whispering to theirselfs.

Is it a wicked thing, to be thinking to run away, when Khadija is by herself, lying dead in Kere village? Is there another options for me? Papa say nothing will happen to me, but Papa make a promise to Mama and he didn't keep the promise. How will he keep his promise now to save me from this troubles?

I wipe my eyes, move away from the window, roll out my mat from under the bed, pull out the black nylon bag from inside the raffia mat and put my belongings inside it.

I don't have much things because three of my four cloths is in Morufu's house. I take my ankara dress, one pant, the black brassiere that Mama gived me when I was first starting to growing breast, my chewing stick, and my mama's old Yoruba Bible. It have a black rubber cover, the words inside small, the edges folding from many years of Mama reading it at night with candlelight in the kitchen. I press it on my chest now, say a prayer to God to help me. To save me from my troubles.

I look around the room, at the cushion Kayus is using as pillow on the green mat in the corner, at the kerosene lantern beside it, and shake my head. How will I be leaving all of this? If I run away now, where will I see Kayus again?

I on the lantern, lift it up as if that will block out the dark of my heart and pull out the one thousand

naira I been keeping there before my wedding. I
remove one hundred naira, fold it, and put it under
the cushion-pillow for Kayus. It is not much, but it
can buy two or three choco-sweets, make him to be
happy. I am trying to not cry as I press my face to
the mat and tell it to be caring of my Kayus for me.

In the afar, I can hear Born-boy, sounding as if
he is just entering inside the compound. I rise to
my feets, run outside to meet him, my nylon bag
dancing in my hand.

Born-boy is carrying two tires on top his head,
looking as if he is just coming from his mechanic
working place. He look shock when he see me.
Blink. "Adunni?"

"It is me, brother," I say. I strong up my face,
arrange it straight, and push Khadija far back in
my mind.

"Why are you standing and looking?" Born-boy
say. "Collect this thing from me."

I collect the tires, set it on the floor.

"What have you come to find here?" he ask.
"Where is your husband? What is in your hand?"

"He send me to come and give Papa money," I
say, holding my nylon bag tight. "To say thank you
for marrying me."

"He is a good man, your husband." Born-boy
swipe the sweat from his forehead with his finger
and flick it at my feets. "Because of him, we are having plenty food to eat now. Did you see the yams

and plantains in the kitchen? Even the community rent, Papa pay for it two months back, did he tell you? Where is Papa? Inside?"

"Papa is"—I swallow spit, try to talk again—"out. With Mr. Bada."

"You are going now? To your husband's house?"

"Yes," I say. "Night is falling."

"Greet him for me, the good man." He look me up and down. "You want me to escort you? It is dark outside."

"No," I say. "Thank you. I am going now, now."

Born-boy stretch his hand and yawn like a dog, his wide mouth snapping close. "Go quick," he say, thinning his eyes. "Wait, Adunni. You sure all is well? You have trouble running all over your face. What happen? Morufu, is he well?"

I lick my dry, cracking lips. "He is well."

"And the senior wifes? Labake and the other one? They do you good?"

Khadija do me good, but now she is dead. "They do me well," I say as my voice is starting to break with tears. "Let me go quick bye-bye."

"Hurry," he say. "Go well. Greet the good man, the very good man."

Born-boy enter the house, and a weak light from the lantern light up the room window. I shift on my feets, looking the sky, the gathering of gray clouds to the center of it. The wind be sounding like a whistle, blowing a sad, cold song. There is a smell inside the air too, of dust that swallow water, and I know that the rains are gathering their self to begin falling.

Now, I think. **Go now.**

I draw a deep breath, look our house on my left, the dusty road on my right, then I press my nylon bag tight to my chest, and I begin to run.

CHAPTER 18

At first I am running, keeping my head down, my eyes on my feets on the muddy path that is leading outside the village.

On my left and right are maize plantations, with wide green leafs. I am thanking it because it is keeping me from the village eyes that is behind the plantations. Light is flashing from the sky, followed by a shout of the thunder. I keep running, my ears catching the sound of dogs barking in the afar, the goats from the nearby compounds bleating **meh, meh,** stamping their feets on the floor as if they are fighting with the earth. Chickens are running everywhere, their feathers flapping every time the sky flash a light. I keep running, sometimes I am skipping when I see rocks or weeds, or when I see old car tires that some devil-childrens leave on the road to cause person to be falling.

One red cock with green thread on his neck jump inside my path from nowhere, making me to knock my leg on a stone. I slow myself and bend down to rub the ankles. The ankles are breathing with pain, and I am trying to not cry. From corners of my eye, I see two girls with bucket on their head. One of the girls is Ruka. The two both of the girls are talking together and laughing, but they kill the laugh when they see me.

"Adunni, our new wife," Ruka say when she is reaching my front. "Where are you going?"

"To fetch water at Ikati river," I say, talking as if all my breath is about to finish. I am standing up now and pointing my hand to the back of my head, where my house is far behind. "Our well is dry, so I need to keep water for, for tomorrow." I try to force a laugh, but I know the laugh will turn itself to crying.

"See!" the girl with Ruka say. "which kind of new wife is this one? Fetching water with no bucket in the rain?" I eye that one. She is looking like the fowl that jump inside my path, with her thin neck and long mouth like fowl beak. I don't know her, why is she asking me question?

"Ruka, please leave this one alone," she say, the fire of jealousy burning inside her eyes. "She thinks she is better more than the rest of us because she is a new wife."

"Adunni," Ruka say, "I keep telling you how fine marriage is making you look. Did Kike marry this morning? Is it true?"

"Yes," I say as another thunder scatter the sky. "Thank you. Let me be going before this rain is starting."

"We will come and dance for you too when you have a new baby!" Ruka say with a wink as she is walking away with her friend. "Bye-bye!"

"Bye-bye," I say, but I don't move, even after they go far, even after the rain is starting to fall. It is a heavy rain, the kind that is shaking the earth and causing the roofs of the houses to be sounding as if a mad person is playing mad music: banging pots, pans, and spoons together. The rain beat my hair, run down my face and into my mouth so that I can taste the coconut oil pomade from my hair, and the salt from my tears and the rainwater. The water is soaking my cloth, making me to be shivering in the middle of the path. I am thinking of what Ruka just say, about coming to dance with me when I have a new baby. Will my papa and Morufu be shocking with anger and surprise when they hear that I am missing? Will they think it is because I kill Khadija that I am running away? Will my papa be having heart pain because of me? Will they put my papa inside prison until they find me come? Or will Papa know that I am running away? And if they find me, will they hear what I am saying about Bamidele?

I wipe my face with the back of my hand and

sniff up the **catar** from my nose. This decisions is too hard, and maybe I am not doing the correct thing. Maybe I can go back home and try to follow Papa to the village chief? But if I do that, they will kill me just like they kill Lamidi the farmer, and Tafa, Asabi's love-boy, and other peoples I cannot remember now.

I think I must go first, then when Bamidele is finding hisself, I can try and be coming back. I take the edge of my dress, twist it and squeeze out the rainwaters, shake it to try and dry it, but the dress just gum his wet self to my skin and give me sneeze.

I pick up my running until I reach the market square. There is one light pole in the center, the golden-yellow beam is making the wet cement floor to shine like glass. In the center of the square, there is gray stone statue of our village king on his throne. His stone eyes is wide-open, and he is holding a big stick, as if he is watching the whole place for thiefs . . . for me.

The rains have stop, but the sky is the black of coal, and the market stalls are empty. All the sellers of tin-milk and sardines, of **garri** and maize, even the mens that are selling electronics like tee-vees and DVDs, they have leave the place. The **mallams** that always use to sell **suya** too have run for shelters. The smell of the dry meat, frying onions, and pepper is still inside the air, making hunger to be vexing my stomach.

I cross the market square and cut to the village

border. There is another statue of the king, like the one in market square, only this one, the king is holding the sign that is saying: **BYE-BYE TO IKATI. THE VILLAGE OF HAPPYNESS.** If you look the sign from the back of it, from where the express is turning inside our village, it is saying: **WELCOME TO IKATI. THE VILLAGE OF HAPPYNESS.** Today I am facing the side that is saying bye-bye with no any happyness.

I see one woman selling **akara** in a pot of black, hot oil, under a red umbrella. She is talking to the **akara,** speaking in Yoruba, telling the beans-cake to be sweeting itself and bringing customers even though the rains have chase them all away.

When she see me, she wipe the sweat from her forehead into the oil, and it make a **sssh** noise, causing black smoke to be rising in the air and pinching my eyes. "You want to buy **akara**?" she ask.

Hunger is flogging me, but I am not having the mouth to eat anything.

"No," I say. "Thank you. No any moneys to buy."

She strong her face, using her eyes to climb from my feets to my head. "If you don't have money to pay for this good food, go away from here and let better customer come."

Just then, I hear a voice calling my name; rough, the voice of a **siga** smoker.

I feel a hot thing running to my head. Who knows me this far from my house? I turn around. Mr. Bada. He is wearing a blue kaftan which is tighting his body. His round, fat head, which didn't have any hair, is shining in the dark as if he use oil to polish it.

"Good evening, sah," I say, kneeling down to greet him.

"You want to buy **akara**?" he ask as he put his hand inside his kaftan pocket and bring out a bundle of money, pull out two twenty-naira note of money and give it to the woman. "Madam, give me six for my Adunni here. She is my friend's daughter. She married Morufu the taxi driver. She is a new wife. Young wife."

The woman didn't even do as if she can hear him as she is collecting the money and folding it three times before she push it deep inside her brassiere.

"Thank you, sah," I say.

"Get up, child," he say. "What are you doing here in this rain?"

"I am going," I cough out words sticking to my throat, "to the next village." **Foolish girl,** I think to myself. **Why are you telling him where you are going?**

"To do what?" Mr. Bada ask. "Where is your husband?"

"My husband, he send me to go and collect car spare part from one workshop."

"Your husband should send another person in this rain," Mr. Bada say as the woman pack six balls of **akara** with the spoon, shake all the oil back inside the pot, and wrap it inside one old news-paper for me.

"Yes, sah." My hand is shaking as I collect the newspaper bag of my food. "My husband will be picking me from the place. Thank you, sah."

"Good," he say. "Go well. Greet your husband for me. You hear?"

This time, I don't stop my running until I reach the next village, until I reach the place where Iya was telling me to come to her if I am ever needing her help.

CHAPTER 19

Iya is living in a face-me-I-face-you house in Agan village, which is the village that is sharing border with our own. She live in one room that is facing another person's room. The room after her own is facing another room. Like that, ten rooms are facing each other, five on the left, five on the right, with a long, thin corridor in the middle.

By the time I reach Agan village border, the night is dark, the moon is a curving of bright yellow light in the sky. The rains visit Agan too, the wind is still blowing cold air on my body, and I am still doing sneeze. The market square in Agan border have more light poles than Ikati, and it is full of peoples selling **zobo** drink, mobile of telephone recharge card, bread, and **suya**.

Mens and womens are talking, laughing, buying,

and selling as if there is no end of day for them. Even some of the sellers' childrens are playing in rainwater by the market stalls. There is one motorcycle under a guava tree across the market square. I walk to the place and see the driver sitting on the floor, his back pressing the tree. There is a chain from his left ankle to his motorcycle, maybe to stop thiefs from stealing it when he is sleeping. There is small gold padlock on the chain where it join his ankle to the motorcycle. He is wearing a t-shirt and a jeans-trouser, and his snoring is rising to reach me over the night noises.

"G'evening, sah," I say, making my voice to rise. "I am wanting to go to Kasumu Road. Sah. It is you I am greeting. Why you are not answering? Excuse, sah?"

When he don't give me answer after I am calling him three times, I kick his leg, and he is trying to jump up, but he is falling back down because the chain is pulling him back.

"You are crazy," he say. "Why are you kicking me like that when you see I am sleeping? You don't have elders in your house?"

"Sorry, sah," I say. "I was waking you since but you didn't give me answer. I want to go to Kasumu Road."

He put his hand inside his pocket and bring out a small key, open the padlock. "Fifty naira for this time of night," he say as he pull the motorcycle from the tree, jump on top of it, and put fire to the engine. "You are coming or not coming?"

"Please, sah," I say. "Fifty naira is much for me. Twenty naira?"

"I swear, after the kicking you give me, you suppose to pay three hundred naira," he say. "Jump on top. I will carry you because of God."

"Thank you, sah." I climb, sit in his back, put my nylon bag inside my lap, and hold tight my breath because his body is smelling like cow manure.

As he is driving through the village, I am seeing lines of houses with iron roof sheets, beer parlors with green and red lightbulbs in the outside, mens with fat stomachs squeezing theirselfs inside small wooden benches outside the beer parlor, drinking, laughing, playing bang-bang music.

At the turning to Kasumu Road, I am seeing shadows of light in the windows of Iya's house and I am hoping that Iya will help me. That she will remember what she say to me that long time ago, when I bring her food. That she will have a kind heart and keep me in her house for a small time.

I pay the man, climb down from the back of his motorcycle, and release one long breath. I walk into the compound, passing the long corridor, which is having one lightbulb in the ceiling that is offing and onning itself as if the electric in it is having problem.

At room number two, I knock on the door. "Iya," I say, "it is Adunni behind the door. Adunni, the only daughter of Idowu, puff-puff seller from Ikati village."

Nobody answer.

I knock it again, tighting my fist and banging it harder. "It is me, Adunni. From Ikati."

Still, no answer. Now I feel like I want to piss and shit at same time and I press my hand in between my legs.

If Iya don't open this door, where will I sleep this night? The market square? I think of that driver and his body smell, and spit is filling my mouth and tears is standing in my eyes as I am knocking and knocking and knocking, but nobody is answering me. I am crying, big loud cry that is tighting my chest and coughing my throat. I am thinking I have make a big, big mistake. How was I thinking that this is a good ideas? Why sometimes I do foolish, stupid things like this? I am crying so plenty that I didn't hear it when the door in my front have open.

I wipe my eyes. The door is open but nobody is there. I look down, and I see Iya sitting on the floor.

"Adunni," she say, and her voice is thin, like it is inside a container with a tight cover on top it. Her two legs are in front of her, looking like cable wire. There is a walking stick on the floor, next to the legs, and I am thinking she didn't eat any food since the last time I bringed food to her because her neck, leg, face, and chest is the thin of a stick. There is no hair on her head too, only patch of gray hairs in the middle of it. She is tying a cloth across her chest, and when she is breathing, her chest is climbing up, down, up, down, sounding as if somebody is sucking hot tea from a cup. Nobody needs to tell me that Iya is more sick than even Mama was.

I kneel to greet her. "G'evening, Iya," I say. "Am I waking you with my knocking?"

"Ah, Adunni," she say. "I hear you are knocking, and I am getting up from my bed, but it is taking long because I have to carry and bring my dead legs with me." Her skin is dragging back on her forehead as she is talking. Her two eyes are open, but she is not looking me. Her eyes are finding something else behind my back.

"What is bringing you to me at this time? Have the rains scatter your house?"

"I am needing your help, ma," I say. "I am inside deep trouble in the house."

"Come inside." She use her buttocks to drag herself back as she open the door wide for me. "We are having half current, so no 'lectricity light inside here. Look to your left, there is a kerosene lantern over there."

The smell of kerosene is thick in the air as I enter. My eye cut to the window, and I cross the room, collect the lantern from the floor, and on the lamp. As I am holding the lantern up and looking the whole place, my heart is falling. There was a box tee-vee, wardrobe, chair, and fan before, but now, is only mattress on the floor and one blue kerosene stove behind it. Two or three cloths are hanging on one kind wooden handle behind the mattress and that is it.

The two both of Iya's eyes are wide-open and stiff, and when I go to sit on the floor behind the door, she is not using her eyes to follow me. She is just looking the window and talking.

"Ma binu," Iya is saying. "Don't be angry. I sell the chair last week. What happen to you?"

As I am telling her the story of Morufu and Khadija, I am fighting very hard to not cry. "I just need a somewhere to be staying for small time," I say. "Maybe until after Bamidele come out and tell them that he is the one that cause it for Khadija to die."

Iya shake her head. "Bamidele is not never coming out, not with a new wife and new baby coming. Even if they catch him, they will drag him to Ikati chief because Khadija is from there. We all know that Ikati village is worst for killing people with no questions. Bamidele will never say the truth about Khadija. Nobody wants to die before their time. Ah, your mama will be too sad for all these things that have happen to you. What can I do for you, Adunni?"

"Help me," I say. "Let me be staying here small, to hide myself. After maybe I can find work in another village and be using the moneys to help myself."

"You cannot stay here," she say. "As you are sitting there, I can only see the smoke of you. Sometimes, I cannot see anything. My eyes is sick. My legs is sick. My body is sick. Everything sick."

"I can help you be taking care of yourself," I say.

"I can cook, wash, fetch water, go to market, you just say it and I will be doing it." But as I am saying that, I am thinking, how will I do that and the peoples from this village will not send a message to my papa?

Iya is shaking her head no. "The end is near for me, Adunni," she say in Yoruba. "My ancestors, they are calling me come." She tilt her head to the side and up in the air, as if somebody from the top of the window is calling her name. "Can you hear it? They are drumming the drums and singing the songs to welcome me." She open all her teeths in one kind of smile, and the lantern light is making it look as if she only have one half of face.

I didn't sure how to answer her or her ancestors, so I am keeping my words to myself.

"Your mother was a kind woman," she say. "God rest her soul." She think a moment. "Stop crying, Adunni. I can help you." She push her head back until she is lying on the mattress. "I have one brother, Kola is his name. We share the same father but not the same mother. He is doing job of helping girls like you."

She is looking up in the ceiling now, eyes open wide with no blink. For one moment, she don't say anything. Then she say, "Tonight we sleep. Tomorrow we talk. Off that lantern so we don't die inside fire before the cock crow."

"Yes, ma." I off the lantern, stretch myself on the floor, and fold my hands under my head, my nylon bag of belongings by my feets. The whole place is quiet, but crickets outside are speaking **kre-kre** far into the night. Sometimes Iya will just start to cough like she wants to cough out all her lung. Other times, she will snore like a generator engine.

I lie there, thinking of my mama, of Kayus, of Khadija, of the time when I didn't have plenty trouble like this. I am thinking all these things until the first cock is saying **coo-koo-roo-koo** at first light and the early-morning sunlight is pouring inside the room from the window.

Just then, there is one kind noise, sound like two animals fighting. At first I am thinking maybe the noise is inside my head, but the more it is coming close, the more it is louding. It is not animals fighting. It is voice of a man, a voice I know very well. It is coming closer with feets that is sounding **bam-bam** like a mad **solja** marching to the war front. As it is reaching Iya's compound, my heart is starting to beat fast because it is the voice of my papa. His most angry of all voice.

He is shouting: "Where is my daughter? And who in this cursed village is bearing the name Iya?"

CHAPTER 20

All my body have collapse.

My head, it is telling myself to get up—**Adunni, get up, get up and run**—but my arms and legs is not making sense with itself. I feel like going to toilet, and as I am thinking of it, hot piss is flooding my dress, covering the whole floor. My heart is in my ears, banging **boom-boom-boom.**

Papa is here. Here in Agan village. What can I do? Where can I go to disappear and never be finding myself?

"Adunni," Iya is calling me from her mattress. I am giving her answer, but my voice, it have gum to my throat. It is not coming out.

"Adunni?" she call again, and the sleep is dragging in her voice. "Is it your papa's voice I am hearing?"

"Yes, ma," I say, but is like she didn't hear me. I

didn't hear myself too. Something have snatch my voice. There is a knocking on her door, **ko-ko-ko.** The door is shaking and Papa is shouting, vexing. "Open this door now!"

Cold is spreading rashes over my body. I am finished. Killed dead. What will I do? Where will I go?

"Adunni." Iya is talking with her breath and I am not hearing her well. "Behind the mattress is one door," I think she is saying. "It is leading to our baffroom. Go there. Quick."

When I don't move, Iya slap her hand on something. "Go. NOW!"

I push myself up as if something just shock me electric in the back. I can see the door she is showing me, it is the place where she was hanging cloth. How was I blinding to this yesterday?

The door is still rattling. "Open this door," Papa is saying. And Iya is answering, "I am getting up from my bed. If you break the door of a old sick woman, thunder will strike you dead."

I push the door open, and I am tumbling into a narrow corridor that is smelling like piss. The piss smell is choking me and making me to cough and bringing water to my eyes.

There is one very big bang, and then Papa's voice: "Why was it taking you long to open door?"

Iya is giving a mumble of answer that didn't make sense.

At the end of the corridor is another door. I enter, swallowing the vomit in my throat at the shits on the floor, some round and brown, like hard-boil egg, others watery like porridge. All of it is stinking. Flies is perching on the shits, jumping and dancing from one shit to another. To my left, beside the broken toilet with no flushing hand, is a baffing bowl with shit stains everywhere. I plant my feets on the only clean space on the floor and hold my vomit as I listen to Iya and Papa arguing with theirselfs:

"Where is my daughter?"

Mumble. Mumble.

"Did something gum your mouth? I say where is my daughter? Peoples say they see her coming here last night."

Mumble. Mumble.

Papa say, "Kayus, this old woman is having ear and mouth problem. Search this room for me. Check it everywhere. Find Adunni!"

I hear **boom, bam, slap,** and I think Kayus and Papa are throwing the belongings in Iya's room this way and that.

Papa say, "What is in this nylon? Is it not Adunni's cloth? Kayus, look it and tell me."

I don't hear what Kayus is saying. I keep shut my eyes, fold myself into myself.

"Is that a door there?" Papa say. "Open it."

Something is tumbling inside the corridor. Feets is making **slap-slap** again. Papa say, "Kayus, go inside that stinking place and check it that Adunni is not hiding inside. YOU HEAR ME?"

"Yes, sah," Kayus say.

As the door is opening, I am holding my breath and pushing myself until my back is rubbing the shits on the wall. I am just praying the wall will open and swallow me and the shits, all of us together like that.

Kayus is standing in my front. Looking me. No blink. Like he is seeing the spirit of Mama and Mama's mama. I am shaking my head, pressing one finger to my lips. My eyes are begging him, my spirit is begging him. **Please don't tell Papa,** my eyes are saying, **don't tell Papa.**

"Is she inside that place?" Papa ask from outside. "Kayus?"

"No, sah," he say. "Nothing here . . . but the window is open, maybe she is running to the market square."

"COME OUT and let us go NOW!" Papa say. "Quick. Morufu and his peoples are waiting. The village chief is waiting!"

Kayus stay like that a moment, mouth shaking as if he is fighting to not cry. His eyes are wet with tears, but there is a pinch of a sad smile on his lips. And when he press his hand on his chest and nod his head, I know that Kayus is wanting me to run away and, most of all, to not allow them catch me.

Thank you, I say with no voice. **Thank you, my brother.**

"Kayus!" Papa shout. "Come on!"

Kayus nod his head slow, our last bye-bye.

Bye-bye, Kayus, my eyes say to him as he is

turning hisself around and running outside. **Bye-bye, my sweet Kayus.**

I remain standing there for a long, long time, with my hand on my chest, with the tears standing in my eyes.

CHAPTER 21

I find Iya sitting on the floor in her room, turning something inside a pot on top a kerosene stove with a long wooden spoon.

There is a fire dancing under it, and when I enter the room, she low the fire, press her up lip to her nose.

"Your whole body is stinking the whole place," she say. "Go and baff. Throw away that smelling dress you are wearing. You have another dress?"

I look my belongings in one corner by the floor, my mama's Bible perching on the ankara dress. "They will come back," I say, watching my cloths. "They saw all my belongings. I cannot use that place to baff. It is full of shit."

She start a laugh that end in a cough. Sound like somebody flushing toilet. "Nobody with sense is using that place to baff," she say. "That place is for shitting. You shit and go. Every month, we clean it room by room. Next week, room number eight will clean it. Go behind the house, beside the well. Baff there.

"I am cooking yam," she add with a smile, as if me and her just finish talking and laughing about yam. As if my heart didn't just nearly collapse finish because of Papa.

"Hunger is not doing me," I say. "Are you check it sure that my papa and Kayus, they have go?"

"Since when?" she say. "They must be reaching Ikati by now. One of the small boys that is helping me in this compound is watching the village border for me. The boy can run very fast. If he sees your papa or brother coming, he will come and tell us."

Iya remove the cover from the pot, dip the spoon inside, and turn it around. I think it is yam porridge she is cooking. It is smelling like pepper and crayfish and palm oil yam, but it is looking like orange shit. Vomit climb my throat, but I push it back.

"I send another small boy to call Kola for me and tell him to come," she say. "Go now, Adunni. Go and wash yourself of all the mess."

"What if Papa come back as I am baffing?"

"Stand there and be asking me foolish questions," she say as she slap the spoon of yam porridge on her palm and lick it for taste. "If your papa come back again and find you just standing there, I will not put my mouth in your matter. There is a room and bucket next to the well. Go quick."

I pick my ankara dress, pant, and brassiere from the floor and leave her front.

The well, a circle of gray wall deep inside the ground and full of water, is behind the building. I throw the bucket inside, draw my water, and enter the baffroom: a square place with cold cement floor, slippery like someone pour raw egg on it. Just like the baffroom in Morufu house, there is green grass climbing up, up the wall to the iron roof.

I off my cloth and begin to pour the water on my head. The cold water is shocking me electric and I am scrubbing my whole body with my palms and the water is mixing with my tears. Scrubbing and crying and scrubbing and crying until it feel as if I will peel my skin and be pouring blood if I don't stop.

When I finish, my skin is breathing in and out from too much scrubbing sore. I wear my brassiere and pant on my wet body like that because I don't have cloth to be drying the water. By the time I go back to Iya, she is eating the yam porridge from the bowl, her fingers full of orange yam, as if she dip her hand inside orange paint.

"You want food now?" she ask, licking her fingers. "It is new yam, new harvest."

"No, ma," I say. "My stomach is turning me."

"Rest your mind, Kola is coming," she say. "He is living in Idanra town, which is not far from here, but he is driving a motorcar and is having one of those telephone things that you are carrying around with you. What you call it?"

"Mobile of telephone," I say. "Morufu is having one. In English-speaking, to mobile means to be letting a thing go up and down by itself."

"That is it," Iya say. Her eyes are shining, as if she is prouding of this her brother and this his mobile of telephone.

I am fighting sleep from my eyes when somebody start to knock again. But it is not angry knock, not like Papa own.

"Open it," Iya say. "It must be Kola. My brother."

I open it. There is one man standing there. He look lanky, with a face like a burned something. There is marks on his face too; two straight lines from under each of his eyes to his jaws area, as if somebody vex and draw number eleven on each of his cheeks with thick black paint.

"Morning, sah," I say, kneeling down.

He bend his neck to the left, eye me up and down, and clear his throat as if he about to start singing a very loud song.

"Is my sister inside?" he ask.

"Come in, sah." I step to one side for him to enter. "Welcome, sah."

He greet Iya with a quick nod of his head, and she pray for him and thank him for the Milo and Lipton Tea he was sending her last month. He ask if she is taking her medicine, and she say yes, three times of the day, even though I didn't see her taking any medicine yesternight or this morning.

When he scratch his throat again, I am thinking maybe he is needing water.

"Did you send for me?" he ask Iya, sounding as if he is vexing, as if Iya is always troubling him. "I don't have any money for you yet."

"I don't care for your money," she say, "but you must help me for this one. The girl that open the door just now is Adunni. Remember Idowu, the woman selling puff-puff in Ikati? Adunni is her daughter."

"Ah." Mr. Kola turn to my side, nod his head yes. "I remember when she was bringing food for you. Sorry about your mother's passing."

"Thank you, sah," I say.

"She needs our help," Iya say. Then she is telling him all the story about Khadija and how my papa is looking for me and how he will be coming back. "Can you find her job like all those girls you use to help? Adunni is very good girl. She is even knowing book. She is speaking good, good English."

Mr. Kola sniff his nose. "Iya, I can help her, but not today. Today is too short notice. I know she is in trouble, but if she can wait maybe one week, I can find—"

"One week is too far," Iya say. "She must go today. This morning. Her papa will come back to find her here. I know it. I cannot let anything bad happen to Adunni. I make a promise to her mother years back, I will keep that promise till I die."

My eyes pinch again with tears when Iya say this, and I press my hands together, bring it to my lips and say a prayer of thank you for her.

"I hear you," Mr. Kola say. "But there is nobody that can give her a job because . . ." He stop his talking, as if he is just thinking another thing. "There is one girl that is supposed to be starting work for me in Lagos today," he say. "Maybe I can put Adunni instead. She seems to be what my boss is looking for. The right age. Can she travel to somewhere far like Lagos?"

Lagos, the big, shining city? The Lagos of plenty **aeloplane** and motorcars and moneys? The Lagos that me and my friend Enitan, we was talking about all the time? And dreaming of going when we have small moneys?

My heart is turning of excitement and sadness. I am feeling much sadness because I was wanting to go to Lagos to see what it is looking like and learn about the place, not because I am running away. But the man is waiting for my answer, and Papa and Morufu can come back anytime now.

"I can travel any far you want, sah," I say. "I am a good girl, sah."

"Let me make the call," he say.

He put his hand inside his pocket and bring out the mobile of telephone. He press the thing one, two, three numbers and put it to his ears. He is talking, moving his head up and down, left and right.

"Hello? Big Madam? Morning, ma. This is Mr. Kola-the-Agent calling. Sorry I am waking you up this early morning. There is a small, important problem. The girl I was bringing today is developing typhoid fever. Too sick to travel long journey. I have another girl. Good one. Her name is Adunni. Yes. Same price. Small girl, yes. Did I ever disappoint you, ma? Of course, yes. She has passed all the medical tests. Thank you." He press the number on the mobile thing again and put it inside his pocket.

"All is done," he say. "Pack your things. We are going to Lagos."

I didn't sure whether to be laughing or crying. My throat is closing as I am kneeling and thanking Iya and putting my belongings into another nylon bag that Iya give me.

"Kola, thank you," Iya say, clapping. "Adunni's mother's spirit is thanking you."

Mr. Kola nod his head, dip his hand inside his pocket, and bring out two dirty notes of money and a key. He squeeze the moneys and put it inside Iya's hand. "Things are hard. The country is not smiling. Manage this till next month." He turn to me, make a beckon with the key in his hand. "Let's go."

I hold my bag tight, but I don't move my feets. I stand there, blinking, looking the man because what if the man be a bad man? What if he will do me bad things in the Lagos?

"Iya?" I say, wanting to ask her if she really know this man well, even though he is her brother, but the words are hiding somewhere inside my brain and I am looking for them, but they are hiding too far so I just stand there, looking the man, blinking.

"Adunni," Iya say, sounding like she will slap her stick on my head any moment now if I don't move my feets. "You better go with him before your peoples are coming back."

The man sniff up his nose, turn around, say, "I will be in the car. If I don't see you after five minutes, I move."

"Pray for me," I say to Iya, bending to where she is sitting on the floor so she can touch my head.

"Good things will meet you in Lagos," she say, pointing a hand to my head. "Your mama's spirit is with you. Go quick."

It is after Mr. Kola on the engines of his car and forward it on the road that the load of everything gather itself and fall on my head, breaking my spirit.

I am leaving Ikati.

This is what I been wanting all my life, to leave this place and see what the world outside is looking like, but not like this. Not with a bad name following me. Not like a person that the whole village is looking for because they think she have kill a woman. Not with one half of my heart with Kayus and the other half with Khadija.

I hang my head down, feeling a thick, heavy cloth as it is covering me. The thick cloth of shame, of sorrow, of heart pain.

CHAPTER 22

Lagos is far like we are driving to the end of the Nigeria. It been three hours or so since we leave Agan village, and we are still on the express motorway.

Sleep is catching me, but the road is having potholes every five minutes of driving and Mr. Kola's blue Mazda car is just doing like electric is shocking it every time we fall inside the pothole. All the jerking is slapping the sleep from my eyes. Sometimes, I am even fearing the car will just division into two and Mr. Kola will gum to one half and I will gum to the other half.

Because of it, I am keeping my eyes on the window and looking outside. The express motorway is having womens, mens, and childrens selling bread, Coca-Cola and Fanta, dried bush meat hanging upside down on a stick, newspapers, fruits, water in a nylon bag. My stomach is vexing with hunger, but I am not asking Mr. Kola to stop for me to be buying food because Mr. Kola is stronging his face and holding the wheel-steering with his two hands tight as if he is afraid the wheel-steering will just fly away. There is a angry line on his front head, a rough folding of his skin.

We been driving in silent since morning, and when I am tired of keeping shut, I ask him a question.

"When will we reach this Lagos?" I ask as I use my palm to cover my eyes from the sun. It is not yet midday, but the heat is much, feel as if the sun is spitting fire from the sky. Everywhere is burning, even the rubber of the car chair is frying my buttocks, and sometimes I am sitting on my palms to be keeping my buttocks cool. When he didn't answer me, I ask him again.

"Soon," he say, looking up in the car looking-glass and cutting to another lane in the road.

"What will be happening to me?"

"You work," he say. "That reminds me. Adunni, listen. I have a medical result in my boot. My doctor friend made it for me. Big Madam wants to be sure you are not carrying sickness." He slide his eyes to me. "Are you carrying sickness?"

"No, sah."

"Good. I will write your name on the medical result and show it to Big Madam. If she asks you if we went to the doctor, you must say yes, we went to Idanra clinic, okay? If you say no, no more work for you."

"I will say yes," I say, shifting in my seat, not understanding why Mr. Kola is lying. If he is lying about doctor, what else he be lying about? Did I really think it well before I was running to leave Ikati and follow this man? I look him, the flesh of his jaws moving up and down as if he is eating the air, and sigh. If he is telling lies to me, nothing I can do about it. I cannot be going back to Ikati or running to anywhere now.

"You will stay with me in this work?" I ask.

"No. I will visit you every three months."

"I will be going to school in this work?" I ask.

He look me one kind, clear his throat. "If you are behaving and Big Madam likes you, she may put you in school."

"If my papa comes back to find me, will Iya tell them where we are going?"

"Iya will die than to betray your mother," he say. "She is a stubborn woman and is not afraid to die. Look, your papa can never find you again, not by Iya. Not by me. Not except you go back to Ikati by yourself. Do you want to go back?"

I shake my head in a quick no, even though my heart is paining me that I cannot never be going back to Ikati. "Who is this Big Madam?" I ask, rubbing my chest, the pain in my heart. "Why are you calling her that?"

"Adunni," he say as he is starting to slow the car because the other cars in front too are slowing.

"Yes, sah?"

"We will reach Lagos soon," he say. "Keep quiet and let me drive."

So I shrug my shoulder and keep my eyes on the road. We pass a woman sitting on a short bench, her back bending over a pot of boiling oil, long iron spoon turning around in the black oil, the spoon pushing the frying balls of puff-puff, like a farmer using a stick to push his sheep here and there. It make me think of a time far back, when I will be standing beside my mama and holding old newspaper in my hand like a plate. Mama will pick the brown puff-puff out of the oil, three by three, shake the spoon until all the puff is draining of the oil, before she will drop it inside my newspaper-plate for me to eat, to taste it for sugar and salt. Me, I will jump and laugh and say, "It is hot, hot, hot," and Mama will say, "Hot but sweet, not so, Adunni, not so?"

I think of how she was telling me to sing when the sickness was biting her body and making it hard for her to move herself from her sleeping mat.

"Adunni **mi**," Mama will say, "my sweetness. Sing away my pain."

When Kayus come to my mind, I push him away. I don't want to think of Kayus, of how he press his hand on his chest this morning, of the sad in his eyes as he was saying bye-bye.

So I start to sing a song my mama teach to me when I was about six years of age, a song of hope and God's love.

I press my nose to the window and start to be singing it from somewhere in the bottom of my stomach:

Enikan nbe to feran wa	One is kind above all others
A! O fe wa!	Oh, how He loves
Ife Re ju t'iyekan lo	His is love beyond a brother's
A! O fe wa!	Oh, how He loves
Ore aye nko wa sile wa sile	Earthly friends may fail or leave us
Boni dun, ola le koro	One day soothe, the next day grieve us
Sugbon Ore yi ki ntan ni	But this Friend will ne'er deceive us
A! O fe wa!	Oh, how He loves.

When I finish, I peep Mr. Kola. His front head is releasing the frown, and his lips is tilting up, as if he is wanting to smile.

"Everything is okay, sah?" I ask. "Is my singing making too much noise?"

"You sing well," he say. "Has anybody told you?"

"My mama was saying so many times," I say.

He say nothing. Just swallow something. After a

moment, he say, "I hope Big Madam will be good to you."

Me too, sah, I am thinking, **me too.**

"Welcome to Lagos," Mr. Kola say. "Wake up, Adunni."

I jump wake up, and wipe my eyes and the stupid spit that have run from the side of my mouth to inside my dress. "Sorry, sah," I say. "We have reach?"

I don't know how long I am sleeping, but now I am seeing so many cars on the street, like when **solja**-ant is gathering their self around cube of sugar. The cars are pressing horns to be talking to each other: **peen, peen.** When one car behind us make the **peen** noise, Mr. Kola strong his face, say something in his breath, and slap his hand on the wheel-steering, **peeen.**

The smell of fresh bread, of pineapples and oranges and paw-paw, of the gray smoke from the buttocks of the car, of petrol, of armpits that have not baff in a long time, all mix together and fill the air.

I draw a breath, and it feel too thick, it block my throat, make me cough.

There are peoples squeezing their self on the road between the cars. Everybody is selling everything they are seeing to sell, even the mobile of telephone and DVD movie. One man is holding something like block-milk and pressing his nose on the window-glass on my side of the car.

"Buy cold ice cream!" he is saying. "Hello, baby girl," he say to me. "No ice cream for you today?"

When we don't give him answer, the man leave our front.

Another man jump in front of our car. He is wearing a green singlet and black trouser, holding a round bottle with foam-water inside of it. Before I can ask what he is doing, he press the bottle-cover and pour the foam-water on the front-glass of the car, pull a brown cloth from his pocket, and begins to wipe the water.

"Get away from my windscreen," Mr. Kola say, pressing the horn, **peen.** "I swear I will jam you with my car. Move out of my way."

But the man is not even doing as if he can hear Mr. Kola. He wipe the glass fast, fast, up and down, left and right. I am trying to not laugh because the cloth is leaving more dirty on the glass than before, and I am thinking maybe it is oil inside the bottle. When he finish the wiping, he shake the cloth, fold it, and put it inside his pocket. He smile, put his hand to his head, make a salute. "God bless you, sah," he say, "we keep it clean for you to be seeing the road."

"Look at this idiot," Mr. Kola say, "he wants me to pay him for staining my windscreen. God punish you."

I didn't sure the man is hearing Mr. Kola. He is just standing there, showing his teeths in a smile, touching his head in salute, and saying, "God bless you, sah," until Mr. Kola move the car front, and the man run off to the car behind us.

"Nuisance," Mr. Kola say. "Idiot. Nuisance."

The car move again to near one boy, about six years of age. His red t-shirt is hanging on his long neck like a hanger, red baffroom slippers on his feets. He is looking me, but his eyes feel like they are far away from this place, lost inside another city, another time of life. He touch his hand to his mouth, wave me bye-bye, touch his hand to his mouth again. There is a signboard on his neck: **HUNGER. HELP PLS.**

"What is this boy wanting?" I ask Mr. Kola.

"He's a beggar," Mr. Kola say.

In Ikati, we don't have begging childrens. Even if the mama and papa of a child is not having moneys, they don't send their childrens to beg. They wash and clean and pick dustbin, and the girls will marry and the mama and papa will collect bride-price and use to eat, but the childrens don't beg for food.

"I am feeling a little hunger, sah," I say after we move the car front again. It twist my stomach with no warning, the hunger, but I am talking with a low voice because I feel shame to be asking for food after all the help him and Iya have help me.

"You want a sausage roll?" he ask as he roll down the window on his side and use his hand to be calling one seller that is carrying tray of small, small bread on his head.

"Sauce or what-you-call-it?" I say.

"It is just bread with meat inside," he say. "Sausage roll."

"Yes, sah," I say.

"How much?" Mr. Kola ask the man.

"One hundred naira," the man say, and pull out one small bread from the tray. "Very hot. Fresh from bakery."

"Give me three." Mr. Kola use one hand to hold wheel-steering and another to pull out fresh notes of moneys from a bundle in his pocket. I watch the bundle, feeling sad at how he squeeze dirty money that cannot buy even two of the sausage for Iya this morning, as he is paying the man with the clean notes.

"Eat two, leave one for me," he say, giving me the bag of food.

The meat inside is small, hard, feel like I am eating salty chewing gum, but I am too hungry, so I swallow it before I finish biting it.

The **okadas** on the road in Lagos is too plenty. Left, right, here, there is just the motorcycle-taxi everywhere, and they are entering in front of cars with no fear, inside out, moving around the road like streams of water. The people sitting on the back of the motorcycle are wearing one kind plastic cap that is too big for their head, and when I ask Mr. Kola what is it, he say, "That is a helmet. Everybody riding **okada** in Lagos must wear it or else the governor will put you in jail."

"You will go to prison if you don't wear helmet cap?" I ask as I wipe my mouth with the back of my hand.

"Yes," he say.

I want to ask more questions because what he is saying is not making sense, but I am seeing something else that is catching my eye: big bus. Plenty of them. Yellow with black lines on it. Some of them is carrying load that is tie to the bus, the other of them are carrying peoples. The one next to our car is having the door open. Some of the peoples inside the bus are lapping other peoples. There is one man holding the door open and his body is hanging outside it. The man is shouting, "Falomo straight! Enter with your correct change!"

"Why is he not sitting inside the bus?" I ask.

"Some bus conductors hang on to the bus in Lagos," Mr. Kola say. "So that they can sell their seat. Thank God, the traffic is moving."

Mr. Kola forward the car, and soon we are leaving all the noise behind us and climbing one road that is going up, up, above one river that is stretching far, far under us, and even if you stretch your neck and look it, you cannot see where the river is ending. On the river, there is a fisherman in the afar, looking like a stick on the water. White boats are going along of it too, canoes carrying peoples.

I drag my eyes away and look up at the green sign

on top the road. "'Third Mainland Bridge. Victoria Is-land. Ikoyi.'" I am reading the sign out loud, because I want Mr. Kola to know that I know English.

"Victoria Island," Mr. Kola say. "**High-land. Not Is-land.**"

I don't understand it. The sign is not reading "high-land," but I keep my words to myself. "Is it where we are going? This Victoria Island place?"

"We are going to Ikoyi," Mr. Kola say, and give me one kind look, as if he is wanting me to be jumping and dancing. "But I will take you to Victoria Island, so you see what it looks like, then we turn around and go to Big Madam's house in Ikoyi. When you get to her house, you will understand. Big Madam has a mansion. Big house. She is rich, Adunni. Very rich."

"That is good?" I ask.

"Money is always good," he say, pressing his lips tight as if he is tired of all my questions.

We are driving like that in the silent, until we climb down from another up road and we are now inside town again. This time, everywhere is just shining and brighting. Tall buildings with wall of glass, and shape like ship, like hat, like choco-cubes, like circles, like triangles, all different shapes and color and size is left and right of us on the road.

"Eh!" I say, my eyes wide, looking everywhere.

"Yes," Mr. Kola say. "It is very nice. Nice but busy. That glass building there is a bank. That blue one, far away, on the edge of the water, is the

Civic Centre. This one here, with the hundred or so windows, is the Nigerian Law School. That hotel there, the very tall one that looks like is full of shining stars, is the top of the Intercontinental Hotel. Very expensive hotel. Five stars. Look, that is the Radisson Blu hotel. Let me link back to Ikoyi from here."

We drive on a street with more buildings and plenty shops until Mr. Kola nod, say, "Look, Adunni, look at that shop, the one with mannequins in the window beside that GTBank, that's Big Madam's shop. She owns the entire building."

I look the tall glass building Mr. Kola is pointing me, catch the shining and blinking blue and green letters on the roof of it: **KAYLA'S FABRICS** inside of the glass. There are two dolly babies with no hand, behind the window too, their skin like the peoples in the Abroad tee-vee. I never see a dolly baby that is tall like me in my life. One of the dolly baby is having costly-looking blue lace pin down on her body, and the other one be naked with two small breast on top the chest like a guava that didn't ripe.

"Eh!" I say it again because only "eh" is coming to my head.

"Her daughter's name is Kayla," Mr. Kola say, keeping his eyes to the road. "That's why it's called Kayla's Fabrics. Good, the traffic here is moving." We keep driving, and Mr. Kola keep pointing to this shop, that mall, that office. Everything is too beautiful and too much loud for me to be following it all because it is filling my head and making it to be swelling big. When the car turn into one quiet road with green leaf trees on the left and right, and there is no more noise and glass and bank, then my head is no more wanting to burst.

"What do you think?" Mr. Kola ask. "Of Lagos?"

"Too much, sah," I say. "Lagos is just a noise-making place with too much light and glass."

Mr. Kola throw his head back and shift the cap on his head and laugh. "'Noise-making place' is a good way to describe it," he say. "Big Madam lives at the end of this road."

"Yes, sah."

"Adunni." He stop the car on the side of the road, turn his whole body, and look me. "You must behave yourself in Big Madam's house. Don't steal. Don't tell lies, and please, do not follow boys."

I strong my face. "Me? Steal? It didn't possible, sah," I say. "I don't tell lies. I don't like boys. I am a very good girl, sah."

"I need to warn you because if Big Madam tells me she does not want you anymore, I don't know where to put you. You understand?"

"Yes, sah," I say. "I don't know where to put myself too. The village chief will kill me dead if I go back to Ikati."

"Now—" Mr. Kola clear his throat three times, which means that what he wants to say a serious thing. "Big Madam expects you to be very hardworking."

"I can be working hard, sah," I say.

"She will give you rules to follow. You must obey them all."

I nod my head yes.

"Eat what they give you. Sleep where they show you. Wear what they give you," he say. "You hear me? Don't start to grow wings after you have been there for a short time. If you do, you will get kicked out. You know you cannot go back to Ikati, so behave yourself. You hear?"

How I can be growing wings when I am not a fowl? "Yes, sah," I say. "What else must I do?"

"Every month, she will pay you ten thousand naira," he say.

"Ten what? For me?" That is too much money to be collecting.

"I will collect the money for you and keep it in a bank," he say. "When I come and visit in three months, I will bring all the money. You hear?"

"Yes, sah," I say. Maybe Mr. Kola is a nice man. He didn't smile every time and he tell a lie about medical test, but maybe he is helping me. "Thank you, sah."

"Now, it is time to go." He on the car engine, drive small, and turn inside one road. At the end of it is a black gate. Mr. Kola stop the car in front of the gate and press his horn, **peen, peen.**

Just then, one tall gray car with front lights like the eyes of a angry cat is coming behind our back. The car is tall than any car I ever see. The car come to a stop, press **peen,** and just like that, the gate is opening wide.

"That is Big Madam in the Jeep," he say. "When we get inside the compound, greet her and then step aside so I can talk to her. You hear?"

"Yes, sah," I say as our car is starting to move.

I look the whole the compound, at the big white house with red roof and two long gold posts in front of it, as if one fine carpenter carve the trunk of a tree, sandpaper it, and spray it with gold paint. I look the short palm trees, three on each side of the road, with trunks like thick pineapples, their long, green leafs spreading out as if to say, **Welcome to this fine, fine house.** I look the yellow, blue, red, and green flowers sitting inside black glass flower-pot here and there in the compound, the gold lampposts with round bulbs like moons in a container, the ten windows at the top of the house, blue squares of looking-glass sitting in a frame of gold. The red stone stairs climbing down from the front of a wide black door is reminding me of a tongue, the tongue of a giant that been eating too many shining things.

As I am looking it all, swallowing the whole place with my eyes and with my heart beating fast, I am thinking that maybe Big Madam is a queen, that this is the palace of the king.

CHAPTER 23

Big Madam's car come to a stop in a space next to another car like it.

Mr. Kola put his own car behind, off his car engine, and we climb down. The man driving Big Madam's car, he climb down too, and run to the other side of the car. I look his fair, smooth skin, the long brown dress he is wearing, the white **fila** on his head, the three dark marks on the side of his forehead, the white prayer beads in his hand, which he keep holding even as he open the car door, bend his head, and step to one side.

"Who is he?" I ask Mr. Kola.

"That is Abu," Mr. Kola whisper, "Big Madam's driver. He has been with her for years. No more questions."

The cool air inside the car is escaping with a

strong flower smell as somebody is climbing out. First thing I am seeing is feets. Yellow feets, black toes. There is different color paint on all the toesnails: red, green, purple, orange, gold. The smallest of the toes is having gold ring on it. Her whole body is almost filling the whole compound as she is coming out. I am now understanding why they are calling her Big Madam. When she come out, she draw deep breath and her chest, wide like blackboard, is climbing up and down, up and down. It is as if this woman is using her nostrils to be collecting all the heating from the outside and making us to be catching cold. I am standing beside Mr. Kola, and his body is shaking like my own. Even the trees in the compound, the yellow, pink, blue flowers in the long flowerpot, all of them too are shaking.

She is wearing a lace **boubou**, which is long up to her feets. The **boubou** is doing shine-shine as if the lace is having eyes everywhere, and blinking the eyes open, close, open, close. She is not having a neck, this woman. Just a round, fat head on top the wide chest with breast that must be reaching near to her knees area. There is one gold **gele** on her head, and it is looking like she just gum a ceiling fan on a hat and put it on her head.

She take two step near to us, then I am seeing her face well. Her face is looking like one devil-child vex with her and paint it with his feets. On top the orange powder on her face, there is a red line on the two both eyesbrows which she is drawing all the way to her ears. Green powder on the eyeslids. Lips with gold lipstick, two cheeks full of red powder.

"Big Madam," Mr. Kola say, lying on the floor to greet her. "Welcome back."

When she open her mouth to talk, one of her bottom front teeths is having gold on top it.

"Agent Kola. How are you?" she say, her voice deep. "That is the girl?"

"The best, ma," he say.

She laugh. Sound like a rumble, a big rock rolling down a mountain.

I kneel down as Mr. Kola is rising from the floor. "G'afternoon, ma," I say. "Adunni is the name."

"Adunni." She look me down, face strong, and then she is asking question upon question. "Can you work hard? I have no time for rubbish. Did Mr. Kola tell you my expectations? Have you done your health checks? Can you speak English? Write? Basic communication?"

I don't know too much about this **expecta-shun** and **communica-shun** thing, so I am keeping my words to myself.

"She is hardworking," Mr. Kola say. "She is healthy, I have her test results right here—you know I have never brought you an unhealthy girl. This one understands English and can read simple sentences. She is intelligent, everything you asked for, ma. She will not disappoint. Adunni, get up."

Big Madam pinch her **boubou** open in the chest area and blow air inside it. "Agent Kola. That is what you always say when you want to sell them to me. The last girl you brought, what is that her name? Rebecca? She is still missing till today."

Which girl was Mr. Kola brought before? Why was she missing? I am looking Mr. Kola, but I know I cannot be asking him the question now. I turn to Big Madam, thinking to ask her who this girl was, but her face be like a circle of silent thunder, flashing angry and making me to be afraid. Did something bad happen to this Rebecca that make her to be missing? And if something bad happen to Rebecca, will something happen to me here too?

"Go inside and wait for me there," Big Madam say. "Let me talk to your agent."

Mr. Kola nod his head yes. "Go inside," he say. "I need to speak to Big Madam. I am coming."

I stand to my feets and look the compound. At the palm trees on my left and right, at the other cars in the place, at the main door in the afar, which look like the door to heaven with the gold wood handles on it. As I am walking away, I can feel the eyes of Mr. Kola and Big Madam entering my back.

When I reach the front door, I look back at the two both of them, head bending close to each other, talking and talking.

The handles on the front door is the gold head of a smiling lion.

It is a statue, but I still check it sure that the lion will not just jump awake before I knock the door. When it open, one short man with skin so smooth, the color of cooling charcoal, is standing in my front. His cheeks are round, swelling, as if he is keeping air inside of it, with mustaches that curve around his mouth. He is wearing white trouser and shirt with a long white cap on his head. There is a long blue cloth hanging around his neck and in front of his stomach with a writing on it: **The Chef.**

"Good afternoon, sah. Big Madam say I should be coming inside," I say, pointing behind my head to Big Madam and Mr. Kola. "Adunni is the name."

"Finally, the new housemaid arrives," he say.

"Housemaid?" Is this the work I will be doing? Mr. Kola didn't say before. All he was asking is if I can be working hard, and I am saying yes.

"I am Kofi," he say, pointing one short finger to the writing on his cloth. "The chef. The **highly educated** chef. If you are here to **werk,** follow me."

Why is he talking as if his tongue have a problem? Saying "werk" instead of "work"?

"Why are you talking one kind?" I ask, looking him close. "Are you from the Nigeria?"

"I'm from Ghana," he say, turning around. "I have lived in Nigeria for twenty years, but my accent is stubborn."

"You have a stubborn accident?" I ask as I follow him inside, feeling pity. "When it happen? It affect your mouth? Hope nobody die?"

He stop walking, look me like I mad. "Where does Big Madam find these uneducated beings? I said I speak with an accent. Not an accident. Okay?"

"Is okay," I say, even though it didn't okay. What he say is just making me more confuse. Maybe he have a accident in his head too.

I look around the room, feel a shiver all over my body. There are gold and black tiles on the floor. The walls are pale red, with pictures of Big Madam and two childrens, a boy and a girl, sitting inside the picture. The boy have a nose like big letter **M** and the girl have teeths that is sitting on top her bottom lip. The two both childrens are wearing long, black robe, with triangle hat on their head. Big Madam is standing in between them, her hands on their shoulders, left and right. There are two chairs far back in the room with wood handles, and two round cushions on the floor, red and gold and swollen like balloon.

There is a smell of shoe polish, of fish stew, of new money. It feel too cold too, and I peep one white box in the wall where the cold air is climbing out from. I see a line of looking-glass on the wall to my left and right, and a clock with big face and big numbers. At my right side, I see a bowl of green water with blue stone at the bottom of it, and small fish swimming around a light pole inside the green water. The fish are having different colors: red, green, black and white, orange.

Different shapes too, and one is even looking like a frog. The light pole is vomiting bubbles, plenty of it, making sound like water boiling too much inside pot.

Kofi point a finger to the fish-bowl. "Take a seat over there by the aquarium. I will be in the kitchen preparing dinner. Your job is to take care of the house. Mine is to cook. You stay in your lane; I stay in mine."

Before I can be asking why he is talking of lane as if I am a motorcar, he enter inside one glass door and close it on my face.

"Ah-kweh-ri-um," I say slowly, looking the fish-bowl, as I sit in the chair next to it and put my belongings on the floor. The seat is soft, the brown rubber of it is smelling like new shoe, the top of it cold on my buttocks. I look the clock. Time is saying fifteen to two.

Have they find Khadija by now? Bury her? What of her childrens, are they wailing cry now because their mother is dead? And me, why am I here, inside this noise-making Lagos, doing housemaid of one Big Madam with too much color on her face? Why am I not in Ikati, in Morufu's house, sleeping beside Khadija and talking quiet talk in the night? Or with Mama, if she was not dead, sitting by her feets on her mat, smelling her smell of flour and sugar and milk?

Why am I doing housemaid work, when all I was

wanting was to go to school? I don't know when or how my eyes is wet of tears again, but this time, I cry quick and wipe it quick and tell my mind to be strong as I wait for Big Madam and Mr. Kola to come.

CHAPTER 24

Big Madam didn't bring Mr. Kola.

She come in by herself, stand in the middle of the parlor, put two hands on her hips, and begins to be shouting at top her voice: "Kofi! Kofi!"

Me, I am sitting in the chair, watching her. I open my mouth, close it back. I didn't sure whether to be saying something or keeping my words to myself.

"Kofi?" she shout. "Ko— Where is this man? KOFI! Are you deaf?"

Kofi jump out from somewhere, holding a wooden spoon. "Sorry, ma'am. I didn't hear you over the blender noise in the kitchen. I was just— Do you need something?"

"What is for dinner?" she ask. "Did you get the oranges from Balogun market? How about the yams? Is Big Daddy's fresh fish on the fire?"

Kofi is nodding his head yes and shaking his head no at same time. "The fish is in the grill. The oranges were not fresh, but I got them anyway. I am cooking white rice and fish stew for dinner. Would you like some broccoli on the side? Steamed or stir-fried?"

"Steamed. Get Adunni her uniform," she say. "Show her to her room."

When she say that, I stand to my feets. "I am here, ma," I say. "Where is Mr. Kola?"

"Once she gets changed, show her around the house," Big Madam say. She is not looking me. She is just talking to Kofi. As if I didn't just talk.

"Squeeze five oranges for me and bring it upstairs," she say. "There are a pile of clothes in the laundry room that need ironing. I doubt she can operate an iron. Show her. If she burns my clothes, your next month's salary will pay for it. Is that understood?"

"Perfectly understood, ma'am," Kofi say.

"Good," she say. "Tell Abu to bring three bundles of the burgundy French lace from the boot. Put them in the reception for me. Caroline will be sending her driver to pick them up. I do not want to be disturbed." She turn around, enter inside another glass door, and close it.

"Is all okay with her?" I ask Kofi, my eyes on the glass door. "Why didn't she talk to me?"

"You don't want her to be speaking to you," Kofi say, talking whisper. "Wait here. Let me turn off the gas cooker and show you around. By the time Big

Madam comes back downstairs, she expects you to already be working."

When Kofi leave my front, I catch my face in the looking-glass. My hair is looking like a bad farm: New, thick hairs are growing over the lines of the plaiting like stubborn weeds on a garden path. All the red beads Enitan put on it so long ago have fall off. My eyes are wide and big and shocking, and my skin, which was smooth and bright and fair, is now the color of spoiling tea with no milk.

CHAPTER 25

Big Madam's house is having rooms here and there, left and right.

The room for shitting is different from room for baffing. Room for hanging cloth is different from room for sleeping in bed. There is room for shoes-keeping, for car parking in the outside, for keeping makeups in the upstairs. All the rooms are having space and gold tiles on floor. We didn't enter inside Big Madam's bedroom, but Kofi say she is having a round bed and another baffroom inside. In the downstairs, there are two parlors. One for visiting people and the other is for Big Madam only. "No one sits in here unless Big Madam asks you to," Kofi say as he is closing the door in front of the second parlor. There is a looking-glass on the wall in every room. "Big Madam is quite vain," Kofi say. "Always looking at herself in the mirror."

There is another room just for eating food with a long table and like fifteen chairs. The chair is gold, the table a long gold slate on top four glass legs. There is a light case with about one hundred bulbs hanging in middle of the ceiling, glass flowerpots full of pink and red and smelling fresh flowers in the every corners of the room.

"Dining room," Kofi call it. "Big Daddy and Big Madam eat here when they are on good terms, which is a rare occurrence these days. Follow me. Yes, this small room here is the library." He open another door and we are inside a room with books sitting inside a dark brown wooden case. So many books are climbing up the case to the ceiling. There is a sofa with correct cushion in one corner, and table and chair next to it, a gold standing fan with three blades beside it. The whole place is smelling of dust, but I am not minding it. My heart is swelling as I am looking it all. Is like I am inside one kind heaven of books and educations.

"You like books?" Kofi ask.

"I want to be reading every day," I say, feeling a pinch of happiness as I am remembering what Kike say to me about feeding my mind with reading of books. I bend my neck, trying to read the title name of some of the books:

Things Fall Apart
Collins English Dic-tion-ary
Africa Bible Com-men-ta-ry

A His-tory of Nigeria
1000 Prayer Points to Secure Your Marriage
The Book of Nigerian Facts: From Past to
    Present, 5th edition, 2014

"Who is owning all this books?" I ask as my eye
is cutting around the wonder of the whole room.

"Big Daddy," Kofi say. "He used to love reading
many years ago. But that was before he lost his job
and turned to alcohol. Now the library is hardly
ever used. I am only showing it to you because you
will need to dust it often."

"Who is this Big Daddy?" I ask. "Is he Big
Madam's husband?"

"Yes," Kofi say, whisper. "Unrepentant alcoholic.
Chronic gambler. He keeps getting into debt and
making his wife bail him out. Shame of a man, if
you ask me. Real shame. He is away on business,
should be back later today. And when I say 'business,' I mean woman business."

"You mean how?"

Kofi round his eye. "He is a womanizer. He has
girlfriends. Plenty of them." He turn his mouth
down, as if he is tasting something bitter so sudden,
then he ask, "How old are you, Adunni?"

"Fourteen years of age," I say. Why is he wanting
to know my age?

"I see," Kofi say. "Come with me this way."

As we are leaving the library and Kofi is opening another glass door and enter inside, he stop a

moment, then look me deep inside my eyes and make his voice so whisper, I am nearly not hearing him. "Be very careful of Big Daddy," he say. "Extra careful."

I am wanting to ask what he mean by that, but he clap his hand two times loud and say, "Right. This here is the kitchen. My favorite part of the house. Come on in."

The kitchen is like nothing I ever see. There is machine for doing every work. Machine for blending, for washing cloth, for water pumping, for heating water. The fridge is like ten times big than the one I use to see inside shop that was selling fridge in Ikati market square. The color of every machine in the kitchen is to match. Everything is red this and that. There is a looking-glass even on the cooking stove. "Is it Big Madam that put looking-glass in this stove?"

Kofi laugh. "That's how the gas cooker was made," he say. "The oven door is made of reflective glass. It is like a mirror." He tap the cooker two times, like he is prouding of it. "This here is a top-of-the-range Smeg with six burners. I call her Samantha. Sammy for short. Fantastic piece of equipment. She is one of the reasons why I remain in this house."

I close my eyes a moment, and I see my mama in this big kitchen, I can see her singing songs as she is licking her palm for taste of sugar in the flour, as she is pressing this button and that button on the

machines to be frying her puff-puff. I open my eyes
to the clear windows behind the kitchen sink, the
wide green fields outside, and I think of Kayus. Oh,
how Kayus will love to be kicking his football there.
A real football, not like the tin of milk he is always
kicking at home. I can hear his voice in my head
now, shouting **Is a goal!** as he score one in the net.
Since he was a small boy, Kayus was wanting to be
like Mr. Mercy, a footballer from the Abroad.

My papa will like to sink hisself in that soft cushion sofa in Big Madam's parlor and be watching
evening news and talking elections with Mr. Bada.
How he and Mama and my brothers will love this
house; the rich and big and powerful of it all.

"Where will we fetch water to wash plate and
cook?" I ask, and the trembling in my voice shock
me. I keep still my voice, clear my throat, make up
my mind not to think too much of a life that can
never be. "Is there a river or well in the afar?"

"Adunni, we have taps," Kofi say. "That is a tap."
He point to the sink area. "Water comes out of
there. Turn that handle to the left for hot water
and right for cold water. See?" He turn the handle and water is jumping out like a angry stream.
We have community taps in Ikati, one tap for the
whole village, but the water from it be dripping one
drop in every one hour. Too slow. He turn it again
and the water off. "That's that. Now, to your room.
Follow me."

We go outside the kitchen to the compound

around the house. There is a lot of grass, more palm trees along the path. We turn one corner and we are facing another small house. It have a red roof too, with two windows, one wood door, two flowerpots full of sleeping yellow flowers.

"This is called the boys' quarters," Kofi say. "All of Big Madam's staff stay here. You will use one of the rooms here."

"Why am I not sleeping inside Big Madam's house?" I ask.

"Because you don't," he say, mouth straight. "I have cooked for that damn woman for five years, and I still cannot sleep inside her house. Right. Here we go." He push open the wooden door. There is a long corridor, with three more doors along of it. Kofi point to the first of the door, twist the handle to open it. "Here is your room. Rebecca used to sleep here until—" He stop his talking, swallow something. "Step inside."

"Until what?" I ask. "What happen to this Rebecca?"

"Who knows? Probably ran away with her boy-friend," he say, shrug. "Your uniform is on the bed. It used to belong to Rebecca. I hope it fits. Her shoes are under the bed. Hope those fit too, other-wise, stuff tissue in them. Go in, get changed, and I will be back to show you what you need to do."

I enter inside the room. The room is the size of Morufu's parlor in Ikati. A bulb is hanging on a white plastic rope from the ceiling. There is a open window in the wall with metal gate behind it. A red curtain cover most of the window, but it leave a crack, enough to allow a small breeze and a blink of light from outside, be like red lips parting a little to show two white teeths. On the bed is a mattress of yellow foam, table and chair in one corner, a brown wooden cupboard beside it.

"That is my uniform?" I ask, picking up the cloth from the bed and spreading it out. It is a dress, long to my feets, with red and white square stamp on it everywhere. "Is it for school? This uniform?" My heart is swelling. Maybe it is a good thing that I run away from Ikati.

"This has got nothing to do with school," Kofi say, dull. "Big Madam expects us, her domestic staff, to wear uniforms. I wear a chef's uniform, and you will wear a housemaid uniform."

The dress don't make noise as it is falling out of my hand and landing on the floor by my feets. "This is not uniform for school? Why anybody with correct sense will be wanting housemaid to be wearing uniform?"

"Big Madam expects us to look professional. You know, like we are working in a proper place. And I agree. I don't know about yours, but my job is an important job. She has important friends. Rich men and women in the society. Now, did Mr. Kola tell you that Big Madam will put you in school?"

"He say if I am behaving myself," I say, "that Big Madam will put me in school. So, when I am seeing the uniform, I am thinking Big Madam—"

"Will educate you?" Kofi cut my words and shake his head. "She has never educated any house-maid in my years of serving her. You are here to work. Face your work. That's that. Get changed and meet me outside your room in ten minutes."

"Have you ever used an iron?" Kofi ask.

We are now inside a small room, with a long, triangle-shape table, a basket full of clean clothes by the door, a white iron sitting on top the table that say **Philips** on it.

"I see one or two of the shops in Ikati are selling irons," I say, pulling the uniform around my neck to be making it fit. "But it is very costly. I never use it in my life."

The uniform is reaching almost to my ankles. The arms space is too wide, and I look as if I am making preparations to be flying. Rebecca's shoe is on my feets. That too is too big, so I am putting toilet paper inside the front, and it is making my toes to curl inside of the shoe and paining me. I think that this Rebecca girl was old more than me. Big too, more than me.

"It is simple to use," Kofi say as he is twisting

one button on the iron. "You just need to plug it in to the socket down there, adjust this dial here to match the label on the back of the cloth. Don't worry, I'll show you how to check the labels. All you need to do is this." He is sliding the iron up and down on the cloth, stronging his face as if the iron is vexing him. "When you finish, always remember to unplug the iron down there," he say. "To prevent a fire outbreak. If you are not sure of anything, ask me."

Kofi's English-speaking and way of talking is sometimes too much, but I am using my brain and picking his words to make sense of it. "I will be making sure that I am unplugging the plug every time. I don't want fire to be outbreaking."

"Good," he say. "Big Madam has a schedule for housemaids. I am sure she will take you through it, but I know she expects you to start work at five a.m. You will mop all the floors in the house, including the tiles on the wall in the five bathrooms. Clean all the windows, sweep the compound, and scrub the paving on the driveway. At night, she expects you to water all the flowers, wipe the mirrors, and dust the beddings in all the rooms."

"Is okay," I say, feeling a sadness all at once. "It is plenty work, but I can be working hard. Mr. Kola say he will bring my moneys for me after three months." Maybe after many months of working here and saving the money, I buy bus fare and go back to a village that is near Ikati. If I am near Ikati, and near Kayus, even Papa, then my heart will not feel like it is full of something heavy.

Kofi pull his eyesbrows back. "You really think Mr. Kola will bring your salary in three months? You believe that?"

I nod my head yes. "He is helping me. I don't have a banking account, so he is keeping money for me. Why are you stronging your face?"

"I am frowning because," Kofi say as he is pressing a button and water is jumping out from the iron onto the cloth, "he told Rebecca the same thing. She believed him, and he collected all her salary and did not show up here again until this afternoon when he brought you."

"You mean he will be running away with my moneys?" I ask, feeling my heart begin to climb up and down, up and down. "Because I swear I will be finding that man and knocking his head with this too-big shoe on my feets. Kofi, are you check it sure of what you are telling me?"

"I only told you what I observed." Kofi shrug his shoulder. "Goodness. For such a young girl, you are feisty. I don't mind you being feisty, but around Big Madam, you stay humble, quiet. You respect her, okay?"

"What is my concern with anything feisty?" I say. "Me, I be respecting everybody if they are respecting me back. Now, tell me true, can I be finding Mr. Kola in this Lagos?"

He sigh, but a smile be bending the top of his lips. "We will have to wait and see what happens with Mr. Kola, okay? Here, take this shirt from me and iron it."

CHAPTER 26

We are now standing in the kitchen and Kofi is blending pepper inside the blender. I use to grind pepper on a stone in my papa's house and in Morufu's house. It was a easy thing to do, just roll the stone front and back, but this machine is too quick, making too much noise, confusing everybody.

I want to understand how one small button on the machine is turning around the pepper, tomato, and onion and disappearing it to become water-pepper, but my mind is still thinking about what he say about Mr. Kola and my moneys and about what he say about Rebecca missing. I feel like something hot is shifting inside my head and burning me with all the things I am not understanding about everything.

"This Rebecca girl," I say, "who was she? Why did she ran away? What chase her from here?"

Kofi stiff his finger on the blender button, but he don't turn to look me. "She was Big Madam's former housemaid," he say. "I already said she probably ran away, which means she used to be here, but she is no longer here. Do not ask Big Madam about her, you hear me?"

"I hear you," I say, shifting on my feets, feeling the hot in my head climbing high. "But will the same thing happen to me too? Will I be no longer here like Rebecca?"

"Don't be an idiot," Kofi say, pressing the blender button and noise is filling the kitchen again.

"But can I talk to Big Madam about another matter?" I shout, over the noise. "Where is she?"

He stop pressing the button, look me over his shoulder. "Talk to her about what? Big Madam does not know where Mr. Kola lives."

"I want to ask her to not be paying my money in Mr. Kola banking account," I say. "Maybe she can give me and I will keep it under my pillow. How about that one?"

Kofi use a napkin-towel to mop the sweat from his forehead. "Look. Don't bother. You cannot reason with Big Madam. She is never in a good mood. She only speaks to you when she wants to. You don't go to her for anything. She comes to you. There is nothing you can do about your salary right now, or about anything, except maybe to find another job. Do you know your way around Lagos? If you got out of the front gate, would you turn left or right to get to the main road?"

"I don't know Lagos." I cross my hand in front my chest. "Why can't I be talking to Big Madam? Is she not a human beings like—" I stop my talking as the door to the kitchen is opening and one woman that is looking like Big Madam is rushing inside like a wave on a ocean edge, loud and crashing. I blink, look her again. It **is** Big Madam, but all the makeups on her face have wash off. Her face is looking like something rotten; like a bad road with mud-holes, her skin filling with oily pimples in every space. She is wearing another **boubou,** blue with gold thread running down the middle of it. The **gele** she was wearing before have come off, and her head is full of short, gray hair, plaited in round-about style. She put two hands on her hips, eyes jumping from me to Kofi, left to right. "What is happening here?"

"I am wanting to talk to you, ma. Serious talk."

Kofi give me one look. His eye is warning me to keep my mouth shut, but I don't even do like I am seeing him.

"Mr. Kola say he will keep my money in his banking account," I say. "But Kofi is telling me—"

"We were just—" Kofi jump inside my words, silent me. "I mean. I was just showing Adunni how to blend peppers, ma'am." His voice is changing tone, and he is talking as if he is fearing Big Madam will blend him with the blender.

"I asked you to show her around the house," Big Madam say. "Did you? Has she done any work since she got changed? Is she smart and sensible? Or do I need to get Mr. Kola here first thing tomorrow to take her back to her village?"

"No, ma'am," Kofi say. "She's a fast learner. A bit talkative, perhaps feisty, but intelligent. She even managed to iron a few shirts. I taught her."

"Adunni." Big Madam look me up and down. Her eye is reminding me of how Papa use to look me. As if I be smelling of shit.

"Yes, ma?"

"Follow me."

As she turn around and walk outside the kitchen, I follow. We pass the dining room to inside her parlor. The parlor is like all the other parlors in the house, with a round, curving sofa, gold tiles on the floor, long looking-glass on the wall. There is a tee-vee on the wall too, flat like a looking-glass. One man is inside the tee-vee, talking something but no sound is coming out. Big Madam fall inside the sofa, and the cushions make a **praa** sound.

She pick up the remote-controlling and point it to the tee-vee, off it, and blow out a angry wind from her mouth. There is a glass table next to her, a cup full of orange drink with ice block inside.

"Adunni?" she say as she pick up the cup and drink the drink.

"Yes, ma."

She swallow, set the cup down like she want to break it, and the ice blocks jump, make a **chink** sound. "Adunni?" she call again.

"Yes, ma?" I say. Is she having ear problem? Why is she calling me two times?

"Don't stand and 'yes, ma' me," she say. "When I am talking to you, I expect you to be on your knees."

I kneel down, put my hand in my back. "Yes, ma."

"How old are you?"

"You mean me, ma?" I touch my chest.

"No, I mean your ghost," she say. "Who else will I be talking to? Will I be asking myself how old I am?"

"Fourteen going fifteen years of age, ma."

"Mr. Kola said your mother died and you ran away from home?"

"Yes, ma." Thank God Mr. Kola didn't tell her about Khadija.

"When did you stop schooling?"

"Primary school," I say. "I was managing nearly almost four years inside primary school before I was stopping. But I like book. And school."

"Can you read and write?" she ask.

I am nodding my head yes.

She reach down and pull up one handbag with yellow feather, look like somebody kill a fowl, dip the poor thing inside paint, and sell it to Big Madam. She pull out a biro, bite the cover, spit it to the floor, give me the biro with no cover. She pull out a notebook and give me that one too. I collect.

"Now open the two ears God gave you and listen carefully," she say. "You will write a list of things we need in the house and give it to Abu, my driver. He does the shopping in the house with Kofi on Saturday mornings. Every two weeks, on a Friday, go around the house, note what we need, and write it in that notebook. Do you understand?"

"Yes, ma," I say.

"I don't know what Mr. Kola told you, but I am a very important woman in the society," she say. "I have very important clients. Presidents, governors, senators, they all wear my fabric. Kayla's Fabrics is number one in Nigeria."

"Yes, ma." What is concerning me with all this things she is telling me now?

"Your job is to keep the house clean and tidy and to do what I ask you to do. When you are not working, you stay in the boys' quarters, in your room. Whenever I need you, I will send for you. Understood?"

"Yes, ma. I am understanding."

"Now." She lean back in the sofa and stretch out her feets. "Massage my feet."

"Like how?" I ask.

She is turning her hand this way and that, as if

she is molding clay. "Use your hands and rub my feet and my toes. Massage it."

I look her feets, skin like dry cement with white cracks on the side of it, and shake my head inside of me. With all the money she is having, her feets be like she work on a building site from morning till night with no shoes. I hold her two feets, twist my nose from the smell as I am using my hands to press the ankles this way and that. I am wanting to ask her about Mr. Kola and my money, but when I look up at her, she is closing her eyes. Soon she be snoring, her throat making a noise like the blender in the kitchen.

I am like that for fifteen minutes when the door to the parlor open, and one man which I am thinking is Big Daddy enter. The man is reminding me of when a balloon have just burst, the shape of it when the air inside is coming out. Big Daddy look like he is having air in the top half of his body, and no air in the rest bottom half. He is wearing a white **agbada,** with a cap on his head. His skin is the brown color of new potato and around his mouth is full of gray hairs. There is a eye-glass sitting on his nose, and behind it, I can see his eyeballs, wide and red, jumping as if he didn't have focus. He stagger front, knock the side of the tee-vee, before he come to my side.

"Who is this one now?" His voice is dragging, like Papa's voice when he drink too much.

"Evening, sah," I say. "Adunni is the name. New housemaid for Big Madam."

"Adunni, **dunni-licious.**" He lick his lips, tongue climbing over his mustaches. "Beautiful name for a beautiful girl." He touch his chest, show a hand full of plenty hair, thick and curling. "I am Chief Adeoti, the one and only. But you can call me Big Daddy. Say it let me hear. Say 'Big Daddy'!"

"Big Daddy," I say.

The man is making me discomfort. I shift, look Big Madam, but the woman is sleeping. I shake her leg, but she just change the gear of her snore. Make it even more louding.

"Big Madam." I pinch her feets. "Big Daddy is asking of you."

Big Madam didn't answer. She is just eating the air and snoring. I tell you true, if I carry the tee-vee and smash it on top her head, I don't think she will wake. Is like she have dead.

"That woman can sleep through a tsunami," Big Daddy say as he fall inside the sofa and off his cap, slap it down on the seat beside him. He off his eye-glass, blow air inside of it, and wipe the glass with corners of his **agbada** before he is putting the eye-glass back on his nose. "What is that your name again?"

"Adunni. Sah."

"Ah. Adunni. Wonderful name."

"Thank you, sah."

"How old did you say you were?"

"I didn't say my age to you before, sah," I say.

He laugh, show teeths that is missing one in

the bottom. "Sharp-mouthed, eh? I like that. I like that a lot. Okay, let me ask properly. How old are you?"

I tell him.

"Fourteen going fifteen, eh? That makes you what? Nearly sixteen going seventeen. Almost an adult. Not so innocent."

"No, sah," I say. "My name is Adunni, not Innocent."

Big Daddy throw his head back and laugh again, rubbing his big hand on his belly. "An ignoramus of the highest order. Come on, Adunni. Humor me some more. What else have you got in store?"

"Nothing inside the store, sah," I say, just as Big Madam is jumping awake.

She is looking around the parlor like she lost and just find herself in a dark forest. "Adunni?" she say, looking me down. "Did I fall asleep?"

"Yes, ma," I say. "Big Daddy have come back."

She look up, see Big Daddy, blink her eye. "Welcome back, Chief. How was the journey? Adunni, go and tell Kofi to serve dinner. Tell him to squeeze some more orange juice."

Her feets is still in my lap. I didn't sure whether to remove it or be waiting for her to remove it.

"What are you staring at?" she shout. "Get up."

"Your feets, ma," I say.

She collect her feets, slap it on the floor.

As I am standing up and leaving the parlor, I am feeling the heat from Big Daddy eyes as it is following me outside the parlor, even after I close the door and enter inside the kitchen.

At night, inside my room, I off the light and climb on the bed and press my hand to my heart, feel it beating hard. My body is paining me from all the cleaning and sweeping, but first time since my mama born me, I am by myself, inside my own room, with my own bed, a real bed with soft mattress.

This is a good thing, to be having all these things, but I feel as if my body is missing a part of it: a eye, a leg, one ear. There is no Khadija here, no Morufu with his Fire-Cracker and stinking, smelling mattress and hard-coconut stomach. Khadija's childrens are not whispering and laughing quiet to theirselfs in the room at the end of the corridor, and who know when I ever be seeing Kayus and Enitan and Ruka in the stream like I use to do before?

I close my eyes as a memory climb over me so sudden: of a time when I was five years of age and me and my mama visit the waterfalls in Agan. I can hear it now, the roaring and thundering of those waters, a noise that was giving Mama a tickle so much that she was throwing up her hands under the shower of it and laughing. But me, as I was sitting on the brown rocks beside the waterfall and watching her, I was fearing, fearing that the water will vex and swallow me and Mama. When my mama sense my fear, she climb down to where I was sitting and pull me to my feets and press my face into the soft and wet of her stomach. "Adunni," she shout, "have no fear. Listen to the wonder of it, listen to the music in the noise!" So I listen and listen until my ears catch a song in the noise—a blowing of a thousand trumpets mixing with the beat of a hundred drums. And just like that, there is no more fear, and soon, me and my mama, we begin to laugh and dance under the water.

I feel the same fear in this big house tonight: the fear of falling waters, of swallowing thunders and crushing rocks, of Big Madam and Big Daddy and Missing Rebecca, but there is no music in the noise of this house, no wonder in anything. There is no Mama to sense my fear and stop it, and when I close my eyes and try to sleep, all I see is Khadija, lying so weak, in the cold wet sand of Kere village, crying for me to help her, to not let her die.

CHAPTER 27

This is how I am doing work in Big Madam's house: Every day, I must wash all toilet and baffrooms.

I must use teethsbrush to be scrubbing in the middle of the tiles and be using bleach to be mopping the floors and walls. I must sweep the inside of all the rooms and outside the whole compound. I must be pulling weed from inside the flowerpot even though Kofi say they have one man that his name is "The Gardner."

Kofi say this Mr. The Gardner will be coming on Saturday morning to be doing flower and grass work, but Big Madam say I must do it first, so I am doing it. When I finish that, I am washing Big Madam's pant and brassiere with soap and water inside a bucket in the outside. The first time I see

Big Madam's pant, I was wanting to die dead. I tell you true, that pant is wide like curtain. Her brassiere is like boat. She like to be wearing two pant and two brassiere every day, so I am washing so many in one week. After I finish washing her brassiere and pant, then I must be putting it inside the machine-washer in the kitchen so the machine too can be washing it.

When I ask Kofi why I am washing first before machine-washer, Kofi shrug his shoulder and say, "Do it and don't complain."

In the evening, I am cleaning window, cleaning looking-glass, dusting table, chair, wiping this, mopping that. I am also massaging Big Madam's stinking feets at night, and sometimes, she open her scarf and ask me to be scratching her hair. I am only stopping to eat in the afternoons. No evening food. No morning food.

"Big Madam says she can only afford to feed you once a day," Kofi say when I ask him why no morning or evening food.

Sometimes, Kofi will call me in morning and give me food to be eating before Big Madam is waking up. Two weeks back, Kofi give me rice and stew with one boil egg. Big Madam was sleeping in the upstairs, so I thank him and sit down on a stool inside the kitchen. As I was biting the egg, Big Madam enter the kitchen. I shock, stiff. Hold the egg in my hand, thinking whether the floor will open and swallow me whole with the egg.

When she see me, she march to my front, collect the plate, and pour the rice on top my head. She snatch the boil egg, smash it in the middle of my head. As I was crying because the pepper from the stew is entering my eyesballs and I am fearing I will be blinding, she was starting to slap, punch, kick me everywhere. "Did I not tell you I don't want to see you eating inside my house without my permission?" she was shouting. "You don't expect me to clothe and accommodate you in exchange for the substandard work you do for me, do you? If you must eat more than once a day, you sit outside and eat your food. Your own food. Not mine. Is that clear?"

She turn to Kofi. "The next time I see this girl eating more than once a day, I will reduce your salary." By the time she finish beating me, the hunger is not doing me again. That was the first time Big Madam beat me, and in the nearly one month I been here, she is beating me almost every day.

Just this yesterday morning, she slap my face because I was singing as I was picking the weed from the grass. She was in her car, driving outside the compound when she just ask her driver to stop the car. She climb down from the car, march to where I was kneeling by the flowerpot under the palm tree in the hot sun, and give me a back-hand slap.

I daze. The sun daze too, blind my left eye for a moment.

"You are shouting," she say. "You are disturbing

the citizens of Wellington Road with that noise you call singing. This is not your village. Here we behave like sane people. We have class. We have money."

As she is shouting on me, I am thinking her own shout must be disturbing the peoples more than my own soft singing, but I cannot be telling her that. When she finish shouting, she release a long breath, nod her head, before she turn around, climb back inside her car, and drive away. When I ask Kofi why she is beating me every time, Kofi say he confuse too.

"Yours is one of the worst I have seen," Kofi say. "She beats you every time she sets eyes on you. Did you annoy her in any way?"

I think back. "No. I didn't do anything."

"In that case, I will suggest you find a way to go back to your village," he say with a sigh. "Adunni, let me tell you something about me. Five years ago, I seriously considered returning to Ghana after I lost my job as the personal chef to the Ghanaian ambassador to Nigeria. It was a highly distinguished job, Adunni, very important. I lived in the Federal Capital Territory; in a wonderful two-bed house in Abuja, unlike the nonsense we have here. I served world leaders. I lived well. But I lost that job when a new ambassador was appointed, a godforsaken idiot who said my cooking was not to his taste." He shake his head as if the remembering of it is causing him pain in the head. "I decided to stay back and find another job. I mean, I had studied accounting

in university and upset my whole family when I decided to follow my passion and become a chef. How
could I go back to Ghana in shame? Especially when
I still hadn't completed my building project? After
everyone back home thought I had an important
job with the ambassador? Me, I am only working
here because I need to finish my house back home.
But you have nothing keeping you here. Nothing.
Go back to your village. Go home."

"But how will I go back?" I ask. "Mr. Kola is
missing, and I don't know my way back to Ikati.
Even if I am knowing the way, to go back is didn't
possible because . . ." I clamp my mouth. "Going
back is didn't possible."

Kofi look me, face down. "In that case, stop
complaining," he say. "Do your work. That's what I
did, what I do every day."

"The beating is too much." My eyes are feeling
hot with tears. "My mama didn't ever beat me like
this, not even my papa." Or Labake. Or anybody.

"Try staying out of her way," Kofi say. "When
she is in the house, get busy outside. When she is
outside, run inside and find work to do there. If she
doesn't call you, don't show your face. Adunni, you
know you talk too much. Must you have an answer
for every question? Learn to shut up. And for goodness' sake, stop singing all the time."

And so, for the next two nights after my talk
with Kofi, I stay in my bed thinking of correct

plans, until finally, one sharp, good ideas for hiding from Big Madam is entering my head.

×

This morning, I was wiping the window outside the kitchen when I hear Big Madam's car driving inside. Quick, I pick up my cleaning cloth, pass the side of the house, enter the library, and shut the door on myself.

I draw a long breath, start to wipe the bookcase. I bring each of the books out one by one, open it, and wipe it. As I am wiping it, I am trying to be reading the writings in the book. I cannot be doing loud reading because of Big Madam, but I am talking inside of my breath.

Many of the books is having big English, so I am only reading the first ten words or so before dropping it until I am picking up the Collins. Is a small but fat book like my mama's Bible with wide letters in yellow and blue color on the page. I open it and see that it is having words and the meaning of the words next to it. I begin to turn the page. The book is putting words letter by letter, like ABC alphabet. Since I am knowing the alphabet, I begin to look for words. First, I am turning to letter I to check the meaning of "innocent" because the way Big Daddy was laughing that day is making me think the word is having another meaning than just a name. The Collins write this about "innocent":

> **innocent**
> adjective: **A person not guilty of a crime or offense.**
> noun: **A pure, guileless or naïve person.**

Why is Big Daddy asking if I am pure? And how I can be pure after how Morufu was making me so dirty in the spirit and body when he drink his Fire-Cracker? The whole thinking back to that time is making me want to vomit, so I close the Collins and pick up **The Book of Nigeria Facts.**

Why it have such a long name, this book? Is a tall one too, be like three books gum together, the cover with the picture of a ball, shining and bright, and the map of the Nigeria inside the ball, the green, white, and green color of the Nigerian flag inside the map.

I put it down, check what "fact" is meaning in the Collins:

> **fact**
> noun: **A thing that is known or proved to be true.**

Is this book having the true answer to the every question I am having? I open the first page of it, peep it. It is full of dust, give me a tickle in my throat, make me cough two times. It seem so full of wise, this book. Many pictures, many things making explanations for many things about the Nigeria and the whole wide world of it. It have dates of when things happen in the Nigeria from before in the past till this 2014:

Fact: October 1st, 1960: Nigeria's Independence Day. Nigeria gained independence from Britain.

What is this the Britain? Is it a fighting enemy? I know "independent" is meaning when you are free. Where they take our free? And how we collect it back from them? I sit down on the floor, keep my eyes on the book:

Fact: Lagos is Nigeria's most populated city. A major commercial hub for the world, the city is blessed with many beaches, and an active nightlife, and is home to one of the largest concentrations of millionaires in Africa.

So this is why all the rich peoples are living in this Lagos. I swallow spit, pull the book more close to me. I have plenty work to be doing, but this book be like two big hands, full of love, drawing me close, keeping me warm and feeding me food.

Fact: In 2012, four students of the University
of Port Harcourt were tortured and beaten
to death in Aluu community after they were
falsely accused of stealing. The horrific act
sparked a global outcry against jungle justice
in Nigeria.

Jungle justice.

If I didn't run from Ikati, from Bamidele's wife
and all the Agan village peoples, maybe they will
make me suffer this jungle justice thing, burn me
with fire because they think I am a thief.

This fact make me so sad, but I keep reading, keep
learning the fact I am understanding and the one I am
not understanding until the book is feeling too heavy
in my hands so I set it down and pick up my cleaning.

When I finish wiping the everywhere in the library, I pull the notebook from my pocket, sit on the
sofa, and as my head is remembering the things that
we are needing in the house, I write it. Sometimes
I am checking the Collins for the spelling:

1. Toilet Tissue paper.
2. Soap.
3. Nylon bag. For putting inside dustbin.
4. Bleach. For toilet dirty.
5. Powder Soap. For Machine-washer.

"Adunni?" Somebody call my name in the afar.
Big Madam. "ADUNNI!"

"I am coming, ma," I shout and, quick, put my notebook inside my pocket and stand to my feets.

When I open the door, Big Madam is outside the library. Her eyes are angry, her whole body looking like she is wanting to just burst.

"Are you deaf?" she ask, hands on her hips. "Why did it take you so long to answer me?"

Before I can talk correct answer, she give me one hot slap.

I daze, stumble back. "**Ye!**" I say, rubbing my cheek. "I was answering you, ma. I was saying I am coming but—" She use another slap to silent my words.

Before I can be thinking about that slap, another one is landing on my back. I fall to my knees and close my eyes and think of Mama, of Ikati, of Kayus, as she is using her palm to be slapping my back, **slap, slap, slap,** like she is one angry drummer beating one angry talking-drum.

But I am not crying; I am just collecting the slap and slapping her back in my mind. When she slap me, I slap her back too, only I don't touch her. I don't count how many slaps before I hear Big Daddy voice, "What the hell is going on here?"

Big Madam give me a kick. "Useless fool," she say, spit on my back. "Why are you not crying? Are you possessed? Is a demon living inside you? Because I will beat it out of you today."

"Florence. Do you want to kill that girl?" Big Daddy say. "You used your mad anger to chase away all the other house girls, and now you want to do the same to this poor girl? Adunni!"

I open my eye, look up. Today is the first day I am seeing him since that time in Big Madam's parlor because he always travel for his woman business. Today he is not having red eye. His word is not dragging. He is looking like a sensible somebody.

"Adunni, get up," he say and give me his hand.

I push myself to my feets. Big Madam is not slapping me again, but it is still feeling like my back is still collecting the slap. The pain feel like somebody rub hot pepper on my skin, before pouring kerosene and lighting matches to my body. The whole of everywhere is breathing with pain.

"Welcome, sah," I say. I don't kneel down to greet him. My knee cannot bend again. Nothing in my body is working correct.

"Adunni. Are you okay?" he ask.

"Okay, sah," I say, even though we all know that I didn't okay.

"Florence"—Big Daddy turn, face his wife—"you are the possessed one."

Big Madam release a long breath, look as if she just finish eating a food that is so sweet, as if beating me is giving her life, hope. She look me up and down, hiss. "She is a useless girl," she say. "A lazy good-for-nothing waste-of-space. I had to search the whole house this evening before I found her in the library, fast asleep."

"And so you found her asleep in there and you

decided to murder another woman's child?" Big Daddy say, his voice climbing high. "I heard you from the driveway, Florence. The driveway! What if you had given her a fatal blow? Damaged her brain? Left her paralyzed? Would your excuse stand in the courts of justice?"

I don't understand everything Big Daddy is saying, but I know he is angry with Big Madam.

"Now, Florence"—Big Daddy hold one finger up, twist it left and right—"let this be the last time you touch this child in this house. I repeat. Let this be the last time you lay a finger on Adunni. IS THAT CLEAR?"

Big Madam say something mumble about paying all bill and prostitute-girlfriend as she is walking away.

Big Daddy turn to me. "Are you all right?" he ask.

"Yes, sah," I say. "Thank you, sah."

"Come here." He open his two hands wide, like he wants to collect something. "Come on. Don't be afraid. Come."

I plant my feets in the ground, look him. What is he wanting me to do? To give him a embrace? Or to what? When I don't move, he come near me and wrap his hand around my body.

I stiff, press my hand to his chest, but he just squeeze tight.

"Don't mind her, Adunni," he say, pressing his mouth inside my neck areas. His mustaches is scratching my skin, breath hot and smelling of butter-mint and small drink. "You hear me?"

"Yes, sah." I talk with my teeths close tight. "Work is waiting for me, sah. Please let me be going to—"

"I want you to feel free with me in this house," he say, cutting my words, holding me more tight. "Florence will not be able to touch you if you let me protect you."

I push his chest hard, collect myself from his hand, and run to the backyard. I was running fast and I didn't see Kofi beside the outside tap, I jam him by the shoulder, nearly falling him and myself and the basin he was holding to the floor. Kofi set the basin on the floor and grip the wall with one hand to steady hisself.

"Adunni!" he shout, offing the tap. "Are you okay? Why . . . What is chasing you?"

I press my hand on my knees to slow my breathing. "Big Daddy," I say. "He was holding me too tight, just now. I collect myself from him and run fast."

"Big Daddy was holding you?" Kofi say, concern. "Why? Where is his wife?"

"I didn't too sure why," I say. "Big Madam just finish beating me, then Big Daddy say he wants me to feel free and that he wants to protect me. What is he wanting from me, Kofi?"

I look Kofi, fear in my eyes. I know what Big Daddy is wanting, but I am afraid to think it. To say it.

"Is that man cursed or something?" Kofi say, talking quiet. "Ah, **chale,** but I warned you to be careful."

"I been trying to be be-careful," I say, feeling tears climb down my cheeks. "I don't want trouble in this Lagos and I cannot be going back to Ikati, but the man, the Big Daddy man, he was holding me tight, making me to fear. The other time, I catch him looking me one kind of way. Help me, Kofi, please."

"Don't cry," Kofi say, shaking his head with a sad sigh. "There must be something . . . I'll think of something that can help you. Stop crying, you hear?"

"Thank you," I say, wiping my cheeks with the edge of my dress as I leave his front to begin my evening toilet washing.

When I finish my work and climb into bed at midnight, my body is sore, my back on fire.

My fingers feel like a stiff curve of plastic, and I know it is because I been holding the cleaning cloth too tight, for too long. I try to sleep, but when I close my eyes, I see Big Daddy's teeths, sharp like a blade, bleeding with blood, coming for me.

CHAPTER 28

Fact: Nigerians are known for their love of parties and events. In 2012 alone, Nigerians spent over $59 million on champagne.

Big Madam is doing big party on Sunday.

She been running mad with preparations for it, shouting every second. "Adunni, wash every corner in the downstairs toilet," she will say, pointing a fat hand with dancing flesh to the toilet door. "Use the new toothbrush I bought yesterday to scrub the grout before you bleach the bathroom tiles. Did you scrub the backyard fence like I asked you to? You did? Do it again. Scrub it until the cement sparkles like my mother's gravestone. Don't forget the mirrors in the dining room."

Yesterday afternoon, a tall white van drive inside the compound. When I run outside to look who is inside it, all I see is one brown cow sitting inside the back of the van, licking the fly perching on his nose. I watch as Kofi drag the cow down and tie the neck to the coconut tree in the backyard with a long rope. "This will be slaughtered for barbecue meat and beef stew on Sunday," Kofi say as he slap the cow on his buttocks and laugh.

"Why is Big Madam doing party preparations?" I ask Kofi this morning as I am sitting outside in the hot sun, washing the gold lace tablecloth. "Is the party tomorrow for Big Madam's birthday?"

"No," Kofi say. He is sitting on a bench beside me, picking beans in a tray. "The party on Sunday is for the Wellington Road Wives Association. Big Madam is the president of the group."

"The what you say?"

"The WRWA," Kofi say. "A bunch of middle-aged women who formed an association as an excuse to get dressed and get drunk. They say they are trying to raise funds, money to help the poor. All lies! They meet once a quarter and host in turns. Big Madam is hosting November's meeting."

"It is not even party for birthday," I hiss, scrub the cloth, dip it into soapy water and turn it around. "So just a ordinary meeting and they are just wasting money anyhow. **The Book of Nigeria Fact** is telling me that Nigerians like to spend millions of money on parties and I was thinking it is not true until I reach this Lagos. Is Wellingston the name of our road?"

"Wellington, yes," Kofi say. "There is no **S** anywhere in the word. This street is full of all sorts of people. Half of them are former military personnel, thieves who stole Nigeria's wealth and divorced their wives of youth to marry younger blood; the other half is made up of wealthy businesspeople like Big Madam, high-flying executives and entertainers, some of whom cannot afford the lifestyle but fight to live it anyway."

He pick up the beans tray, shake it so that the beans is jumping in the air and setting back on the tray with a rattle noise. As he is doing so, he is blowing the dirty among the beans into the air. Kofi set the tray down. "Three years ago, some idiot wife thought it'd be a good idea to form an association just because they happen to live in one of the richest streets in Lagos. I see it as another excuse to throw a party. That's all these people do with their money. Throw parties and press dollars on each other's foreheads and chests like it is a form of medication. Do you know that the exchange rate is now one hundred and seventy naira to one dollar? **Chale,** unless Buhari becomes president next year, nothing can move this country forward. Nothing."

I am not understanding why Kofi is always saying Nigerians are spending this and that when him too, he is using the Nigerians money to be building his house in his Ghana country. I see when the visitors of Big Madam give him money, how he will squeeze it tight and slide it inside his pocket with a big smile and a big thank you. Why didn't he refuse the money if it is thief money? He too is among the problem wrong with Nigeria.

Kofi cough into his hand, wipe it on his white trouser. "Big Madam goes to parties every weekend. She supplies fabric to half of Lagos and makes millions. **Chale,** look at the insects crawling from these beans. The bastards have drilled holes through the bag! What was I saying? Yes. The WRWA. They have about ten to fifteen members. It's always a competition. The last host, one Caroline Bankole—Big Madam's closest friend, the filthy-rich housewife of an oil and gas businessman—she killed three goats for a party of ten people, hired a celebrity private chef—an overpaid buffoon—and served wine older than my great-grandfather."

"Is Big Daddy working a job?" I ask, looking Kofi's fingers as he is cracking the shell of the beans. "Big Madam is having a job. She is going to her shop every day. But not Big Daddy. Why?"

"Big Daddy is a fool," Kofi say. "He used to work in a bank. He authorized some loans for some of his friends. Billions of naira. Of course, the friends did not pay back. Bank filed for bankruptcy, I mean it closed completely about two years later. That was about"—he strong his face and think—"about fifteen years or so back, long before I came here to work. I have always known him to be a colossal nuisance, spending Big Madam's money on women, NairaBet, and booze."

"Booze is what?"

"Drink," Kofi say. "Beer. Stout. Alcohol."

"Cham-pag-nay?"

Kofi laugh. "Cham-what?"

"I see it in **The Book of Nigeria Fact,**" I say. "Nigerians are spending million to buy it too. They spell it **C-H-A-M-P-A-G—**"

"Ah! Champagne!" Kofi say. "It is pronounced **sham-pain.** Oh, yes, Big Madam and her friends pop bottles of those at events like it costs nothing."

"Is it like the **ogogoro** that we drink in the village? Or the gin?" I ask. "If you are drinking it too much, it will make your eye to be looking like this." I twist my eye, move my eyesballs from left to right, and Kofi laugh again.

"You've been here for three months," he say after a moment. "If I recall, you got here in August. What are you going to do about your salary?"

I squeeze soap from the tablecloth. "I didn't sure yet," I say. "I keep wanting to talk to Big Madam, but I am fearing she will beat me."

"Let's see what happens in a few more months." Kofi put the tray down, wipe his hand on his laps, then look over his shoulder, as if checking to see if someone is coming. Then he dip his hand into the pocket of his trouser, bring out a folding newspaper. "Take this," he say. "Have a read and let me know what you think."

"I should read newspaper?" I say, looking his hand. "Why?"

"Just read it," Kofi say. "**Chale,** I had to find time to go to my former job at the embassy before I could get a hold of this edition of the Nation Oil newspaper for you. There's something in there I hope you can enter for."

I shake the wet from my hand, pinch the newspaper with the tip of my finger, and shake it open. It is just one page, a tearing from a newspaper page, with plenty writings on it. "I should read the whole everything?"

Kofi sigh. "Adunni, look at the heading to your left, above the obituary."

I look it, read out loud, slowly:

CALL FOR APPLICATIONS:
OCEAN OIL SECONDARY SCHOOL SCHOLARSHIP SCHEME FOR FEMALE DOMESTIC WORKERS

Ocean Oil, Nigeria's foremost oil servicing company, in collaboration with Diamond Special School, invites female domestic workers aged between 12 to 15 to apply for its annual scholarship. Now in its seventh successful year, the scheme is dedicated to ensuring that bright, talented, and vulnerable Nigerian girls who are working in a domestic capacity are able to commence or complete their education. Mr. Ehi Odafe, chairman of Ocean Oil, initiated the scheme in the memory of his mother, Madam Ese Odafe, who worked as a maid in order to support her children through school.

The scheme will cover tuition at the prestigious Diamond Special School for up to eight years for five students and, where applicable, boarding fees and a reasonable sustenance for the duration of the scholarship.

To qualify, applicants must be female, aged 12 to 15, and be working as a housemaid, cleaner, or in any domestic capacity.

The submission must be accompanied by an essay of no more than 1,000 words from the prospective scholar, stating why she should be considered for the scheme, as well as a signed consent form from a guarantor and referee, who must be a well-standing Nigerian citizen. Closing date for all applications is 19th December 2014.

The list of successful scholars will be displayed in our offices in April 2015. Names will not be printed in any media outlet in order to protect identities.

"What is all of it meaning?" I ask Kofi as I set the newspaper by my feets, press it down to keep it from flying in the wind. "It is plenty English, but I see something about schooling."

"A chance to go to a school you won't have to pay for," Kofi say. "They will give you a house to live in too, all for free. The chairman of Ocean Oil was a friend of my former boss. An amazing guy. He always ensures his staff send details of the scheme to the embassy every year, in case any one of us has children that might want to apply."

I nod, not really believing everything Kofi is telling me. "And all the things they are asking for, how can I send it to them?"

"Abu took me to the Ocean Oil office on our way back from the market yesterday," Kofi say. "I picked up the application form for you and kept it in my room. Adunni, this is your only chance at freedom." His voice is tight, nearly angry too. "If you remain here, that . . . bastard may harm you. We keep saying Rebecca left with her boyfriend, but who knows? Sometimes I wonder if that man had something to do with it. Adunni, I have a daughter like you in Ghana and I cannot imagine . . ." He shake his head. "Forget that bastard, think about your future. There is no future here for you, and from what you told me, none in Ikati either. This is all you have."

"But the time is short to be entering for it," I say. "How about if I manage and be better in my English until next year, then I—"

"You can't delay it," Kofi say, nearly shouting. "You are fourteen. The cutoff age is fifteen. You need to apply now. Are you afraid?" Kofi ask. "Because the Adunni I know will jump at this chance without thinking."

I don't answer.

I don't want him to know that I am very full of fear. That I been wanting something like this for so long, and now that Kofi is telling me about this thing, I am afraid to enter for it.

Afraid to even think of how to enter.

"Listen, I know it is scary. You will need to write a compelling—a very good—essay to be selected, but you are bright. It is very competitive, and very selective, but one thing I am sure of is this: You can do it."

"You think?" I ask.

"I know you can." He shrug. "But I won't force you to apply for it. It is up to you, **chale**. I have done my best. Once my house in Kumasi is complete, I am out of here."

I blink back my tears. "How can I make my English better and write a essay all before December? What is a essay anyway?"

"A story. In this case, about yourself," Kofi say. "Did you ever do composition in primary school?"

"I know composition," I say as I pull the newspaper from my feets, fold it, and keep inside my brassiere. "I been knowing it since when Teacher teach me in Ikati."

"Chale," Kofi say, "you can nail this thing. Just try it. We just need to find someone who can stand as a reference and guarantor for you because I can't. I am not a Nigerian citizen, and I am not sure my position as a chef, as important as I believe it is to the survival of humans, will help you. Big Madam or Big Daddy are out of the question. I have a few Nigerian friends I can ask to help, but they need to meet you first. That will be difficult, but not impossible. I am just concerned that we don't have a lot of time. The deadline is just over a month."

I hear everything Kofi is saying, and I see how much he is wanting me to enter this scholarship, and I swear, I want to enter it with all of my life, but I didn't sure I can enter it or even be writing any essay or be finding someone to be referencing me all before December.

"But why do you keep calling me **chale** all the time, Kofi?" I ask, wanting to change my focus from the whole essay thing. "Are you always forgetting that Adunni is my name?"

"'**Chale**' is one way of saying 'friend' in my language."

"I am your friend?" I ask, smiling. Kofi sometimes is kind to me, like today. But many times, he is just doing as if he didn't know me. Sometimes, if I greet him in the morning, he will not give answers, and other times, he will talk to me and give me food. "Me too, I am your friend," I say. "Thank you very much for the scholarship thing."

"I am going to soak the beans." He stand to his feets, pick the beans tray. "You've washed that tablecloth enough. It is going into the washing machine anyway. Leave it and go find something else to do."

When I enter my room at night, I sit on the edge of my bed, pull the newspaper out from my brassiere.

I been trying to push the thing to the far back of my mind since Kofi tell me about it, but I keep thinking of it, keep thinking, what if? What if I enter and they pick me and I am going to school?

I wide the newspaper on the bed, use my hand to straight it, and thin my eyes to read the whole thing with the moonlighting from the window. Big Madam sometimes don't like us to be onning the light at night, but it is too dark to read, so I stand to my feets, go the window, and try to pull the curtain so I can be having more light, but inside the space between the metal gate and the window, there be a string of something shining.

I peep it well, confuse. It look like beads, a long, elastic string of it. Who owns the beads?

I hold my breath and pull, and it make a **shree** sound until it curl up in my palm like a small snake. I hold it up. What is this? It seem too big to be a neck-chain. The colors of each bead, the yellow, green, black, and red, make me think of Ikati, of some of the girls in the river that are wearing beads on their waist, and when they are dancing and playing, the beads will be making a clapping sound.

I was wanting beads when I was small, but my mama say she don't like them, so I don't ever be wearing them. Who owns these waist beads? I keep looking it, swinging it in my hand, and with each swing, I see that for every four beads in the thread, there is a red one, the red of Agan village, a kind of red that is orange under the moonlight and blood-red under the dark.

Was it belonging to Rebecca? Was she from Agan village? And why did she off her beads and hang it on the window metal gate?

I confuse even more. All the girls that are wearing beads in the village don't be ever offing it from their waist. Never. They wear it from when they are like three years of age and don't ever off it.

"Rebecca," I whisper to the night air, "if you run away with your boyfriend like Kofi say, why did you not take your beads with you? Why did you off it?"

There is no answer to my question, no any sound at all, except of the generator humming outside, so I turn back, put the beads under my pillow, and climb my bed, with the newspaper folding in my hands. I try to sleep, but I feel heavy, cold. Something evil happen to Rebecca. I know it. Feel it inside of me, curling around my bones like the waist beads under my pillow.

I hold tight the newspaper, crunch it in my hands.

December is not far.

If I can try to make better my English, find a reference, and enter the scholarship, maybe I can free myself from this place, from the evil of it.

But who, in the evil of this big house, will help me?

CHAPTER 29

Fact: With over 250 ethnic groups, Nigeria has a wide variety of foods. The most popular include jollof rice, skewered pieces of grilled and peppery meat called suya, and akara, a delicacy of bean fritters.

Middle of the afternoon on Sunday, the whole compound is filling with different cars.

Is like nothing I ever see. Cars with shape like **aeloplane** and **helikopta,** like boat and bucket. Some of them short with no roof, others are tall like Big Madam's car. All of them are looking too costly. I don't see the womens coming down from the car because Big Madam say I should be weeding the weed in the backyard grass.

I ask her why she is wanting me to weed grass on Sunday afternoon, and she pick a stone from the backyard and use it to knock me hard in the head and call me idiot "for daring to ask me questions."

As I was pulling the grass in the outside on Sunday, Kofi call me to the kitchen. "I am going crazy here," he say. "Go and wash your hands. I need your help." I wash my hands, and Kofi give me a tray full of small, fried meat with green pepper and onions with toothspick in the middle of the meats.

"Here is the stick-meat," he say. "Take it inside the living room and serve all the women."

I look the tray, at the way Kofi arrange the meats in a circle style around the edge of the plate, with one small tomato in the center of the plate.

"I should just give them the meat?" I ask. "One by one? And the tomato, what am I doing with that one?"

"That is not a tomato," Kofi say with a sigh. "It's a cherry. It is used to garnish the plate. Leave it as it is. Adunni, I beg you, don't touch the food. Do not attempt to pick up the food for anyone. If you touch it, Big Madam will pour it all into the bin and ask me to cook a fresh one. If that happens, **chale,** I will skin you alive. So, keep your mouth shut, your head down, and hold out the tray and curtsy like this—" Kofi bend his knee quick, stand up. "I repeat, do not speak to anyone. Serve the food and come back here. Is that clear? Now where on earth did I put that pot of jollof rice?"

As I enter the parlor with the tray, I turn to the first woman standing in front of me. Her skin is a rich dark color, shiny, smelling of bitter oranges and firewood, a sharp, strange smell that slice my nose and cause it to tickle. She is wearing a tight green dress, short to her knees area, the round top of her smooth breast peeping from the neck of it. Her hair is low-cut, the brown of a tree bark, with one line on the side of it, a parting from her ears to the middle of her head. Every makeups on her face is green color, except of the blood-red of her lipstick. Even her eyesballs are a sharp green. I keep my eyes to the floor as I am giving her the tray.

"Who is this one?" she ask, talking with a high, cracking voice, the voice of a too-much smoker. "Florence, is this the new maid you told me about?"

"She's as useless as they come," Big Madam answer from one corner of the parlor as somebody laugh from somewhere by the tee-vee.

"Where do you find them?" one woman ask. My eye cut to her. She is wearing ankara dress, blue and white, with shine-shine stone around her chest areas. There is a wig on her hair, big and round, as if she gum hair on a football and put it on her head. The powder on her face is the orange of evening sun, her lips the same brown of the court shoe on her feets. "From your agent? Mr. Kola? I told you to stop using local agents, you won't hear. The agency I use, Konsult-A-Maid, they get me the best. All foreign."

"I've told you guys this several times," Big Madam say, "Mr. Kola is cheap and reliable. When Rebecca left, he found this one quickly. I don't need a foreigner to clean my house for me. My children are abroad, so there is no fear of her harming them. You people that hire all these expensive Filipino

nannies for your children, tell me, do they do better than these ones? All of them are useless. Having
white skin and a strange accent does not make you
a better worker. I hear some of you even pay them
in dollars? Why on earth will I pay a housemaid in
dollars in my own country? And with the current
exchange rate? God forbid!"

Green Eyes pick the meat, her nails long, green
color match her eyes, the tip of it curling into the
finger. I am fearing to think how she is using that
long nails to wash her buttocks in toilet.

"What is her name?" she ask. "Come on, girl.
Raise your head. What is your name?"

I lift my head. Kofi say I must not be talking,
but this woman is looking me with her green eyes,
blinking, waiting for me to give answers. She make
me think of a cat, a black cat with brown hair and
green eyes and long nails.

"Adunni is the name, ma," I say.

"Well, at least this one speaks English. Who re-
members that girl that Florence had for like a week?
That stole half of your kitchen food. What was
her name?"

"Chichi," Big Madam say. "Possessed child of
the devil. I sent her back to the hell she came from
after I caught her urinating into the cup I use for
my morning tea."

"Rebecca is still your best house girl ever.
Well-spoken, respectful girl. She was what, twenty?"

I stay stiff when I hear Rebecca's name. Maybe

one of these womens will know. Maybe Big Madam will say something.

"Who cares?" Big Madam ask. "Does anyone want some cocktails? I also have some peppered snails on the grill. There's **suya** too, fresh and spicy."

"Florence, did you get to the bottom of what happened with Rebecca?" Football Head ask. "I always liked that girl," she say. "Did she run away? Florence? Did you go to her family?"

Big Madam say, "I could have sworn someone requested homemade piña colada."

"They all run away in the end, don't they?" another woman say. I peep that one too. Her whole body is one straight line. No breast, flat chest like floor. Her hair is long to her back, straight, the black of charcoal. Her eyeslashes is sticking outside of her face; like a short broom sweeping the red powder on top her cheeks. "Why would Florence bother traveling to goodness-knows-where to search for Rebecca? We all know that house girls are notorious for getting pregnant for one local idiot and disappearing. Hey, you. Bring that tray here."

"Yes, ma," I say as I move my feets, carry the tray to her, and keep my eyes on the gold tile on the floor. "Here, ma."

She pinch two stick of meat and pick it, fingers like matchstick. "Take it round to the girls," she say.

I raise my head. "Which girls?" I ask. "You mean the womens?"

The woman, she throw her thin head back so

quick, I am fearing it will just snap off, fall to the ground, and roll to the outside.

"Did she just call us 'womens'?" she say, laughing, her eyes filling with water. "My days. That is hilarious. Kiki, Caroline, Sade. She just called us 'womens.'"

There is laughters all around me, be like one kind crazy chorus.

"Sorry, ma," I say. "I didn't think sense."

"What is wrong with you guys?" somebody say, over the laughters. She sound like she is far, far back of me, her voice as if she lick plenty honey before she is talking. I want to peep her, but I cannot be turning my head well, so I keep my ears on her voice and lock the sound of it in my heart.

"We are women," she say. "I don't get the need to embarrass this girl. Not amusing in the least bit. Not at all."

"What is Tia moaning about now?" Green Eyes whisper to Football Head.

Football Head twist her nose like her own mouth is smelling. "All she does is complain about the ozone layer. Lost soul."

"She needs to get laid and have a baby." Green Eyes sniff a laugh as Thin Woman pinch another stick-meat.

"Adunni, you know you are meant to be at the backyard," I hear Big Madam say as I turn around. Her red **boubou** is sweeping the floor, the yellow bows on shoulder area jumping up and down. She is holding a wineglass, the red drink inside turning around and around as she is walking and talking. "Serve the stick-meat and get out of here. If I hear your voice again, I will break your head with my cup."

"Yes, ma."

"I hear Senator Abdul is backing Jonathan's campaign," Green Eyes is saying as I am turning away from Big Madam. "He was one of his most vocal critics. I guess money has changed hands."

"My husband has a meeting at Aso Rock tomorrow," Thin Woman answer as she pick another two stick-meat from my tray, bite on it as if it vex her. She so thin. Where all the food is going to?

"Whenever he gets summoned to the Presidential Villa to discuss oil revenue and all that, he always comes back home with a suitcase of dollars," she say, chewing. "With the election imminent, I can only imagine he will be returning with a truckload of cool cash. I must be a good girl so that he can sponsor a day trip to Harrods next weekend. That Gucci croc-skin bag is calling me."

"The 5K one? With bamboo handles?" Green Eyes say.

"5K what? Dollars?" Football Head ask.

"Pounds, baby," Thin Woman answer. "UK pounds. I'll be rocking it for Senator Ladun's fiftieth. Got my shoes from Harvey Nicks last month. It's a stunning pair of six-inch red bottoms. The perfect match."

Honest, honest, these rich people have a sickness of the head. Because why anybody will wear
red buttocks on their feets? Who own the red buttocks? Maybe this night I can check **The Book of
Nigeria Fact,** maybe it will tell me why rich people
of the Nigeria are wanting to wear red buttocks
as shoe.

"Gucci is so not my thing," Green Eyes say. "You
know how long I waited for my Hermès Birkin?
Eight bloody months. I swear, nobody in Lagos has
that bag. By the way, I heard Lola's husband got his
side-chick pregnant. She's expecting twins."

"Can we please discuss the fund-raising for the
Ikoyi orphanage?" someone ask, but before I can
check who it is, Thin Woman say, "I knew it would
happen! I knew it. I warned Lola, didn't I? I told her
to organize some boys to beat the bleach out of the
chick's skin, but she was quoting scripture, saying
God will fight her battles."

I keep carrying the tray around, hearing them
talk and talk about the shopping, about buying
costly bag and shoe with dollar money and pound
of money, and about one husband giving side-
chickens pregnant.

I reach the last woman. She is standing by herself in one corner, looking like she lost and find
herself here by one kind accident. She is wearing
t-shirt, pink color, with blue jeans-trouser, white
canvas-shoe on her feets. She look more young than
the other womens here, with her slim, egg-shape

face and skin the color of a roasting cashew nut. Her head is full of plenty tiny twists, like a million millions of them, some of it is hanging in front of her face, the curly tip of it bouncing on the round top of her nose, and the rest of it is pack up in a band at the middle of her head. There is no make-ups on her face—only red lipstick on lips which is looking like the cherry in the middle of the plate. There is one earring inside her nose, a spot of gold to the left of her nostrils.

I hold the tray for her, and she give me a smile, show white teeths with iron gate around it. "We **are** women," she say in her honey voice. She is talking whisper, but it is loud for me to be hearing her. "Don't mind them."

Honest, honest, her voice is doing music inside my ears, and I am just feeling something in my belly, like I want to be singing. Laughing. I take my eyes from her face, keep it on her white canvas-shoe, on her short, thin legs inside the blue jeans-trouser. She pick the meat, fingers small, nails short and neat. "Thank you," she say.

Thank you.

That is something I don't ever hear in this house. I look her face, blink. Why is she saying thank you? For just holding tray? For nothing?

"Thank you," she say again, with that music voice. "I certainly hope you enjoy serving your madam Florence."

"Kind of you," I say. "To say thank you to

me. Nobody have say thank you to me since I leave Ikati."

"It's okay," she say, touching my shoulder, gentle. "Go on now."

The touch is like electrics on my body. I shock, drop the tray, the stick-meat scattering the floor by my feets.

"Are you all right?" the woman say.

I look all the stick-meats, the remaining six of it on the floor, and all I want is my mama. I want her to not be dead, just for two or three minutes only, so she can bring herself come here and tell Big Madam to not beat me, or maybe she can magic and hide me until all the meats is no more on the floor. Or maybe she can—

"Don't cry," the woman say. "Here, let me help you get those. Step back a bit so I can—"

"No, no," I say, wiping my tears. "I get it myself, ma."

As I bend to pick the first meat, I feel a quick cold air, and something heavy is landing on my head as the honey-voice woman is shouting, "Florence, what the hell?" and I want to tell her that yes, my head is very hell, because it feel as if my head is frying inside a fire, burning, burning, burning, and I am thinking the ceiling have come down and crash on top my head, but when I look up, I see Big Madam. She is holding one leg of her red shoe, and before I can say another one word, she smash the shoe right inside the middle of my head.

CHAPTER 30

Fact: Zamfara state in northern Nigeria was
the first to make polygamy legal, in 2000.

C an you hear me?"
Her voice is making my inside to be warm,
but my head is still hot, my brain is running up
and down inside my skull, **boom, boom, boom.**
Everywhere around me is black. I feel something
wet on my face, my eyes. It is cold, soft, a cloth?
"Open your eyes."
I am smelling her scent, of coconut oil, butter, a
white lily flower.
"Adunni," she say again. "Open your eyes."
We are in the outside, at the backyard. My back
is lying on the wall near the outside tap, and she is
bending in front of me, kneeling down with one
leg. Behind her, the sun is bright in the sky, throwing sun rays over the grass fields in the afar. She is
giving me a smile, the gate on her teeths blinking

in the sun. I want to smile back, but when I try, my head is pounding of pain, it collect the smile from my lips, crush it.

"It must hurt," she say.

"Very hot," I say.

She nod. "I'll see if I can get the cook to give you some paracetamol."

Something wet is climbing down my face, and before I can be touching it, she use a cloth and wipe it. The cloth is the gray cleaning cloth from the kitchen, but when she wipe my face, the color is changing to red.

"I am bleeding blood?" I ask. "Big Madam wound me bad?"

"It looks worse than it actually is," she say. "How are you feeling?"

"Like Boko Haram is bombing inside my head."

She smile. "Your madam was very upset. She said she asked you to do some work outside. Why were you serving guests?"

"Kofi ask me for help," I say.

She throw one look back at the house, where there is noise and laughters and music. "I think I might just sit here with you for a while."

She sit on the floor next to me like me and her are best of friends since we was small childrens. "It's my second time attending the WRWA," she say, after a moment. "My husband wants me to get to know our neighbors better. He thinks I am too uptight. How's the head? Better?"

"Yes, madam," I say. "Better. You are a kind person."

"Forget the 'madam,'" she say. "Just call me Tia."

"Madam Tee-ya?"

"Ms. Tia," she say.

"Ms. Tia." I smile. "I like it if you like it."

"How old are you?"

"Fourteen, ma."

"Fourteen?" She strong her face a moment, think. "That's not right . . . Florence should know better than to hire an underage girl as a maid. I should speak to her—"

"No," I say, nearly shouting, and when she look me, concern, I force myself to smile. "I mean, don't be talking to Big Madam about me, please. Just leave me here like this." How I can be telling this woman that I must stay here until I enter the scholarship? That I have nowhere else to be going except of this place?

"Okay," she say, slow, dragging the word. "I won't say anything. Tell me, where have you come from? You said something about Ikati when you served me the stick-meat. Where is that?"

I tell her I don't know where it is, but I know it is far because we are driving for a long time before we are reaching Lagos.

"I don't need to ask if you like it here," she say. "I can tell you aren't happy."

I down my face, shake my head. "Are you living far from here?" I ask.

"We moved down the road last year," she say.

"Well, I did. My husband has always lived on this street. I used to live in England. You know England? The UK?"

I think of that rich man Ade. My mama's man-friend. "I am hearing of the UK of the Abroad," I say. "And I am seeing it a bit in the CNN news tee-vee."

She scratch her jaw with her fingernail, as if she is thinking of something deep. "Did you go to school?"

"I was going to school for small time. I didn't able to finish because of no money and because my mama was dying, but I am trying to be learning English and speaking better because I am want-ing to enter one exam very, very soon. I keep read-ing **The Book of Nigeria Fact** and the Collins."

"The Collins? Oh, you mean the dictionary?" She turn, look my whole face, inside my eyes, as if she is seeing me for the first time ever and at the same time she is searching for something deep inside of my eyes. "I am surprised that Florence is putting you through school. You could ask her to get you some storybooks, you know?" she say. "A few books on grammar should help with your forthcoming exam."

"Yes, madam. I mean, Ms. Tia." How can I tell her Big Madam is not putting me in any school?

"Do you know Rebecca?" I ask, thinking of her waist beads still under my pillow. Maybe Ms. Tia can help me.

"I heard the women talking about her," Ms. Tia say. "I don't think I ever met her. Why are you asking?"

"I am just asking," I say. "She was working here before, and now she is missing. I ask Kofi, but he say maybe she run away with her boyfriend."

"She probably did," Ms. Tia say, shrug. "Stuff like that happens all the time."

Talking to this Ms. Tia is making the pain in my head to be stopping small. Her honey voice is like medicine, her laugh like cool water on my hot head. I don't want her to hurry and go, so I am asking her more questions, saying everything that is coming to my brain, so she will stay. "Did you live in the Nigeria after they born you? When did you go to the Abroad?"

"I was born in Lagos. My primary school education was here in Lagos as well," she say. "In Ikoyi, actually. My dad then got a job in an oil company in Port Harcourt, and so we moved over."

She say the word "Port Harcourt" as if it is a song, her tongue wrapping around the words, making them dance.

"I spent most of my life in Port Harcourt before I left for university in Surrey."

"Why it is Sorry?" I ask. "Is it a sad place?"

She raise her hand, cover her eyes from sun rays with a smile. "No, it's nice. Different."

"You have any brother or sister?" I ask. "Where is your mama?"

"I am an only child," she say, shrug, voice level, flat. "My parents are still in Port Harcourt; my dad still works for the oil firm. My mum was working as a librarian at the University of Port Harcourt until she got sick last year."

"Your mama sick?" I say, feeling much pity. "Sickness is the worst of all things to happen to a mama. When my mama was sick, I didn't able to balance myself. I was crying every day until she dead. Even now, sometimes, I cry nearly every day. Are you crying every day too?"

She sigh, say, "No, I don't cry. I am so sorry to hear your mother passed. Sounds like you were close."

"My mama?" I smile soft. "She was everything to me. My best of friend. Everything."

"Good for you," she say. "I . . . uh, how to say this? I relocated . . . came back home to Nigeria last year."

It don't sound like she is having much feeling for her mama. Or like she want to talk of her.

"Why did you move back to the Nigeria?" I ask. "Because your mama sick?"

"Because I wanted to," she say. "I got an amazing opportunity to join a small, lovely company called the Lagos Environmental Consultancy, and I knew I had to take it. And"—she pluck a twist of hair from her face, twist it around her finger—"because I fell in love and got married to my husband." Her voice is taking a new, strange, high tone as she is talking of her husband, her eyes brighting up. "His name is Ken," she say. "Kenneth Dada. He is a doctor. A good man. He helps women get pregnant."

My eye cut to her stomach. It is flat under the t-shirt she is wearing. Is she having childrens of her own?

"I don't have children," she say, as if she know what is in my mind.

"You don't have childrens?" I ask as a lizard run out from behind the flowerpot. He stop, look me and Ms. Tia, blink his eyeslids real slow, as if he is fighting sleep. He nod his orange head up and down, before he cut to the other side of the compound.

"Nope," she say, eye on the lizard. "Don't want any."

"You don't want any at all, **at all**?"

Honest, honest, I never hear of a adult woman not wanting childrens in my life. In my village, all the adult womens are having childrens, and if the baby is not coming, maybe because of a sickness, then their husband will marry another woman on top of them and the adult woman will be caring for another woman's baby so that she don't feel any shame. I look her face, concern. "Will your husband marry another woman on top of you if you didn't have childrens?"

When she laugh, it sound like bell ringing quiet. "No way," she say. "People choose not to have children for all sorts of reasons."

I nod, feel as if I understand what she mean a little, even though she is a adult woman.

"Not too long ago," I say, thinking back to when I was drinking leafs in Morufu's house to stop my pregnants from coming, "I was so very afraid of borning childrens because in my village, they want us girls to be borning childrens early. But I am wanting to finish my schooling. My mama, before she was dead, she fight so much for me to finish my school. She was the best mama in the whole wide world of it. So I make up my mind that after I finish my schooling and I find a working job, then I will find a very good man to marry. My papa didn't always be kind to me and he didn't want girls to be going to school, but I am different from my papa and I will not marry a man like him. No. I will work hard and born my own childrens, and me and my husband, we will send them to a very good school, even if they are all girls-childrens. Then one day, I will go to Ikati and show my papa, then he will be proud of me when he see my own childrens and my own money."

I feel sad as I am thinking this, thinking that maybe, one day, Papa will not be too angry that I run away from Ikati. "I have a old friend from my village, Khadija was her name. She tell me that childrens be bringing joy," I say with a smile. "Maybe one day, I will feel that joy too, and share it with my papa, make him a happy old man."

She nod slow, looking me for a long time until I begin to feel discomfort.

"What about you?" I tilt my neck, surprise myself

with the question I ask her: "You finish schooling. You are working a good job. So, what is your own sorts of reasons for not wanting childrens?"

When she strong her face, I am thinking I cause her to be angry. Now, she will remove her shoe and smash it on my head just like Big Madam, and my brains will scatter finish. But she didn't remove her shoe. She just look me sharp, her eyesbrows drawing together in a line. Then she push herself up, dust the sand from her buttocks.

"I hope your head gets better soon," she say. "It's been lovely chatting with you."

As she is walking away from my front, I am thinking, why did I open my big mouth and say something so foolishly foolish?

CHAPTER 31

Fact: Nigeria's film industry is called Nollywood. With over fifty films produced weekly, the industry is worth about $5 billion and is the second largest in the world, behind India's Bollywood.

The day after she was nearly breaking my head, Big Madam call for me.

I meet her where she is sitting in the sofa in her parlor, one leg hanging across the chair handle, the other one on a cushion pillow on the floor. The tee-vee is on, loud, showing one old Yoruba movie. The man in the tee-vee is wearing red cloth with cowries hanging from it and holding a white fowl. There is black paint with white dots everywhere on his face. He is talking to the fowl, begging the fowl to make him rich.

"Ma?" I say, kneeling in her front, keeping one eye on the tee-vee. The man is now dancing on one leg, turning the fowl around and around.

Big Madam press the remote-controlling to stop

the tee-vee, making the man to hang one hand and one leg in the air, like a statue about to fly.

She turn to me. "How is your head?" She keep a straight face as if she is wanting me to tell her that my brain have dead.

"My head is okay, ma," I say.

"Next time, I will make sure I crack your skull open so that when I give an instruction, you will store it in the right compartment," she hiss. "You know I have zero tolerance for rubbish. I said stay outside when I have visitors. Don't come into my parlor. Do. Not. Enter. My. Parlor. What part of that didn't you understand?"

"I understand now, ma."

"You are very lucky Tia Dada was in this house yesterday," she say. "If not, God knows that I would have killed you with beating. I don't even know who invited that one with her thin voice. Imagine her intervening, telling me she will call the police because I disciplined my own housemaid. Which police can she call in Nigeria to arrest Big Madam? Does she know who I am? Me that I supply fabric to the who-is-who in Nigeria? Where will they see me to arrest? Who is the policeman that will arrest Chief Mrs. Florence Adeoti? Where does she think she is?" Big Madam pinch the top of her gold **boubou,** blow air inside it.

"I blame Dr. Ken. When we told him to settle and marry Molara, he said no, he wants a woman that will understand his needs. What foolish needs? Look at what he now ended up with. An unfriendly, empty barrel. One whole year of marriage and no sign of pregnancy."

My chest is burning that she is talking bad about Ms. Tia. I am feeling fire in my heart, angry fire, and I am wanting to shout on Big Madam to tell her that Ms. Tia is having honey voice and a kind heart, that Ms. Tia didn't pregnant because of all sorts of reasons, but I am fearing she will slice my throat with knife if I say anything.

"How many ears do you have?" she ask.

"Two, ma."

"Now, pull your two ears. Yes. Pull them. Like this." She pinch my right ear with her nails and pull down to my shoulder. "Listen well. I am traveling next week. I will be going to Switzerland and Dubai. I will also stop over in the UK to see my children. I will be back, by God's grace, in about two weeks."

"Yes, ma."

"When I am away, you must behave yourself. Kofi must not tell me that you did something you shouldn't have done. You hear me?"

"Yes, ma."

"Do you have a list of the things we need in the house?"

"I will write it after I am finishing from here," I say. "I will give to Abu."

"Big Daddy will not be around either," she

say. "He will be traveling to Ijebu to see his poverty-stricken family members. If he comes back from Ijebu before me, stay away from him. If he comes to the backyard, you go to your room. If he calls for you, don't answer him. It is only when I am around that you answer Big Daddy. I don't like leaving my house girls alone in the house when I am traveling, honestly."

She shake her head. "My sister in Ikeja will be traveling at the same time. I would have taken you there to stay with her for my peace of mind." She pick the remote-controlling and press it to on a film in the tee-vee. "I have told Kofi to look after you. He will keep an eye on you. Whatever Kofi asks you to do, you do it. I must not hear one word of complaint from him or else I will dump you on the streets. I won't even ask Mr. Kola to come and get you. I will dispose of you like the trash that you are. **Sho ti gbo?** You hear me?"

"Yes, ma," I say. "Can I ask you one question, ma?"

"What is it?"

"It is about Rebecca, I been wondering if—"

"Get out of my sight," she shout so sudden, my heart nearly collapse. "How dare you ask me questions about Rebecca? Who is she? You must be an idiot for that question." When she bend down to begin to off her left shoe, I jump to my feets, run from her front, just as she throw the shoe and bang the glass on the door, nearly breaking it.

In the backyard, I find Abu at the outside tap.

He is rolling his trouser up to his knees. His blue prayer kettle is on the floor beside him.

"Abu," I say, breathing fast. "Good afternoon."

Me and him don't talk much, but when we see, we greet ourselfs with a smile, and sometimes, I am helping him to wash the car tire when he is needing to go for his afternoon prayer.

"**Sannu**, Adunni," Abu say. He turn the tap and pick his kettle to fill it up. "Why are you running? Can I help you?"

Like Kofi, Abu too have a way of talking. He like to be using **F** instead of **P,** so when he say "help," it sound like **"helf,"** and if he say he want to drink Fanta, it sound like he is saying **"Panta."** At first I wasn't understanding him, but now it is not too much a problem. Everybody in the whole world be speaking different. Big Madam, Ms. Tia, Kofi, Abu, even me, Adunni. We all be speaking different because we all are having different growing-up life, but we can all be understanding each other if we just take the time to listen well.

"I was running from Big Madam," I say, then I start to laugh. I laugh and laugh until my chest begin to pain me. "I just ask her a simple question now, and she just start to off her shoe to throw it at me. Honest, that woman is having many problems. Anyway, she say I should give you a list. For shopping."

"Keep it for me inside the car," he say, offing the tap. "When I finish my prayer, then I will go to Shoprite with Kofi."

"Okay," I say, then low my voice. "Abu, I been wanting to ask you something. You remember Rebecca?"

Abu spit to the left of me, wipe his mouth with the back of his hand. "The one that was working for Madam before you? I know her well."

I nod. "Thank you. Do you know why she is missing? Kofi keep saying he don't know. He thinks she run away with her man-friend. I just ask Big Madam, and she throw a shoe at me, so I say, let me ask Abu, maybe Abu will tell me."

"**Walahi,** Adunni, you are looking for big trouble." Abu grip his plastic kettle, turn around, and begin to walk fast from me. "If Kofi says she ran away, then hear what Kofi is saying and leave it."

"Abu! Wait!" I shout, but the man turn a corner by the boys' quarters and disappear into his prayer room.

CHAPTER 32

Fact: Funmilayo Ransome-Kuti, the mother of music legend Fela Kuti, was a renowned feminist who fought for equal access for women in education.

Ms. Tia bring herself back the day after Big Madam travel to the Abroad.

I was washing the downstairs toilet, head deep inside the commode, when Kofi tell me I have a visitor. At first, I was fearing, thinking that Papa have come with the whole village to come find me. But in the reception, I see Ms. Tia bending down to her feets and tying the shoe rope around her white canvas-shoe. She is wearing a tight black trouser and a singlet top, and when she raise up her head, she give me a smile.

"Hi," she say.

"Hi to you too," I say. "You are the visitor asking of me?" Maybe she is still vexing because of the foolish thing I say that last time. "Please don't vex about what I say," I say. "Sometimes I like to talk too much and—"

She hold up her hand, silent my words. "I actually came by to apologize. I shouldn't have walked away because you asked me a question I get asked all the time. It was wrong of me. I am sorry."

"You are giving **me** apology?" I shake my head, not understanding the woman.

"My conversation with you that day, it kind of . . ." She scratch her head, move the twists out of her face, curl them behind her ears. ". . . moved me in a way I cannot explain. It's just so strange."

What is she talking about?

She look around the reception. "Your madam is away, right? She mentioned at the last meeting that she was going away. I hope my being here is not . . . I mean, it is not a problem for you to talk to me now, is it?"

"No problem," I say.

Both of us don't talk for a moment. Then she say: "What you said the other day. Questioning my reasons and all that. It dug up something inside of me."

"What did it dug up?" I ask, fold my hand in front of my chest, looking her.

She rub her hand up and down, finding something to fix her eyes on, the floor, my face. "So, two days ago, I was going for my morning run on the Lekki-Ikoyi bridge. I was all good, running at a great pace, when right there, right in the middle of the bridge, I had an epiphany."

"Epi— What you call it?"

She wave her hand up in the air, her eyes wide, brighting. "A moment of realization. About my wanting children and all that . . . all because of the conversation we had." She start a laugh, change her mind, and kill it. "Am I confusing you?"

"Too much," I say. **And yourself. You are confuse of yourself too. Rich people have plenty brain problem, honest.**

"I am just a little excited, that's all," she say. "I will head home now. Do take care of yourself, and good luck with your exams." She start to turn around, and I know that if I let her just go like that, that I will never see her again. So before I can think of my action, I jump forward, grab her hand, hold her.

She stop, look me, my hand, my fingers crawling around her arm and squeezing. "Are you okay?"

"Sorry, ma," I say. "Please don't be angry."

"What's wrong?" she ask.

I wait for her to shout, but she don't shout. She sound calm. Her eyes sort of melt, a question of a smile on her face. I low myself to the floor and begin to talk. "You ask me about exam," I say as I put one hand inside my brassiere and bring out the newspaper and press it into her hand. "I don't have any exam, but I need your help, ma. I need somebody to make reference for me."

"Reference? For what? Oh, please stand," she say, pulling me to my feets. "What's in the news-paper?" She open the newspaper, read it silent, her eyes moving up and down the paper. "I see," she say, folding the paper and giving it back to me. "A scholarship scheme for domestic workers. What a brilliant initiative. I assume Florence has nothing to do with this?"

"She will kill me if she find out about it," I say. "But I must try and enter it."

"What's the urgency?" she ask.

My eyes fill up, and I press my fingers to my lips. "This is all I been wanting all my life. Please . . ." I stop talking, swallow the tears in my throat. "The final age for entering is fifteen. Please."

She shift on her feets. "I honestly . . . don't know you well enough to be able to stand as a guarantor—"

"Big Madam is traveling now," I say. "So I collect my independent just like Nigeria, but my own is for just two weeks, not forever and forever. You can ask me any question, tell me to do anything, I will do it. You can know me in two weeks. I will show you my real self in the next two weeks and you can write it inside the form and tell them I am a good girl, working hard every time. Please."

She start a smile, then change it to a short laugh. "You are the most amusing girl I have ever met in my life. Adunni, I would love to help you, but Florence and I don't get along that well," she say.

"If she finds out I gave you a reference or acted as a guarantor—"

"She will never forever find out," I say, eyes full of something sure. "I will keep it a secret forever and ever and ever. She is always beating me in this place. This is my chance to be free. Please," I say again. I just want her to say yes, that she will help me. "Can you help me?"

She sigh. "I guess it's the least I can do in exchange for how you helped me." Before I can ask when I ever help her with anything, she say, "You need to write an essay of a thousand words in the next few weeks?"

"Yes, ma," I say, heart beating fast.

"Let's see." She look the ceiling, then look me. "Ken is out this week. The articles for the month have been processed. I can probably move that meeting with the environmental agency tomorrow evening, and finish off the report on Kainji Dam a day or two late. Can I do this?"

I don't know if she is talking to me, or talking to herself, or both me and herself together, but I wait, keep looking, keep hoping she will say yes.

"Adunni. Listen. I can free up some time this week and maybe a few more days in the next week. Since your madam is away, I could swing by in the evenings, and I could, you know, teach you a bit of English to help you prepare for the essay and brush up your speaking, and that way, I can get to know you hopefully well enough to write a pretty good

reference. If you can get some time off in the evenings and—" She stop. "You look dazed."

I daze. Very daze. "You will help me and be teaching me?" I put my hand on top my chest. "Me?"

I don't think of whether what I am about to do
is the correct thing, I just jump front, put my hand
around her, and hold her tight. She smell of rich
people's sweat and something like mint leaf. She
is laughing as I leave her be. She didn't angry that
I am giving her embrace, and I feel sad and happy
that this rich woman didn't push me back and spit
on me like Big Madam.

"Sorry I am holding you like that," I say. "It is giving me excitement, this teaching me better English
and helping me. Will you reference me too?"

"It shouldn't be a problem," she say, shrug her
shoulder. "No **wahala** at all. I'll come by tomorrow
evening. What time would work?"

"By seven, seven thirty, I am finishing all
my housework."

She wide her eyes. "You work from what time
till seven?"

"I am waking up around four thirty, five, in the
morning," I say. "I am doing my work, cleaning,
sweeping, washing, everything, till seven, seven
thirty. But if Big Madam is in the house, then I
am working till sometimes eleven or twelve in
the midnight."

"From dawn till midnight? That's madness." She
talk in her breath, but I hear every word of it.

"See you tomorrow evening." She wave two fingers in the air, turn herself around.

"Thank you, ma," I say. "See you."

At night, I sleep a good sleep. I see Khadija and Mama inside my dream. The two both of them have become a happy bird with wings of rainbow color, flying high in a sky with no cloud.

CHAPTER 33

Fact: There are over 50 million users of the internet in Nigeria. It is predicted that, by the year 2018, over 80 million Nigerians will be using the internet, placing the country in the top fifteen globally for internet usage.

"Why are you locking your teeths inside iron gate?"

I ask Ms. Tia this question on the first evening that she is teaching me school. It is six fifteen, and the sun is climbing down from the sky, making the whole place have a orange glowing light. Me and her are sitting in the outside, under the palm tree, the one beside the outside tap, near the kitchen. There is no breeze, the air is stiff, the smell of the onions Kofi is peeling is in the air.

The two both of us are sitting on the floor, me in my uniform, her in her blue jeans-trouser and t-shirt. Today, her t-shirt is white. They write **GIRLS RULE** on top the front in black biro. She have on a white canvas-shoes on her feets. She so small, sitting beside me, her size make me think of Khadija.

"Gate?" She look up, squeeze her nose. "On my teeth?" She laugh. "My braces?"

"Brazes? That is what you call it?"

"Yes, braces," she say. "I had crooked teeth when I was growing up. My teeth were growing on top of each other. I looked a bit like a baby shark. They come off in a year. I guess they do look like tiny iron gates." She use her tongue to climb the braces, feel them one by one. "So I was thinking, we should start with the simple stuff, your tenses."

She pick up a pencil and exercise book from the floor, take the pencil, and write **ADUNNI** on top the cover of the exercise book. Her writing style is full of plenty curves, everything joining each other, making me think of the henna Enitan drawed on my hand when I was doing my wedding. "I checked online for a beginner syllabus," she say. "A syllabus is a plan for how we would work, what I can teach you."

"See-lah-bus," I say, talking slow.

"Good pronunciation. Where was I? Yes. I checked online. On my phone." She lift her leg, dig inside her pocket, bring out her phone. She draw something on her phone with her finger, and light is coming on inside it. She hold it up and I am seeing plenty words like a newspaper.

"I would suggest we start with the intermediate course." She turn the phone to herself, begins to read from it. "This website has courses that can help. It's the BBC website."

I look her, blank.

"I have also found some free-to-learn online courses," she say. "Some days, I will teach you. Other days, I will give you my phone to just listen and learn."

"On which line?" I ask.

"The internet," she say. "That's what I mean by 'online.'"

"The **inta** . . . net." I see this in **The Book of Nigeria Fact,** but it only make me think of a cloth with plenty holes inside, of the hairnet on Labake's head.

"Here." She take the phone, turn it to myself. "This phone connects me to the internet. Think of it as a place where you can connect with people anywhere in the world and access almost any information. When you connect with your phone or computer to the internet, you are going online. You can shop, make friends, send emails, do loads of stuff online."

"You can be going to the market on this online?"

She nod. "I buy stuff from shops online. Food, clothes, whatever I need, really."

"That will be costly," I say. "Why not go to the real market?"

She laugh. "I don't have the time to go to the proper Lagos markets. When I do go, my crappy Yoruba doesn't make things easy, plus I am pretty useless at haggling. 'Haggling' means asking the seller to sell stuff below the asking price. Anyway, I am crap at it, so I always end up feeling frustrated and leaving."

"Maybe I can follow you one day," I say. "In Ikati, I was always buying things for my mama at low price, more low than the market womens are selling it, because we didn't always have the money. I can show you how to do this haggling, or what you call it?" I smile. "I want to help you a little, just like you are helping me now."

"That'd be so wonderful," she say, smiling back. "Thank you."

"How did you and your husband meet each other?" I ask. "Was it in this Nigeria? Or in the Abroad?"

"I actually met my husband online," she say. "On Facebook. We dated for a year, long-distance, not the easiest thing. We got married about eighteen months ago in Barbados."

"Is Facebook inside the online too?"

"Let me show you." She press something on her phone and show me. I see the white and blue color of the Facebook, see small pictures of Ms. Tia, plenty photos of many peoples but nobody in all the pictures is facing their book. "It is a social networking site," she say. "People from all over the world can find each other on it at the click of a button. Say I want to find— Oh, here we go, Katie just sent me a message." She press a picture of the girl face. "That's Katie, my friend. We used to share a flat."

The Katie friend is laughing with all her teeths. Her skin is pale like chicken skin, after you have peel all the feathers. Her nose is the shape of question mark, long with a quick curving at the tip of it. Her hair look like a waterfall, the red of blood, pouring from her head to her shoulders. "She is not from the Nigeria?"

"She's British," Ms. Tia say.

I think on what she say a moment. Then I say, "Your friend collect our free. But we collect it back on October 1st, 1960."

"The British government did," Ms. Tia say with a small smile. "Not Katie or any individual."

"One day, I collect my own free back from Big Madam," I say.

"You will," Ms. Tia say. "One day."

I look the Katie picture again. "I didn't know that peoples like you can be living in the Abroad because when I am watching news in the tee-vee with Big Madam, I am only seeing peoples that look like Katie."

"What, you only see white people when you watch the news?" She force a quiet laugh. "That's not— I mean there are loads of black people on TV in England and in— Actually," she sigh, low her voice, make it somehow sad, "you have a point. There aren't enough black people anchoring the news . . . or in parliament . . . or in top positions. Not enough."

I didn't too sure I understand what Ms. Tia is

talking about, or why she is calling her Abroad peoples white and black when colors are for crayons and pencils and things. I know that not everybody is having the same color of skin in Nigeria, even me and Kayus and Born-boy didn't have same skin color, but nobody is calling anybody black or white, everybody is just calling us by our name: Adunni. Kayus. Born-boy. That's all.

I look Ms. Tia, wanting to ask her if it matter much that a person is one color or another color in the UK of the Abroad, but she is pinching her lips with her teeths and still looking sad, so I keep my words to myself and tell her another fact: "Mr. Mungo Park was discovered River Niger."

"What?" she say.

"Is another fact," I say. "In **The Book of Nigeria Fact.** Mr. Mungo Park, a man from the British, was traveling to Nigeria and just discovered the River Niger. But he is not from the Nigeria. How he can discover a river that been in the Nigeria for since? Somebody from Nigeria must have show Mr. Mungo Park the river, point him the way to the place. Who is the person? Why didn't they put the person's name inside **The Book of Nigeria Fact**?"

"Maybe because . . ." Ms. Tia pinch her lip with her teeths, think. "I am not sure, actually. It is something to think about."

"Like Kofi," I say. "He cook all the food since

nearly five years, but everybody is blinding to him. When the visitor come and eat Kofi's fried rice, they are always saying well done to Big Madam, that the rice is very sweet, and Big Madam is always smiling, saying thank you. Why she cannot say it is Kofi that make the food? She is taking the thank you for another person work."

"Because she's not thinking about it," Ms. Tia say. "Maybe because she's paid Kofi a salary. It doesn't mean it's the right thing to do. I'll just log out of Facebook."

"This Facebook thing," I say. "I can find anybody I am looking for inside it?"

She nod her head yes. "Most times."

I think of Bamidele, whether I can find him inside this place. "Can you find somebody they are calling Bamidele?"

"Bamidele?" She press her phone, shake her head. "Adunni, there are too many people called Bamidele on here. What's his surname?"

"I didn't sure," I say.

"I am not sure," she say.

"You say what?"

"I am correcting you. It is 'I am not sure,' not 'I didn't sure.'"

"Ah," I say.

"Right. So, our first lesson is to get you to understand your tenses. Thankfully, you have a very good understanding of English, can even manage some complex words, but your tenses need work. Are you ready for this?"

"Yes," I say, "very ready."

"Here," she say, eyes bouncing with a twinkle. "Take the notepad and pencil. Let's get started."

CHAPTER 34

Fact: Nigerians did not need a visa to travel
to the United Kingdom until 1984.

Honest, honest, English is just a language of confusions.

Sometimes, I am not even understanding the different in what Ms. Tia is teaching me and what I already know. In my mind, I am speaking the correct English, but Ms. Tia, she is always saying I am not saying the right thing. Even though it take a lot of begging for her to help me at first, she now seem so happy to be teaching me, and every day, by seven thirty, she arrive like happy childrens, bouncing on her two feets, holding exercise book and pencil, wanting to teach me. It is tiring me sometimes, her teachings and corrections, but I know that the more better I am learning, the more better the chance for me to enter the school.

But sometimes, we just talk and talk.

Yesterday, I tell her more about me. That I was running away because my papa was wanting to sell me to Morufu because of community rent, and how I was meeting Mr. Kola, and how he was bringing me to Big Madam's house. I tell her about Mama, and how I am missing her, and when I start to cry, Ms. Tia rub her hand on my back around and around and say, "You'll be fine, Adunni, you'll be just fine." But how she know I will be just fine? All she need to do is enter a **aeloplane** and she will see her own mama in Port Harcourt. But me, which **aeloplane** can take me to heaven?

My mama is nothing but a sweet memory of hope, a bitter memory of pain, sometimes a flower, other times a flashing light in the sky. I didn't tell Ms Tia that I ever marry Morufu or about all the things he did to me in the room after he drink Fire-Cracker. I didn't tell her about what happen to Khadija. I didn't tell her because I have keep it inside one box in my mind, lock the box, and throw the key inside river of my soul. Maybe one day, I will swim inside the river, find the key.

She tell me more things about herself too. That she and her papa are "incredibly close," but she and her mama been always fighting because her mama was "too demanding" when she was growing up. She say her mama didn't let her to have many friends when she was growing up, and so now she don't know how to keep many friends. She say too that they didn't teach her how to speak Yoruba because they are mix of Edo and Ijaw, and now she feels one kind of shame that she cannot speak Yoruba because she wants to be talking with her husband's family in Yoruba, so I tell her I can be teaching her and she smile and say, "That'd be amazing!"

Then she tell me she is wanting childrens. Well, she is wanting, but her husband is didn't too serious about the wanting of the baby like her, but now they are starting to try for the baby. When she say this, her eyes fill up with tears, and I sense that she feel a release inside of her spirit, as if she take off a load that she been carrying about for a long time. When I ask her why she change her mind to be wanting childrens, she bring out her phone and press the internet thing and give me.

"Listen to that," she say. "It's a lesson in oral English. Listen and pronounce."

I don't like those oral English-speaking lesson. I am not hearing the people when they are talking. Their voice is fast, fast, like something is chasing them with cane and making them to talk with no stopping to breathe, but because Ms. Tia is always looking me, I am forcing myself to be saying what the phone is saying. Like yesterday, it was teaching me how to say one word: "cutlery."

I say: **"Kotee-leer-ree."**

The phone say: **"Kutluh-ree."**

Ms. Tia say: **"Kutluh-ree."**

I say: "How is my own differing from your own?"

Ms. Tia say: "How is mine **different** from **yours,** Adunni. 'Different.' Not 'differenting.'"

Then she teach me the different in her own different and my own differenting.

That is how we are doing. We will start talking, then I will say something, she will twist her nose, begin to teach me, and then we just forget the thing we are talking about before.

But this evening, before we start our English lesson, I sit down on the floor beside her, say, "Ms. Tia? Mind I ask you something?"

"Yep," Ms. Tia say. "Ask me anything."

"Mind I ask you again why you change your mind about wanting childrens?" I say.

She sigh, pick a stone by her feets, throw it into the grass, then pinch her bottom lip with her teeths, bite it hard, and blink, blink, blink. "I told you how my mother was a tough woman," she say. "She still is, but the sickness has softened her a bit, made her weak. My mother demanded perfection in every way. Over everything. As a child, I didn't have friends. Every moment was spent studying. She wanted me to be an accountant. I hate numbers. She also wanted me to get married at twenty-two and have children immediately because she wanted to be a grandmother before a certain age. She insisted I move back to Port Harcourt after my studies, but I met Ken and moved to Lagos instead. My mother had a manual for how my life would go and I rebelled—got stubborn—at every decision she made for me. She made me so unhappy that I couldn't imagine having a child and doing what she did to me to my own child. I didn't think I would be a good mother. I didn't even want to bring children into this world. I mean, look at the state of things! I was happy to voluntarily reduce our population to save our planet, so I spent a year traveling—before I met Ken—campaigning against population growth."

She pause a little, steady her voice. "But when my mother got sick last year and was diagnosed as terminal, meaning she would not ever get better, I started to see her, to see things, in a slightly different light. Maybe the sickness softened her, but many times, she would cry and hold my hands, as if trying to say sorry for how things were with us. As I went back and forth to see her in Port Harcourt, especially over the last few months, I began to wish I had a baby to take along with me, to give my mother a reason to fight to live. I'll be honest and say that it was always just a quick thought, never a strong enough urge to make me discuss with Ken or to change my mind. But the day we met"—she peep me, smile—"you said something about your father being a bit mean, but that did not stop you from loving him. You said you'd take your time to find a good man at the right time so that your children will enjoy what you didn't. You made me realize that I could be a good mother. That I could **choose** not to be like my mother. You don't know this, but what you said that day, it struck a chord inside of me. Made me dig up a long-buried desire."

She face me, tears shining in her eyes. "And now, I know it is what I want. I cannot stop thinking about it, about having a little boy or girl, just one, because I still believe in my environmental causes." She laugh soft. "I will raise my child in a loving, balanced home, and hope she can become as smart, intelligent, and amusing as you are."

"You will be a good mama someday," I say, blinking back my own tears, "like my own mama was. Ms. Tia, you are not like your mama. You are a good person."

She take my hand, hold it tight, say nothing.

"What did the doctor think?" I ask. "About you changing your mind?" I take to calling her husband "the doctor" since she tell me about him. She doesn't mind it.

"At first he wasn't keen," she say. "He got upset, said I was backing out of the plan. But we didn't have an agreement as such. When we met, he said he didn't want kids and I was cool with it, so we got married." She smile a shy one, then say, "He's come round now, we're trying. I know it will happen."

"Very soon," I say.

She nod, give me my exercise book and biro. "Can we now get on with our work for today?"

Six nights have passed, and now I am in my room, reading the paper Ms. Tia give me.

She write ten sentences in the paper, and tell me to pick which one is correct English and which one is not correct English. I am sitting up on my bed, pencil in my hand, looking the paper, when I hear a noise in the back of the cupboard. Like a rat scratching his nails on the door.

I climb down from the bed, pick up one leg of my shoe, hold it. If that rat peep his head, I will smash it. I wait, breathing fast, quiet. The noise come again, a creak. It is coming from outside, behind my door. I turn to the door, pull it open.

Big Daddy is standing there, looking shock. He is wearing trousers, white singlet on top, slippers on his feets. His body have a smell, of too much drink.

What is he doing on this side? In the boys' quarters?

"Adunni." He keep his eye on the chest area of my nightgown. "How are you?"

"Sah?" I say, kneel and greet him, hold my nightgown with my hand, pull it close, covering my chest. "I am fine, sah. Good evening." I remember what Big Madam say, her warning not to answer Big Daddy, so I stand to my feets, make to enter my room.

"Come back," Big Daddy say, licking his top lip, and something full of hope die inside of me.

"Come here," he say. "Don't be afraid."

I look to my left, my right. By now Kofi is sleeping deep, snoring.

"You are a very beautiful girl," Big Daddy say. He push his eye-glass down on his nose. "Intelligent too."

"Thank you, sah."

"My wife is away," he say.

"Yes, sah."

"She's threatened. My wife. Threatened by every damn female around me. Frustrating, I tell you, very frustrating."

"Yes, sah."

"She has nothing to worry about," he say, sway on his feets, shake his head. "I mean, my wife. She has nothing to worry about."

I am not saying **yes, sah** again. I just stand there, keep my back to the wall, fold my hand in front of my chest, and lock my nightdress well.

"I want to make a proposal, Adunni," he say. "A proposal. That is not the name of a person, you know."

"What is it you want, sah?" I slap away a mosquito from my arm, yawn. "Sleep is catching me."

"You don't have to hurry away from me, Adunni. I am a gentleman, you see."

I don't see anything, so I didn't give him answers.

"All I am trying to say is"—he clear his throat—"I want to help you. To give you money to spend." He sway, jam the wall with his shoulder. "You understand?"

"No, thank you, sah." I take one step back, open my room door. He take a step near me, put his feets in the middle of the door.

"Please, sah, go away before I shout." I am talking with a low voice, but my heart is banging itself inside my head, **bam.** If this man wants to rough me now, who will I call? If I shout from here, will Kofi hear me?

He push his eye-glass up his nose, hold up his two hand. "Hey, no cause for alarm, here. No point in making—"

"Good evening, sir." Kofi just appear from nowhere into the corridor. He is not wearing his cooking cap, and his head is a smooth, round ball with no hair on it. He is tying a white cloth around his waist, no shirt on his thick flesh of chest. I never been so happy to see a almost naked man in my whole life.

"I heard some noises," Kofi say. "It woke me up. Sir, do you need something? A light snack perhaps?"

Big Daddy shake his head. "No, Adunni called for, for help. I think she was, I don't know, threatened by some noise. I was just, yes, just leaving. Thank you."

Before me and Kofi can talk, Big Daddy turn around and walk away into the night. A moment later, and a door slam.

"You are lucky I was not asleep," Kofi say.

A shiver run up and down my body, prick my flesh. "Thank you, Kofi."

"Big Madam will be back next week," Kofi say. "Have you started on your essay? You and that woman, the doctor's wife, have spent the last week working on it, right?"

"She is teaching me better English so that I can write it," I say, and the thought of it is filling me up with light, with a warm hope that is chasing away the shiver in my body.

CHAPTER 35

Fact: Child marriage was made illegal in 2003 by the Nigerian government. Yet an estimated 17% of girls in the country, particularly in the northern region of Nigeria, are married before the age of 15.

After that night, I am not sleeping very well. Sometimes, I will sit on the bed, holding Rebecca's waist beads, as I am reading Mama's Bible, or learning English with the book Ms. Tia give me. Other times, I will keep my eyes on the ceiling lightbulb, trying to be listening over the generator humming outside, checking it sure that Big Daddy is staying in his house. But it seem like Big Daddy is behaving hisself. He didn't come back to find me yesternight, or the one before that, but I know he is thinking of how he will come back when Kofi is not there. Before then, I must think of what I can be doing to be keep him afar from me. After much thinking with no solutions, I make the decisions to tell Ms. Tia about it.

This evening, as we are sitting behind the kitchen,

me on the short wooden chair and she standing in front of blackboard (Ms. Tia buyed a blackboard and bring it home yesterday. It is square, the size of the tee-vee in our parlor in Ikati), she set it on top the tall kitchen stool and is writing on it with pink color chalk.

"Big Daddy come to me three nights back," I say as she is wiping the blackboard with a cloth. "He enter into my room."

She turn around, wipe her hand on a tissue in her back pocket. "What happened? Why did he come to your room?"

"I don't know," I say. "But I know it was not to greet me good night. He was finding something, and I am fearing it is a bad something."

"Did he say anything to you?" she ask, look over her shoulder. "Is he home?"

"He have go out," I say. "He is not coming back till very late."

"He **has gone** out," she say. "What did he say to you?"

"He was talking nonsense," I say. "But I was fearing that he wants to rough me."

She look up, like the words I am speaking is appearing in the air, shake her head. "'Rough'? Like you mean, touch you inappropriately? In a wrong way?"

"Yes," I say, make my voice whisper. "Kofi come in and stop the man." I feel a quick colding as I am thinking it. "I am afraid, Ms. Tia, and that is why I want to leave this place. To enter the school."

"Listen, Adunni," she say, take two steps close, bend herself so that she is sitting on her feets and looking me eyeball to eyeball. "You must be very careful. Does your room have a lock?"

I shake my head no. "It don't have a lock."

"It **doesn't** have a lock," she say, smiling because of how I twist my eye. "It is confusing, I know. We'll get there. Your madam is back in two days, right?"

"On Saturday," I say. "Tomorrow after tomorrow."

"The day after tomorrow," she say.

"We won't be able to see each other that often anymore," she say, with a voice that seem full with sadness. "Florence won't approve."

"No," I say, feeling sad too.

"Unless we can think of something that'd get her to let us hang out together."

"Like what?"

"If I can find a way to maybe . . . I don't know . . . tell her something, a reason why we need to see each other? I could maybe get Ken to speak to her. She respects Ken, and he can tell her that we need you to come with me to the market a few times, or something? We definitely need more time to work on your essay."

"You think she will agree?"

"We can only ask," Ms. Tia say, "but do you

want me to speak to her about what happened with her husband?"

I wide my eyes, shake my head no. "Tell her, **ke?** She will beat me stupid, and she may send me away. I don't want her to send me away, not yet."

"Fine. I won't say anything just yet, but you must ask her for a lock. Tell her you want her to fix a lock in your room. Can you do that, Adunni? She won't beat you if you ask her to do that, will she?"

"I don't know," I say. "I can try it."

"You have to," she say. She stand up, shake her leg like it have dead and she want to give it life. "Be very careful around your madam's husband. You must tell me if he ever comes back to your room, okay?"

I feel all sorts of feelings that she is keeping her eyes on me, watching for me. "What are you teaching me today?" I ask.

"The present continuous tense," she say. Her voice is strange. Tight in her mouth. She walk to the blackboard, write, **VERB: BE (ING form).** She face me. "I know that makes no sense at first glance, but I will explain it."

I bite on the buttocks of my pencil, keep my eyes on the blackboard.

"Basically, we use the present continuous tense to talk about the present. For something that is happening now. So, for instance: I am **standing** in front of you. 'Standing' is present continuous tense.

These words are usually identified by adding '-ing' to the verb. You know what a verb is?"

"Action word. Doing word," I say. Teacher was teaching me that one in Ikati. I didn't ever forget it.

"Good. Can you think of an example of the present continuous tense?"

"I am sitting on top the chair," I say.

"Brilliant!" she say, clapping her hand. "'I am sitting on the chair' is correct. You don't need to add 'top' to the sentence." She face the blackboard, start to write: **SITTIN** . . . and stop before she can write the letter **G.**

Her hand is shaking. She turn around, say, "I think I need to sit." She stagger herself, sit on the floor near me, pull her knees up, and rest her head between the two of them.

"You feeling fine?" I ask, looking the twists of her hair resting on the top of her knees. "Want to drink ice-cold water?"

She raise her head, give me weak smile. "I am tired. I am hoping that, you know, I might be pregnant . . ."

"You think?" I wide my eyes, cover my mouth. "How you know?"

She laugh, pick a twist away from her nose. "I am just kidding. It's a bit too soon."

"When last you see your monthly visitor?" I ask.

"It's due in a few days," she say.

"It won't come," I say, nod. "It won't ever come."

"You are too sweet," she say. "It's just, Ken's mother, she's on my case."

"The doctor's mama? Why?"

She blow out a breeze inside my face, her breath smelling like toothspaste. "She was at our house this morning," she say. "She comes once or so a month."

"Why?" I ask. "Is that why you were looking sad just now? What is she finding?"

"She comes to ask if I am pregnant," she say. "Can you imagine that? She has come every month in the last six months to say: 'Where are my grand-children? When will I carry my grandchildren and dance with them?' Like I've hidden them in an attic somewhere. If she wants to dance, she should go to a bloody nightclub." She keep talking before I can ask her who is bleeding blood. "It's been a bit stressful dealing with his family, especially because we kept our decision not to have kids away from them for so long."

I talk slow, thinking on my words, my English. "So she don't . . . doesn't know that the doctor didn't want childrens until now?"

Ms. Tia shake her head no.

I slap a fly away from my nose. "Then tell her that you need time, that you and the doctor have just start to be trying. And if she cannot wait, then she can be facing her son and fighting him."

Ms. Tia shrug. "Oh, she won't believe me. She says it's been too long. She's tired of waiting."

"Very soon," I say, "the baby will come and then she will stop looking for your trouble."

Ms. Tia give me a look, sigh, then push herself back up to her feet and pick up the chalk. "Let's finish this off," she say. "I'll talk to Ken tonight about us going to the market together."

CHAPTER 36

Fact: Nigerian senators are some of the highest-paid lawmakers in the world. A senator earns around 240 million naira ($1.7 million) in salary and allowances per annum.

Big Madam come back all happy and smelling like brand-new cloth.

She climb out of her car, go straight inside the house, and starts to open all the doors, to check which place is dirty and which is clean. She seem happy with it all, even pat my head two times when she see how the toilet tap is clean, bright. I make myself try and talk to her, ask her how her childrens are behaving theirselfs, if the cold in the London is not too much. She tell me the boy "is working in IT," and the girl, Kayla, is having engagement with a man.

"A banker," she say, laughing as she open the second door and peep inside the toilet. "They are getting married next year. He is the son of Senator Kuti. His name is Kunle. Very handsome boy. First-class graduate of the London School of Economics. I raised my daughter well. She took her eyes to the market and brought back a diamond. A rich, handsome boy." She laugh again. "This bathroom is very clean," she say. "Adunni, you kept my house well. Very good. Very good of you."

I thank her and follow her behind, dragging her load of Abroad shopping.

"Put my suitcase here," she say when we reach upstairs hallway, in front of her room. She put herself inside the sofa in the hallway, fan herself. "I forget how hot this country is when I travel out. What kind of cursed heat is this one? Adunni, put on that AC and fan for me. Put it on full blast."

I put on the AC switch on the wall, and the fan on the floor. Cold air blow inside the room as I kneel down in her front and wait for her to be commanding me on what else she wants me to be doing.

Her mobile phone ring, she pick it: "Yes, I just came in from the airport. You heard? Good news travels fast. Thank you. Thank God. He is Senator Kuti's son." She throw her head back, laugh. "It is God-o. He is the divine connector. He connected my Kayla with the Kunle boy. The wedding? Next December. Yes, we have just over a year to plan. But there will be an engagement ceremony next summer, a big one. Of course, I will supply the fabric. Come and see me in my shop tomorrow and I will share more details with you. Let me rest my body. I will call you later."

She end the call. "My phone has not stopped ringing since I got off the plane. Where is Chief?"

"He has gone out," I say.

She hiss. "As usual. Useless man. I hope he didn't disturb you when I was abroad?"

I think of what Ms. Tia say, about having a lock in my room. "No, ma," I say.

"You can go," she say. "Come back later to scratch my head. My feet have missed your massages."

"Yes, ma." I stand, kneel again. "I have something to ask of you, ma."

She pull her box, zip the zip. "What is it?"

"I want a . . ." I scratch my head, trying to arrange my words well. "A lock to put into the door of my room."

She turn her head, look me, eyes sharp. "Why?"

"Nothing, ma. It is just, sometimes. Because I am a growing woman, I want . . ." I bite my lip, confuse. Everything Ms. Tia tell me to say have become birds with wings and fly away from my mind.

"Did Chief come to the boys' quarters?" She lean close, look inside my eyes. "Adunni, tell me the truth. Did my husband come to your room?"

I shake my head no, nod it yes. "No, ma. I mean, not him. It is the rat. The rat was making noise, so I want to lock the door. From the rat."

"From the rat, **abi?**" She thin her eyes. "I understand. Get up and go, I will get the carpenter to fix a lock for you."

"Thank you, ma," I say, and stand. "I will come back around evening time, for hair scratching."

There is no answer as I walk away from her front.

I return upstairs in the evening for the hair scratching.

As I fold my fingers to knock on Big Madam's door, I hear plenty noises behind the door. I stop my hand, wait, and listen, even though I know it is bad to be doing so. It is sounding as if two people are in a big argument. I bend my head, listen well.

Somebody slap something, then Big Madam is shouting: "Chief, when will you stop disgracing yourself? **Haba.** Adunni is not yet fifteen, Chief. What were you looking for in her room?"

When Big Daddy answer, his voice is dragging, heavy with drinking. "Did Adunni tell you that I came to her room?"

"The girl asked me for a lock, Chief. Why will she ask me for a lock if not because you have carried your useless self to her? You have no answers, do you? Useless man."

"Watch your mouth, this woman," Big Daddy say. "Before I deal with you."

"You can't do anything," Big Madam shout back. "I put my money in your pocket so you can hold your head up. So that you can be a man. Do you think I don't know about Amaka in University of Lagos? You put two hundred thousand naira of my money into her account just last week, didn't you? Or about Tayo? That thing with skinny legs in University of Ife, did you not send that one to Zanzibar, just last month? I know them all. But to bring it to my house again? Under my roof? Ah, God will deal with you. How can you keep chasing our common house girl for cheap sex? A nonentity? How low can you stoop, Chief?" Big Madam starts to cry loud, wailing, saying, "Why won't you love me? What more can I do to make you see me as I am, as a woman worth loving? A woman who has sacrificed so much for you? Your children have refused to come home for Christmas because they don't like how you treat me, and yet I remain in this marriage because I love you!"

"So this is why Kayla hasn't called me in two months?" Big Daddy roar the question, use it to silent Big Madam's wailing cry. "What have you been telling my children?!"

"I don't need to tell them anything, Chief," she say, more quiet now. "They are not blind. They grew up in this house, saw how you have always treated me! Why are you doing this to our home?"

Then she begin to ask Big Daddy how low he is going in chasing a nobody entity like me until I hear a noise. Like somebody punch a pillow. A slap. Two slaps. Three slaps. I put my hand on my chest, feel my heart beating fast. Is it because I ask of a lock that Big Madam and Big Daddy are fighting like this? Am I the cause of the troubles between them? Ah! Why didn't I keep shut my big mouth?

Will Big Madam send me away? And if she does that, where will I go? When Big Madam starts to curse Big Daddy and his family, I take one step back, and another step, and then I am running down the stairs, through the kitchen, until I reach my room in the boys' quarters.

CHAPTER 37

When I reach my room, I find Kofi standing in front of my room door, giving me a vexing look.

"I have been killing myself, cooking since morning," he say, wiping the sweat from his forehead with his apron cloth. "The doorbell rings, and I start shouting your name in the main house like a crazy person because the last time I checked, you were the housemaid. I didn't realize you had retreated to the boys' quarters."

"Who is treating who?" I ask. "Is Big Madam needing a doctor? Have she dead?"

"I said '**re**treat.' Follow me. We have guests."

"Who is the guest?" I ask as I pick myself and follow him. "Where is Big Madam? Everything okay with her?"

"Big Madam is fine," Kofi say, walking fast, making me run to catch him to hear what he is saying.

"They had a fight. **Chale,** your mouth will kill you one day. Why did you ask Big Madam for a lock to your room? I told you to be careful. You didn't have to ask for a lock. There are options. You should have consulted me. For instance, you could have dragged the cupboard in your room, pushed it behind the door. Or placed a rat trap at the entrance, watch it snap the useless man's foot shut when he comes to your door. Now that would be a scene to watch. Imagine Big Daddy hopping around on one foot, howling in pain, but unable to tell his wife the source of the pain. Ha!"

"I didn't know it will cause them to be fighting," I say, wiping new tears. "Wait, you are walking too fast."

"I have chicken drumsticks in the deep fryer," he say. "I don't have time to stroll and chat."

"But Ms. Tia say I should ask for lock," I say. "I ask, and now, I am in big trouble. Will Big Madam send me away?"

"I don't know," Kofi say. "Ms. Tia happens to be married to a filthy-rich doctor and has no problems in life. She should not be dishing out advice to a semi-illiterate with the IQ of a fried fish."

"IQ fish?" I ask. "You are frying some with the chickens?"

Kofi stop his fast walk, give me a long, vex look, begin his walking again. "You better pray that the

wedding will keep Big Madam's mind too occu-
pied to think about replacing you before you hear
back from the scholarship people," he say. "That is,
after she recovers from this recent battering from
Big Daddy."

"Why is Big Daddy always beating Big Madam?"
I ask.

We reach the kitchen back door, and Kofi goes to
the fryer on the kitchen table, bring out the basket
of frying chickens from the hot oil. The chickens
are golden brown, the smell of it filling my mouth
with spit, my stomach twisting with hunger. Big
Madam is back home now, so no more eating of
morning food.

"The guests are in the reception area," Kofi say,
picking one chicken thigh from the basket and tearing it with his teeth. "This is spectacularly seasoned.
Perfect balance of salt and spice. What are you staring at? Go and make the guests welcome, and then
go upstairs to let Big Madam know that she has
visitors. I pray you come back down alive."

Ms. Tia and the doctor are sitting in the visitors'
parlor. When I kneel down to greet her, she gives
me a smile, but not a smile like she knows me, or
have talk to me before. It is a stiff smile, a drawing of her lips in a tight line, like I am one kind of
stranger, a stranger she met from long ago.

"Adunni, right? How are you? Nice to see you again," she say, putting her hand on the lap of the doctor. "This is my husband, Dr. Ken. We are here to congratulate Madam Florence and Chief on their daughter's engagement. Kofi says they are upstairs. Can you let them know we are here?"

She face the doctor. "I told you I met Adunni at the WRWA meeting. She's the one I said might be best placed to come with me to the market, to teach me how to improve my haggling skills and all that. That is, of course, if her madam does not object."

The doctor is a tall man with eyes that make me think of stale brown water. He has bushy eyebrows, mustaches that start a journey from under his nostrils and end it in the middle of his jaw. He is wearing a white shirt, button up to his chest to show gold chain with gold cross hanging on his long, smooth neck. He has on a short, brown knicker that stop at his knees, showing legs with plenty curling hair. There are slippers in his feet, brown, smelling of rich rubber.

He nod his head, look me up, down, down to up. "I have heard a few interesting things about you," he say. His voice is polish, smooth, words flowing from his mouth like he is using oil to wrap his word before talking. He and Ms. Tia, they fit theirselfs. Honey voice and oil voice. Pity they have small troubles because of childrens.

"Yes, sah," I say. "Good evening, sah. I will call Big Madam and Big Daddy to come downstairs.

You want ice-cold drink? We are having cold Fanta and fresh juice and wine drink in the fridge. Which one do you want?"

He wave a hand. "Water for me, thank you."

As I stand, the doctor is whispering to his wife: "You do know that there are other women, posh, well-spoken, on Wellington Road, that would gladly go to the market with you, right?"

And Ms. Tia, she laugh her bell-ringing laugh and say, "Babe, trust me, I know what I want. She's perfect for the job."

CHAPTER 38

Fact: Many Nigerians have superstitious beliefs about pregnancy. One such is the belief that attaching a safety pin to a pregnant woman's clothing will ward off evil spirits.

"Tia's weekly column is coming along nicely," the doctor is saying as I bring a tray of tumblers into the dining room. "The blog recently hit five thousand subscribers. Have you had a chance to read it?"

"Who has time to be reading about the environment when there is money to be made?" Big Madam say with a laugh.

She is sitting on the dining chair, beside Big Daddy, Ms. Tia, and the doctor. Big Madam's face is full of all sorts of makeups, be like she melt a rainbow, wipe it on her face. Her teeth are bright white under the red and gold lipstick, her lips swollen by the corner of it. She and Big Daddy are smiling, looking like they didn't just nearly kill theirselfs with beating.

"Put the glass cups there," Big Madam say to me. "Right in the center of the dining table. Yes, right there."

"But she still complains that she is bored," the doctor say as I am bringing the cup from the tray and putting it on the table. "I have told her to mix with the likes of yourself, Madam Florence. With the other classy women on our street. But she'd rather stay home and complain."

"What she needs is children." Big Madam pick the cup, look it well, wipe it with her hand, set it down. "Mrs. Dada, when you are chasing children up and down in your house, you will not even think of complaining. Where will boredom sit in a house full of children? It cannot happen. Adunni, put one glass cup in front of Chief. What is delaying you people from having children? You have been married for over one year. I was pregnant the first time Chief touched me on the night of our wedding." Big Madam laugh a shy laugh. "I hope you are not exploring life and traveling the world before you start birthing children-o? If you are not careful, your womb will just expire." She laugh again, but nobody is joining her to laugh. "And when it eventually happens, you must hide yourself. When you start to show, remember to put a safety pin on your dress so that no one will uproot your baby from the womb with evil eyes."

Ms. Tia sit stiff, like something starch up her whole body.

"When shall we expect to hear good news?" Big Madam keep talking like something curse her mouth. "When shall we come and eat rice and chicken?"

"We only just started—" Ms. Tia begin to say, but the doctor press a hand to cover his wife's hand, say, "We will keep trying. It will happen in God's time. I just want Tia to be happy. The last thing I want is for anyone to pressure her." The doctor look at his wife with love eyes, then nod his head yes, as if in a question.

"That's right," Ms. Tia say, sounding like her voice is a sharp pin in her mouth. "Keep trying. No pressure."

I cough, put the tumbler in front of Big Daddy, feel the heat from his look on my hand.

"I should tell Kofi to serve the food now?" I ask. "And the orange juice?"

"God's time is the best for these things," Big Daddy say. "Babies are a gift. A miracle."

"Indeed," the doctor say.

"Orange juice?" I ask again, but nobody is giving me answer so I stand back, press the tray to my chest. Ms. Tia's head is down, like she can see her sad face on the glass table and is feeling sorry for herself. The doctor take her hand under the table and hold it.

"One thing that might help take her mind off the pressures of trying for a baby," the doctor say, "is to go out more often. Tia loves to explore cultural stuff. She's thinking of redecorating the house, and she's asked if maybe your house help"—the doctor nod at me with a soft smile—"can go with her to the market one of these days. To help teach her to, uh, to haggle."

"Which house girl?" Big Madam say. "Adunni? What does that one know? She is a stranger in Lagos-o. An illiterate thing, completely useless. She cannot follow anybody to any market. And why can't Mrs. Dada haggle by herself? Is she not a Nigerian? What does she need Adunni for?"

"I can haggle." Ms. Tia lift her head. "Or at least I try. But it'd be nice to have some help in the market. Adunni speaks Yoruba fluently. She is intelligent, and I am comfortable with her—more than I am with most people. I think we can discover things together."

"'Discover things together,' **ke?**" Big Madam laugh, shake her head. "Is my house girl a search engine? No, no. Please. I don't want Adunni to—"

Big Daddy hold his hand up. "Actually, Florence. It is a good idea," he say. "In fact, you can have Adunni help you out one evening in the week."

Big Madam look like she want to use her eyeballs to bullet Big Daddy, kill him dead for that stupid talk.

"Are you sure?" Ms. Tia say. "I mean, if it won't be a problem, that'd be amazing."

"Not a problem," Big Daddy say. "I insist. Dr. Ken is a dear, dear friend of ours, and if his wonderful wife asks us a small favor, who are we to refuse?"

Ms. Tia smile to the doctor. "Babe, did you hear that?"

The doctor look like he confuse. "I don't think Madam Florence thinks it is a good idea to—"

"It is okay," Big Madam say, shocking everybody. "She can come and help you go to the market one day a week for a short time only. A very, very short time. I need her here for the housework, so please, if you think you need her for longer, I can recommend Mr. Kola, my agent. He can get you a good house help for a reasonable price."

"That is so kind of you," Ms. Tia say. "I am ever so grateful. Thank you."

Big Madam grunt, say something nobody hear.

My heart start a skipping beat. Does that mean that me and Ms. Tia will be seeing ourselfs once in the week? And we can be learning more things before I write my essay? That is the best good news I ever hear since I reach Lagos.

Big Madam turn her head to look me. "What are you still doing there? Get inside and bring our juice before I wipe the smile off your face with a slap."

CHAPTER 39

At night, I say my evening prayer to be thanking God for entering Big Madam's mind for letting me go out with Ms. Tia one day in the week.

I am also thanking Him that, even though Mr. Kola didn't come back with my money, I am not in a coffin in the ground, using the soil inside the earth as a wrapper and as a pillow. I say prayers for the new year 2015 coming, that it will be good and a happy year for me, the year I will enter school. I remember Khadija, tell God to make her feel good in heaven, give her big bed and plenty food. I tell God to take care of my mama too.

I remember Ms. Tia too, that she will get pregnant and have one child in the next year, because she only want one, not two or three childrens, and that it will not cause troubles with the doctor mama. And Papa, that God will give him a kind heart and make his mind at peace.

I don't pray for Kayus. Thinking or praying for Kayus will make my heart full of sadness. Today is a good day, no sadness for me. When I finish my prayer, I feel a free that I didn't feel in long time, and when I smile, it climb from inside my stomach and spread itself on my teeth.

I set to removing the plaiting on my hair. My hair was a rich black color, thick as a sponge, use to break all my mama's wooden comb when I was growing. It has a smell now, of bleach and dusty oil, and it take me a whole one hour to remove all the plaiting, and when I finish, I look my hair inside the looking-glass, sitting like a cloud around my neck, warm and full of grease. I shake my head, watching as the hair bounce itself on my shoulders, and I laugh as I remove all my cloth, take a cloth, wrap it around my body, and leave the room.

It is dark outside now, the moon look like God plant a glowing egg into a flat black slate with stars scattering theirselfs around it, some fading and blinking, others staying still, forming one kind of strange shape in the sky. I walk quick, cutting the grass, laughing as some cricket jump out from it and make a **kre-kre** noise. As I cut to the part of the house where we spread clothes on the line, I see the shape of a man coming in the dark, walking like he has one half of a leg: Big Daddy. I stop, press my hand to my chest, and keep looking him. He is on the phone, talking to somebody, voice low but loud enough for me to hear him:

"Baby love, I said I was sorry," he say. "I will make it up to you, I promise. Why don't we meet tomorrow night at the Federal Palace Hotel? Or at a special— Adunni!"

He sort of freeze like a statue when he see me. He press the phone to his ear and wide his eyes until it be as if his forehead is one big eyeball. The woman inside the phone is still talking, sounding like she swallow a bee, speaking **bzz-bzz,** but my ears can pick the low "Baby love, are you there?" of her words.

"Good evening, sah," I say as Big Daddy shake out of his freeze and slide the phone from his ear. It is a phone I have never see him use before, a black, slim, costly-looking thing, the size of a matchbox. He press the phone, and the numbers on the face of it glow, coloring his face a strange green too, before he put the phone into the pocket of his ankara trouser—same one he was wearing in the morning.

"What are you doing here?" he ask. "Wait. Were you listening to my conversation?"

"I am going to the washing line," I say. I am not caring if Big Daddy is talking to another woman outside when his wife is sleeping in the house. "I didn't hear anything, sah."

Big Daddy nod his head. "Good. Because I was speaking to my pastor, my pastor's wife, I mean.

We are, er, planning a special service tomorrow at a hotel. Isn't it a beautiful evening?"

"Good night, sah," I say.

"Come back here a minute. Don't you think I deserve a dash of gratitude after what happened today?"

"Dash of grati-what?" I ask, pulling my cloth tighter on my chest.

"If you don't know what it means—"

"I know what it means," I say. "What am I thanking you for?"

"For how I intervened at dinner this evening," he say, voice low. "With the Dadas. Come on, stop playing stupid," he say, throwing a look behind his shoulder, where the light in one of the top windows in the house off itself, and someone draw a curtain. "I know you and Tia Dada have been meeting for tutorials of some sort. I saw her once or twice while Florence was away. She was sitting with you back there, behind the kitchen. I like that she is trying to educate you." He lick his lip. "I support it. A hundred percent. And that is why I made that suggestion in the dining room. My wife would never allow you, by the way. She is not as generous as I am."

"Thank you, sah," I say.

"Your madam is this close to kicking you to the streets." He hold up two fingers, bring it up to his eye level. "This close. But for my intervention. I can let you continue to meet Tia Dada one day a week for as long as you want, but on one condition."

315
ABI DARÉ

"What is the one condition?" I slap a mosquito from my shoulder, peep my hand. It has become a spot of blood. "Be quick, sah, I want to go, mosquito is biting me here."

"Did mosquitoes not wine and dine with you in the village you came from? Look at her, complaining about mosquitoes. These useless housemaids. They have a taste of luxury and start to feel entitled. Listen. All I want is for you to allow me to help you. To be kind to you. You understand?"

I look at the man, at the sack of him, his gray beard like beads of silver cotton wool around his chin, and hiss a silent hiss. "If you want to help me," I say just as the idea is coming to my mind, "find Mr. Kola, sah. Tell him to bring all my money for working here since August. We are now in the first week of December, sah, it has been five months of working with no salary."

"Mr. Kola? Who is that? The agent?" Big Daddy sniff a laugh. "Why would I waste my time and resources to find Mr. Kola? For peanuts? How much is your salary? I will pay you double, triple. Listen. If you allow me to help you, you will have more than enough to spend."

"I want the money I have worked for, sah," I say as I begin to walk away from him. "Good night."

"Adunni," he call out, but his voice is not loud, I know it is because he is afraid of Big Madam hearing him.

"Adunni, come back here," he say, whispering. "Come back here."

I reach the clothing line—a thin wire tied between two trees behind the boys' quarters—snatch my dress from it and throw it over my shoulder.

How is Morufu and Big Daddy different from each other? One can speak good English, and the other doesn't speak good English, but both of them have the same terrible sickness of the mind.

A sickness with no cure.

CHAPTER 40

Fact: As of 2012, Nigeria was estimated to have lost over $400 billion of oil revenue to corruption since independence.

The man in the tee-vee has been talking elections for one hour now.

I am sitting on the floor, massaging Big Madam's feet and keeping one eye to the tee-vee. He is holding a microphone, his neck long in the gray English jacket he is wearing as he is speaking. "The question in everyone's mind as 2014 draws to a close is this: Will the giant of Africa continue to be propelled into further instability, bloodshed, and economic woes under the fedora-hat-wearing man who never had shoes as a child, or will Nigerians arise and vote for change under Muhammadu Buhari, the retired major general who was once the nation's head of state? We have four months until the nation decides. Until then, keep your eyes glued to your favorite channel."

"Buhari can never rule us again," Big Madam say, twisting her feet in my hand. "Scratch that place for me, Adunni, yes, that place by my heel. That's it. Perfect. God forbid that Buhari should become president."

She is not talking to me, but she is looking me, looking my hand as it is going up and down on her feet. "Buhari is going to deal with all those who benefited under Jonathan. Ah, my God will not let him win. Buhari is an enemy of progress. What corruption is he promising to fight? All lies! Nigerians have been blindfolded by this promise-of-change nonsense. They think the man is the next Obama. I pity them. That man has no heart. He will finish the country with his military-man ruling style."

There is a knock on the door, and Ms. Tia comes in. She is wearing her same style of t-shirt and jeans-trouser. This time, they write **NAIJA GIRL** on the t-shirt with shining alphabet. She give me a smile and a wink, nod her head at Big Madam.

"Good morning, Madam Florence," she say. "Hope you are enjoying your Saturday."

Big Madam put up her nose in the air, as if about to sniff a smell. "Mrs. Dada."

Ms. Tia keep her smile. "So, I figured that since it's a Saturday morning, and we, uh, agreed last week that Adunni could come with me to the market . . . I just thought to check if, you know, today might be a good time, say around two?"

"Adunni is busy," Big Madam say. "Keep massaging, rub my big toe well," she say to me.

Ms. Tia give a laugh that sound like it pain her. "Right. I thought we agreed—"

"We did not agree anything," Big Madam say. She collect her feet, push herself up on the sofa. "I offered you my house help as a favor. I don't owe you anything. Today, she is busy. Come back on Monday when I am at the shop."

Ms. Tia sigh. "I'll check back in next week."

My heart is heavy as Ms. Tia make to be going. Big Madam hold up her hand. "Wait, Mrs. Dada. As I mentioned to you last week, my agent is called Mr. Kola. He is a very reliable agent. Reasonably priced too. I can give you his number, and if you don't want Mr. Kola, because I know people like you can like to feel posh, you can try the agency Kiki talked about at the WRWA meeting. What did she call it? Konsult-A-something?"

"Konsult-A-Maid," Ms. Tia say. "I will come back on Monday." She reach the door, put one hand on the handle. "What time on Monday?"

"Before midday," Big Madam say.

"That's fine," Ms. Tia say.

"Find yourself your own maid," Big Madam say as Ms. Tia is leaving the parlor. "I am not a housemaid charity. Enjoy your afternoon, Mrs. Dada."

Ms. Tia nod her head, keep her mouth in straight line. "Have a lovely weekend."

Before Monday, I am using all my brain to be learning English.

I am reading the Collins, doing my best to be learning more hard words.

I turn the pages of the Collins and pick any three hard words I can find and I cannot wait to use the words for Ms. Tia. I learn:

1. Assimilate
2. Communicate
3. Extermination

I am also doing my best to learn my present tense with all she has been teaching me. When she comes on Monday morning, the sun is big in the sky, the heat biting inside of my armpits as if I put one hundred pins under my arm as I am waiting for her by the gate. When I see her running down the road, I raise up my hand and give her a wide smile. She didn't bring any motorcar, she say her house is just in the afar corner, and that we can be jogging there because car smoke is always causing problems for something in the ozone.

"How was your weekend?" she ask as we are walking down Wellington Road. It is a quiet road, no cars passing, red and green and brown roofs of big houses peeping over curved, high fences.

"I assimilate all my work," I tell her, and she stop, give me one look like I am saying something so foolish.

"You've been reading the dictionary?"

"I am communicating the Collins," I say, and she throw her head back, laugh a loud laugh that is echoing around us and causing one bird in the palm tree in our front to fly away. She laugh so hard, she stop to put hand on her knees to keep herself from falling.

"Adunni, you are something else. Listen, a dictionary alone would not help you to speak or write better," she say, wiping the tears under her eyes with her finger. "Work with me at my pace and you will get there. You still have two weeks before the deadline, so take things a little bit easy on yourself, okay?"

I want to answer her with, **But I want to extermination my bad English,** but I change my mind because I didn't sure the word is fitting the sentence. So I say, "Okay."

"Your madam was so not impressed by my visit on Saturday," she say as we reach the end of Wellington Road. "I thought it'd be great if we could maybe, actually, go to the market together today. I sense she won't let us continue to hang out, unless of course her husband can convince her to.

"Such a shame really," she say. "We'll have to make do with whatever time we have. Right." She stop walking as we pass one light pole in front of a gray gate with grass in front of it. "That's my house. It's the first house when you come in from Milverton Road. Ready to come in?"

I nod my head yes, feeling something tremble inside of me.

Ms. Tia doesn't have a gate man like Big Madam. She open the gate herself and we enter inside her compound. The house is sitting like one fine queen behind a field of grass. The green on the grass is not dull like the one in Big Madam's compound, this one is a green color that seem like it is breathing and alive. The house is white, with blue windows and a red roof. There are squares of blue glass on the roof, about thirty of them, all joining each other with white lines and dots, blinking under the early-morning sun. Flowerpots sitting in gray stones line up the floor all the way to the front door of the house, where a round grass decoration of red bows and gold bells is hanging on the front of it.

"It's not as big as your madam's," Ms. Tia say. "Ken wanted us to live in a very big house—think five bed, five bath, swimming pool, the works. I couldn't imagine it. And the cost of keeping a house of that size in good shape and energy sustainable? Unthinkable."

"What is that glass in the roof?" I ask.

"Solar panels," she say. "It gives us electricity from the sun. I cannot stand generator noise or the thought of damaging the environment with the fumes."

"One day, I will find a way to put the solar

something in the houses in Ikati," I say, look up the roof. "Many of the village houses don't have light, but Ms. Tia, if we can do this solar thing, if we can collect the light from the sun and put it in all the houses, then the village will be better for it. We will not be needing anybody to give us light or be finding money for costly generator. We just take our light from inside the sun."

"What a brilliant idea, Adunni," Ms. Tia say, looking me with wonder. "I must raise this at our next meeting at work. There must be another agency we can partner with, to find a low-cost way of installing the panels in some villages. Maybe Ikati can be one of our first. Come on this way, Adunni. Careful of that pot of geraniums. Please take your shoes off right there."

I pull off my shoe, feeling my heart warm and swell up with something proud as Ms. Tia talk of putting the solar in Ikati. I cannot even think of how beautiful Ikati will look, if all the houses and streets and shops are having light.

She kick off her own shoes too, keep them on one short wooden table outside the kitchen door. We enter her kitchen. I don't think any human being has ever eat or even enter the kitchen before.

"You cook inside here?" I ask, looking the machines on the kitchen table, a coffee-making machine and a kettle, shining and new like somebody just off-load it from the package. Everything is white, too white, too clean, smelling of bleach. I am thinking that Ms. Tia have real fear of dirty, and a fear to be owning plenty things. The tiles on the floor, kitchen cupboards up on the walls, the toaster in the corner beside the cooker, and the water filter machine near it is all a sharp white.

"What?" she say. "Why are you giving me that look? Ken does most of the cooking, and I just make sure I clear up nicely when he's done. Want something to eat?"

I shake my head no, even though I am hungry. Where will she find food for me in this empty kitchen?

She pick a towel, white, from one of the drawers, shake it, and wipe the table that is clean. "I am really looking forward to going out today. It will help take my mind off things."

"What things?" I ask.

"I got my period again," she say, shrug. "Not sure why I was so hopeful this time around. It messed up my whole week. And to make things even more crazy, my mother-in-law is now asking me to go with her to some prophet. She wants me to take a bloody bath."

"Blood baff? For why?"

"Sorry, no. Not blood bath. She wants me to take a bath, at some stream. She says she knows a prophet that would wash away my childlessness. She'd mentioned it a few times in the past, but I kept thinking I would get pregnant and wouldn't have to. But now she's insisting."

"We do it all time in Ikati," I say. My mind cut to when Khadija died because she didn't baff. "Maybe this it will help, make things very quick and speed up for you, so that in one year time, you born a baby. Just one."

Ms. Tia push up her eyebrows. "That crap doesn't work, Adunni. Does it?"

I shrug my shoulder. "The crap is working sometimes in Ikati. It may help you, make the baby come quick."

"It's just . . ." She grip the towel tight, make it a ball. "The thought of some nasty old man running his hands through my body in the name of giving me a bath. It's . . . ugh. Repulsive."

"Try it," I say. "It will make the doctor's mama happy too, keep your whole marriage free of her troubles. And when the baff begin to happen, close your eye tight like this, block away all the ugh." I close my eye, squeeze it tight. "Think of good, good things when they are baffing you. Things like the baby name or baby clothes. Or your friend Cat-tee."

"It's Katie." Ms. Tia laugh, and I open my eyes. "I would love to name my baby Adunni," she say. "If it's a girl. 'Adunni' means 'sweetness,' right?"

"Yes," I say, feeling my heart swell. "I can be helping you take care of the baby too."

"Like a little aunty," she say. "I'll think about the bath."

I look at her sad face. "Maybe I can follow you?"

The words fly out from my mouth before I remember what happened to Khadija at the river.

"Actually," she say, before I can change my mind, "that would make a world of a difference, if you can come. We can ask your madam for one more day for us to go out, and we'll use it for the bath?"

"You think?" I ask.

"I think," she say with a wink. "The bath probably won't happen until next year, but we can tell Florence that it will be our final outing together. Hopefully, the scholarship results will be out by then. I'll agree a date with my mother-in-law and get you to come with me."

"And the doctor?" I ask. "He knows about this baff?"

"He does," she say, folding the towel. She open the machine-washer and throw it in. "He says it is harmless, and that if it makes his mother happy, I should consider it for my sanity. He sent me a bunch of roses at work, as if to say sorry for the stress she's putting me through. Anyway, come with me," she say, "I've got a surprise for you."

CHAPTER 41

Fact: Some of the earliest art sculptures in the world originated in Nigeria. The Bronze Head from Ife, which is one of the most renowned, was taken to the British Museum a year after it was discovered in 1938.

We enter a corridor with pictures of Ms. Tia and the doctor on the white wall.

It show them laughing, kissing theirselfs, doing real love, real marriage. I feel kind of sad, thinking about Morufu and the marriage he was having with me, Khadija, and Labake, the cold and bitter and pain of it. Can I ever find real love one day? And with a fine and kind man, just like the doctor?

"Come on this way," Ms. Tia say, opening one door at the end of the corridor. "Here's the living room."

Ms. Tia has no tee-vee. Nothing with electrics in the parlor. The whole air is smelling of something like washing soap and lemongrass. There is a white, round sofa—never seen anything like it—with many cushions, all white and round shape. A tree with plenty silver brushes on the branches, as tall as a small child, is standing by the wall in the corner, decorations of stars and glass angels and gold bulbs on it. Christmas tree, I think, remembering that Big Madam ask Abu to buy one just last week from the market, only Ms. Tia's own is white, not green. There are flowers inside clear glass vases too, four of them, with little cards inside, and when I peep one, I see it is from the doctor to Ms. Tia. Seem like he like to give her love-flowers every week.

There are two drawings on the wall. One of a woman wearing an ankara dress, and one of a clay head. It doesn't have eyes, this clay head. Just holes inside the head for eyes and nose and mouth. And it has marks on its face; thin, long lines drawed from the forehead to under the eyes to the jaw. As if somebody vex and use long nails to be scratching the face everywhere.

"Got those paintings from the Nikè Art Gallery. It's an amazing place in Lekki," she say, pointing to the one of clay head. "That scarred one is my favorite. It is a painting of the Bronze Head from Ife. A masterpiece. Do you like art?"

"I read of it in **The Book of Nigeria Fact,** about how we were letting the British to steal our art," I say. "Where is this surprise?"

"Take a seat. Get comfortable, I'll be back."

I sit down inside the sofa. She come back holding a blue jeans bag.

"Here," she say, eyes wide and bright as she bring

out three books from the bag. "I got you an early Christmas present, some of the best books on grammar," she say. "This here is called **Better English.** I had a quick read through and it's amazing. Perfect for you. The remaining two are equally good, but get through **Better English** first."

I collect the books, feel water pinch my eyes. "Thank you," I say. "You are too kind, too much."

"That's not all." She put her hand in her pocket, bring out a phone. It is slim, black, the size of a small child's hand. "This is as simple as it gets. Perfect to hide away from your madam too. I have loaded it with some credit—"

I don't let her finish, I jump on my feet and the three books fall from my laps and slap the floor as I am giving her embrace.

"Thank you, Ms. Tia!" I say, holding her tight as she is laughing. "Thank you!"

"It's not a big deal, Adunni," she say when I leave her be. "I am really concerned about what you said happened with your boss's husband. When you said, he . . . you know, came into your room. Did you eventually get the lock sorted?"

I nod my head yes. "Big Madam send a carpenter and put a lock there."

"And now, you also have a phone." She press the phone, and it make a **njing-njing** noise, give me a tickle. I laugh and she laugh too. "I will teach you how to send a text message. I have stored my number on here as Tia. It is the only number saved on your phone. If you are ever in trouble, send me a text. Just type one simple word: 'HELP.' And I will try to be at your house as soon as I can. I have also stored several recordings of myself pronouncing certain words. Have a listen."

I collect the phone, turn it around in my hand, my eyes are not believing that me, Adunni, a small girl from Ikati village, is owning a mobile phone. Even before my papa is owning one. My heart is swelling with thank you for it.

"Your madam must not find it, okay?"

"Even if you don't teach me that, common sense is telling me that one. Is it having Facebook on it?" I ask, looking at the phone again, like it is something that just fall from heaven and land in my hand.

"No," she say. "I cannot let you get on the internet until you know exactly what you are doing. And"—she bite her lip like she thinking deep for a moment—"if your madam's husband ever tries to touch you, you fight, okay? You fight with everything in you. And scream. Fight and scream. Remember those two words, okay? Promise me that you will do that?"

I nod my head yes. "He did not come near me again since that time." I know I am telling a small lie, but I don't want Ms. Tia to come to Big Madam and be causing fight. I am fearing of what will happen to me if she cause a fight.

"And if it ever happens again—God forbid—but if that bastard comes near you again, I will have him bloody arrested and damn the consequences." She blow out air with her nose and mouth, blinking her eyes fast. I feel something move inside my chest. Why is this woman so kind to me? What can she see in me when even me, I am not seeing anything in myself sometimes? I fight the stubborn, foolish tears pinching my eyes, but it come out anyway.

"Aww, I didn't mean to make you cry," Ms. Tia say, wiping her finger under my left eye.

"What you see in me, Ms. Tia?"

She shake her head, hold my two hand up, make it like two bars so she can peep my face, the real me behind the bars. It feel like she is climbing out of herself and entering my own soul, my heart.

"Tell me, what do you want most in life?" she ask.

"For my mama to not be dead," I say, my voice breaking. "For her to come back and make everything better."

"I know," she say with a soft, sad smile. "I know, but can you think of something else you want?"

"To go to school," I say. "And now, to win the scholarship."

"Why is this so important to you, Adunni?"

"My mama say education will give me a voice. I want more than just a voice, Ms. Tia. I want a louding voice," I say. "I want to enter a room and people will hear me even before I open my mouth to be speaking. I want to live in this life and help many people so that when I grow old and die, I will still be living through the people I am helping.

Think it, Ms. Tia. If I can go to school and become a teacher, then I can collect my salary and maybe even build my own school in Ikati and be teaching the girls. The girls in my village don't have much chance for school. I want to change that, Ms. Tia, because those girls, they will grow up and born many more great people to make Nigeria even more better than now."

Ms. Tia is nodding her head yes as I am talking. "You can do it," she say. "God has given you all you need to be great, and it sits right there inside of you." She drop my hands, point a finger to my chest. "Right inside your mind, in your heart. You believe it, I know you do. You just need to hold on to that belief and never let go. When you get up every day, I want you to remind yourself that tomorrow will be better than today. That you are a person of value. That you are important. You must believe this, regardless of what happens with the scholarship. Okay?"

I look deep into Ms. Tia's eyes, at the spot of something gold in the brown of her eyesballs, and my heart sort of melt. I know she is saying all this from the good of her soul, but it is not so easy when you are born into a life of no money and plenty suffering, a life you didn't choose for yourself. Sometimes I wish I can just believe for a good life and it will magic and happen for me, just like that. But maybe, to believe it in my mind is the start, so I nod my head, drag it real slow up and down as I am saying: "Tomorrow will be better than today. I am a somebody of value."

"Beautiful, Adunni. Just beautiful." Ms. Tia sort of cry-laugh. "Come on now," she says, picking my hand. "The car is outside. Let's head to the market."

A black Toyota car, Ms. Tia call it a Uber, pick us up from the front of her gate.

The man driving, Michael, he nod his head and pull the collar of his shirt to his jaw when he see Ms. Tia. Then he tilt his neck to one side, and I am thinking maybe he ate small poison before leaving his house this morning because of how he is doing like a sickness is worrying him. Before he start the car, he look up in the mirror and lick his lips.

"Yo, miss," he say, "you're kinda hot, you know?"

I look at Ms. Tia. Is she feeling hot?

But she roll her eyes and say, "Can you please put on Wizkid or turn it to Cool FM?" because she "is not in the mood to chat today."

"Aiight," the man say. "No need to be rolling those brown eyes at me."

Then he turn on the music and start to drive. We drive in traffic for a whole hour, climbing the up-road and down it, through lines and lines of cars horning every minute, until the man turn into a street that is full of million-millions of people. Michael stop his car in front of a red food shop—Frankie's—with picture of three pink cakes and a child eating ice cream in front of it.

"Aiight, ladies," Michael say. "This is as far as I can go."

We climb out of the car, and with another nod, Michael drive off.

"Why was he nodding and bending his neck? Is he okay?" I ask Ms. Tia as she grab my hand and we begin to squeeze ourselves between the too many human beings in the market.

"I am sure he is fine," Ms. Tia say, looking around. "Now, where on earth do we start from?"

I look around too, feel something dizzy.

The Balogun market is one long stretch of street, full of so many people and noise. I think that maybe God pack a whole city inside a suitcase, travel to this street, open the suitcase, and let the whole city out. Every single noise in the world must be sounding right here, right now, at the same time: I hear the **peen, peen** from cars, the **meh** of goats, **"Allah hu Akbar"** and "Praise the Lord" from the loudspeakers hanging from a building of a mosque and a church side by side of each other.

The bells of food sellers, their shining balls of **akara** and puff-puff inside a glass box on the heads of the sellers, the voices of men and women and children selling everything they are seeing to sell: pants and bras and shoes and ice cream and pure water in a bag and dried shrimps inside a roll of bread and hair wigs and everything. From where we are standing, the people look like a carpet of heads sailing on water, like tiny ants, millions of them, moving along a path.

I try to look my feet, but all I see is darkness, there is no space between me and Ms. Tia, and the person beside me, who is pressing into me, is speaking loud on his phone about a "container from China" and how it must not lost.

"Hold on tight," I think Ms. Tia is trying to say, but a loudspeaker from above my head is swallowing her words with the noise-making announcement in Yoruba about a strong herb medicine to cure manhood problem. There are cars in the middle of the street too, the yellow-and-black taxi of Lagos state, not moving, just staying there, pressing their horn. A man is banging on the windscreen of a car, shouting at the driver to "move this thing, bastard!"

The rest of us keep going straight, slowly, pressing into people, smelling different odors from different people: women's stale monthly bleeding, stinking sweat, strong flower perfume, incense, fried bread, **siga** smoke, and dirty feet. Some women are sitting under colorful umbrellas—pink, red, yellow, white—on the side of the street, shouting at the people passing to come and buy "fresh fish and coconut candy" and "one hundred percent human hair." Others keep walking with us, their tray of things on their heads.

"Where are we going?" I shout to Ms. Tia as one man from nowhere just pull my hand out from her own and shout into my ears, "Fine girl, follow me, come and buy gold leggings, original." I snatch my hand from him, and another man, wearing a pink singlet with holes and dark sunglasses on his face, push a small white fan to my chest. "Buy fresh breeze. Original breeze to blow away your troubles. Hundred naira for five minutes?" I shake my head no, keep holding Ms. Tia tight, my heart beating at everything and everybody.

As we pass a stall selling shoes leather and rubber and all sorts of shoes, all climbing up, up to the top of the shop, a woman with a small bowl full of bottles on her head press an ice-cold block to my cheeks and shock me with it and say, "Cold water. Very freeze, very pure." She put up one hand, pull out a Coke from the bowl on her head, press the bottle to my chest. "Or you want Coke? We have Mirinda, 7up. Which one?"

There are buildings to our left and right, but all the buildings are covered with things hanging from the windows: trousers and shirts and suits, gray telephone wires crossing the top of our heads from one building to the second building, tangling up with all the signboards for church and mosque and herb medicine.

Ms. Tia keeps walking, gripping my hands. "We will take a turn by the left of the fish seller's stall," she shout. "It's a crazy world out here!"

It doesn't feel like we are moving.

I feel as if the crowd is a moving machine,

floating me along with the people, until we turn left and then the crowd is not as much as the first street. This road is a long stretch of people selling beads and ankara fabric, and before I can ask Ms. Tia if this is the right place to stop, a man wearing a black t-shirt with the word "PRANDA" on it smile at Ms. Tia, pull the giant red beads on his neck, and say, "Madam, we have everything you want. Which one?"

"For goodness' sake!" Ms. Tia say, swiping a hand on her forehead. "I'm just after some fabric."

"We have designer t-shirt too," the man say and bend to a bowl by his feet, pick up a white t-shirt. "Very original. Brand-new." He spread out the shirt, and Ms. Tia eye the word on it—"Guccshi"—before she shake her head no and start to walk away.

"I need authentic ankara," she say. "That's all I am here for."

"But we have Channel bag inside," he say, pulling my hand with his own hot, sweaty hands.

"Why don't you go to Big Madam's shop?" I say to Ms. Tia as I snatch my hand back from the man. "I have never seen anything like this in my life. Is this Lagos?"

In Ikati, the market is like a quarter of this, and everybody is quiet, and everybody is knowing each other, talking peaceful.

"It is Lagos," Ms. Tia say with a tired laugh. "Florence's fabrics are bloody expensive. This way."

We jump over a stinking gutter in the road, full of black water with little frog-fishes swimming through the wet **siga** and tissue and newspaper inside it. We cross to the other side of the street, where there is another line of shops full of fabrics.

"Finally," Ms. Tia say as we turn to a stall the size of a toilet, with a wall of colorful folded ankara hanging from the ceiling to the floor. The woman in front of the shop, round like a rolling drum, was singing a Yoruba song and folding a fabric into two, but when she sees us, she drop the cloth, point to the wall of fabric behind her.

"Welcome, mummy," she say to Ms. Tia. "We have Woodin, ABC Wax, New Satin, anyone you want. Everything here is original. Wash it and wash it, but it will not change. See this one. Latest." She pull out a folded yellow and green pattern of ankara and press it into Ms. Tia's hand.

"This is stunning," Ms. Tia say, speaking in her clear, clean English. "So soft to touch. Simply exquisite. Can I have like three of these? Six yards each? I want to make bedsheets and pillow cases out of them for the guest rooms."

"London mummy," the woman say to Ms. Tia, "for you, six yards is six thousand naira. You want three? I have three. Sit down, sit down, let me pack it in a London nylon bag for you."

Watching the way Ms. Tia's eyes are lighting up at the fabric is making me long so sudden for my friend Enitan. She was always having a light in her eyes too when she see a new color of a eye pencil or a lipstick in the market. Only thing is, most times, Enitan will not have money to buy anything, so we will just look at the makeups, laugh, and keep walking. Ms. Tia has all the money and can buy things that she doesn't even need, and sometimes, like today, I wonder about Enitan, and about Ms. Tia, at how different two of them are, how Ms. Tia and I are friends, but not like me and Enitan.

"Adunni!" Ms. Tia wink at me, and I nod, bring back all the memory of how my mama was teaching me to be arguing price with the market women in Ikati.

"No way," I say in Yoruba to the seller. "Six thousand naira for six yards? God forbid. It is too costly. Sell it to us for three thousand."

"Four thousand five. Last price," the woman say, snatching the fabric from Ms. Tia as if she vex her. "This is original. Latest."

I smile at the seller, say, "Mama, I am your daughter-o. If you sell it for us for three thousand, I will come back here next week with her. We will buy plenty from you. We have come from very far in this hot sun. Collect three thousand from us. Please."

The woman sigh, say, "Bring your money."

I turn to Ms. Tia. "She will collect three thousand. Pay her."

Ms. Tia laugh, say, "Adunni, this is exactly why I brought you here with me."

Two hours later and my two legs are swollen.

My head feel like a hot, burning football. My throat is dry, tongue clipped. Ms. Tia keep shopping like something curse her, buying this and that, making me low the price until my mouth is too dry to keep talking. She is so excited, too happy with how I am saving her money, and every time we finish with a seller, she will clap her hands and say, "You are a genius! We must do this again!"

We leave the market just as the sun is going down, as the sky is turning orange. We walk slow, Ms. Tia dragging her feet and her nylon bags full of shopping (she refuse me to carry anything for her, she says her own two hands are working well), until we find ourselves in front of Frankie's Fast Food, where Michael dropped us off in the early afternoon.

"Would you like something to eat?" Ms. Tia ask.

"Yes, ma," I say, licking my lips. "I am too-too hungry."

"'Starving' is the word you need, Adunni. 'STAR-VING.'"

How can she even think sense to be correcting my English in this hot sun and after all the walking?

We enter the cool, air-con shop, and I pick the third seat by the door, slide into a red leather cushion chair that look like a rich man's bench, with a high wood table in the middle of it and pictures of giant meat pies and sausage rolls and sliced boiled eggs on the walls to my left.

"I will order something for us," Ms. Tia say, dropping her bags of shopping and walking away.

She return a moment later, set a tray full of meat pies, sausage rolls, small yellow cakes, and orange juice on the table.

"That was crazy fun," she say, sliding in with me. "We should do this again. One more time, maybe after the bath. I will ask Ken to speak to Florence. Go on, eat something."

I look at the food, swallow spit. I don't think I have eaten anything like this in my whole life, and I wish that I can have Kayus and Enitan here with me, eating this plenty food, laughing and talking. The feeling come quick, drag down my spirit.

"This is so much," I say, forcing a smile to pick up my spirit. "So much food."

"Well, you are starving. Go on, eat."

I taste the meat pie, close my eyes as my teeth sink deep into the bread of the pie and break it, as the thick, warm soup of meat and potato flow out of the bread and melt on my tongue.

When I open my eyes, Ms. Tia is watching me, smiling.

"You really shone today," she say. "Confidently haggling with those women."

I shrug, pick a sausage roll, bite it.

"My mum's unwell, again," she say as she pick

up a fork and knife and begin to slice the cake into small cubes. She pinch one with a fork, eat it. "I'll be going to Port Harcourt next week. I will be there over Christmas and the new year. We've completed the application form, and I have written your reference and printed out the supporting documentation as a guarantor. All we need now is the essay. Adunni, you need to write it very soon. Can you work on it over the next two days, and bring it to my house?"

"I will try," I say. True thing is, I have been waiting for the right time to pick up my biro and write it, pushing the day forward, afraid of what I will say, how to make it the best.

"Make sure your handwriting is clear, and that you use a good pen. When you are done, fold it and slide it under my front gate. I will take it to the Ocean Oil office myself to make sure it gets delivered before I leave for Port Harcourt. Can you bring it in two days?"

When I don't answer, she pick up my hand, hold it tight. "Are you scared?"

"A little bit," I say, wiping the crumbs from my mouth. "I am afraid of what to write."

"Write from your soul," she say. "Write your truth. From a place—" She drop my hand, stop talking. Her eyes are on the swinging front door, her face looking shock. I follow her eyes, see what she is seeing: the Thin Woman from the WRWA meeting. She is wearing a black English suit, but with a skirt, the collar of her jacket like she about to fly up in the air.

"Shit," Ms. Tia say, whisper. "It's Titi Benson. She's coming this way. Duck, Adunni. Now. Duck."

"A duck?" I say, looking around. "Inside this restaurant?"

"Get under the table," she say, talking through her teeth. "Now."

I climb under the table, hide behind the bags of shopping, my heart beating fast.

The Thin Woman, her legs like thread, is walking to our table, and I am not understanding how her legs is not breaking into two with how she is strolling so fast on her high-heel shoe.

"Tia Dada," she say, stopping at our table, her smell of costly perfume swallowing up the smell of my meat pie and sausage.

"What are you doing in Balogun market?" she say. "Let me guess—running a report on the pollution in the area?"

"Titi," Ms. Tia say, sounding like the cake is a brick in her throat. "Good to see you. How are you?"

"I'm good," Titi say. "That is a lot of food. Are you expecting someone?"

"Yep," Ms. Tia say, then laugh a painful laugh. "Nope. It's all mine. I am famished. Ridiculously so."

"Ah, famished," Titi say, voice like a sudden singing-song. "Are you trying to tell us something? Is there a bun in the oven? How far gone—"

"I am loving the bag," Ms. Tia cut in. "So chic."

"I know, right," Titi say, stroking a hand on the blue box of a bag that is hanging from a thick gold chain on her shoulder. There are two gold letter **Cs** crossing each other on the clip of the bag, and it look too costly, just like her black shoe.

"Do you know I've had this boy for three years?" she say. I can hear a smile in her voice. Like she is proud of her boy of a bag. "It's the most stunning calfskin. And **your** bag is lovely. Italian?"

Ms. Tia's bag is shape like a half a triangle and made with black and pink leather with a gold pin as a button. "My bag is Nigerian," Ms. Tia say. "I mostly wear Nigerian brands."

"Well, you simply cannot go wrong with Chanel. Anyway, I am running late for a board meeting at the First Bank on Broad Street. I couldn't resist stopping over for Frankie's meat pie. Definitely better than the crappy Niçoise salad the CEO at the bank orders for our board meetings. So depressing. Got to run. My love to Kenneth. Take very, **very** good care of yourself and the bun! Ta-ta!"

The woman walk away, her shoes making **clack, clack** on the floor.

I wait another six, seven minutes before Ms. Tia put her hand under the table and beckon for me to come out.

"Why am I hiding?" I say when I climb out and stretch my back. "Big Madam knows I followed you to the market. And why is that woman asking you about a bun inside oven? All she ever thinks about is food!"

"Florence knows we are going to the market," Ms. Tia say, sounding tired. "But she doesn't know I'm taking you out to eat. She doesn't know how close we are or that I have been helping you with anything. If Titi had seen you eating here next to me, she would have asked questions. For your own good, no one can know how close we are. Not yet. Do you get it?"

"I get it," I say, picking my meat pie and cursing Thin Woman in my mind for making my meat pie go all cold and hard.

That evening, as I enter the house and see that Big Madam is not back from the shop, I finish all my housework quick and then enter my room. Even though my whole body is tired, and my eyes are calling me to be sleeping, I pick a paper and pen, and try to write the essay.

At first I write it anyhow: what my name is, where my mama born me, how my papa and brothers are living in Ikati. I tell a story of a life with small money but a lot of happiness, make up all the good things that I can make up in my head, but when I finish writing it and I read it, I feel sick in my stomach. It is full of so many lies, the paper looks like it is swelling up, about to burst.

Write your truth, Ms. Tia say. **Your truth.**

I tear to pieces the paper, and throw it to the floor. Then I swim deep inside the river of my soul, find the key from where it is sitting, full of rust, at the bottom of the river, and open the lock. I kneel down beside my bed, close my eyes, turn myself into a cup, and pour the memory out of me.

I write about Morufu, and what he did to me when he drink Fire-Cracker. About Khadija, and how she died, and how I was running. About Papa. And Mama and Kayus and Born-boy. I tell the school that this scholarship is my life. That I need it to live, to become a person of value. I tell them that I need it to be able to change things, to help other girls like me. And at the end of it, I tell them I have a deep love for Nigeria, even though my life has been full of suffering in this country. I add three of the most interesting of the Nigeria Fact that I know, and when I finish writing, I feel weak, as if I just finished swimming a wide ocean with half of my body: one hand, one leg, one nostril.

I try to think of a good title for the essay, something catching, but no more words are coming to my head. My brain is no more having strength to think and so I use the first title that is coming to my tired mind:

The True Story Essay of Myself by Adunni, the Girl with the Louding Voice

And first thing in the morning, before fear will make me change my mind and write another essay, and before anybody is awake, I run to Ms. Tia's house and slide my essay, folded like a rectangle, under her gate.

CHAPTER 42

Fact: Muhammadu Buhari was the head of state of Nigeria from 1983 to 1985. In 1984 he enacted the War Against Indiscipline, a rule remembered for human rights abuses and restriction of press freedom.

Christmas comes and goes like a stiff, silent wind. Big Madam and Big Daddy go out every day until New Year's Day, visiting everybody and coming back home late, tired, drunk, and smelling of jollof rice, fried meat, and drink. Kofi travel back to Ghana to see his wife and children for Christmas, and me, I stay in the house, cleaning, washing clothes, reading books in the library when I have a chance, and remembering Christmas in Ikati with a twist of sadness in my spirit, how everybody will gather in the village square and blow knockouts and bangers and share **zobo** drink and choco-sweets until late in the night.

Today is the first working day in the year 2015, and Big Madam say I must follow her to her shop, because her shopgirl has gone to her village and she needs me to help her. We are in her car now. I am sitting in front, and Abu is driving through traffic, nodding his head to the radio speaking news in Hausa on a low volume.

Big Madam is at the back seat, speaking to her friend Caroline on the phone. "It will be terrible," she is saying. "If Buhari wins the elections, Nigerians will not understand what hit them. No idea! That man has an evil agenda. Do you remember what we went through in the '80s? How people lost their livelihoods because of War Against Indiscipline? I was flogged once by his demonic soldiers as I waited for a bus at Obalende in 1984. Who knows what will happen if he wins? I know at least three of my customers that have promised to check out of the country on a self-imposed exile. Why wait for tragedy to befall you? It is a nightmare. We are doomed. We need to call a meeting for the Fabric Sellers Association of Lagos to make sure the women in our area can convince our people not to vote for him."

I turn to look at her, to hear what she is saying about Buhari because I like to be learning new things. She is nodding her head up and down, speaking. "I hear you, Caroline, I hear you. But I don't see how this can be good for us. That man can make a law that will affect my business. Ninety percent of my income comes from selling fabric for weddings, funerals, engagements . . . ha. It will be a disaster if people start to reduce their spending on fabric. A real disaster." She catch my eye, say, "Please, hold on, hold on."

Before I can turn away quick, she knock the side of my head with her finger that have a gold stone ring on it. I feel the pain in the middle of my brain.

"Will you keep your eye on the road and stop listening to my conversation? Idiot."

I hear her pull something from her bag, jingle like a bunch of keys. She throws the thing to the front seat. It miss me, land on the floor by Abu's feet, where the car foot pedals are. Abu slide one eye to me, then face his front and keep driving like nothing happen.

Big Madam keeps talking on her phone. "Sorry, Caroline. Adunni was listening to my conversation. Imagine the godforsaken idiot? No, she's coming with me to the shop. Glory went home for Christmas and has refused to return. Adunni will help me today while I wait for a replacement shop assistant. Anyway, I found a cruise package I think you'd love. My wonderful Chief will be sponsoring me, as usual. No, not the Royal Caribbean—let us talk about it later. How far away are you? Okay, that's not far. There is no traffic on Awolowo Road, so I should see you soon. Bye."

I rub my head, feel hot tears burn my eyes. I know the meaning of "forsake." I know it means when somebody has leave you by yourself. When you are of no use to the person. A wasted waste.

I am not a wasted waste; I am Adunni. A person

important enough because my tomorrow will be better than today. I talk to myself, as I have been doing every day since Ms. Tia teach me, until Abu turns the car into the gate of Big Madam's shop.

The steps climbing up to Big Madam's shop is made of white marble, and deep inside each step is a bulb of white light, shining on our feet.

At the top floor is a room the size of her parlor, and I look around, blinking at how bright it is, the wonder of it all. The air is cold with air-con air, smelling like perfume and money.

There are no noises of cars or market women here. No smelling people. Just glass shelves, lining up right from the floor all the way to the ceiling, like a wall of glass around the whole room. Inside each glass is a small ladder sitting under a bright white bulb of round light. Fabrics, the most beautiful I ever seen in my life, are folded into each step of the ladder. There are fabrics with flowers, hundreds of them, so that it look like Big Madam uproot a flower garden and fold it like a cloth to sell. Others have stones, shining ones, different colors, purple, pink, red, blue, white, black, even some colors that don't have a name. There is one of net, one like a curtain material, heavy-looking, another like a sponge, thick and full. Up in the ceiling, I count sixteen lightbulbs deep inside it and round like eye-sballs of light, all in a case of silver metal.

The same dolly babies from when Mr. Kola was pointing the shop to me, two of them, both naked, are still standing behind the front window. A sea of white lace is around their feet, and two vases made out of basket weaving and full of dried yellow flowers sit by each dolly.

In the middle of the shop, there is a purple chair with gold feet, the cushion back of it curling a little. There are magazines on the glass table to the side of the chair, arranged like an open hand fan, and I catch the title of the top magazine with my eyes: **Genevieve.** There is a picture of three Nollywood actress on the cover, looking rich and happy.

"Put my handbag on the till," Big Madam say, pointing to the glass shelf on my left with a small computer sitting on top, next to a pen and a pad of paper. Behind the shelf is a chair, tall, with a round seat. There is a tee-vee on the wall too, flat like the one in Big Madam's parlor.

I put down her handbag, wait for her to tell me what to do.

"My storage is behind that door," Big Madam say, setting herself in the purple sofa and kicking off her purple shoes. "I don't think it is locked. Open it, and right on the floor, you will see a bag full of fabric. Bring that bag for me."

"Yes, ma," I say, turning to the door behind me.

I twist the gold handle, blink into the dark store-room. It is too dark to see much, but I can make out rows and rows of ladders, full of lace materials, too many to count, too far to see the end of it. I pick the nylon bag behind the door and close it.

When I enter the shop floor, I see Caroline. She is wearing blue jeans-trousers that look too tight, with a gold t-shirt that stop on her belly. There are high heels on her feet, pink with a sharp, pointing tip. Today, her eyes are not green but the gold-brown of honey. How is she able to keep changing her eye color? Or is she wearing a special eye-glass deep inside her eyes?

She wrap up her head with a red scarf and when she nod at me with a quick smile, the two big, round earrings in her ears dance up and down.

"Is this my guipure?" she say, snatching the bag from my hand and peeping into the bag. "Florence, did you give me the best in your collection? I want to make a waist-snatching dress for a special somebody."

Big Madam laughs like a horse. "Who is the special person? Eh? You this woman, the day your husband will catch you, I will not beg him to take you back."

"It is not my fault that he is always offshore," she says as she pulls out the fabric and spreads it out, the lace pouring to the floor like a giant red wave, the stones in the material blinking under the bright lights. "Today he is in Saudi, tomorrow he is in

Kuwait, chasing dollars. A woman needs a man to warm her bed."

"I hear you," Big Madam say. "Who is making your dress?"

"House of Funke," Caroline say. "Florence, ah, this guipure is fantastic. The burgundy is just alive! Look at the pattern on the edges, my goodness. How much for me?"

"One hundred and fifty thousand," Big Madam say, picking the magazine on the table and fanning herself with it. "For you and for **everybody.** Do you need all the five yards?"

"I am thinking of making a midi-dress," Caroline say, talking to the fabric. "So three yards should do. I can't wait to see what magic Funke will work on the neckline. I may add more stones in it because I want it blinged to death!"

"This new man must be special," Big Madam say, yawning. "See how you are smiling."

Caroline say, "Florence, 150K is too much. Knock 50K off for me, **abeg.** I will send Adunni to my car to go and bring the money now."

"Knock off what?" Big Madam slap the magazine down, sit up straight. "We are talking about Swiss lace here, Caro. Isn't your new man worth it? In fact, there is a new brocade that just landed. Luxury embroidered. You will love it. I can imagine you making a jumpsuit with it, maybe for another date with this your new man. It is a lovely champagne-gold, and I have the perfect velvet turban to go with it.

The governor's wife just got off the phone with me.
She wants three yards of it for a special lunch at the
US embassy. Shall I get it for you?"

I look Big Madam, wondering when she ever
talk to any governor's wife just now, but she keep a
straight face.

"Florence!" Caroline shake her head with a
laugh. "You will make me bankrupt, I swear. How
much for the two, three yards each? Do you have
the turban in store?" She turn to me. "Adunni, run
downstairs. My car is in the parking lot. My house
girl is sitting in the front seat. Her name is Chisom,
tell her to give you my handbag and bring it up
for me."

As I turn around and leave them, Big Madam is
saying, "Before I forget, there is one turquoise tulle
fabric I think you would love . . ."

The four doors to Caroline's black Jeep are wide-
open.

A girl is sitting in the front seat, talking on a
mobile phone that is pressed between her ear and
her shoulder. She is nodding to the phone, laughing
too, as she pick up a spoon full of jollof rice from a
bowl in her lap and eat it.

The driver, a man with a black cap covering his
face, is sleeping in the driver's seat, which he push

all the way down. His two legs are up, in the space between the wheel-steering and the open car door. The man doesn't even move as I go near the car.

"Hello," I say, looking the girl, pressing a hand to silent the hungry noise in my stomach. "Are you Aunty Caroline's housemaid?"

She look nothing like a housemaid. Her hair is full of thick, neat plaiting all the way down to her back. Her dress, bright yellow and pink with patterns of a bird in a tree, look nothing like my own. I don't see her feet, but her fingers, which she is using to hold the spoon, is having nails the same pink color of her dress.

"Let me call you back," she say to her phone.

"Or are you her daughter?" I ask. Maybe she is Caroline's daughter. She look like a daughter, dress like a daughter. Speak like a daughter too.

"Hello," she say to me.

"I am looking for Chisom," I say. "Aunty Caroline's housemaid. She said I should bring her bag up to the shop."

"I am Chisom," she say, eyeing me from up to down. "You are Big Madam's maid?"

"Yes," I say. "She say I should bring her bag."

"Sure," the girl say, then turn to the back seat, pick up a black leather bag with big letters **L** and **V** stamping everywhere on it, and give me. "What is your name?" she ask as I collect the bag.

"Adunni." I swallow the hot spit in my mouth

as I watch her. She pick up the plastic cover of the jollof rice bowl and put it on the bowl, covering the rice and fried meat.

"**Bia,** Adunni, why are you so skinny like this?" She look at me a moment, then at the bowl, then she laugh. "Do you want my remaining rice?"

I drag my eyes away from the bowl. I cannot collect the rice because Big Madam will beat me. But maybe I can find a corner to eat it quick?

"Rebecca was always hungry," Chisom say. She slap her hand on the cover to lock the rice well, then hold up the bowl to my face. "Take my food. My madam will buy me another one."

"You know Rebecca?" I wide my eyes, forgetting all my hunger, the rice. "How? Do you know what happened to her? Was she from Agan village?"

Chisom shrug. "She used to talk about Agan," she say. "Me and her were not too close, so I don't know if she was from there, but whenever I see her here, I will give her food. Then one day, she didn't come again."

"When did she stop coming to the shop?" I ask.

Chisom think a moment. "Maybe around the time she was starting to get big. Before then, she was skinny. Like you."

"She was getting big?" My heart begin to beat fast as I think of the waist beads under my pillow. Maybe she take them off because she was getting big, but the beads are inside a elastic string, so it can stretch and stretch and she don't really need to ever take it off. I sigh. "Chisom, did she tell you—"

"Adunni!" Big Madam shout from upstairs. "Is Caroline's bag in Saudi Arabia? Do you need to apply for a visa before you can access the bag, **ehn?** If you make me come downstairs and find you, I will—"

"I am coming, ma," I shout before Big Madam will complete her sentence.

I turn around quick, nearly falling over as I run to the stairs, and just before I start to climb, I look back and see Chisom laughing, shaking her head at me.

"Your shop is very fine, ma," I say to Big Madam as we leave the shop, and Abu is driving up a short bridge.

"So very big, beautiful." My stomach is very hungry, and keeping silent too much is making my mouth to smell a foul odor, so I keep talking, even though Big Madam is sitting in the back seat, breathing hard, not answering me.

"Just like heaven," I say. "All the lights in it, shining beautiful. The smell too, like perfume. The fabrics? So costly. So nice."

Abu slide his eye to me, as if to ask if I am mad, but I keep talking: "And all those peoples coming into your shop and calling on the telephone, very big Nigerian people. Your children must feel too proud of their mother." Then I keep quiet.

As Abu is turning into the road that is leading to the house, Big Madam say, "You think so?"

At first, I am not sure she is talking to me, so I whisper my answer, say, "I think so."

Big Madam laughs. A real laugh. I turn around to look at her in the back seat. She is smiling. At **me.** With me.

"You are very good at selling to everybody," I say, forgetting all of my hunger, and Chisom, and everything that was worrying me. "All the customers that came inside today, you sell to all of them, making good money. You make it seem so easy to do business. Honest, ma, if I am ever wanting to be selling clothes, ma, I want to be selling just like you."

"Like me?" Big Madam press her fingers, full of gold rings, on her chest and laugh again, and her eyes, which were red and tired, are now lighting up the whole car. "Adunni, I started my business from nothing," she say, pushing herself to sit up and lean forward. "Fifteen years ago, I was selling cheap materials from my boot, going from place to place, looking for customers. I wasn't born into wealth. I have worked hard for my success. I fought for it. It wasn't easy, especially because my husband, Chief, he didn't have a job. If you want to be like me in business, Adunni, you will need to work very hard. Rise above whatever life throws at you. And never, ever give up on your dreams. Do you understand?"

I nod. Keep my eyes on her. Feel something share between me and her. Something warm, thick, like a embrace from an old friend.

Then Abu press the horn, **peen,** and Big Madam blink, look around. "Ah? Are we home already? Adunni, what are you staring at me for? Will you fly out of this car and get inside the house before I slice your head off? Idiot!"

I climb out of the car, tumbling over everything we just shared—the warm look, the quick smile, the hope that maybe she can be ever kind to me—and run quick inside the house.

CHAPTER 43

Fact: Nigeria has the largest Christian population in Africa. A single church service can
record a congregation of over 200,000.

Buhari win the elections.

Kofi danced as if him and Buhari are sharing
the same mother and father. "Change has come,"
he say as the tee-vee announce the announcement last week, pulling off his white hat from his
head, throwing it up and catching it with a laugh.
"Change has come! Nigeria will thrive! This is what
we have been waiting for!"

Papa was always following elections news, and I
wonder now, with a pinch of sadness in my heart,
if he too danced for this news, if he is still thinking
of me.

But Big Madam was ever so mad. She curse and
curse Buhari so much, I am fearing the man will
fall dead any day from now. She say he is a witch
doctor. That he does not know English. Now that

makes me think, if he does not know English, and he is a new president, maybe Adunni too can be a president one day?

Today is the first Sunday in April, and we are going to Big Madam's church for the Women in Business special thanksgiving service. She say I must follow her to help her carry the bag of fabrics she wants to gift to the women in her group. I have never been to church since I came to Lagos, and I am feeling excited as I climb into the car and sit in the front with Abu.

Big Madam and Big Daddy sit in the back. Big Madam is wearing her **boubou,** but this one is a heavy gold material, so heavy I have to carry the edges so she can climb into the car. There are white, shining stones on the shoulder and sleeves, a thick line of silver lace around the neck. Her gold **gele** is like a tiny ship in the middle of her head, her earrings a string of five red beads that drag her ears down to her shoulder.

I am still wearing Rebecca's shoes. The edge of the shoe is now cutting, and yesterday, I used a needle and a thread to sew it back. I like the shoe, it makes me feel as if I know Rebecca from before, as if I am carrying her along with me on my feet everywhere, sharing her life, her secrets with her. I know that very soon, I will know what happened, why she just disappear and why nobody in this house is wanting to talk about her.

Ms. Tia is still in Port Harcourt, she text me

just this morning. She say her mama has been in hospital admission since new year and that things have "finally settled down, so should be on the next available flight back to Lagos." She say too that her husband, "bless his heart, has been coming to Port Harcourt every Friday to be with me."

I read the message three times, before I reply: **OKAY. SEE U SOON.**

"Do you have money for church offering?" Big Madam asks Big Daddy now, as the car is climbing up the bridge that looks like it is hanging by the many threads, thin white fingers on the left and right side of it. I think this is the Lekki-Ikoyi bridge that Ms. Tia uses for her morning running.

"What kind of stupid question are you asking me, Florence?" Big Daddy says. "Did you give me offering money?"

Big Madam grunts, opens her bag of feathers, and brings out money, bundles of it, a brown rubber band around the bundle. "That is fifty thousand naira," she says to Big Daddy, dragging a fat bundle out from the rest. "Use 10K as offering. The forty thousand is your donation for the Good Men conference next weekend. Chief, please make sure you donate the money, because the last time I gave you two hundred thousand for the Over Fifties Men's Retreat, the church secretary never received it."

Big Daddy snatch the money and push it deep into the pocket of his green **agbada.** "Why don't you wait till we get to church so you can take the microphone and announce to the congregation that you gave your husband, the head of the family, the man in charge of your home, two hundred thousand naira for retreat, and that he spent the money? Useless woman."

Big Madam nods, but her jaw is shaking, shaking like she is fighting to not cry, and I feel something pity for her. When she faces the window and sniffs something up her nose, Abu loud up the radio and **The News on Sunday** fill up the car with noise.

We drive like that, with nobody except the radio talking, until Abu climbs down the bridge and cuts a turn by the left of a roundabout.

When Abu brings the car to a stop, Big Madam climbs down, but Big Daddy stays in the car. He says he will be joining us after; he wants to smoke a small **siga** first, to make his mind open to be hearing from heaven.

The church is a round hat-shape building with a gold, heavy-looking cross on the tip of the roof. The windows, I count fifty of it, is made of colorful glass with drawings of doves and angels on it, the whole compound full of tall cars like Big Madam's Jeep. Everybody coming in is dressing like it is a birthday party or wedding celebrations, with high heels, **geles** of all sorts of rainbow colors, costly-looking lace, and plenty makeups on the face of the women.

In Ikati, our church is having just roof and bench and drum for the music, and people be wearing cloth to church like they mourn, sing like they mourn too. This one, from even outside, I am hearing plenty music, makes me want to dance.

We climb up the stairs, enter a place that looks like a parlor with no sofa. It is cool in there, with many people laughing, talking, smiling to each other, saying happy Sunday. In front of us is the front door of the church, two glass doors with red carpet on the floor in front of it.

There is one woman standing in the front of one of the doors like a gate man; she is wearing too-tight black skirt that look like it is giving her breathing problem, and a red shirt that look like it belongs to a child that is two years of age. It push all her breast up to her neck. Under her plenty makeup, pimples be pinching all her face, make her look like she had a measles sickness that didn't finish healing itself.

"Good morning, welcome to the Celebration Arena," she says, giving Big Madam a wide smile that stretch her lip, and all the pimples around her mouth gather to one angle.

"I assume this is your housemaid?" she says, looking at me like I am wearing my cloth from back to front.

I kneel, greet her. "Good morning."

"Adunni, get up and bring my handbag," Big Madam says. "Yes, she is my house girl," she says to the woman. "Am I correct in thinking that she cannot enter this church auditorium? I need her after the service to bring fabric from the car."

The woman shakes her head. "She can't. She will go to the housemaid service at the back. I will take her there and bring her to you later. Go on in, ma'am. God bless you."

I am standing there, watching, as Big Madam enter the glass door, as a shock of cold air and singing voices escape and reach me.

"Why am I not following my madam into the church?" I ask the woman after the door has swallowed Big Madam inside of it. "Where will I find her when she finish? I don't know anywhere in Lagos. I don't want to lost."

The woman stretch her lips into a quick smile. "Don't worry, you will be fine. Follow me. This way."

We cut to the far, far back of the church. She is walking on her red high-heel shoe as if the floor is a tightrope. We pass one path with a bush to the left and right of us, like a parting of short, full hair on a flat head. We reach a house. It is the first time I see a gray house in Lagos that make me think of Ikati. It has no paint or door or window. Beside it is another small house, with no door too. I smell the piss before I see the round edge of the white toilet bowl, the broken brown tiles on the floor. It look like they just builded this house anyhow and throw it to the back of the church, after they finish using all the money for the fine church in the front.

"That's where the housemaid service happens,"

she say, covering her nose with a hand, the red of her pointed fingernail pressing into her cheek. "There's a problem with the toilet flushing system, but that's on the queue to be fixed. Hopefully should be sorted out before next Sunday. Anyway, have a seat with the rest in there. The preacher will be here soon. We'll come and get you after the service, okay?"

I step inside, see about five girls sitting on the floor, their head down. They all look the same age of me: fourteen, fifteen. All are wearing dirty dress of ankara or plain material with shoes like wet toilet paper, tearing everywhere. Hair is rough, or low-cut to the scalp. They smell of stinking sweat, of a body that needs serious washing, and they all look sad, lost, afraid. Like me.

"Good morning, everybody," I say, trying to smile, to see if I can talk to one of them, to make a friend.

But nobody is answering me.

"Good morning," I say again. "My name is Adunni."

One of the girls look up then, hook her eyes on me. There is no kindness in her eyes. Nothing. Only fear. Cold fear. She say nothing, but with her eyes, she seem to be saying: **You are me. I am you. Our madams are different, but they are the same.**

I look around, see Chisom at a far right corner, pressing her phone. I forget the rest girls, walk quick to her. There is a white wire inside her ears, and she is nodding her head to a silent music and eating a chewing gum. She look happy in her blue church dress, black shoe, and clean white socks, and as I bend low in her front, I wonder if she is a housemaid like me and the rest girls here, or if Caroline is just having a different way to keeping her own maids.

"Chisom," I say.

She blow a bubble with the chewing gum, use her tongue to kill it. Then she slap the floor near her for me to sit, pull out her earphones. "Skinny!" she say. "How are you?"

"Adunni is the name, but fine, thank you," I say. "Is this your church?"

"No," she say. "My madam goes to another church. We only came for the Women in Business program. Why are we sitting here? On the floor? I asked that usher with plenty pimples, but all she said was, 'It is protocol.' My madam said I should follow her and that she will complain after the service. What is 'protocol'?"

"I don't know." I sit down and pull my knees up like the other girls. "Your madam is very nice to you," I say. "Why?"

"Because she is a nice woman," Chisom says, "and because me and her, we understand ourselves. I take care of her, and she takes care of me."

"Like how?" I ask. Maybe if she tells me, I can try and take care of Big Madam, make her kind to me.

"I know things about my madam," Chisom says.

"Things nobody else knows. All her secrets, every-thing, I keep them for her. Me and her are more than madam and housemaid. We are like sisters. But you, and all these girls here? There is nothing you people can do to make your madams nice to you. Nothing. Most of them are just wicked, any-way." Chisom put her wire thing back inside her ear, begin to snap her finger and shake her head.

I wait a moment, then elbow her. "Chisom?"

She pull out the wire, give me vexing look. "What?"

"That day at the shop," I say, talking soft, "you said Rebecca was thin before, then she begins to get fat. Do you know what happened to her after she was getting fat? Why was she fat? Did she run away?"

"I don't know," Chisom says. "Me and her didn't ever talk much, but when I saw her, she looked big. And when I saw her the second time after the first time, she was getting more big, then I understand."

"You are confusing me, Chisom," I say as one man enter the room. He is wearing suit like a worker, holding a big black Bible under his arm. "Hello, everybody," he say, looking round with a smile at all of us sitting down. "I am Pastor Chris. Today we will—"

"Understand what?" I ask Chisom. My heart is beating so loud, it drown everything the pastor is saying. "Tell me, what did you understand?"

"Rebecca told me she was getting married," Chisom says, whispering. "She was very happy, but seemed so afraid. Next thing, they say she didn't come back home from going to the market one afternoon. But—"

"I said can we all rise up?" the pastor says, clapping his hand. "You two in the corner, stop chatting. Stand up!"

"Wait," I say to Chisom, not even looking at the pastor's face. "Who was Rebecca marrying?"

"I don't know, but I think—" She cover her mouth. "**Shh,** the pastor is coming this way."

I was not able to speak to Chisom again after that.

Her madam, Caroline, she came to find her in the middle of our own service and to take her to the big, fine church in front, and after the service, I stand beside the church gate and try to find her. I use my eyes to search all the women and men in their fine dresses, eating meat pies and laughing and talking about the church service, but I don't see her and I don't see Caroline too. I was thinking to maybe enter into the church building to keep looking for Chisom, when Big Madam pull me by my hair and drag me inside the car.

We are in the car now, driving home silent.

Big Daddy is at the back snoring loud, and Big

Madam is on her phone talking to somebody about a "supply of organza material for two hundred wedding guests."

When we reach home, Big Madam and Big Daddy climb out of the car, but I don't climb out. I don't want to enter the house. I want to stay here, in this car, and hide myself forever.

Everything Chisom said about Rebecca is not making sense. If she was marrying somebody, then why didn't Kofi know? Why didn't anybody know? I sigh. I am tired. Hungry. Confused. Angry at myself too, for thinking something bad happened to Rebecca when she was happy and getting married and maybe just decide to run away because she didn't want Big Madam to stop her marriage plans.

Just like how I too don't want Big Madam to stop my scholarship plans.

But why did she take off her waist beads if she was just getting married?

I sigh again.

My hair, which Big Madam was dragging in church, is paining me in the brain. My body is looking like a map, showing different marks of where Big Madam has been beating me so much. There is one on my back, a wound, she used her shoe heel to open it two times, causing it to smell bad for a week, after it was nearly drying. There is another behind my ear, one to the left of my forehead.

How will I free myself from this place? The end of April seem so far, even though it is only few weeks from now. Even then, I don't know if I will win the scholarship, and even if I win, will Big Madam let me go from here? I feel a longing so deep for Ikati, for my life of before, a pulling that twist my heart and cause me to start to cry.

"Adunni," Abu say, and I look up, forgetting he was even in the car. "**Haba.** What is making you cry?"

I wipe my face. "Everything, Abu," I say. "My life, Rebecca, everything. I am just tired."

I put a hand on the door handle, make to push it open.

"Wait," Abu say. "Why is Rebecca making you cry? She is not here."

"Yes," I say, then I tell him about the waist beads, and what Chisom say.

Abu keeps nodding as I am talking, and when I finish, he sigh and say, "May Allah be with her."

"Amen," I say. "I just keep feeling that maybe she was in trouble, and that maybe what happened to her will happen to me. I feel close to her. She was from Agan village, which is not far from my own village. But now, I think she is okay. She was just running away to marry and I was worrying myself for nothing."

"Adunni," Abu say, then look over his shoulder to where the house is so far away. "I want to show you something. Something I saw inside the car . . . after Rebecca was missing."

"What? What did you see?"

"Not now," he say, looking over his shoulder again. "The thing is inside my room. I will bring it to you when Big Daddy is maybe sleeping at night, or when he is not in the house, **ko?**" His face look so serious, eyes so wide with fear, that I feel my heart starting to beat.

"Okay," I say. "When you come, knock the door three times, I will know it is you. I don't like to open my room door at night for anybody."

"Eh," he say, nodding, "I will knock it three times and wait for you outside your room."

"Till then," I say as my phone make a vibrate in my chest. I climb out of the car, walk a little away from Abu and hide behind one of the flowerpots, before I pull out my phone.

Another text message from Ms. Tia:

**About to board a flight back to
   Lagos. See you tomorrow afternoon for bath.
Your madam is okay for you to come
   with me to the "market." No need
   to reply. xx**

I smile a little, wonder what "xx" mean, before I put the phone back in my brassiere and run inside to begin my afternoon housework.

CHAPTER 44

Fact: The Yoruba ethnic group considers twins to be a powerful, supernatural blessing, believed to usher in great wealth and protection for the families they are born in.

H ey," Ms. Tia say when I meet her in the compound on Monday afternoon.

She is sitting under the coconut tree, and when she sees me, she push herself up and dust the sand from her buttocks. "My days, look at you! You are awfully thin. Has it really been nearly four months since I last saw you?"

"Yes," I say. "Since before Christmas."

She gives me a quick embrace. "I flew into Lagos a few times between Christmas and now, but only to check in at the office. I would have stopped by to see you, but I couldn't. Did you get my text messages?"

"Yes," I say. "How is your mama? Is she feeling fine now? Are you and her trying to be more close?"

I pull the padlock of our gate, open it, and we go outside on the street, begin to walk to her house.

The black smooth road is a stretch in front of us, looking like it is full of oil under the heat of the sun, the top of it like thin waves of water.

She nods. "She had a chest infection and we nearly lost her, but she somehow managed to pull through. Things are a lot better between us . . . thanks for asking. Did you have a nice Christmas and new year? How's your Big Madam? Have the beatings stopped? You've lost a lot more weight."

She is always asking if the beatings have stopped, but my answer has never changed itself. "Just yesterday, after church, she poured water on my head," I say. "Somebody used the downstair toilet and didn't press the flush well. There was shit inside. She says it is me that do the shit. She beat me, saying I am a devil-child, and a big, fat liar. She doesn't ever give me food to make me fat, so why is she calling me fat? She made me put my hand into the toilet, pick up the shit one by one, and carry it to our own toilet."

Ms. Tia makes a face like she wants to vomit. "That's just . . ." She shakes her head and doesn't say anything again until we reach her gate, where one car is parked in the front of it.

Ms. Tia slow her walking. "That's my mother-in-law's car," she says, her voice low. "I told her you are coming with me. Ken talked her into letting you come. I can't even believe I agreed to do this, but who knows? Maybe the bath would work, make all this . . . the stress from her, from everyone, make it all stop." She shake her head, then talk low, to only herself. "I've been off the Pill since late last year. We've been doing the right things, but nothing yet. It's bloody frustrating."

The Pill is Tablet. Tablet is Medicine. Like the one Khadija made for me in Morufu's house to stop me from getting pregnant. If Ms. Tia is no more taking the medicine for stopping baby, and they been trying for months now, why is the baby not coming?

I put my hand on Ms. Tia's shoulder and tell her it will be fine, just like she is always telling me.

She gives me a wet smile and pulls my hand. "Come on, let's do this."

Ms. Tia's mother-in-law is a thin woman with a nose like a teapot.

She looks just like Dr. Ken with no mustache to the jaw, and with a short black wig on her head. She is wearing a costly-looking red lace dress with stones on it, and when I greet her, she just sniffs up something in her teapot nose.

Ms. Tia climbs into the car, sits beside the woman, and me, I sit in front with the driver.

"Moscow," the doctor mama say, talking to the driver. "We are going to the Miracle Center in Ikeja. The one by the Shoprite roundabout. Remember it?"

Moscow, a man with head that looks like it is

full of dry cement, too heavy for his neck, says yes, he can remember the place, and begins to drive. He put on the radio, and I sit there, feeling cold from the air-con and hearing the radio woman talking like she is from the America about new Buhari president and how Nigeria will be better because of it.

Ms. Tia and the doctor mama, they don't talk in the back. The only noise inside the car is from the America-talking woman in the radio. She is speaking so fast, the only word I am hearing from all she's been saying in one hour of driving is "Obama."

The go-slow is the worst I ever seen in my life. Outside, the other cars in the road are pressing horn like mad people, the drivers cursing. After about three hours, the driver turns into one gate, stops the car, and puts off the engine.

The doctor mama say to Ms. Tia, "We are here. Here is a scarf for you to cover your head with. This is a holy ground. You could give this newspaper to that one in front. She also needs to cover her hair. Why you'd bring a stranger, your neighbor's housemaid, along to something so sacred, so personal, is completely beyond me. I cannot understand it at all."

"She has to come with me," Ms. Tia says. "That is what we agreed. If she cannot come with us, I will leave. She can have the scarf; I'll use the newspaper."

"And go in looking like what? A destitute? Tia,

please, behave yourself." The woman is talking like she is just tired of Ms. Tia and her many troubles.

"I invited her," Ms. Tia says. "It is unfair for her to use a newspaper to cover her hair when she didn't ask to come here."

"You will not go in there with a newspaper on your head," the doctor mama say.

"No, I won't," Ms. Tia say, folding her hands across her chest and pushing out her top lip like a vexed, small child. "I am not moving an inch from here unless Adunni wears the scarf."

The doctor mama whispers something in Yoruba. I know Ms. Tia is not understanding it, but the woman just asked if Ms. Tia is having brain problem, where the doctor find this kind of crazy Port Harcourt woman from the Abroad to marry.

I don't want them to be fighting because of me, so I face the back seat. "I can take the newspaper," I say. "I can even wear it like a dress if you want. Where is it?"

I give Ms. Tia a look, begging with my eyes for her to give me the paper.

Ms. Tia nods, picks up the newspaper from the seat, and gives me. I wrap the thing around my head, fold it here and there. It tears many times, but last, last, it resembles one kind mash-up cap.

"See? It looks very good," I say, giving them a wide smile with all my teeth.

The doctor mama hiss, open the car door, and

climb out. "Meet me inside," she say, slamming the door and walking away.

Me and Ms. Tia, we look at each other and burst into laughter.

The prophet of this Miracle Center is one short man with bowlegs like two letter **C**s facing each other. It make him look like he is bouncing around instead of walking.

He has a sleeping eye, so even when he is awake, you will want to tap him to wake up. He is wearing a long red dress with a white belt around his stomach. A white cap with a slanting purple cross sits on his head, a small gold bell in his hand. When me and Ms. Tia enter the church, he bounces up, rings the bell, **gran, gran,** says to us, "Welcome to the zone. Sit down."

The place is having about thirty wood benches, just like my classroom in Ikati. The doctor mama is sitting on the end of one bench, so me and Ms. Tia, we slide to that same bench. At the front of the church, behind the wooden altar with long brown cross in the middle of it, is a picture of one man. I think it is Jesus, but this Jesus looks hungry, with vex face too. He look a bit like Katie in the London too, with long brown hair.

Why is Jesus looking like somebody in the Abroad? Maybe Jesus is from the Abroad?

There is a sharp smell in the air, and my nose follows it to the three green mosquito coils on the floor, bringing out gray, waving smoke. There are red candles on the floor too, I count fifteen of it around the leg of the altar.

"**Alafia,**" the prophet says.

"He says peace to you," I whisper to Ms. Tia. "'**Alafia**' means 'peace' in Yoruba."

Ms. Tia says "**Alafia**" back to the prophet.

Me, I greet the man good afternoon.

"**Alafia,**" he says to me, and rings the bell one time.

The doctor mama, she begins to talk to prophet in smooth Yoruba. She says Ms. Tia marry her son and was not having a baby in over one whole year since the marriage. That she is tired of praying and shouting for a baby, and she thinks maybe Ms. Tia has one evil spirit that is swallowing the baby. That Ms. Tia bring the spirit when she was coming and the evil spirit needs chasing off to go back to the Abroad. She cut her eye to me when she says this because she knows I am understanding her.

Me, I keep my eyes on the prophet's feet. He doesn't have shoes on. Toenails look burned.

"So, you brought her for the powerful bath," the prophet says in English. "This is the land of solution, amen? The land of miracle. Twenty-four-hour miracle." He coughs. "Did she bring cloth to change into? Because she will throw away the cloth she came here with. She has come with a garment of sorrow and barrenness; she will return with a garment of twins. Amen?"

"Just one baby," I whisper.

"Twins," the doctor mama says, eyeing me. "Amen. Two boys."

"I have a pair of jeans and a fresh t-shirt in the boot," Ms. Tia say.

"Good," the prophet says. "Young woman, kneel here so I can pray for you first."

Ms. Tia slides off the bench and kneels. Me and the doctor mama too, both of us we kneel. The prophet bounce to his feet, begins to go around Ms. Tia. He will go around one time, ring bell one time, his dress spreading up around him like the wings of an eagle. He will go around her two times, ring the bell two times. He does this like seven times, until he begins to look like he daze. I keep hearing the bell inside my head for like two minutes after he stopped ringing it.

When he begins to jump, up and down, clapping his two hands, saying, "Eli . . . jah . . . baby . . ." The doctor mama nods her head yes, yes, yes, and says: "Baby boys, baby boys."

Ms. Tia peeps open one eye, looking like she is wanting to laugh, then close it back.

We stay like that on our knees, until the prophet man finish his bouncing and he says it is now time for the baby-making baff.

CHAPTER 45

Fact: Some of the richest pastors in the world live in Nigeria, with net worths reaching up to $150 million.

The prophet is bouncing in front of us, taking us through a path of red sand.

Green plants, full of thorns, with branches shaped like a hand with broken fingers, are sitting in clay flowerpots on each side of the path. Where the path ends, one woman, wearing the same dress as the prophet, meets us with a smile that looks like it is upside down. She reminds me of a housefly, this woman, with her lean body and arms which is full of hairs where her dark skin is showing, wide eyeballs that stretch a little to the side of her head, and the long, thin purple cloth around her body like slim wings. She is wearing the same cap as the prophet too, but her own looks like it is swelling. I peep a red wig under the cap, looking like something a car climbed over and crushed plenty times.

She kneels in front of the man. **"Alafia."**

The man nods his head, puts his hand on her cap. "Peace to you too, Mother-in-Jerusalem."

He turns to us. "This is Mother-in-Jerusalem Tinu," he says. "She is the head of our female birth-makers. She is a powerful woman in the baby-making miracle ministry. You can call her Mother Tinu, she won't mind. She will take our sister here with her to the river. Men are not allowed, so I will wait behind."

Ms. Tia makes a noise like something pinched her. "Right now? Can we not, like, do this later? I just need time to think. To gather my thoughts."

"Have you gone around her seven times with the bell?" Mother Tinu asks the prophet. "Because once that has happened, the bath must follow. No going back." She smiles. "It will be quick."

"Can Adunni still come with me?" Ms. Tia asks.

"Foolishness," the doctor mama says. "Utter foolishness."

"Adunni, you can come with us," the Mother Tinu says. "You must keep your eyes closed throughout the ceremony. This is not a film cinema."

"Yes, ma," I say.

"Go," the prophet say. "After the bath, meet me in the church to collect the special cream you will use to rub your body."

"Cream too?" Ms. Tia says. "Well, how about a suite at the Ritz-Carlton and a limo ride back home? You said this was just a bath."

"We can discuss this later," the doctor mama

says, talking with her teeth grinding together. "For now, please, just comply."

"Follow me," Mother Tinu says.

We follow her behind, turn left into another path. The red sand is wet under my feet, cold, with rocks pushing into my shoe.

We walk until we see a hole formed with brown rocks with a round opening for people to enter. There are voices in the air, plenty women singing afar off, a moaning song of no words, a song of sorrows.

Ms. Tia is holding my hand tight, her nails pinching my skin, nearly drawing blood.

"What the hell?" she whispers into my ears.

"This is not the hell," I whisper back. "This is holy ground." I like Ms. Tia, but sometimes, she can like to ask questions that don't make sense.

"Those women are in the spirit, preparing for you," the Mother Tinu says. "Beyond this cave lies the sacred river where your bath will take place. Did you bring clothes to change into?"

"I already told the man I had clothes in the car," Ms. Tia says.

"I believe you have paid?" Mother Tinu slides her eyes from Ms. Tia to the doctor mama. "Because we have a strict policy here. No pay, no bath."

"Pay?" Ms. Tia says. "We have to pay for this?"

"I have handled it," the doctor mama says with a stiff voice.

"In that case, let us go," Mother Tinu says.

"When we finish the bath, Adunni, you will run to the car and bring the clothes.

"This way," she says to Ms. Tia. "You need to bend your head to come in. It is full of rocks inside; we don't want you to bang your head. You have come to seek solution, not headaches." She laughs by herself.

We bend our necks, walking like old people into the cave place. It is a small space, so we line up ourselves: Mother Tinu in front, me behind her, Ms. Tia behind me, and the doctor mama last. It is dark too, the ceiling low, with rocks deep into the roof of it. I bang my head on some rocks, bend myself lower, almost crawling, until we come out on the other side. Now we are facing a riverbed with tree branches hanging low as if worshipping the muddy floor in front of the river. The river is dark green, the water curling like a tongue around the gray rocks on the edge, licking the golden-brown leaves between the rocks. The place takes me back, back, to where I was watching the sky, the gray covering the orange as the sun hide itself and gave way to rain, to a time when Khadija was warring with God for her soul. It is dark here too, as if the rains are coming, only this time it is the leaves that have become a blanket over the sky.

There are four women kneeling in front of the river. They tie a white cloth around their chest, white scarf on their head, a string of cowry beads around their neck. They sway here and there on their knees as if the wind is rocking them, as if the dipping tree branches are whispering a soft, sad song into their ears.

"Ooo," they keep saying, "ooo."

"I don't like this," Ms. Tia whispers, gripping my hand even more now. "I don't like this one bit."

"I don't like it too," I say.

"Can we delay this for a bit?" she is still whispering into my ear, still pinching my flesh.

"Silence!" Mother Tinu shouts from our front, and Ms. Tia jumps.

"No whispering around the baby-makers," Mother Tinu says. "Wait there. Don't move one step further. I will get the holy cloth and holy brooms."

As Mother Tinu is walking away, Ms. Tia says, "Brooms? What for?"

I never heard of anybody ever using brooms in Ikati to wash theirself. I know of sponge, and black soap. But not broom, and not in a church. The talk of broom is making me feel discomfort. "I don't know," I say. "Maybe we will sweep the floor first?"

"Adunni, you heard the woman," the doctor mama says. "Shut your mouth."

Mother Tinu is now walking back to us. She is holding a folded white cloth and what look like a pack of long brooms. She reach us, and I see that she is holding four brooms. Each of the brooms is made up of long, very thin, and very many sticks tied together with a red thread around the top of it.

We use this kind of broom for sweeping the floor in Ikati. What are they using it for here?

"Take this," Mother Tinu says, giving the cloth to Ms. Tia. "Take off your clothes and put them on the floor. Tie this white cloth around your body, and the smaller one on your head."

Ms. Tia collects the cloth, and slowly, she pulls off her jeans, her t-shirt. She is wearing a pink brassiere and pink pant of lace material. Her stomach is the flat of floor, her skin smooth. There is a mark to the left of her belly button, darker than her skin, looks like a tiny upside-down map of Africa. She press the square of folded cloth between her breasts, saying nothing. Not one word. Her lips just shake and shake, like she wants to burst with angry words, but something is holding her back, tying her down.

"Come on, Tia," the doctor mama says. "We have to hurry. Tie the clothes around you, take off your bra and underwear. Those must go too. Is that right, Mother Tinu?"

"Yes, everything she came in. Be quick, please."

"Leave her to take her time," I say, my voice sharp.

"Shut your gutter mouth," the doctor mama says.

Ms. Tia ties the cloth around her chest and on her head. Next, she drops her pant to the floor, and pulls her brassiere out from her chest, drops it to the floor too.

"Now," Mother Tinu says to us, "will you two take a few steps back please?"

Me and the doctor mama, we take two steps

back and stand far from each other like enemies in a battlefield.

I watch as Mother Tinu takes Ms. Tia to the edge of the river.

I watch as the women stop their moaning, stand up on their feet at the same time, and collect the brooms from Mother Tinu at the same time, as if they been planning the movement for weeks.

I watch as one of the women pulls off Ms. Tia's cloth, exposing her naked, as she begins to whip her with the broom. At first, Ms. Tia is looking shocked. She is standing there, mouth open like small letter **O.** When it seems that she is understanding that they are flogging her, that she is collecting a whipping instead of a washing of water and soap, she starts to fight back. She kicks her legs and screams and says what the fork and what the hell, but the other three women, they hold her hands, and her legs, and cover her mouth, with no feelings on their face. No frown, no smile. Nothing. They struggle, pull Ms. Tia to the wet, muddy ground. One woman standing by Ms. Tia's head twists her two hands behind her back and ties them with a thick brown rope I didn't see before, and the other wraps the rope around her leg, making it tight with one thick knot.

They step back, pick up the brooms, and begin to whip.

I want to jump in front, to fight them with my life, to tear them away from my Ms. Tia, but something is gumming my legs to the floor, my hands to my side, and I am not able to move any part of me.

And so I watch as they whip, and whip, and whip, as Ms. Tia is rolling on the ground and screaming, until her fine smooth skin is having puncture from the sand, and until her whole body is becoming the red of the earth.

CHAPTER 46

By the time the women finish the flogging, Ms. Tia is no more shouting and screaming.

She is just staying on the floor, bleeding blood, her back full of so much marks. Mother Tinu collects the brooms from the other women and throws them into the river, puts her head up, shouts, "THE EVIL OF CHILDLESSNESS HAS BEEN CHASED OUT. PRAISE BE TO THE LIVING HIM!" The other four women, they clap their hands and say, "ELI-JAH!"

They pull Ms. Tia up, scoop water from the river edge, and pour it on Ms. Tia's body, ever so gentle, as if to say, **Sorry, sorry we flog you.**

When Ms. Tia turns, and I see her face, my legs become rubber. Like something yank out all my bones. I fall, pushing a cry deep inside of me. Ms.

Tia's face is full of so many whip marks, like the drawing hanging in her parlor, the one of clay head with no eyes and no mouth. Only this one is Ms. Tia. And she has eyes and mouth and ears and is feeling so much pain. And her eyes, her eyes have a look, of a wild animal, of a hunter that is wanting to kill.

A cry is boiling inside of me and I want to release it, but I feel a warm hand on my shoulder: the doctor mama.

"I didn't know," she says, whispering. There are tears shining in her eyes, her voice shaking, fingers on my shoulder shaking too. "I didn't know that they'd do this to her. That it would be this brutal, this bad. They told me it was just a bath. An ordinary, harmless bath. If I had known, I wouldn't have . . . I should have stopped them. My son is going to . . ." She sighs, snatching her hand from my shoulder. "Go and bring her clothes from the car."

I pick myself up and drag myself away from the place. My stomach is turning, the beans I ate yesternight seems to want to climb out of my throat. I stop my walking a moment, bend my knees by a short bush. I cough, pressing my stomach, but nothing is coming out. I wipe my mouth with my dress and make myself to keep walking.

Behind the church, from the open window, I see a woman on the floor, kneeling, holding a red candle in her hand, nodding, shouting "AMEN" and the prophet, he is bouncing, turning around, shouting, "ELI . . . ELI."

And the Jesus in the picture is no more vexing His face.

Now, He just looks tired. And sad.

CHAPTER 47

We drive home like dead bodies in a coffin.

Nobody is talking. Or moving. The car feels too small, coffin-size, the cold air from the air-con so dry, my lips feel like fish scales. We are breathing though. Hard, fast breathing. Slow, heavy breathing. We are saying many things with our breathing. We just don't talk. Don't say a word.

But there are words in my head, many things I want to say. I want to tell Ms. Tia I am sorry I made her come here. I want to ask why the doctor didn't come too. Why didn't he come and get a beating like his wife? If it takes two people to make a baby, why only one person, the woman, is suffering when the baby is not coming? Is it because she is the one with breast and the stomach for being pregnant?

Or because of what? I want to ask, to scream, why are the women in Nigeria seem to be suffering for everything more than the men?

But my mouth is not collecting the questions from my head, so I just keep it there. Keep it hanging, turning inside my head, causing a banging head pain.

The doctor mama try to make small talk with Ms. Tia. "I promise you that I had no idea what was going to happen—at least not to that extent," she says. "I wanted to stop them, but how could I go against so many women? And I thought of your miracle, your baby . . . Is there a, a way we can keep this between us? We can find a story to tell Ken, but he must not know that I allowed something so horrible . . . Think of what could happen in nine months, Tia."

Ms. Tia keeps her eyes to the window. She doesn't give the doctor mama any answer. Not one word to anybody. She is just sitting there, breathing fast, hard, her fingers on her lap are curling into each other so tight, the skin is nearly splitting.

We drive for about fifteen minutes until the go-slow in one street forces us to slow down, where one man selling ice cream in front of us holds up one block of ice cream and presses his nose to the window.

"Buy ice cream!" he says, and the closed window makes his voice sound as if he is chewing a cloth and talking at the same time.

But when he sees Ms. Tia's face with all the lines and marks, he becomes stiff, looking at Ms. Tia for a long, long moment, worry and concern all over his face, until the driver presses his horn to make him jump back.

The house is quiet when I enter.

Big Madam's car is not anywhere in the compound. Where has she gone? It is late now, around eight o'clock, and by this time, Big Madam will be sucking oranges inside her parlor, watching Sky tee-vee or CNN news channel and cursing Nigeria. I walk fast, my feet crunching the dry grass, until I reach the back of the kitchen. From the kitchen window, I see Kofi's buttocks up in the air, the top half part of his body inside the oven. I knock on the window, and he brings his head out from oven, makes a beckon.

I enter, greet him good evening. The whole place is smelling of sweet cakes. It turns my stomach, making me want to crawl somewhere and vomit the nothing in my stomach.

"Where have you been?" he asks, wiping his hand on the apron around his body.

"With Ms. Tia," I say. "Did Big Madam ask of me?"

"She's out," he says. "Her sister, Kemi, had an accident. She had to go to the hospital from the shop.

Not sure she'll be back anytime soon. Big Daddy is watching the news in the living room. Completely useless, that man. His sister-in-law is in hospital and he asked me to bake him cupcakes to have with his evening coffee." He rubs his hand together. "Oh, but I must show you the latest pictures of my project in Kumasi. The roofing is almost complete, and I had to ship the floor tiles from— **Chale,** why the long face? What happened? Did the school reject you? Did you hear from them?"

"I didn't hear from them," I say. "Any work for me to do this night?" I am so tired, but I want to wash and clean and scrub until I scrub away this afternoon out from my mind. Bleach it all away too. Make my mind white, blank.

"Well, there are some clothes that need ironing upstairs, but you don't look well. Go and lie down. If anybody asks, I will find something to say."

"Thank you," I say.

I turn around.

"Adunni," Kofi calls.

I stop, look him.

"Are you hungry?" he asks. "I can give you some cupcakes. You like cupcakes, don't you?"

"No, thank you," I say. "Good night."

He gives me a long look, sighs. "It will all make sense one day," he says. "One day, things will get better."

"I know," I say with a tiny, tired voice. "Tomorrow will be better than today."

"Abu is looking for you," Kofi say, "Shall I send him to your room?"

"Not this night," I say. I want to hear what Abu wants to say about Rebecca, but I don't want to hear it tonight. This night, I just want to crawl inside my bed and close my eyes and not think about anything or anybody.

"No problem," Kofi says. "Go and sleep."

CHAPTER 48

The sleep is not coming.

I find the sleep, beg it to come, but it is not coming. My eyelids feel like they are full of wet sand, as if I put a stone inside the middle of my eyeballs so that when I try to be closing it, it is scraping my eyes, causing it to hang in the middle of the open and the close. My chest is paining me too, paining from all the things I saw today, from a deep longing for Mama. I want her so much, just for one minute, so I can tell her about Ms. Tia, about what happened today, about the wicked things those women are doing in the church, things that are making God and me and Ms. Tia sad.

A sound cuts my thinking, two short **hoo**s of an owl in one of the trees, and I sit myself up, and peep the crack in the window, at the full moon in the sky casting a glow over the fields, at the grass looking like they are full of tiny blue-green light-bulbs, at the metal fence surrounding Big Madam's house, high and round and endless, and I wonder if I will ever leave this place, if things will ever be better for me.

When I go back and lie down on my bed, I don't sleep. I stay thinking about my life, Ms. Tia, Big Madam and her sick sister, about Big Daddy not even caring of his wife, about all the money rich people have and how the money is not helping them escape from problems, until the night turns and brings the morning light.

At the first light, I wash myself, wear my uniform, and find Kofi in the kitchen.

"Morning, Adunni," he says, slapping a egg on the edge of one glass bowl to crack it. "Do you feel better today?"

"Has Big Madam come back?" I ask.

Kofi shakes his head, yawns. "She's still at the hospital with her sister. I'm making breakfast for that glutton." He starts to turn the egg with a fork. "I didn't go to bed until midnight because of his cupcakes, and at four a.m., he sent me a text to bring up some scrambled eggs. What do you need Big Madam for? You know what to do. Get the broom—"

"I am going out," I say as I leave the kitchen. "If Big Madam comes back and asks of me, tell her I am . . . Tell her anything you want."

"Adunni," Ms. Tia says. "It's really early. Come on in."

She doesn't look good, Ms. Tia. Her hair is all hiding, packed up under one black scarf. Her eyes are all red and swollen, her face is looking as if they roasted her inside a fire instead of flogging her with brooms. The lines are all black and brown and angry, but it is her eyes that give me a shiver; the all at once red and angry of it.

"You been crying?" I make to touch her face, but she pulls herself back, twists the rope of her robe, and makes a tight bow in front of her stomach.

"Thanks for, for yesterday," she says. "I am sorry I made you come with me. It must have been horrible for you . . ." She presses two fingers to both of her eyes, keep it there a moment.

"I am sorry I didn't save you," I say. "I tried, but my legs, my legs was not working well."

She pulls my left cheek with a sad smile. "There was nothing you could have done. This was not your fault, okay?"

"Okay," I say. "The doctor mama, she said she didn't know those women will flog you. I don't think she is too much a bad woman."

Ms. Tia nods her head, real slow. "It doesn't matter," she says as she turns around and walks far into her compound. I follow her until we reach her kitchen back door. She didn't make to enter, so I stand there, the early-morning grass like a carpet of crushed ice under my feet.

"You haven't got shoes on," Ms. Tia says. "It's chilly."

"Your face," I say. "Is it paining you?"

"I will be fine," she says.

"Rub palm oil on your face every day. In no time, it will vanish. Then your skin be like a baby's own again."

She pulls me and gives me embrace so quick, I shock. "Thank you," she says. "You are one brave girl."

"What did the doctor say?" I ask, whispering. "When he saw your face, what did he say?"

Ms. Tia put her hands on her face and scrape her cheeks up and down as if to scrape away the stain of the memory. "He and his mother had a big fight. He accused her of hurting me. She said she was only trying to help. He told her she can't help, and he asked her to leave our home. When she left, he told me that the bath is useless, and that he—" She draws a breath, her chest climbing high. Then she begins to talk real fast, and her words are running inside theirselfs and almost confusing me.

"He cannot get me pregnant," she says. "His mother didn't know. He didn't tell anyone. Ken is infertile, unable to— That's why his ex, Molara, left him, why he started to help other families, I think, because he knows what they are going through. He said because we'd briefly discussed not having kids, he didn't think he needed to tell me he . . . Shit. Shit!" She kicks the back of the door, it shoots out, makes a bang on the wall. "Shit!" she says again, and when she starts to cry, I know she is not really needing the toilet.

"He didn't tell you this before you married him?" I say when she slows her cry and presses her finger to her eyes again.

"I had no idea," she says, her voice sounding like she put her throat in a blender, grind it with sand. "If I had known, we could have sought alternatives right from when we decided to start trying. At first he didn't tell me because he didn't think I needed to know, and then when we discussed having kids, he was afraid I would leave him if he told me, and I honestly don't know how I feel about that.

"And as if I hadn't had a crappy enough day, I got a call at midnight. My mum's infection is back. I'm going away for a few days. I leave first thing tomorrow." She sighs. "Maybe that's a good thing. It'll give me a chance to process everything."

"Tomorrow will be better than today," I say with a soft smile. "Not so?"

She coughs out a dry laugh. "I wish I could get those women arrested," she says. "That barbaric act must stop. It's bullshit."

"Very bullshit," I say, even though I am only knowing of cowshit and goatshit.

Ms. Tia laughs again, dips her hand inside her pocket, and brings out tissue. She blows her nose as if she wants to uproot it, then smash up the tissue and throws it into one white dustbin behind me. "I will try and stop by at Ocean Oil office as soon as I get back, to check the list, to see if the results have been published."

I feel the words escape from Ms. Tia's mouth, feel them hang like a cloud over my head, feel them drop down, cover my spirit, and drag me to somewhere far, somewhere like a dream. "And what if I enter?" I whisper. "How, what will I tell Big Madam?"

She focus her eyes on the space behind my head. "I will do the talking. I will tell her you got a scholarship and that you have to go."

"And what if . . ." I am afraid to say it, but I try: "What if I don't enter?"

"Adunni?"

"Yes, Ms. Tia?"

"Yesterday I tasted your normal," she says, picking up my hand.

"My normal?" I ask. "How it taste?"

"I read your essay, Adunni," she says. "You've been through so much, so bloody much, and yet you always have a smile, you cheeky thing, you always have a damn smile on your face. When I got flogged in that church, I felt a fraction of—" She drops my hand, drawing another breath to steady herself before she picks my hand again. "I felt a fraction of what you have had to endure for months. I tasted your normal, Adunni, and I have to say, you are the bravest girl in the world. And all this bullshit happening to me, that's nothing compared to what you've been through. Nothing."

My throat is a rock, a rock filled with water, with something else that I don't know what it is.

"My own bloody marital issues aside, I'll be back in about a week, and when I do, I will go and find out if you got it. If you did, I will get you enrolled. We will go shopping and buy every single thing you need to make you comfortable. And when you do get in, I will come visit you every time I get a chance. I will stand by you and support you in every way I can. I know it will be tough to get your madam to agree, but I will fight her with everything I have, every single resource. I will get her bloody arrested if I have to. This is your chance. You worked hard for it. Nothing will take it away. And to answer your question: If"—she hold my hand tight—"if, God forbid, you don't get selected, I will figure out something for you. You cannot continue to stay with Florence. No way. I just need time to figure something out, but let's wait and see what happens with the scholarship first, okay?"

I nod my head yes, and I am wanting to say thank you, but the tears are coming from my eyes and I am wanting to catch it with my hands, but she is gripping my hands so tight, the tears are sliding down my cheeks and down my neck and inside my dress.

CHAPTER 49

Fact: Despite the creation in 2003 of the National Agency for the Prohibition of Trafficking in Persons, to tackle human trafficking and related crimes, a 2006 UNICEF report showed that approximately 15 million children under the age of 14, mostly girls, were working across Nigeria.

Kofi is catching sleep in the backyard when I get back to Big Madam's house.

He is lying on a bench, his white chef-cap folded on his eyes to block the early-morning sun, and with his two hands across itself on his chest, he is resembling a dead person that is waiting to enter mortuary.

"Kofi?" I say and clap my hand two times. "Are you sleeping?"

"No, I am swimming," he says. "In the ocean."

He slaps the cap to the bench, pushes himself up. "Abu has been looking for you. He's getting frantic. Says he has to see you about something. What is it? And where did you run off to?"

"Tell Abu to find me in my room later," I say. "I went to Ms. Tia. I was full of worry for her. But all is okay now, I think."

"Why were you worried for her?"

I shrug, shake my head. I want to tell Kofi, but I cannot ever be telling him something so deep about Ms. Tia.

"So what if Big Madam was home?" he say. "Look at the filthiness of this compound! If that woman causes Big Madam to sack you before you can plan your way out of here, **chale,** I swear, all I will give you is tissue paper to dry your tears."

"How is her sister?" I ask. "Is it bad?"

"Her sister is in surgery," Kofi say. "Big Madam called a few minutes before you got here. She wants me to cook some fish stew and send it with that idiot she calls her husband. I don't think she'll be back for a few days. Why do you look so happy?"

I laugh, even though nothing is causing me a tickle. Something pinch my feet in that moment, making me want to dance, so I jump up and begin to sing to a song that has been in my head since I left Ms. Tia's house:

Eni lo j'ayo mi   **This is the day of my joy**
Lo j'ayo mi   **The day of my joy**

Kofi is watching me with a smile as I am turning around and around, going up and down, waving my broom in the air.

"Did Mr. Kola finally bring your salary?" he asks when I stop dancing. "Or, wait, let me guess? You heard back from the scholarship people? The results are out this week or next week, isn't it? Is that why you are so happy?"

"No any news about scholarship yet." I tap the broom head and begin to sweep the dry leaves. "And I didn't ever see that nonsense Mr. Kola man since he dropped me in this house. Mr. Kola is a slave trader. Him and Big Madam, they are slave-trading people like me. Only difference is I am not wearing a chain. I am a slave with no chain."

"Preparing for the scholarship has helped you learn a lot." Kofi puts his cap on his head, slaps it down. "So, illuminate my understanding. Tell me what you have been learning about the slave trade."

"The Slavery Abolition Act was signed in the year of 1833," I say as I sweep around his feet. "But nobody is answering the abolition. The kings in Nigeria from before, they were selling people into slave work. Today, people are not wearing chain on their slaves and sending them abroad, but slave trading is continuing. People are still breaking the act. I want to do something to make it stop, to make people to behave better to other people, to stop slave trading of the mind, not just of the body."

"**Chale,** I swear, if you can pull it off," Kofi says

with a side smile, "then kudos to you. And who knows, maybe someone will talk about you too one day. You know, as part of history."

I stop my sweeping, stand myself up to his level, and look him in the eyes.

"Not his-story," I say. "My own will be called her-story. Adunni's story."

CHAPTER 50

It is midnight.

The rain outside has been beating the roof like a gun shooting shots, the air smelling of the dust of the earth, of the hope of my independent. I am lying on my bed, talking to Mama, telling her about Ms. Tia and the doctor hiding things from her, about my scholarship result coming out very soon, when there is a knock on my room door.

Ko, ko, ko.

Three knocks. Abu.

I push myself up from the bed, run to the door, push the cupboard a little from the back of it, and open the lock. "Abu," I say. "Sorry I was not free yesternight when you were looking for me."

"Sannu," Abu say, greeting me with a quick bow of head. But he doesn't try to enter my room and

I don't ask him to enter. He stand outside, throw a quick look to the left and right of the dark corridor, before he puts a hand in his pocket, brings out a folding paper. His face is a shadow of fear, his **jalabiya** wet with rainwater and gumming to his chest. "I left Big Madam in the hospital so I can give you this thing. Adunni, this thing I want to give you, you cannot say it is from me. You did not get it from me. **Walahi,** if anybody ask you and you say it is me, I will tell them you are lying!"

"What is it?"

"I found it in the car, about a week after Rebecca was missing. It was inside the 350 Benz Big Daddy is always using to go out," he say. "I have been keeping it for too long, but now the load of it is weighing me down, making it hard for me to say my prayers. **Dan Allah,** Adunni, I beg you, take this thing from me! Take it."

He presses the paper into my hand as if it is an evil curse that he doesn't want to hold with his own hands, and folds my fingers to cover it. "Adunni, hear this because after today, I will not talk about this thing again. See. The day after Rebecca was missing, I went to wash the 350 Benz because Big Daddy asked me to wash it. I washed outside, but inside the car . . ." He draws a breath. "Inside, the front seat was wet. Wet like somebody poured water on it. So I stop washing, run to Big Daddy to ask who wet the front seat. He said he did not know. I asked Big Madam, she said maybe Glory, her shopgirl, maybe she poured water by mistake. I asked Glory, she said she didn't pour any water on the seat. It was when I found this letter after one week of Rebecca missing, and I read it, that I know why the seat was wet. And since then, I have been keeping the letter, carrying the load."

"Why are you telling me about wet seat?" I ask, confused.

"The letter"—Abu shakes his head, as if the memory is causing him pain, as if I didn't just ask him a question—"it was deep inside the seat belt buckle. Inside. I only saw it because I was trying to buckle it, to wipe it clean, and the buckle was refusing to work. When you open the letter, look it well, you will understand everything I am saying. I am going back to Big Madam in the hospital. **Sai gobe.** Good night."

Before I can say one word, Abu bow quick, turn around, and disappear into the darkness.

I fold out the paper with shaking hands. A short letter with no end. The writing is small and neat in black biro, and each letter is measuring the same tall and wide size, the same space in the middle of the letters, but near the end of the letter, the writing is changing to rough, like the person was hurrying up, and what is that stain on it?

I hold the letter up in the light. The edge look like it was inside a struggle, like the scattered teeth of a mad man, or the edge of Kofi's bread knife, and near that edge is a print or two of a finger dipped in blood. I look at it well, at the red-brown color, the stain of dried blood, around the fingerprint, and I think, as my heart is starting to climb a ladder of fear, that the person who was writing this was bleeding blood.

My room seem to turn around on itself as I try to steady my jumping heart, to set myself and read:

My name is Rebecca. I am a housemaid of Chief and Florence Adeoti, which we are calling Big Madam and Big Daddy. I am pregnant for Big Daddy. Big Daddy forced me to sleep with him at first, then he promised to marry me if I am sleeping with him all the time. Sometimes, when Big Madam is at home, Big Daddy will put sleeping medicine inside Big Madam's cup of juice at night so she will sleep when he is coming to my room.

When I found myself pregnant, Big Daddy was very happy. He said he will marry me and that me and Big Madam will be his two wives and live in this house together. Since he told me, I have been so happy.

This morning, he said we are going to the hospital to see the doctor, but I want to write this letter because after eating the food Big Daddy bought for me, my stomach has been paining me, and I am somehow afraid that Big Madam will be angry about

About what, Rebecca? Why didn't you finish the letter? What happen to make you stop writing and hide it inside the seat belt buckle?

I fold and fold the paper until I cannot fold it again, until it is a small, hard rectangle, a bullet-looking thing. My whole body is shaking. Big Daddy is the boyfriend that Kofi and Chisom were talking about. But why did she take off the waist beads? Why is there blood on the letter? Did he kill her? Or did he keep her somewhere?

I squeeze the letter in my hand, feeling something bitter form inside my heart like a rock as I climb my bed and lie there like that for nearly one hour, thinking about Rebecca, fearing so much for what happened to her, that when there is a twist on my door handle, I don't hear it.

When it comes again, I sit up straight. At first, I think it is the rain, maybe it caused a twig outside to crack, snap to the floor, but when the cupboard groans from behind the door, when it begins to move, I sit up.

"Abu?" I say, standing. I didn't lock the door on myself when he left, but I pushed the cupboard just a little to block it. Did Abu turn back from going to the hospital to meet Big Madam because maybe he wants to tell me more things about Rebecca? "Abu?"

I don't hear any answer from Abu, and my room door is still opening, still pushing the cupboard door more and more back, still scraping the floor.

"Who?" I whisper, standing still beside my bed, afraid to move. "Who is there? Who is it?"

Big Daddy. I know it is him. I can smell his drink from where I am standing, can feel his evil inside my room.

I want to move to the door, to push it back, but I know I don't have the strong power to match his own, so I bend myself low, slide under the bed, and close my eyes.

When he enters, I lie still, make myself a wood log, a dead body. I hear the shift of his feet on the floor as he is coming closer, the ruffle of his cloth. My hand feels something like a ball of cloth and I grip it, hold it tight as if it will save me from Big Daddy.

"Adunni?" His voice is a whisper, dragging with drink. He stops near my bed, his feet so close, so near my mouth. His big toe is ugly, looks like a bending arrow, the toenails long and black, curving into the floor. I think to snap his nail off with my teeth, to bite his toe till he bleeds.

"I know you are here," he whispers.

The bed creaks and hisses as the mattress is pressing down on my face, the spring inside pressing into my head, my shoulders, my chest, as if to drill a hole through my bones and flesh. His body on the bed is crushing, closing my chest down, down, until I cry. A soft cry, inside of me, but he hears it.

"Aha!" His face is looking at me. There are eyes everywhere on his face, evil-wicked eyes.

"Aha!" he says again as he grabs my feet and drags me and all the dust from under the bed. He falls on top of me, his whole body stinking like sweat of three years.

Fight.

Is that Ms. Tia talking or my mama?

Adunni, fight. Scream.

I scream until my voice is tearing, until I am not hearing myself, until my scream is entering the rain noise and coming back as a thunder. He tries to cover my mouth with his palm, but I knee his stomach; it makes a **pffts** sound, and he groans, slaps my face, dazing me a moment.

"Behave yourself," he grunts. "Behave!"

His two hands are nailing me down now, trapping me under his body, but I bite his cheeks, taste the salt of his blood, the drink in his skin, and spit it on his face.

I hear the snipping of his trouser zip. The grunt as he is pressing me down on the floor. His breath is smelling of rotten teeth, of something sweet: the vanilla scenting Kofi is putting in his cupcakes.

Fight.

My hand is dead. My legs are pinned down. How can I fight? I keep to twisting my head left to right, right to left, saying **no, no, no,** but his palm, wet and hot, is pressing on my mouth and catching my no and pushing it into my nose.

Mama, I cry inside of me. **Save me, Mama.**

There is a sudden flash of light from outside, the

same blink from the past, from the day with Morufu, only this time, it comes with a shout of thunder, a powerful rumble, and I know Mama is here. Mama is fighting for me. **Fight, Adunni. Fight.**

I gather all my strength, clamp my teeth on his hand, sink it into his flesh. When he shouts, I twist from under him, snatch up my mama's Bible from the bed, and smash it on his head. His phone, which was lighting up with a number and making a noise in his pocket, fly out, land on the floor, twist around and around like a fan, and keep ringing and ringing.

Big Daddy howls like an animal. "Bitch," he says, coming for me.

Just then, the door is bursting open and the earth is shaking and Big Madam is standing in the middle of the door, inside my room, and Big Daddy is zipping his zip and pushing Big Madam out of his front and running out of my room.

Big Madam, looking like she is dazed, walk like a ghost, pick up Big Daddy's ringing phone from the floor, and press it. Then she is staring at it, and staring at it, and I don't know what she is seeing inside the phone, but it is something very bad and very scary and I think more scary than what was happening with me, because Big Madam, she smash her knees to the ground of my room, put her hand on her head, and is starting to wail: "Chief, ha! Caroline! Baby love? No!"

She look such a sorry sight that I forget about myself and Rebecca and Big Daddy for a moment.

I just want to help Big Madam and beg her to stop crying, but she keeps looking at the phone, keeps pressing it, and her mouth keeps opening wide, wider than I ever see, wider more than the River Benue, which is one of the widest of all the rivers in the whole of Nigeria.

CHAPTER 51

Everything after that just fly away so quick, as if I blink it all away.

I remember Big Madam sitting on the floor in my room, crying and crying, and then, when I finally make a move to touch her, she stares at me like she is seeing me for the first time in my life, before she push me away and run out, run far to the main house.

I am by myself in the room now, but I can still smell him.

His sweat. His rotting teeth. The drink. I smell fear too. The hairs on my hand are standing up, as if rising to the fear with respect, saying, **Welcome, sah, welcome, ma.**

The rain outside is now stopping and there is no more thundering noise and everywhere is so silent, but there is the faint moan of a woman about to born a baby afar, a woman inside a deep, deep well, a dull trapping noise that fills my whole room with something thick that I am not seeing with my two naked eyes but I am feeling inside of my heart, and so I pick myself up and run to the main house.

First thing I see when I enter the parlor is Big Madam's wig. It is hanging from one of the mirrors on the wall, looking like the skin of one dead bush-rat. Cushions are all over the floor, near the tee-vee, by the standing fan, around the feet of the sofa. Big Madam's gold high-heel shoes are scattered here and there, her feather handbag is open, and lipsticks, eyeshadows, pencils, money, everything is crawling out from it.

Big Madam is sitting on the sofa. She doesn't open her eyes when I enter, don't even do as if she can hear me. She keeps her eyes closed, and with the tears running down her swelling face, I feel the block of bitter inside me begin to melt. There is blood around her mouth, and she is pressing the place near her jaw with shaking hands. She is moaning still, but not loud like before. Now it just sounds like she is breathing out noise with her mouth.

"Where is Big Daddy?" My whole body is dripping wet with rainwater and anger, the letter in my hand is a wet leaf. "Where is he?"

She opens her eyes, slow, as if her eyelids are too heavy, but she will not look at me. She looks drunk too, like she's been drinking the drink of sorrow and pain.

"I have a letter, ma," I say. "From Rebecca."

"Rebecca is gone," she says, voice dragging. "Gone—"

"I know, ma," I say. "But she write something here. In this letter."

I bring out the letter. The biro ink on the paper is changing color because of wet, the words fading in some parts. "I should read it for you?" I ask.

She shakes her head, opens up her hand, and I give her the letter. She stares at the paper, at the words in it, but I don't think she reads it, her eyes are too swollen, nearly blind with pain. She puts the letter on her chest as if she wants to use the paper to wrap the pieces of her breaking heart, to pack it and seal it up.

"Chief has killed me," she says after a long, long moment. She is not talking to me but to herself and the air. "I could understand the other girls, I tolerated them, I even took care of his mess. But this time, he went too far. Chief Adeoti, you went too far!"

I turn myself around and go to the kitchen. Kofi is not there. I fill a bowl with warm water and take a cloth. Back inside the parlor, I dip the cloth in warm water, squeeze it out, and then slowly begin to wipe the blood from Big Madam's mouth, the tears from her eyes, the shaking from her hands. And at first, she struggles, but I hold her two hands tight until she slacks herself and closes her eyes, until she accepts that sometimes even the strongest of people can suffer a weakness.

I sing the song my mama was teaching me when I was growing up in the village, the same one I was singing when I was first coming to Lagos, and when I check, Big Madam's eyes are still closed, but this time, she is snoring softly, so I pluck the letter from where it has floated to the floor, and go to my room.

CHAPTER 52

Fact: About 30% of businesses registered in Nigeria are owned by women. The continued growth of these businesses, which is critical to sustaining the economy, is largely hindered by limited access to funds and by gender discrimination.

Chale, what the hell happened in this house last night?"

Kofi is standing in front of my room door, blinking as if somebody slapped his head with a big plank of wood. "What's going on?"

I couldn't sleep all night.

My mind felt like it was inside the washing machine, tumbling and tumbling, until this morning when Kofi knocked the door of my room, freeing me from the tumbling of the mind.

"The living room was in a state when I got in this morning," Kofi says. "Big Daddy is not home, and Big Madam looks like she got hit by a lorry. What happened?"

"Where did you go?" I ask, keeping one hand on the door, the other holding my nightdress. Kofi

didn't ever behave to me in a bad way, but after yesternight, I cannot be talking to any man without
fearing he will jump on me.

"Big Daddy gave me some time off," he says.
"Last night, he asked me to take a break, to go away
for the night. Since Big Madam was at the hospital
with her sister, I took the opportunity to go and see
my old friends at the Ghana High Commission. To
be honest, I was skeptical when he gave me some
time off, but I was so tired from cooking for Big
Madam's— What happened?"

"Nothing," I say.

"**Chale,** talk to me. Did Big Daddy come here?"
His face falls, and he presses a hand to his chest.
"I should have known when he insisted I should go
away for the night. Adunni, talk to me. Why are
you just standing there and staring? What did he
do to you?"

"Nothing," I say. "What do you want?"

"Did he rape you?" Kofi asks, his voice climbing
high. "Did that imbecile rape you?"

The word "rape" sounds like a knife-cutting, a
stabbing, a word I never heard of in my life, but
I know I am not needing the Collins to check
the meaning.

"He didn't rape me," I say, voice soft. The memory of it is still giving me shivers, still causing my
heart to bang in my chest. "Big Madam opened the
door before it happened."

Kofi spits on the floor. "**Kwasea.** God punish him."

"Did Rebecca go to school?" I ask. "How was her English? Was she sharp in the brain?"

"Rebecca? She spoke good English but was very naïve for her age," Kofi says. "Her former boss—before Big Madam—educated her. Sent her to a private primary and secondary school and even took her on holidays with the family. When the woman died, Rebecca came here to work. Why are you asking?"

"Nothing," I say. If Rebecca was a wise girl, she will know that Big Daddy cannot marry her and keep her in the same house with Big Madam. She will know the man was telling lies. Now I know that speaking good English is not the measure of intelligent mind and sharp brain. English is only a language, like Yoruba and Igbo and Hausa. Nothing about it is so special, nothing about it makes anybody have sense. "Do you have a sample of anything she write?" I ask. I want to be sure so that Big Daddy will not say it is somebody else that write that letter. I want to be sure that Big Daddy will suffer for Rebecca because Bamidele didn't suffer for Khadija.

Kofi shakes his head. "Abu might have something; she always gave him the shopping list. I would ask him, but he's been away as well since last night. He should be back this morning."

I make to close my room door, but Kofi blocks it with his hand. "Big Madam wants you," he says. "She said you should come straight up to her room, right inside. Why would she ask you to come to her room? She never asks anyone into her room—least of all you. What am I missing here?"

"Thank you," I say, and close the door.

"Come on in," Big Madam says when I reach her bedroom.

Her whole face is a sore wound and I stand there a moment, not moving, even though the door is wide-open. She is wearing a long red robe that looks like red silk wings around her body. Her hand is on the door handle, holding it open for me.

"Come in," she says again, turning and walking away. "Shut the door, take a seat on that chair."

I step in. There is a round bed right in the center of the room, with feather cover-cloth and like fifteen pillows, I am not sure how she will find space to sleep in the bed. There are pictures of her children when they were young lining up the wall on my side, of them laughing inside playground, and one of Big Madam when she was young. She looks so slim in the picture, her skin smooth-looking, I am almost wanting to touch it, to say sorry for how her face will swell in the future because of Big Daddy.

A strange smell, a mix of toilet bleach and dirty feet, fills my nose, and I see the dressing table on my left, filled with big bottles of cream and a nylon makeup bag that is full of all sorts of powder, eye color, pencils, and lipsticks. I catch the names on the bottles: InstaWhite Plus Skin Milk, Skin Fade (New & Improved), Bright Bleaching Mix.

Why is Big Madam wanting to bleach her skin? And with these smelling creams? She is looking fine in the picture of herself on the wall, with her skin before. Is this why her face keeps having different colors, why her legs are brown on the ankle and the knees but the rest is a pale, sicking yellow, sometimes green?

I sit down in the long purple chair facing Big Madam's bed and fold my dress in my lap. "Kofi says you want to see me. I am here."

She looks at her nails as if she is checking it for swelling. "I must ask you, Adunni. Yesterday, did Chief, did he—"

I shake my head no. "He didn't rape me."

She snaps her head up, tight her eyes. "You know what 'rape' means?"

"Yes, ma," I say.

"Tia Dada, Dr. Ken's wife, she called me yesterday. She told me she wants to come and see me, to discuss your future. What stupid future? Who does she think she is? How much of your salary has she ever paid? Or does she think you are one of her environmental projects?" She draws a breath. "She hung up when I asked her that question, and I swear, I saw red. My head was boiling. I left my sister in hospital and told my driver to take me home. My plan was to find you and give you the kind of beating that will reset your brain and throw you out into the streets, because Adunni, you have brought me nothing but trouble since you got here. Tia Dada is not my mate. She cannot even be up to forty years old, and she is hanging up the phone on me? I was going to deal with you first, then face her and deal with her, but what did I find in your room instead? My husband." She stops talking, but her lips keep shaking.

"Chief goes to church. He is a member of the Men of Virtue group. How can a man go to church for so long, for years, and not find God?" Big Madam ask this as if she lost, confuse.

"Because God is not the church," I say, keeping my chin down, my voice low.

I want to tell her that God is not a cement building of stones and sand. That God is not for all that putting inside a house and locking Him there. I want her to know that the only way to know if a person find God and keep Him in their heart is to check how the person is treating other people, if he treats people like Jesus says—with love, patience, kindness, and forgiveness—but my heart is running fast and beating hard and making me want to piss, so I pinch something from my uniform, a red thread, and roll it around and around in my fingers until it is a small knot, a thread-full-stop.

She presses a hand on her knees, leans forward. "Adunni, I have been thinking about Tia's phone call. Do you know what Tia Dada wants to discuss with me?"

"No, ma," I say, whisper. "I don't know."

Big Madam nods her head slowly. "If she wants to take you away from here, will you go with her?"

I nod.

"Because of what Chief did?"

I am not sure of what to tell her, my mind is wanting to say many things, but I am fearing she will vex for me, so I only say a small part of what is coming to my mind. "Because you are not very always kind to me and Kofi. You beat me and make me cry to miss my mama. And because of Big Daddy."

I bite my lip to stop talking, but in my mind, my mouth keeps on moving: **Because if Rebecca was your Kayla, you will not rest, not for one night or one day, until you are finding her. And because you are slave-trading me and you are letting Big Daddy slave-trade you.**

She leans back and closes her eyes, and when she starts to speak, her voice is so low, as if I am no more in her front, and she and herself are talking to each other: "How could Chief do this to me? To us? How do I carry on without Chief by my side? What do I tell people when they ask me what happened?"

He wasn't ever by your side. Except maybe when he is blowing you in the face.

"What do you mean by that?" Big Madam snaps her eyes open, voice sharp.

Was my voice in my head, or was I speaking out? I start to shake my head no, to make up one lie, but she says, "Adunni! What. Do. You. Mean. By. That? Tell me exactly what you mean before I grind you to powder."

I twist the edge of my dress around and around my finger until the blood is no more flowing to the finger. "It is Big Daddy, ma. He is a bad man. Very wicked."

I raise my head as something twist a tap inside my mouth open, and the words, bitter and true and sharp, start to pour out. "He beats you nearly every time and fills you up with so much anger and sadness that when you see me and Kofi, you pour all of the anger out on us, on me most of all. Your husband, he makes you sad and . . ." **And mad.**

"Sorry, ma," I say, when I see how her eyesballs are nearly climbing out of her head. "You asked me to say what I mean and, and I am just saying what I mean. The end." I push out a breath, feeling like a balloon that is losing all the air until it is becoming flat, with no power to float again, so I stand to my feet, real slow, and look around the room like a fool because I don't want to look at her face.

"Can I massage your feet?" I ask. "Or scratch your hair before I go? Yesterday, I sang a song and you fall asleep. Can I sing for you? A song that my mama—"

"Go," she says, waving me to the door, her eyes wet, angry. "Get out of my sight!"

CHAPTER 53

At night, there is banging on the gate, a crazy horning, as if the person driving the car put his hand on the horn and slap, slap, slap it. When the sound doesn't go away after three minutes, I stand up from my bed and peep out of my room.

"That fool has been horning for close to thirty minutes," Kofi says from where he is standing in the corridor, scratching his eyes and yawning.

"Which fool?" I ask, coming out of my room and closing the door. I stand beside him, and together we look to the darkness, where the night is one thick wall of black, and the crickets and the horning are filling the air turn by turn, making it one kind crazy melody sounding song: **peen— kre-kre—peen—kre-kre.**

"Big Daddy," Kofi says. "He's the one horning

like a maniac. Big Madam instructed Abu and me not to open the gate for him, which is very strange."

"Why is it very strange?" I ask.

"Because she has never instructed us not to let him in. Not even when she is sure he's been to see his girlfriend."

"You've seen his girlfriend before?"

"He has a few," Kofi says. "I have seen one of them—a girl he picks up at Shoprite. Skinny thing. Looks like a twelve-year-old. A gust of wind would snap her in two on a good day. But that's the fool's problem." Kofi bend his neck, eye me. "So, what did Big Madam say to you when she called you to her room?"

"Nothing," I say as another horn noise blast the air. "Why did Big Madam say we don't open the gate?"

Kofi shrugs. "As I said, she's never done that before. If anything, she'll direct me to make sure Big Daddy's food is served, no matter how late he gets back home. You should have seen her when she gave us the instruction, Adunni. Her eyes were raw, full of something I have never seen before. Something like steel. Resolve."

"Did you ask Abu? For the list for shopping?"

"Ah, yes." Kofi puts his hand into his trouser pocket, brings out a paper. "Here it is. The last shopping list she wrote before she . . . you know."

I take the paper, open it. The writing—a list of

shopping for Fairy Soap, White Rice, Cling Film, Tissue Paper, and Bleach—is the same as the letter.

My heart sighs. "Kofi, did you ever see her and Big Daddy together?"

"A few times." Kofi frowns, his forehead flesh dividing into three thick lines of skin. "I had caught him leaving Rebecca's room a few times. They seemed close, unusually so, especially when Big Madam was away. I asked her about it, told her to be careful with him, but she always laughed and said I was jealous. Why would I be jealous of a fool? I know how every single maid we've had always seemed to interest him. Which was why I warned you to be careful of him from the very first day. I warn every single maid that comes to work in this house."

I feel a chill, it comes so sudden, causing the hair on my hand to stand up. "Did Big Madam go to Rebecca's house in the village? To find her?"

Kofi shakes his head. "I heard Mr. Kola went a week or two after she disappeared. Big Madam, as far as I am aware, did not go anywhere."

There is another horning, and Big Madam, her voice like five thunders, screams from the main house: "Go back to the hell you are coming from, Chief! No one is opening this gate for you."

Who knows what that man did to her? My eyes surprise me, bring out tears. I wipe it quick. "I am going back into my room."

"Same here," Kofi says, yawning again. "Looks like the fool is going to spend a night with mosquitoes in the car. It's the least the bastard deserves for all he's put everyone through."

Big Madam stays locked up for the two days. She doesn't go to her shop or to church or to anywhere. She stays in her room and sleeps. In the morning, Kofi will take up her food of yam and egg, or bread and boiled egg, or toast and tea, and she will only bite a pinch, send the rest down, which Kofi will give me to eat. At night, she will send for me to come and massage her feet. She doesn't talk when I massage her feet, she just sits there, trapping her tears with her eyes. I want to show her the letter again, but I sense that her heart is so heavy, it weighs her down, too down to even hear what I want to say.

Big Daddy is nowhere around the house. We don't see him, and we don't ask questions, but we whisper to ourselves, me and Kofi, or Kofi and Abu, or me and myself. We talk about where Big Daddy is, and if he will ever be coming back, but it is all empty talk, nobody is knowing anything, nobody is seeing anything.

The third evening after Big Daddy left the house, Big Madam sent for me to come to her room.

This time, I find her sitting in the purple chair, holding her phone to her ear. She waves at me to wait, and so I stand to one corner and keep my hands behind my back. She is looking a lot better, the sore red under her eyes is now the purple of the chair she is sitting on.

"Chief's people are coming here tomorrow," she says to the phone. "No, I don't think you need to come. You need to concentrate on getting better. I know they want to beg me to take him back in. One of his useless sisters sent me a text message last night; Chief has been demanding money from them. He couldn't even fuel the Mercedes. I always used to put petrol in that car." She laughs a sad laugh and shakes her head. "Ah, Kemi, I have been a fool. A big fool."

Yes, ma, I say with my eyes. **A very big fool.**

"Where was his family when I was struggling to build my client list? To raise our children? To pay the bills? You are my sister." She wipes her left eye with a finger. "You know what I went through with this man. How I suffered to support our family with my business. I never told you this, Kemi, but for years, I would bring home the money I made and give it to Chief, and he would pocket my money and still beat me and carry his girlfriends. Still, I gave him clothes to wear, took care of him. I covered his shame. I turned a blind eye to his nonsense, but for him to do this . . . with, with Caroline Bankole from the WRWA! Right under my nose. No, please don't tell me to calm down. No, I am not imagining things. I wish I was.

"I told you how I found the phone he'd been calling her with. The fool stored her number as 'Baby Love.' Baby love? From Chief? He has never called me anything love! . . . Kemi, why are you asking me these senseless questions? What do you mean by 'Are you sure?' Of course I am sure! I confronted her! She said it was the devil's fault. The devil? Does that even make sense? This is a woman I called my friend. My friend." She presses a shaking hand to her mouth to cover her crying noise, and my heart is shifting as I think of Caroline Bankole, the cat with green eyes and bitter orange smell, of the woman who is kind to Chisom because Chisom is keeping her secrets, of the night Big Daddy was talking on the phone behind the boys' quarters.

This must be what Big Madam read in his phone the day she found it in my room, why she is still keeping Big Daddy locked out from the house, why she is looking like she will just die any day now from the pain and shame of it all. And me, I was here thinking she was sad and angry because Big Daddy wanted to rape me.

Big Madam is now listening and nodding and sighing, but I cannot hear what the other woman is saying. "I don't know what prayers would do for me right now, Kemi," she says finally. "Go and rest, you need it."

She throws her phone to the bed, and when she looks at me, her eyes dig a hole into my heart and pours her sorrow into the hole, burying me with it.

"Massage my feet," she says, stretching out her two legs in front of her. "My ankles are swollen." I nod my head, bend, pick up her feet and put them in my lap. I rub my thumb and fingers on her ankles, her toes, slowly, as if to press away all the pain that she has been carrying for so long, releasing her from the prison of herself, her pain.

We stay like that a moment, she releasing the pain, me working it out from her legs, her body.

"I am going to have him arrested," she says suddenly, as if she is just thinking of it. "Yes, that is it. He will be arrested for Rebecca's disappearance, and I will make sure he rots in jail unless he can produce that girl." She rests her head back, closes her eyes. "Adunni?"

"Ma?"

"The night that . . . that Big Daddy tried to . . . Do I recall you saying Rebecca wrote a letter?"

"Yes, ma," I say as hope is rising inside me. I have been waiting for her to ask me about it, waiting for when she will do something to help Rebecca.

"I want to see it," she says. "To read it properly. Bring it to me first thing tomorrow. For now, I need to sleep. My eyes sting. Sing for me."

"Yes, ma."

And so I sing as if my mama is sitting in that purple chair, as if I want to empty out all my voice and cause it to make Big Madam feel all better. I sing as if I want to make Rebecca not missing, to make Ms. Tia's husband not having problem of making Ms. Tia pregnant, as if I want to stop myself from feeling sad that Big Madam is feeling sad.

When I finish my song and look up, Big Madam's eyes are closed. Soft puffs of air escape from her open mouth, but her jaw keeps on twitching every one or two seconds, as if she is biting on the remaining peace left inside her soul, fighting to hold it with her teeth.

But the peace is stubborn; it slips out of her grip and crashes around us.

CHAPTER 54

Fact: A 2003 study of over sixty-five countries suggested that the happiest and most optimistic people in the world live in Nigeria.

I have been awake since five, lying on my bed and listening to a peacock screaming like a bush baby afar in a neighbor's house, to the wind sweeping the leaves from the coconut trees against the window-louvers in my room, to the faraway sound of Kofi banging pots and plates in the kitchen.

My body feels stiff, like I need some oiling to move, some housework to keep me moving. I stand, pull out Rebecca's letter from under my pillow, fold it into a neat square, and push it into my brassiere. After I wear my uniform, I put on my shoes, taking my time to push the thinning leather rope of it inside the buckle, because I don't want it to cut and give up finally.

Outside, the air is cold, and a thin cloud of wet is covering the grass. The sky is so clear; there is no end to the blue-gray of it. I walk quickly, and find Kofi in the kitchen, slicing a loaf of bread with a big knife.

"Good morning," I shout to him as I pick the broom behind the kitchen tap in the backyard, tap the head, and begin to sweep, again, slowly, as if the floor is the long, long hair of a dear friend, and my broom is the comb.

"Adunni," Kofi calls, "I have been waiting for you to come out. Come, come. Drop that broom."

I put the broom on the floor, wipe my hands, and enter the kitchen. I stop in front of the gas cooker, near him. "What happened?"

"I just got off a call from my friend at the embassy," he says. "He says the results came out yesterday. Once I finish my morning work, I will go and find out if you got in."

"Thank you, Kofi," I say. "Ms. Tia too will check it. Has Big Madam gone to her shop?" I ask Kofi.

"Not today," Kofi says, still whispering. "We have guests in the reception. Big Daddy's two sisters. The fool himself is there too, they came in a few minutes ago. Big Madam says we shouldn't let them into the living room, so they are all at the reception."

Can Big Daddy try and do something bad to me today? With everybody here?

"Adunni." Big Madam enters the kitchen wearing a black **bou-bou,** the black of a mourner. Her eyes are the sad of a young widow, the purple around them a fading mark. "What are you doing in here? Go and find food to eat."

I touch my chest. "Me? Find food to eat?"

"Do you have the . . . that letter?" she asks.

"Yes, ma," I say. "You want it now, ma?"

"I will call you when I need it," she says. "Kofi, keep Adunni at the back and find something for her to eat. I am expecting a police officer. Chief and his family must remain in the reception. Serve them food if they want, but please don't let them into any other rooms in the house apart from the downstairs toilet."

When Big Madam leaves, Kofi shakes his head. "Police officer? What for? You told me Big Daddy didn't rape you. Why did you lie? What letter is she talking about?"

"Big Daddy didn't rape me," I say.

And then I tell him about Rebecca's letter.

I stay in the backyard, sweeping, until Kofi calls me.

"I should bring the letter?" I ask as I enter the kitchen. He is standing beside the door that is leading to the reception, pressing his ear against the glass of it. There is flour on his nose, a big dot of white powder on his smooth skin.

"Don't say a word," he whispers, pressing a finger to his two lips, **sshh.** "Just come and hear what they are saying."

I walk to him, my heart sounding louder than my feet as I stand beside him and press my eyes to the cloudy glass of the door. I can see shadows: of Big Madam, a big black mountain sitting behind a setting sun; of Big Daddy, his **fila** perching like a small, sleeping ostrich on his head; and of two women, one tall and the other short, the **geles** on their heads a shadow of two giant hands.

"Where is the police man?" I ask Kofi, talking low.

"That one." Kofi presses his finger to the shadow of a man standing far left. Big Madam's voice is the loudest of all, and she is sounding very angry:

"Officer Kamson, as I briefed you on the phone, I want this man, my husband, taken away and questioned. I have reason to believe he is involved in the disappearance of my former housemaid. I think he might have harmed her. Take him with you to your station and detain him!"

"Do you have any evidence of your allegations, Madam Florence?" Officer Kamson asks.

The letter! I shout in my head, pressing my nose against the glass of the door so hard, I am fearing it will crack any moment now. **Tell the police about Rebecca's letter.**

"Come on, Florence," Big Daddy says. "This is just ridiculous. What do you think I did with Rebecca? Of all people, Rebecca? So what if she is missing? She could have run away!" He turns to the police officer. "Officer Kamson, listen to me. I swear to the god of my fathers that I do not know anything about that girl's disappearance. I have my weaknesses, but to cause a girl to disappear? Why would I do that?"

"Shut your mouth!" Big Madam's shout is so sharp, it makes everybody jump, including me and Kofi. Kofi even bangs his head on the glass door, but before anybody inside can turn to look at us, Big Madam says: "Why don't you tell Officer Kamson about the affair you've been having with my close friend Caroline Bankole?"

The silence, it falls like a sudden storm, a thunder with no boom.

Big Madam's breathing in and out is the only noise for a long, long moment until one of the two sisters falls inside the sofa and puts her hand on her head. "God forbid. This is the devil at work."

"The devil, my foot," Kofi whispers. "The devil, my left testicle."

"Madam Florence." Officer Kamson shifts from one foot to the other. "I understand you are upset with your husband, rightly so. But you invited the Nigeria Police Force here for a reason. Why do you think your husband might have a hand in Rebecca's disappearance? Housemaids are known to jump from employer to employer, aren't they? As far as we are aware, she hasn't been reported missing. And"—he clears his throat—"if you suspect she was having an affair with your husband before she disappeared, ma'am, then it would make sense to invite you both for questioning."

"Me?" Big Madam says as her hands fly to her chest. "Did your boss not tell you about me before he sent you here? I am telling you to take my husband away and detain him and you are talking about investigating me. Questioning me. You must be crazy!"

"Florence, please," Big Daddy says, and everybody turns to look at him. He drops to his knees in front of Big Madam. "Please ask Officer Kamson to go away so you and I can talk about this Caroline thing, man to wife. It was a big mistake, a terrible, terrible mistake. I can explain everything."

Big Madam shakes her head and wipes her face with the edge of her **boubou.**

"Please," Big Daddy's sister says, "let us put this issue about Rebecca going missing to one side so that our brother can move back home. Look at him, on his knees! He is suffering enough as it is. He has nowhere to live. Please, Florence, take him back. Tomorrow, we will gather everybody and have a family meeting to discuss the other matter."

Big Madam pushes out a deep breath. She seems like she is losing the fight of life, and I want to jump and bang the door and tell her to show them the letter from Rebecca. To tell them about me. But Kofi, he can sense my jumping spirit, my angry soul, and he presses a hand on my hand, as if to say, **Slow it, Adunni. Take it slow.**

"You can go, Officer," Big Madam says with a low, quiet voice. "I think . . . I will be in touch when we need you. Sorry for the inconvenience." Turning to Big Daddy, she says, "Chief, I never want to see you in my house ever again. Abu will pack your things. Get them from him at the gate. Do not forget to hand him my car keys."

Officer Kamson's cough breaks the second shocked silence. "I think I will, er, take my leave," he says with a quick salute. "Please remember that we are here to serve. I hope you will resolve what appears to be a mere domestic matter. Call us when there is something to investigate."

I cannot let the police man be going away without the letter, without knowing what happened to Rebecca, if they will ever find her, or if she is dead. **No. No. No.**

"No!" I say this inside my head, but I think I mistake and press one remote-control to loud my voice because my voice is not inside my head really, it is outside of everywhere and filling the whole kitchen, and all the shadows in the parlor are turning to look at the door, at the place where me and Kofi are standing, where I am banging the glass of the door with my two fists, and where Kofi is using his hand to cover my mouth as he is dragging me away from behind the door.

Outside, in the early-morning sun, I am sitting on a stone in the garden. My eyes keep filling with tears that is choking my throat and making me to cough. I was not able to fight for Khadija, and now I am not fighting for even Rebecca. It crushes me to know that I have so much power with the letter, but no power at all if Big Madam is not giving the letter to the police. I am not sure how long I am staying like that, crying sore, until Kofi comes outside.

"**Chale,** you are still crying?" he says. "I can bet on my new house in Kumasi that Big Daddy will be back. It will take a lot of begging on his part, but she will take him back one day because she needs him more than he needs her. Is it not sad that, in this part of our world, a woman's achievements can be reduced to nothing if she is not married? Anyway, get up. You are needed."

"Needed where?" I ask, looking at him with eyes swollen and sore of pain from too much crying.

"Big Madam wants you," he says. "She's in her reception."

"What does she want me for?" I ask, but Kofi shrugs.

"She's in a foul mood. Good luck."

As I wipe my face and enter the kitchen, my phone vibrates in my chest. I pluck it out to peep it quick: a text message from Ms. Tia that seem like it been waiting there for nearly one hour:

Adunni!! You got in!!
You won a place in the scheme!
I am not waiting ONE MORE DAY!

I will fight Florence if I have to.
I am coming to get you now!!
Pack your stuff.
xx

I stand there, in the middle of the kitchen, my back to Kofi as he is putting plates and spoons into the dishwasher with a happy whistle, as he is busying himself with work, forgetting about Adunni and all her troubles.

I read the text message again: with my voice trapped inside of my chest, a whisper in a container, with my eyes wide-open; and then with my eyes closed inside a deep darkness, the words running bright, a ribbon of fire, of hope.

CHAPTER 55

When I enter the reception, Big Madam is sitting in the sofa by the aquarium and looking at the floor.

Ms. Tia jumps when she sees me, and I draw a breath, comforting myself with her scent of coconut oil and lily flower.

She is looking much better now. Her hair is sitting in a big puff on her head, pushed back with a red band. And her face is no more having plenty lines, the skin smooth again.

"Your face," I say. "It is looking good."

"Palm oil worked its magic," she says with a wink. "Are you okay? Have you been crying?"

"I am okay now," I say.

"Adunni, listen," Ms. Tia says. "Your madam and I have had a lengthy discussion about your future. She is aware of the scheme and says you can come with me today, but she insists on having a word with you before she can release you."

Big Madam stands, beckons with her fingers. "Follow me."

"Florence . . ." Ms. Tia's voice is low, like a warning.

"I just want to have a word with her," Big Madam says, "alone."

"Then I will step out," Ms. Tia says as she nods at me, leaves the reception, closes the door quietly.

Big Madam holds out her hand. "The letter?"

I shake my head no.

"Hand me the letter this minute, or I will make it very difficult for you to leave. I don't care what Tia threatens. In the end, you will be the one to suffer if I make things difficult for you."

My heart is heavy as I put my hand inside my brassiere, bring out the letter, and give it to her.

She snatches it and starts to read, her eyes scanning the letter, reading fast, her face showing no feelings. Not even as she sees the dried blood. Then slowly, she starts to tear the letter to pieces.

I watch in shock, as small by small by small, a rain of black ink paper is pouring out from her hand and floating to the floor. A question—two questions—hit my mind so hard, it nearly stops my breathing.

What if it was Big Madam and not Big Daddy that caused Rebecca to disappear and bleed blood?

And if so, is that why Rebecca was writing that she is afraid Big Madam would do something bad to her? Why Big Madam did not arrest Big Daddy with the police? I think back to the night I told her Rebecca wrote a letter, and how she seemed not too shocked. Sad, tired, but not shocked. She didn't even read it! The only thing that seemed to nearly run her mad was the Caroline Bankole thing.

I look at her face, searching for answers, but all I see is a blanket of sadness and sorrow and pain.

"Ma, there was blood on that letter," I say. "On the letter you just teared up."

"I know," Big Madam say, her voice low. "I saw it."

"Why did you let the police go?" I ask. "Why did you tear the letter when you know Big Daddy may have killed her or wounded her or caused her to—" My voice is starting to rise, and Big Madam is holding up her hand, fear crawling all over her face. "Stop raising your voice, Adunni."

"What happened to Rebecca?" I ask. "If you don't tell me now, I will shout and shout and tell everybody what happened. That you killed Rebecca."

She laugh a shock of bitter laugh. "Me? Kill a human being? Is that how low you think of me?" She sigh. "Adunni, I do not owe you any explanation, but I will tell you this. Rebecca is not dead. She was not harmed. I know Chief got her pregnant. I have always known. The day she left this house, I drove her away."

"What about the blood?" I ask. "On the letter? Why is it there?"

"Where did you find the letter?"

"Under my bed," I lie, because I don't want to put Abu in trouble, and because of that, I know I cannot talk about the wet seat in the car, which I now know was maybe full of blood too before somebody washed it off. "What happened to make her bleed?"

"This will remain between you and me," Big Madam says, watching me. Inside her eyes, I see one hundred mouths wide-open, screaming a warning. "The day Rebecca left, I was at home, unwell. My husband did not know I hadn't left for the shop. He and I were not on speaking terms—we hardly are anyway. I needed Rebecca to make me some food, since Kofi had gone out, and because I called for her with no response, I was forced to go and find her in her room. When I got there, she was in so much pain. She was moaning, holding her stomach, trying hard to twist out her waist beads. She was in a bad state, in real agony. She said she drank something, something my husband gave to her. She must have been in the middle of writing the letter you found under your bed, before the pain started, because I noticed it on her bed as I rushed out to get her help."

"I saw the waist beads," I say, "on her window."

She took them off because her stomach was turning with so much pain.

Big Madam shrugs. "She might have left them there as we got ready to leave the house. I ended up dragging her to the car myself because no one was home. I had sent Abu to deliver an urgent fabric order on the mainland, and I don't know where Chief went. I suspect he gave her a drug to cause a miscarriage and took a stroll, left her to bleed out the baby. His baby."

She stops a moment, sway on her feet a little, then still herself. "I drove her to hospital. On the way, Rebecca started to bleed. Turns out she was nearly four months pregnant—I don't know how I missed her growing bulge—and that she was losing the baby. She told me my husband was responsible. And that the bastard had promised her marriage.

"Immediately the doctor was able to control the bleeding, I got her discharged, took her mobile phone off her, deleted all the messages she and Chief had been exchanging, and drove her to the nearest motor-park. I gave her some money, told her to get out of Lagos and never return. She never returned to her village, because Mr. Kola would have found that out and told me, but she has stayed away from my life. And me, in my foolishness, I asked Mr. Kola to get me a much younger girl as my next maid. I didn't know I was married to an animal. A beast. Age matters not to him. Nothing, absolutely nothing, matters to him." She sigh. "Go and get your things, Adunni."

I look at the scatter of paper on the floor, not moving from where I am standing. "How do I know, ma, that you are not lying?" I ask, but I think she is saying the truth. I think too that Rebecca took the letter with her to the car and hid it there, maybe by mistake or because she had hope that somebody would see it.

"Our conversation is over," Big Madam says. "Go now and get your things and leave my home." And then, raising her voice, she says, "Mrs. Dada, you can come back in. Adunni and I are done."

Ms. Tia returns inside, sees the scatter of paper on the floor, says, "What the hell?"

"Adunni and I are done," Big Madam says again. "She can go and get her things."

I run all the way to my room, and when I reach it, I take off my shoes and arrange them under the bed. I peel off my uniform, fold it, keep it on the bed. I wear my dress, put on my sandal-shoes from Ikati.

I look around slowly, at the bed, the cupboard in the corner, Rebecca's shoes on the floor, the folded uniform on the bed.

I set at packing my belongings into my nylon bag: my mama's Bible, the nine hundred naira I brought with me from Ikati, my pencils and note-pad, my **Better English** and grammar books. I pick up Rebecca's waist beads, look at them for a long time, and, with shaking hands, drop it into my bag too. If she is from Agan, maybe one day I will see her and give it to her.

I feel a strong pull of sadness as my mind drags
me back to Ikati, back to when I was about five or
six years of age and playing in the village stream
with Enitan, splashing water on our faces, laughing with no sense of what life will bring for all of
us. My mind rolls again, like a tire set down from
the top of a mountain, as I think of Mama and her
laugh, which was the sound of ten quiet sneezes;
of Khadija, my friend, and the many nights we lay
together on the mat in her room, sharing stories
into the far deep of the night. I think of Rebecca,
and I say a prayer that wherever she is, she will
find peace.

It is when I think of Kayus—who I had been
locking up in my mind for so long, for fear of running mad with the pain of missing him—that my
knees make a sudden bend.

I fall to the floor and start to cry: for Mama,
who spent all her days—sick and well—to gather
school fees money, sometimes frying one hundred
puff-puffs to sell under the hot Ikati sun, and many
times, returning home at night with tears in her
eyes because she didn't sell even one. I cry for Papa,
who thinks that a girl-child is a wasted waste, a
thing with no voice, no dreams, no brain.

I cry for Big Madam, with her big house, the big
cage of sadness around her soul. For Iya, who was
kind to me because my mama was kind to her. For
Khadija, who lived and died for the love of a man
that left her to die. And for myself, for the loss of

everything good and happy, for the pain of the past and the promise of the future.

My cry is a soft wail, both a whipping and healing to my heart . . . until someone calls my name from afar, a sound that stops the wail so sudden, as if something snap off a rushing stream from the source of it.

I wipe my face, push myself up, and pick up the cloth-hanger inside the cupboard. Kneeling on the bed, I pull and twist and stretch out the hanger until it is a thin line, a metal pen with no ink. Slowly, I begin to scratch the wall with the tip of it. I scratch and scratch, blowing away the chippings from the white paint, curving and carving letters deep into the wall until my neck and fingers are paining from too much bending and scratching.

When I finish, I climb down from the bed, pick up the nylon bag of my belongings. At the door, I look at the wall, at what I scratched into it. The **C** is one half of a square and the **A** is almost a triangle, but I can read the words:

ADUNNI & REBECCA

I leave the room, closing the door on the memory of the sad and the bitter and the happy of it all, knowing that even if everybody forgets about Rebecca, or about me, the wall in the room we shared will remind them that we were here. That we are human. Of value. Important.

CHAPTER 56

"I got in, Kofi!" I shout when I get to the kitchen. "I am going to school!"

Kofi drops the round of dough in his hand, cuts to where I am standing, and gives me a quick embrace. "Ah, Adunni. I overheard the doctor's wife talking to Big Madam just now! You got in! Congratulations." He sniffs, wipes one eye with the edge of his apron. "I know the school, and I will come and visit you at some point. But whenever you visit Ms. Tia, please call my number. I have stored it in your phone."

I wide my eyes. "You know I have a phone?"

"**Chale,** I knew from the day you got it. I even know the code. I have stored my name as **Chale.** Call me sometime, my friend?"

I start a crying laugh, a happy one. "Thank you,

Kofi, my friend," I say. "For pushing me to enter the scholarship. For everything."

Kofi wave away my thank you. "All I did was to give you information and encourage you. I would have done the same for my daughter. You did all the hard work. You and that woman, the doctor's wife." He low his voice, "So, what did she do with the letter?"

"She teared . . . tore it all up," I say, my voice low.

Kofi's eyes are sad. "If I had suspected that anything terrible happened to her, I would have done more for her."

"No more we can do for her," I say. "Big Madam told me what happened."

As I tell Kofi, his eyes grow from sad to wide, then to calm. "Let us hope she is okay, wherever she is. You did your best for her." He pats my cheeks two times. "Go and enjoy your new life. When my house is complete, you can come and visit."

"And what about all my salary? Should I ask Big Madam about it?"

"Forget that, **chale,**" he says. "I've always told you to apply wisdom in all your ways. This is a rare chance at freedom, you better take it and run!"

I leave Kofi and run to the main house, but before I go to Big Madam and Ms. Tia, I pass by the dining room and step into the library. "Thank you," I say to all the books in the shelf. "Thank you," I say to **The Book of Nigerian Facts,** touching the cover with the shining map and the green-white-green color of the Nigerian flag, the lettering of many, many facts inside the pages.

"Thank you," I say to the Collins and all my book friends, for helping me find my free in the prison of Big Madam's house.

I stay like that a moment, quiet and still and looking at the bookshelf, as if it is the grave of my mama, and my thank you is the sand I am pouring on the coffin, only this time my sadness is mixing with joy and thank you.

I stay there until I know it, until I feel a warm release inside of me that it is time to go. When I walk away from the library, I don't close the door. I leave it open for the spirit in all the books to be following me.

"That took you forever!" Ms. Tia says as I reach the reception area. She is dancing on her feet, eyes like fire. "All packed and ready to go?"

Big Madam is sitting in the chair beside the aquarium, head bent low, turning and turning her mobile phone in her hand.

"I am ready," I say.

"Mrs. Dada." Big Madam raises her head. I have never seen her look so sad, confused, and angry all at once. "Adunni is a, a very smart girl. She . . . she served me well. Good luck with her. And Adunni." She pushes herself from the sofa and comes to stand in front of me, eyes like a low-burning fire, a tired flame. "It would be better for you to mind your business and face your future," she says, slowly, almost whisper. "Face your life. **Do. You. Understand. Me?**"

I understand the silent warnings in the four words that make up her question: **You must not say a word to anybody about what was in that letter. About what I told you. Do you understand me?**

"I understand," I say. "Bye-bye, ma."

Big Madam nods, but she does not respond. She turns away from me and leaves the room, shutting the door with a quiet **click.** For a moment, me and Ms. Tia, we keep our eyes on the door as if expecting her to come back. But she does not come back. Instead, her feet stamp up the stairs, the sound fading with every stamp, until a door slams so hard, the whole house shakes.

"Goodness me!" Ms. Tia says quietly. "Can we get the hell out of here, like this minute?"

We leave the reception, shut the door, and start to walk to the gate.

"Why did she ask to speak to you privately?" Ms. Tia says as we walk past the first set of flower-pots. "You guys were speaking for quite a while. Is it about the torn paper on the floor? Was it a letter?"

I start to think of a lie to close the matter, to forget talking about it ever again, but I know I cannot let Big Madam put me in a box of fear, a prison of the mind, after freeing me from the prison of her house.

"Yes," I say. "The letter is about Rebecca, from Rebecca." I look back at Big Madam's house, the big and powerful and sad of it. "I will tell you every-thing later tonight."

It feels good to say this to her, to tell her that me and her will talk, face to face, mouth to mouth, not with any text message that you cannot be showing your sad or angry feeling or any feeling.

It feels good to give Big Madam back her box of fear. To put the key on top of the box and leave it in her compound, in her house, where it belongs.

"How are things with the doctor?" I ask Ms. Tia. I am walking a little faster, taller. "Better?"

"So much has happened," she says with a sigh, "but I think we will pull through."

"You think?" I ask, stopping to roof my eyes from the morning sun, to look into her face.

"I think." She nods. "We have decided to ex-plore something called adoption. Do you know what that is?"

I shake my head no and start to say I will check it in **The Book of Nigerian Facts** before I remem-ber that I am leaving the book behind. That I am leaving this life behind and facing a new one.

"I will tell you about it," Ms. Tia says as she takes my hand and holds it tight. "Because tomorrow will be better than today, right?"

At first, I am not giving her any answer.

My mind cannot be imagining a day better than today, with the endless blue-gray in the sky and the smell of new hope and new strength in the air, but I know another day will come when I will see Papa and Kayus and Born-boy, when I can visit Ikati with no fear, or maybe they can visit me.

A day will come when my voice will sound so loud all over Nigeria and the world of it, when I will be able to make a way for other girls to have their own louding voice, because I know that when I finish my education, I will find a way to help them to go to school.

A day will come when I will become a teacher, send money to buy Papa a car, or build a new house for him, or maybe I can even build a school in Ikati in the memory of my mama and of Khadija, and who knows what else tomorrow will bring? So, I nod my head yes, because it is true, the future is always working, always busy unfolding better things, and even if it doesn't seem so sometimes, we have hope of it.

We begin the five minutes of walking to Ms. Tia's house in the early-morning silence through the big black gates that I used to wipe four times a day with that thick yellow cloth in the kitchen, down Wellington Road with its houses full of screaming peacocks—the rich man's fowl—and then finally into Ms. Tia's compound, where the white house with a mirror on its roof is blinking, blinking at me as if to say, **Welcome, Adunni, welcome to your new free.**

ACKNOWLEDGMENTS

I would like to thank:

God, for every breath, for every word, for this gracious gift and for the ones to come.

Felicity Blunt, for all the hard work you poured into this. You are amazing and incredible and simply the best. Emma Herdman and Lindsey Rose, my spectacular editors on both sides of the Atlantic, who worked with me with deep kindness, courteousness, and consideration—thank you both for your excellent suggestions and patience while I worked through the edits. The fantastic team at Curtis Brown UK, ICM Partners, Scepter, and Dutton, including Jenn Joel, who championed and pushed this book in the US, Rosie Pierce, Melissa Pimentel, Claire Nozieres, Louise Court, Helen Flood, Amanda Walker, Jamie Knapp, Leila Siddiqui, and all the wonderful people who have worked, and continue to work, tirelessly for this book.

Caroline Ambrose, for creating the Bath Novel Award, for helping to birth destinies, and for working so hard to give writers like me a chance. Winning the Bath Novel Award in 2018 changed my life. Julia Bell, for those conversations in your office, or in class, and for selflessly driving the Best Workshop Group Ever. The Birkbeck MA #SuperGroup, for the crucial feedback and encouragement during our MA and for the many Thursday evenings since then. Professor Russell Celyn Jones, for reading the **very first** three thousand words, and for opening my eyes to the possibility of fulfilling a lifelong dream.

My precious family. Professor Teju Somorin, for advocating for and championing my advancement in every way. engineer Isaac Daré, who always called me "Duchess," because, in his eyes, I was royalty, and because he, despite his schedule, made time to read and give feedback on everything I ever wrote. Segs, who is rare and wonderful and everything in between. Yemi, who believed in me from day one, and my daughters, who are my heartbeat, and who inspired and informed this novel in many ways. Mrs. Modupe Daré, Mrs. Busola Awofuwa, Sis Toyin, Aunty Joke, Olusco, and the girls, for warm food to eat, for a word in season, for love and encouragement, and for all you do. Wura of Glitzallure Fabrics, for the last-minute, quick calls to educate me on fabrics. I love you all more than words can say.

Adunni, for sharing your world with me. You came at a time when I felt most frustrated in my writing journey. Hearing your first words in broken, desperate English, first as a whisper in my ears one morning, and then as a persistently loud voice for nearly three years after, changed everything for me, for you, and hopefully for girls like you. And to you, dear reader, for this journey, and hopefully for more to come.

Thank you.

A NOTE ON SOURCES

While **The Book of Nigerian Facts: Past to Present** is not a real book, the facts about Nigeria gathered in this book are all available online.

ABOUT THE AUTHOR

Abi Daré grew up in Lagos, Nigeria, and has lived in the UK for more than eighteen years. She studied law at the University of Wolverhampton and has an MSc in International Project Management from Glasgow Caledonian University as well as an MA in Creative Writing at Birkbeck, University of London. **The Girl with the Louding Voice** won the Bath Novel Award for unpublished manuscripts in 2018 and was also selected as a finalist in the 2018 Literary Consultancy Pen Factor competition. Abi lives in Essex with her husband and two daughters, who inspired her to write her debut novel.